PRAISE FOR THE AUTHOR

IN TWENTY YEARS

"Scotch hits a grand slam with this novel . . . With wonderfully fleshed-out, relatable characters, this is an absolute must-read that lovers of women's contemporary fiction will devour in one sitting."
—*Library Journal,* starred review

"Told from five vastly different perspectives of characters who are deeply developed and relatable in their flawed ways, this novel captures the nostalgia many feel for the friendships and simple nature of youth . . . Heartfelt . . . Well written and memorable."
—*RT Book Reviews*

"Allison Winn Scotch is the ultimate beach read. If you plan to sink your toes into the sand and need a fab book to kick back with . . . this is the one."
—*Parade*

"The perfect beach read."

PopSugar

"Both heartbreaking and funny, this novel explores how we cope with the disappointments of adulthood and come to terms with our past."
—*Real Simple*

"A story about youthful dreams and middle-age reality, this is a page turning book to talk about."

"Winn Scotch's highly anticipated, thought-provoking, and emotional sixth novel tells the story of complex yet relatable characters questioning the paths they have chosen in life (and who can't thoroughly relate to that?)."

—*New You* magazine

"A story of learning to accept the past and confront the future, *In Twenty Years* is a heart-wrenching read, highly recommended."

—*Midwest Book Review*

Between Me and You

ALSO BY
ALLISON WINN SCOTCH

Between Me and You

A Novel

ALLISON WINN SCOTCH

LAKE UNION
PUBLISHING

Text copyright © 2018 by Allison Winn Scotch
All rights reserved.

Published by Lake Union Publishing, Seattle

www.apub.com

Amazon, the Amazon logo, and Lake Union Publishing are trademarks of Amazon.com, Inc., or its affiliates.

ISBN-13: 9781503941229
ISBN-10: 1503941221

Cover design by Ginger Design

Printed in the United States of America

For anyone brave enough to fall in love.

Nobody has ever measured, not even poets, how much the heart can hold.

—*Zelda Fitzgerald*

1

BEN

NOVEMBER 2016 (NOW)

I told myself that if she showed, that would be the sign I needed.

If she showed, maybe we could find a way to rewind, rewrite, do it all over. Do it all better. Do it all again, only differently.

It's silly; it's something out of a Hollywood ending, and I'd know that better than most. It's not how I'd write it, but it's how the studio would want it, what would appeal to the demographic they were courting: *Men will want to go home and screw their wives, call their girlfriends; women will weep and know that love conquers all.*

I snort to myself, though it's lost in the bluster of the wind, the squeal of a motorcycle racing too quickly down Ocean Avenue, empty on this overcast Sunday morning.

Did I ever believe that? Did I ever pin my hopes that love could conquer all? It feels like so long ago: when we met each other, when we loved each other without conditions.

A familiar tornado of grief spins inside me. Though it's not just grief for her. It's for both of us. For me too. How naive we were, how we lost ourselves to so many things—her career, mine for a while, Joey, our mourning, everything that piled up to be the weight of too much. Me more than her, I suppose, though I never admitted this aloud. It was easier to point fingers, make her feel responsible, even though I know, if I peel back enough layers to my core, that I was equally so. More than equal. She was always sturdier than I was, elusive in the way that an actress needs to be: permeable, which also made her more adaptable to all the shit that came our way. I was who I was, always had been, and hadn't been able to adapt, to duck right when a left punch was thrown, to duck left when the right one came at me too.

But still, maybe today we can right ourselves.

We can. We have to.

I say this aloud, against the wind, as if putting it out into the universe, here where the earth dives into the sea, makes it true. *We can right ourselves.*

It's so romantic, so unlike who I've become, that I'm surprised to discover how much I believe it, how much I mean it. How much I *need* it. I need her. I want her; my stomach turns at the notion of just how badly I do. I've staked our future on her showing. Which is presumptuous and also dumb, since I have conveyed none of this to her.

But she knows where to find me, knows exactly where I'll be.

I check the time on my phone. Not that I've told her I'd be here. Like a stupid script, some dumb chick flick, I'm throwing it to fate: *If she shows, we'll give it another go.* Call off the lawyers, which she said she didn't really want anyway. Did I want them? A year ago I was certain, but bruises fade until you can't detect them across your healed skin, and now, even when I search for those welts, I find I'm unable to see them. Feel them, yes, sometimes if I press myself in the right places I can still *feel* them, but that's probably the point. That you can still detect the pain but don't have a constant reminder. That's the only way to fix us: *This is where you hurt me; please don't do it again.*

So here I am, casting about, looking for the familiar bounce of her step, the way her hair fans back and forth as she walks, the way her spine points exactly north with perfect posture thanks to endless years of Pilates and yoga and whatever else the studio pays for and implores her to do.

I lean over the white picket fence that lines the park's running path, tilt toward the ledge below, the drop-off that crescents into the beach, then the vast expanse of ocean. When we first moved here, we lived just around the corner in a one-bedroom bungalow that felt made for us. We'd stumble down this same path on the weekend mornings, hands linked, toward the farmers market or for a beckoning cup of coffee. She'd be exhausted from her late shift at the bar; I'd be wired from a night of writing too late.

I press my palms against the fence, straighten out, then head down the sun-bleached steps toward the water, the air swirling and smelling of salt and nostalgia.

She'll know to find me down here, where I always am on his birthday, where something beckons me year after year, as if this ritual brings me peace. *She'll come,* I tell myself. *She has to. I need her to.*

The beach is mostly deserted. It's too cold to swim, and the sun is battling a swath of thick clouds that won't dissipate until late afternoon, just before sunset, when it's too late to enjoy the beach anyway. There are a few lone surfers, bundled in their rubber wetsuits, a determined jogger every now and then. I kick off my flip-flops by the concrete path's edge, then step onto the sand, my arches and heels leaving imprints, tracks, as I go. We also used to do this, take morning beach walks in those heady early days of our marriage. We never had a destination or an end point in mind. We simply walked to keep each other company, talking for hours. Sometimes my calves would be sore the next day. I shake my head: I haven't thought about all of this for ages, years.

Jesus.

Somehow between those days when the sunrises melted into the sunsets and now, we got here. *Here.* I blow out my breath, remembering New Year's, remembering Sundance, remembering Joey's birth, remembering the lot of it. We weren't always split in two; we weren't always beyond repair.

My feet are in the chilly seawater now, sending a jolt up through my ankles, to my calves, my thighs, nearly to my heart. I stretch my arms upward, like I'm offering myself to the gods of the ocean. It's not the first time I've considered it: swimming as far out as possible, seeing what happens from there. But I'm not brave like Leo. I reconsider: I'm not *reckless* like Leo either.

I find a pack of old cigarettes in my pocket. I've never enjoyed smoking, how it makes me light-headed, its disgusting aftertaste. That it will slowly kill me. For a while there, I didn't care, though. Now, I'm wiser. Now, maybe I'm more hopeful. So I raise an unlit cigarette to my mouth, let it linger because I like its heft, but not its consequences. Like so many things in my life, I've learned to straddle the middle and just try to get out alive.

A lithe, blond surfer swims in, just a hiccup down from me, shaking the water off, then offering a little wave. I drop the cigarette back into the pack, then smile back, wondering if she means to wave at *me*, if this lithe, blond surfer has mistaken me for someone else. Not that I'm so bad, not for forty-two, which is midlife in theory but here in Los Angeles could really be an extension of prolonged adolescence. Hell, some of my friends still haven't married; a few still run around with starlets in their lower twenties, especially those who have done well for themselves: drive the Porsche, have a spread with a view in the Hills. Sometimes they'll ping me and say, "Come out dude, let's roll, let's score." But none of that feels important like it used to: the Porsche, the house made of glass in the Hills. Initially, in those first few early months of being single, sure, well, who wouldn't find that liberating? Now I just want her. Our old life.

"Hey," I say to the surfer. "Nice morning for the waves?" I self-consciously run my fingers over my dark stubble that is peppered with a tiny bit of gray.

"Killer," she says. "The best." And then lofts her board under her arm and glides away toward the parking lot. "See ya."

I peer around. The beach is deserted again.

She's not coming.

I lose my breath for a beat, punched in the gut with the realization. I actually *believed* that she was as hopeful as I was, that she was willing to forget how broken we'd become.

"Dumb, dumb, dumb, dumb, dumb," I mutter aloud.

It was a stupid bet I made with myself, a stupid way out from the corner we've backed ourselves into. The Hollywood ending. But Hollywood endings aren't really life, aren't anything more than what I'd type into a draft before hitting "The End."

My dad always told me that I was too romantic. *Being a writer?* he'd scoff. *Not exactly what we had planned for you.* He'd pour himself a scotch, adjust his tie, and gaze at me in the way that I could read only as disappointment.

As if anyone's plans for anyone else can set their path. The same lesson I learned with Leo, and the irony isn't lost on me. I should have said that to him then; I should have known better. *Do what you want, do what you love. Be happy.*

Instead, I lived to whittle down my young romanticism to prove my dad wrong. To show him that I had mettle, that grit wasn't lost on me, even if I wanted to spend my days concocting fictional characters who allowed me to lose myself in other places, other worlds.

The wind kicks up, blowing the salty air over me, and I inhale deeply enough that my chest puffs up, and then I squeeze my eyes shut and remember why I came here this morning. I came here not just in hopes of seeing her, but to remember *him* too. How much he loved the ocean. How he wanted to retire here and surf. I should have told him to, but how was I to know? How was any of us to know?

"I'd have done it differently, you know," I say aloud. To him, to her, to myself too. No one answers, of course. Just the continuous beat of the waves breaking in front of me, the ever-present swirl of the wind. "If I could go back and do it all differently, I would."

I turn and head back to the concrete path where I abandoned my flip-flops.

A figure is running down the path in the distance. My gut spins— an honest mix of elation and nerves. But then I see the red hair in a ponytail flopping back and forth. I squint because I wonder if my brain is playing a trick on me, that I'm seeing something, a mirage, that isn't really there.

But then she's in front of me, startled a bit herself, out of breath, sweat running behind her ears.

"Ben," she says. "Oh my gosh, hey."

"Hey." I lean forward and kiss her damp cheek. "I didn't . . ."

My heart races, my brain goes to static. *Amanda.* Not at all whom I was expecting, not at all whom I'm ready for. I have to apologize for a million things, I'm sure. I stutter again. I was prepared to make a speech, to get down and beg for absolution, and yet, she isn't here and Amanda is, smiling and seemingly open, and my pulse is hammering so quickly that I don't know how I'm still standing.

Maybe this is the sign, that romantic one in the movies that the audience is clutching their seats and waiting for with their hearts in their throats. Even as I hear myself think it, I'm not sure I believe it, but what the hell?

My mind refocuses: on how good she looks, on how lovely she smells, on how something lights inside of me that feels a little feral, a little wild, like it used to whenever I saw her, even when we shouldn't have been seeing each other at all.

"God, Amanda, it's been forever," I say.

She laughs. "Not forever. What, a year or two?" She smiles. "OK, I know exactly how long it's been. Since May last year. Eighteen months."

"That seems right." I hesitate. "You don't hate me?"

She smiles again, easily. "It was all a mess. So no, I don't hate you."

6

I nod, unsure of what to say next. I know what I came here for, but like so many things recently, I find that I'm willing to abandon my principles because they're inconvenient. Write a shitty script? Sure! Leave with a different woman? Why not! I unexpectedly think of my dad again—*Fuck you!* I want to tell him—and how disappointed he'd be with this sliding scale.

"I just . . . I remembered what today was." Amanda's already pink cheeks turn redder, nearly matching her hair, and I push my dad out of my thoughts. "I . . . I thought you might be here. Remembered how you told me you'd do this." She shrugs. "God, that sounds like a stalker thing to do. Really, I run down here most mornings. I just . . . I thought you might be here today."

My brain is playing catch-up, assessing this unforeseen turn. Amanda showed. Tatum did not. I determine that this has to mean something, even if it's not what I wanted it to mean when I woke this morning and resolved to win back my wife.

Finally I say: "Amazing how you knew. Of course I'd be here . . . I'm glad you found me."

2

TATUM

OCTOBER 1999

I made a bet with Daisy that I could get at least three numbers by midnight.

It's not something I'd do normally, this bet, these numbers, but she is pushing me outside of my comfort zone, part of an acting exercise assigned to us by Professor Sherman—*Move past your comfort zone into that sticky territory of inhabiting someone else*—and so I agree. Besides, it's better than deflecting the cheesy pickup lines that come with being a bartender, the lecherous looks of patrons who somehow think you're up for grabs, the self-criticism that would otherwise clang around my easily infected brain. By playing the part, slipping into a role, it's easier to step outside myself. That's half the reason I want to be an actor in the first place. I can be anyone I want to be.

So of course I said yes to the bet.

"They can't be trolls, guys you'd never go out with to begin with," Daisy said, pouring a shot of whiskey down her throat, untying her black apron and passing it to me when we swapped shifts. I knotted it around my own waist as we traded places: me behind the bar, her on a rickety stool in front of it.

"Got it," I said, nodding. "No trolls."

"And no drunks." She held up a finger, then another. "So no trolls and no drunks. Because then it's too easy. Because then you'd get, like, three numbers in three minutes."

I laughed. "You're overestimating my appeal."

"Shut up," she said, and wrapped her blond hair into a bun at the nape of her neck. "Don't do that."

"Do what?"

"That thing you do: act like you're not worth it, act like you don't deserve it." She leaned over the bar and poured herself another shot. "Besides, this is supposed to be fun. This is supposed to be about making them believe you are whoever you want to be."

"So it's about the chase," I said. "Well, and about the assignment."

"Here's to the chase," she replied, and flipped her empty shot glass over against the wooden bar. "And maybe some sexy-ass men."

"Here's to that." I laughed because why not.

So now it's 11:47, and I have one more number to go when I see him at the end of the bar. Nursing a beer, which I hadn't poured for him, which tells me that he ordered it before I came on my eleven p.m. shift. One beer over the course of an hour. A lightweight. A sipper. Probably a bit of a geek, not unlike me when I'm not donning whichever mask I'm assigned for the day or the evening. Nonthreatening. I like making these assumptions; it helps me compartmentalize who he is, who I might have to be in reaction to that. Like a casting call: *We are seeking a nonthreatening kind of geek (who is also cute!) to play off the role of man-eater bartender (who is also pretty in a generic way).*

I grab the dirty rag and wipe down the countertop, making my way toward the corner. Three undergrads, definitely not legal, push their way toward me and snap their fingers to get my attention. My cheeks blaze with something like lower-middle-class embarrassment, but it's dark, and I'm not *me* right now, so I flush that inbred shame away. *These girls.* They're all the same: NYU rich kids who come to Dive Inn with their parents' credit cards or their hundred-dollar bills and act like the world is imploding when they're not immediately served their vodka twists. Outside of the bar, outside of this role that I slip into, these types of girls make me duck my head, dart around them on the street. They are better than me in ways that seem inexplicable, unattainable. But here, in this bar, on my turf, with my apron as a sort of shield, they are my adversary.

"Excuse me!" one of them shouts, then snaps again.

"Don't snap at me," I say, my decibel level stronger than my will. "I'm not your goddamn dog."

"What?" she says, possibly because she can't hear me over the stereo and the voices that are all raised to match the music, or possibly because she simply has never been spoken to in such a way.

"Don't. Snap." I like the way that feels, this bravado.

She recoils. "Oh my god, I just wanted a vodka tonic."

"I need ID."

I don't technically need ID, since we pretty much serve anyone—bar policy—but I'm on a roll now, the distance widening between who I am outside of the bar and who I am behind it.

Her head jerks back like I've slapped her, and her eyes skitter with fury. She leans over and whispers to her friend, then says: "The last lady served us no problem. Look." She holds up an empty glass.

"I'm not the last lady." I shrug. I'm impressed with my swagger, feel very strongly that Professor Sherman would deem my performance "true to life."

"I left it in the booth, in my purse."

I start wiping down the bar again, as if I'm already bored with this. Easing my way toward phone number three.

"Hey, Freckles!" she yells, referring, I imagine, to the band of freckles that run across my nose. "Don't you want a fucking tip?"

At this, the guy at the end of the bar looks up from staring at the foam in his surely warm beer and watches us.

"I'd love a tip," I say. "From someone who's twenty-one."

"Here's a tip," she shouts, standing taller on the foot of the stool, which is teetering, imbalanced. "You're working for *me*, back there, behind there. I am not working for *you*. Got that?"

"Yeah." I laugh, the blood rising to my cheeks again. I turn the other direction. "Got it loud and clear. But you're still not getting served."

"Bitch!" she yells, just before the stool topples over and she disappears from my view and there's a commotion on the floor as her friends huddle around her. My whole face is fire now, I can feel it, hot and shameful, but I squeeze my fingers together into tight fists and remind myself that tonight I'm not who these girls want me to be, I'm not who anyone thinks I am. I am the part I promised Daisy I would play. I curl my hands into balls so tight, my knuckles clench and my nails dig into my palms. Then I release them and let the blood flush back into the recesses of my body. He's watching me—*Phone Number Three*—so I keep my eyes down, just scrubbing the spilled beer, wiping in concentric circles until I stop right in front of him. I check the clock above the exit. I have seven minutes to lock him in. Win the bet, ace Daisy's assignment.

"I hope you don't take her personally," he says, nudging his chin toward the hubbub by the fallen stool. "I went to high school with her older brother. I think being an asshole is genetic."

I laugh easily, like she hadn't just set off a grenade inside of me, and reach for his glass.

"Free refill for you."

"I don't need one." He waves his hand. "I'm on my way out."

"You turn into a pumpkin before midnight?"

He smiles, and he's cuter than I realized from afar. Straight nose, great teeth. Not that I'd taken him to be a troll, because trolls are off-limits per the rules of the game, but the shadows of the bar concealed his blue eyes, his defined chin, his strong shoulders.

"Nah, just . . . I have an early shoot tomorrow, and the person I was meeting tonight never showed."

"A shoot? I'm intrigued." I plop elbows onto the bar, then my chin into my palms.

"Grad student," he says.

"Are you at Tisch? I've never seen you before; I'm there for theater."

"I'm there for writing, MFA," he says. "You know, about to set the world on fire as the next big screenwriter." He shrugs, looks away. "Or something like that. I don't know, talk to my parents and they'll tell you I gave up my very lucrative analyst position at Morgan Stanley for a graduate degree in film."

"Banking boys are so boring. No wonder you quit." I grab the tap and refill his beer anyway, then slide it back to him. "Eh, tell your parents to screw themselves."

He honest-to-God snorts at this. "I'm still living with them, so that's a little hard."

"Yikes," I say.

"Tell me about it." He sighs.

"Well, truthfully, I could probably never tell mine to screw themselves either," I admit. "Sorry, bad advice. I'm trying something new tonight." I shake my head, refocus. I can already hear Professor Sherman chiding me for slipping so gracelessly out of character.

"I thought bartenders only gave amazing advice?"

"Only in the movies." I laugh. "You're shit out of luck with me."

I wipe my hands on the towel, which is really more for show than hygiene, since it's damp with old booze and pretzel crumbs. I extend my right hand.

"Tatum Connelly."

"Ben Livingston." He clasps my palm more firmly than I expect, and I wince. "Sorry," he says. "Habit. Trained that way by my dad since I was six."

"Fun childhood."

"My dad's only paying for grad school on the promise that I win an Oscar."

"So win an Oscar," I say.

"Uh . . . OK." He grins. "Now you sound like him: 'If you're going to do something, Benjamin, you'd better at least be the best!'"

"There are worse role models," I say, because God knows, I know that there are.

"I'm probably making it sound worse than it was." He sips his beer. "You know, to make you feel sorry for me or something."

"Fun childhoods are overrated," I say, because I would know. But because I already slipped once, and I'm not about to betray any part of who I really am again and instead will conceal myself completely in who I need to be for the night, I add: "But why would you want me to feel sorry for you?" I bite my lip, coy, flirtatious, exactly what would be demanded of this role in this moment.

"Oh, I don't know, so when you get my phone number, you might take pity on me and actually call," he says.

I chew on a swizzle stick to disguise my surprise at his forthright-ness. "What makes you think I want your phone number? And even if I *did* want your phone number, why then wouldn't I call? For your infor-mation, as a female bartender, I get numbers thrown at me all the time."

"Well, good, because I don't hand out my number to strangers."

"I'm not a stranger," I say. "I'm Tatum." I wonder, briefly, if I should have made up a name, like Jocelyn or Tiffany or something else to go fully method in this conversation, but it's too late. More proof, I remind myself, that I need to hone my technique, need to work on really living the part, not just trying it on. Sherman is always saying that: *When you go, you have to go all in or else the audience will pick apart your inconsisten-cies like hawks on a dead deer.* He literally said that. Verbatim.

He laughs. "But you don't want my number, Tatum, so we don't have anything to worry about."

"Well, I don't want your number, in fact."

"Perfect," he says.

"Great," I reply. Then: "Well, what if I do want your number?"

"I already told you: I don't give my number out to strangers who scare me, knowing your name aside."

"Something else you learned in your childhood?"

"They trained me well." He raises his eyebrows, flirting.

"What if I'm not a stranger?" I say. "What if I tell you something about my own less than fun childhood that assures that I'm just Tatum, your local friendly bartender!" I wiggle my fingers in my best jazz hands and push my face into a showbiz-style grin. I spy the clock. Less than a minute. *Shit.*

"I'll consider it," he says.

"I started working when I was twelve, have had a job ever since," I say. "So, no fun for me."

"Hmmm. Nope."

"Oh, come on," I say. "Are you going to make me beg?"

"Yes," he says. "I am going to make you beg. Very much so. Come on, give me your best begging face."

I stick my lip out and furrow my brow, folding my hands in front of me as if in prayer. "Please? Pretty, pretty please?"

I hear Daisy cackling before I see her; then she pops up on the stool next to him, shoulders shaking, tears in her eyes.

"What?" I double-take. "Were you, like, crouching underneath the bar? Listening to this the whole time?"

She nods, laughing too hard to speak.

"What? Judging my technique?" I eye the clock—12:01. I lost the bet, which doesn't mean much other than bragging rights, other than more proof that maybe Sherman is wrong about me, that I'm *not* the best one in the class.

"Just ensuring that I won." She hiccups. "Also, I wanted to witness Ben giving you shit because I knew it would be adorable. No, hilarious actually."

"Nice," I say. "Supernice." Then, to Ben: "I take it you know her?"

"Ben wrote a short about dating I did a few months ago," she says. "I told him about our little pickup contest, and he wrote it into the script."

"That *Women Are from Mars* short?"

Ben nods.

"That won an award last semester, didn't it?"

He shrugs. "I just wrote the script. She starred. And the dude who directed it, another guy I grew up with, actually got the award."

"All you fancy Manhattan kids," I say. "The next Scorseses. But you, don't do that." I jab his shoulder.

"Do what?"

"Dismiss any notions of greatness, act like you're not worthy of winning some award." I point at Daisy. "She tells me that all the time. So now I'm telling you."

Even in the dim light, I can see his face redden. He's not so different from me, outside of this bar. Uncertain, unsure.

"I'm serious," I say. "Like, if that had been my film, I'd be standing on top of this bar, screaming about it with a microphone."

He watches me, assessing, and for a moment I wonder if he's going to dare me to do so, put my money where my mouth is, prove him wrong and jump on the counter and yell like a banshee—and I pray that he doesn't, doesn't call me on this ridiculous bluster, because I can take a part only so far before my self-awareness kicks in. But he checks his watch and glances toward the door, then fishes his wallet from his back pocket and flattens forty dollars on the wood paneling. "I should go; looks like I'm getting stood up."

"Well, that sucks." I grab a glass from below the bar and pour myself a beer, ignoring two borderline-legal kids with backward baseball caps who are waving me down. "And you don't owe me forty bucks."

"It's midnight, and you lost the bet," he says. "A big tip—an actual tip, not a smart-ass tip from that girl who went to my high school—is the least I could do." He hesitates. "Anyway, I actually feel kind of bad about setting you up to lose. I really never do things like that." He points at Daisy. "She begged me. So I apologize, and please, take the tip."

"I did," Daisy says, nodding. "It was too perfect not to. But yes"— she holds up her right hand—"I can attest that Ben, whom I have known since childhood, is the rare breed of actually decent man who is not a total asshole."

"Nice," he says.

"She's not from here," Daisy interrupts. "She's only very recently become acquainted with New York men."

"Ohio." I shrug. "We only breed nice men in Ohio. Nice men who don't trick us into losing."

"Thus, the forty dollars." Ben inches the bills toward me.

"Well, I *don't* like losing." I frown. "And I do like big tips."

"No one really likes losing," he says. "And I think everyone likes good tips."

"Are you making fun of me?"

"No." He holds his hand over his heart. "I swear, I am not making fun of you. And I have Daisy to testify that I am indeed a non-asshole New York guy who wouldn't do that sort of thing."

"We went to elementary together," she says. "I've known him since forever."

"I suppose losing a bet and getting forty bucks is better than getting stood up, so my night is not quite as bad as yours," I admit. "So, fine, I will see your forty bucks and raise you a tequila shot. On the house." I reach behind me for the cheap tequila that the undergrads are more than happy to overindulge in. I never do shots on the job, but it feels exactly like what the persona would do, so shots it is.

"I'm not sure if I'm quite being stood up . . . it's complicated." He sighs, and for a moment, it's like I can see his whole childhood across his face: his aspirations, his disappointments, his hopes that he still pins himself to. "My girlfriend's in her third year of med school. She's just . . . busy . . . occupied—that's the word she uses—she's 'occupied' all the time. Saving lives and whatever, so . . . I mean, how can I argue with that?"

"Sounds like you need a new girlfriend," I say.

"Probably, probably. But I'm one for loyalty. I don't bail until the ship is sinking." That look again: nothing but naked openness, like he is still eleven and hasn't yet been jaded by the ways of the world.

"Meaning you're loyal, but she might not be?"

He laughs. "What are you, like, my therapist too?"

"So I couldn't have gotten your number even if I hadn't been set up by my so-called best friend?" I slam three shot glasses down and dump the tequila in each.

He shrugs and smiles. "Hey, Daisy put me up to it."

"Well." I toss the shot back too quickly, and it burns all the way down. "I guess you owe me one." I smile at him now as Tatum, not Tatum the bartender, not Tatum the brave.

He smiles back as Ben.

"Well," he says. "I guess I do."

3

BEN

JULY 2015

"Constance is sick," Tatum says. "Or else I'd have sent her to get him." It was part of our separation agreement: that Constance, our nanny, would do most of the handoffs, though we'd gotten more casual about it in the four months since I moved out. Tatum shrugs and stares at my pathetic doormat, which is gray and muddy and in need of a wash. But how do I wash a doormat? I don't even know. We both let our eyes linger on it for a beat too long.

"I'm throwing that out," I say, and point downward. "I'm getting a new one later today." I don't know why I care about impressing her; I'm *angry* with her; I am *untangling* myself from her. These are the words I use with Eric when he takes me out after work to nurse my wounds. He tells me to consider a real therapist, not my best friend from college who is now my producing partner and is not really good at advice for shit, especially since he is still single at forty-one and trolling Tinder.

"OK," Tatum replies. "Though you could just wash it."

This irritates me for no reason at all. Rather, it irritates me because of course she is right. I *could* simply wash it, which I'd just told myself five seconds earlier. But coming from her, it feels like proselytizing, not wise counsel, like she's saying it just *to be* right. For fuck's sake, why is Tatum always right? Of course I can wash the stupid doormat.

"You don't have to point out my shitty doormat," I say. My eyes twitch when I realize that, in fact, I was the one who pointed out my shitty doormat in the first place. God, when am I going to stop being such an asshole just for the sake of it?

"I wasn't . . . I just . . ." She stops, shakes her head. "I don't want to *do* this, Ben." She checks the time on her phone. "Is he ready? I have a meeting in an hour."

Of course she has a meeting in an hour. Tatum's time is no longer her own, hasn't been for years now.

"So let him stay longer; I'll watch him."

"It's my day."

I soften. "But you have a meeting, and Constance is out sick. Come on, Tate. We're having fun."

"Ben." She uses that impatient voice that I sometimes heard her use on set (when I used to visit) when someone would have the misfortune of suggesting a creative tidbit that was totally beneath her. For the most part, Tatum was accommodating, as far as A-listers go. No temper tantrums, no outrageous diva demands. But it wasn't as if she couldn't skewer you with a raised eyebrow, couldn't decimate your ego with one word. *Ben.*

Also, it wasn't as if she didn't make plans without considering anyone else's schedule, wasn't as if she hadn't grown used to everyone around her saying yes. Except for me. (But I now live in a two-bedroom apartment two miles away from the new house in Brentwood, so it's not working out so well on my end either.)

"Tate, come on."

"The therapist said that consistency was key," she says. And it's true, the therapist we found for Joey to help him through the divorce *had* said that constancy—a united front—from us was imperative. Joey had been moodier since we told him the news: explosive mood swings from a previously docile child, crying jags that felt unending, whereas he barely cried before, even back when he'd broken his arm. *Consistency,* Dr. Cohn kept reiterating.

"OK," I say as she waits expectantly for a fight.

"OK." She nods.

I start to ask her who will be watching Joey—he's only seven and can't stay by himself—but I realize the answer will only spark another fight: Tatum's father. To whom I have been unkind, shamefully unkind, until it grew too late. Until Tatum and I each held our own scorecards, and he was one of the chits she was able to hold against me. Rightfully so. I chew my lip. I could apologize now, I could say: *God, I was such a stubborn dick for reasons that were all about me,* but she has never apologized for her own sins, so I'm not about to fall on my sword. Besides, attorneys have been consulted, retainers have been paid. Apologies are too long in coming and won't amount to much anyway.

"Joe!" I call over my shoulder. "Hurry up, Mom's here!"

"Two minutes, Daddy," he calls back.

"Sorry," I say. "We were knee-deep in *Madden* on the Xbox." Back over my shoulder, I shout: "You'd better not be cheating, kiddo!"

Tatum presses her mouth into a thin line, then removes her sunglasses and squeezes the bridge of her nose. This is her exasperated face. The one I usually see now. Even when it's simply because Joey is playing *Madden* for an extra two minutes.

"I'll get him," I say. Mostly as an escape from the unbearable discomfort between us, not because I want him to leave me a second sooner than he has to. I'm alone so often now, too often.

"All set." I reemerge with Joey and his bag that is filled with his dirty laundry from the past two nights. *Shit.* Am I going to get a passive-aggressive text about how I should have washed it?

I hold my breath, and I can feel Tatum holding hers too; we're both waiting for an explosion of Joey's tears or a kick to my shin or a fist to my side. Yelled protests that he doesn't want to go or he doesn't want us to divorce or just that he doesn't want something. Anything. It doesn't have to be specific these days with him. Instead, he stands on his tiptoes and pecks my check, then wraps his arms around my neck. I loft him off his feet, and he giggles. I feel myself soften and glance at Tatum, who seems to uncoil too.

"Be good for your mom, kiddo," I say before I set him down, and he reaches for Tatum's hand.

"I'm always good for Mommy," he laughs, giggling like he used to, like he wasn't now being split in two.

I watch them go and know that I can't say the same.

With Joey gone, the apartment is so quiet, so empty, I'm not sure what to do with myself. I play *Madden* to kill some time, but it's just pathetic to get worked up over fake football without your seven-year-old son there. I should work. I know that. Eric and I are back on set, managing the writers' room, breaking the story arcs for the next season of *Code Emergency*. But what I should really do is write. Like I used to, like I know I can. Not managing a staff of exhausted thirtysomethings, not crafting some bullshit hospital drama that I could outline while I sit on the can.

I mill about my apartment, running my hands over the empty walls, pausing in corners, turning, starting again. Seeing her today, here, has rattled me. It's easier to pretend she doesn't still inhabit part of me when we go days or even weeks now without stepping close enough to touch. I might see her face on a magazine cover or flip past one of her movies on late-night cable, but it's not the same as breathing in the same air, smelling her faint perfume, the same custom scent from Barneys she's worn for years, wanting to reach out and brush her arm when I think of something clever to say.

I can hear her in my ear, telling me, like she always used to say: "If you can dream it, you can be it," but I've been in hibernation for so long, screwed things up so deeply, that I'm not even sure what I dream. But slowly I'm awakening; slowly I feel myself melting into something like my old self, someone who once dreamed the same things as she did. Who promised to write something for her but then lost himself to other people's visions of what they wanted from him.

I should write it now, today, even if she doesn't need me any longer. Maybe that's the best time—when she doesn't need me. Prove to her that I understood why she asked me all those years ago—*because we were better together.*

But instead I keep walking from room to room in the apartment and staring at the vacancy—not that it's all that big, certainly nothing compared to the house in Brentwood with its high fences and higher ceilings where Tatum now lives alone with Joey, the house that was meant to be our enclave, to protect her from the outside world, protect us from . . . everything else. I let Joey pick out all the new furniture, decorate his room any which way he pleased, so his walls are a jarring bright green and his rug a shocking electric blue, but still, even with his bed unmade from the weekend, it feels barren.

I haven't lived alone in fifteen, almost sixteen years.

I shut Joey's door without a sound, as if I might disturb anyone, though it will just be me until Joe heads back to me on Wednesday, when Tatum flies to London to scout for her next film, which, incidentally, she's also directing.

I grab the scotch, my dad's old drink, from the kitchen counter, where I'd abandoned it earlier after my round of *Madden*, and refresh it.

I down the glass in a single gulp. That helps. Helps numb me to all this *shit* and how *fucked* we are and how *furious* I still am even though we split up months ago. The rage isn't just about us. It's about so many other things too. Things I need to let go of but instead find myself venting about over beers with Eric. I know that makes me childish; I know

I need to grow up. But at this moment, growing up feels overrated, especially when the scotch helps so very much. I tried grown-up with Leo. Look how well that worked.

I pour myself another because seeing her today has shaken me, and one more will ease me into forgetting how my pulse accelerated at the sight of her, how I wanted to reach out and grab her cheeks and press her against the wall and kiss her, but also how much I wanted to shake her shoulders and say: *You wronged me.* She could just as easily do the same to me. I know. I know all of this.

I suck down the shot, then run my finger around the lip of my glass, licking off the residue of the alcohol. I weave back into Joey's room, fall into his bed, where I've been sleeping during the nights he spends at Tatum's. He sometimes asks when I'm going to come home. Tatum thinks it's best that we just explain that we're not getting back together, that he have concise parameters of what to expect so he can mourn his old family unit and embrace a new one. She's probably right—*she's always right!*—but I've been in this place for only four months. Four months is nothing; four months is a sliver of time when perhaps, like Joey, I can still make believe that we can be put back together. Which I do want some days. So I try to reassure him with vague platitudes, as if that reassures me too. Maybe, even though we almost hate each other, we'll find our way back together? My promises sound as false to my own mind as they do when I try to offer reassurances aloud to Joey.

"Ben," my mom said the other night when she called, as she does daily now, like she still worries about me even at forty. "Marriage is a series of small forgivenesses." I could hear Ron in the background, talking to one of their houseguests. They'd bought a place in Sagaponack, mostly retired there now. "If you get caught up with one forgiveness, all the others you may need move out of reach."

"I know," I said.

"I don't think you do."

"Mom," I snapped.

"Your dad wasn't perfect."

"I never assumed as much." God knows that I'd never even considered that he was perfect. I thought of his rigidness, of his push to mold Leo into something Leo never wanted to be. I blinked quickly to abate a rush of tears when I considered my own push to mold Leo into something he never was.

"She's not perfect either," my mom offered.

"It's me," I said, my voice breaking. "I'm the one who's turned everything to shit."

"Well," my mom said. "If you thought that you were a perfect specimen of man, you should have just come and asked me. I could have told you otherwise. Also, Ben love, it goes both ways. You both probably turned things to shit."

I laughed because my mom never swears. At least she never used to.

"Perfection's not the point, honey," she said before she returned to her weekend guests. "Forgiveness is. *Acceptance* is." Then: "Maybe you can write about this?"

I told her that I was trying to, *God am I finally trying to,* and then she said she loved me and hung up. She had her whole life now too, and after Leo I stopped begrudging that and instead tried to find comfort in her happiness.

I rise from Joey's bed, my knees cracking, my empty stomach roiling from too much scotch. I shut his door tightly. Now all the doors are closed in the apartment, and though it's just as quiet as it was when they were open, I feel more settled, like maybe the space is smaller, like maybe I have less space to occupy. I root around the half-filled pantry for something for dinner. Joey's in a big soup phase, so I have a varied assortment: corn chowder, split pea, tomato bisque. A far cry from the catered and gourmet meals that Tatum had sent to our house each morning to adhere to her diet. I settle on three bean. I pop open the lid, which promptly gets stuck between the gelatinous soup and the side of the can, and I slice my thumb open as I try to pry it out. The blood rushes out quickly, faster than the pain hits my nervous system, and I'm momentarily stunned, wondering where this wound came from, wondering why it doesn't hurt more acutely. Then the pain comes: a sharp pinch radiating all the way up my arm.

I suck on the cut and use my good hand to dump the soup into a bowl.

I press the Start button on the microwave and bend over, peering inside the oven as my soup goes round and round. The buzzer beeps when it finishes, but I stay there for a few seconds after, crouched, staring, still pressing my thumb against my tongue, unable to recognize that the time has passed, unable to recognize that the time is up before I'm even fully aware that it started.

4

TATUM

DECEMBER 2000

Ben sneaks a small bottle of vodka from the inner pocket of his down coat, which is too puffy and threatens to swallow his chin.

"You saved my life; you know that, right?" He leans in close, shouting in my ear.

"You barely know me," I shout back. "And you're already giving me credit for saving your life?"

He grins and shakes his head. Around us, the crowds' cheers rise in swells that envelop us and carry us up with them.

"It's a small miracle you got me here on New Year's Eve," he yells. "This is a native New Yorker's worst nightmare."

"Well, you said you'd do anything I wanted in return for doing your film for free." I gaze up toward the flashing billboards, the neon lights. "This is what I wanted."

Also: *him*, this is what I wanted to do with him. Times Square at midnight. With a boy I might want to kiss for the rest of the year by my side. I didn't really think he'd come; I didn't really think I'd ask. But when I'd called Piper, my little sister, who was still back in Ohio and who would be spending her New Year's Eve in Bud Jones's basement—the same Bud Jones who got his nickname from the amount of pot he smoked in high school and who threw the same depressing New Year's Eve party, with a flat keg and blinking multicolored lights looped in the shape of breasts—I realized I had to: I had to dance in Times Square at midnight; I had to celebrate that I was no longer relegated to Bud Jones's metaphorical basement. I had to celebrate how far I'd come.

Ben had called a few weeks ago. We hadn't really spoken since that night at the bar. Sometimes I'd see him around the Village and wave, a little stutter of the hand, but we always kept walking with a bob of our chins. But then Daisy got the chicken pox, and he needed an actress for his graduate film, and that was how he ended up being indebted to me and by my side in Times Square on New Year's Eve. Also: I really wanted to kiss him.

He was single now. Daisy told me as much when I stopped over at her place with an oatmeal bath from Duane Reade and some trashy magazines. I'd gotten the chicken pox when I was six, when the entire first grade went down for the count over a particularly brutal Ohio winter. My mom let me sit in front of the TV all day, and then three days later Piper was covered in spots and joined me, and I was mostly miserable but also happy that my mom had canceled her shifts at the hospital and snuggled next to us while we watched *Kids Incorporated* or she tried to explain the drama on *Days of Our Lives*.

"He dumped his girlfriend," Daisy said, picking at a particularly gruesome blister on her left forearm. "A while ago now. So, totally single. Totally eligible."

"What happened?"

"Something about how she applied to residencies only outside of New York. He broke it off before she moved out of the state and left him behind. He got drunk one night and rambled on about loyalty and how it was all he really wanted."

"Ouch," I said, because it wasn't as if I couldn't relate. I may have been the one to move out of state, but mostly it was because I was fleeing the life I wanted to leave behind. Leave behind the shame of Aaron Johnson, the football player I lost my virginity to in high school, who I believed had loved me, but who ditched me a month later for Julie Seymour, a girl on the field hockey team, and utterly detonated my teenage confidence by refusing to return my calls, refusing to acknowledge me in the hallway or after school when he picked up an item at the pharmacy where I worked (under horrifying lighting and wearing a poop-colored apron); or with others like Brandon and Mark and Eddie in college, all of whom managed to strip me—piece by piece, slowly enough that the damage was almost undetectable—of whatever self-confidence with boys I had left after Aaron and all the chaos of my home life. All of whom somehow convinced me that the current version of myself wasn't exactly what they were looking for. That maybe if I were just a bit smarter or just a bit skinnier or just a bit prettier, they wouldn't have grown bored or listless or looked elsewhere.

"He's a good guy," Daisy said, wincing, scratching with more fervor.

"You shouldn't be doing that; it leaves scars."

"We're actors," she replied. "Scars are what make us interesting."

Tonight, Ben's younger brother, Leo, elbows his way through the New Year's Eve swarm and lands next to us, dragging a girl I don't know but have been told is named Caroline, who is a freshman at Barnard; Leo's a sophomore at Columbia. ("My parents' second wind," Ben said. "The baby of the family in every way.") Tonight Leo is just the right amount of tipsy, and it's impossible not to giggle when he stumbles and flattens himself against Ben to stop himself from falling, and then kisses his cheeks when he is steady.

"My big brother." He grins. "You're always looking out for me. Get him to tell you sometime about how he took the blame for my stash of pot freshman year in high school."

Ben shakes his head. "Mom and Dad threatened to stop my tuition payments for college."

Leo laughs. "Dad is always busting our balls."

"Just trying to bring out our potential," Ben says, and though I don't know him well, I can see he's deflecting. "And mostly, he's busting mine."

"Well, that's what makes you the best big brother in the world," Leo crows. He looks toward me. "I assume you are the lovely lady who somehow got my uptight brother into Times Square right now?"

"Tatum," I say, extending a gloved hand, which he ignores as he pulls me into a hug as if I'm family.

"This is the sickest thing I have ever done."

Ben laughs. "And that's a high threshold."

"No, dude, seriously, don't be a downer. We're gonna remember this forever. Times Square in New York!" He cups his gloves around his mouth and tilts his head toward the night sky. "Hello, 2001! Let's see what you got!"

Caroline passes around an open bottle of champagne concealed in a paper bag, and we all drink generously, the bubbly matching our effervescent spirits, the alcohol warming us in the frigid Manhattan air.

The wind kicks up, and the snow starts to fall: thick, pregnant flakes that feel like they'll stick almost immediately. Leo and Caroline huddle together, him wrapping his scarf around her and tugging her closer as if their lips are magnetic, each unable to be without the other. In seconds, Ben's wavy dark hair is frosted in white, and he reaches out and brushes a few errant flakes off my eyelashes. There must be ten thousand people in Times Square, and I peer up at the Jumbotron, wondering where we are in the sea of faces and bodies that are mashed together, a pulsing wave ready to flush out the previous year, harken in a new one.

Ben and I gape at Leo and Caroline for a beat, self-conscious, awkward in that new way when you're waiting for the other one to kiss you, when you're too new to each other, too unsure to do anything more than bite your lip or stare at your shoes.

"Leo's always been like this," he says. "All the girls in my grade thought he was the cutest. Imagine losing girls to your younger brother. And he was, like, eleven!"

"I find that hard to believe."

"I'm too nice a guy." He shakes his head. "That was never Leo's problem."

"Ah, the curse of the nice guy." I don't mention that Daisy told me she thought that breaking up with the medical school girlfriend gutted him through the summer, that Daisy told him to go out and screw a few randoms, but he chuckled and said that wasn't his style. And she had said: "Not a guy's style? Casual sex is every guy's style!" Which had made him blush a little deeper, laugh a little harder.

"Well," I say now, "I don't think you're *that* nice. I mean, you were a bit of a tyrant on the shoot."

"I was the director; that's my job. I was trying to make the day, get the light. Also, since we're here and I'm being honest, I can admit to asking for an extra take or two because I thought you were so spectacular."

Now it's my turn to deflect, because I've never been great at accepting compliments unless I'm playing a part. "Well, I hope you write that into your Oscar speech. 'I apologize to Tatum Connelly for being a tyrant. And for making her do extra takes just for the hell of it. It was part of my job!'"

I can see his eyes wrinkle into a grin underneath his muffler. "It was just some stupid short to fulfill my thesis. *Romanticah* isn't winning any Oscars."

"Well, not with *that* attitude it's not."

"All I want is some funding, maybe expand it into a feature, maybe get an agent with it. Oscars aren't exactly on my radar."

"I thought you told me once that you promised your dad an Oscar—that was part of the deal."

He shrugs his puffy shoulders. "Did you not hear what Leo just said about my dad? Kind of impossible standards."

"Well *my* mom always says, 'If you can dream it, you can be it,'" I say. "So why not dream it?"

I don't add: *She's sick again.* She called a few days ago and broke the news because she didn't want to tell me when I was home for Christmas, but she told me not to worry, that it doesn't look so bad, that they caught it again before it spread too far. She hadn't betrayed a hint of it for the three days I'd been back; that was all the vacation time I could afford when I could pick up overtime work at the bar and jump-start my bank account for the new year. She looked tired, sure, but she almost always looked tired from her shifts at the hospital, and on Christmas Eve, she and Piper and I curled up on the couch, like we did when Piper and I were little, and watched *It's a Wonderful Life*.

And it never once occurred to me that the insidious seeds of cancer had returned.

Tonight, on the last night of the year in the span of the millennium, I try to forget that my mom is sick again, that after her call I thought the walls of my tiny student apartment might crater on top of me. But I am an actress: I can pretend to do anything, be anyone. So I compartmentalize my fear and reach for Ben's hand. I will tell him tomorrow because I know on instinct that I can tell him, and he will find a way to make it a little better. For now, my glove finds his, and it feels right, it feels sturdy, like I'm holding on to something grounding.

He says: "You've always wanted to do this?"

"Times Square? Oh, my gosh, I grew up watching it with my sister every year!"

"No." He laughs. "Acting. Movies, theater, all of that."

"Oh, it's the only thing I really ever felt like I was good at."

"Besides bartending."

"Besides that, yes, of course."

"Because you're terrible at making bets."

31

"Ugh." I groan loudly enough to be heard over Caroline and Leo, who are cheering at Boyz II Men, who have just wrapped their set, beamed in on the large screens from Hollywood. "I'm sorry, but that was fixed! Stupid Daisy."

He squeezes my hand through our gloves, and I squeeze back, like we have a secret code, like there is an electric pulse running through him into me and back again.

And now there are only a few minutes until midnight, and the snow is both furious and beautiful, eye-opening and blinding, and we have given in to the excitement of the other thousands of people here, of Dick Clark's voice over the enormous speakers that surround the block, of the twinkling ball that's projected across the screens a hundred feet above us.

"I'm glad you made me come here," he says, his breath billowing in a plume of white steam. "I've lived here all my life, and I'd never have done this without you."

"I'm glad that Daisy got the chicken pox," I reply, and his blue eyes widen then crease into happiness.

"I'm glad that I didn't give you my number last year," he says. "My heart couldn't have taken it at the time."

"I'm glad that I didn't ransack your heart, and so you're not dead and that dumb ex-girlfriend didn't have to revive you with her fancy medical knowledge, and then, either way—dead or alive—you wouldn't be here with me now."

He nods. "I'm glad that I'm here with you now." He peers toward the sky. "God, it's like I'm seeing this city for the very first time." He finds my eyes again: "It's like I'm seeing a lot of things for the very first time."

The crowd has started cheering, counting down, jumping and throbbing and clamoring for midnight, the start of something new, the promise of beginnings.

"Me too," I say.

"I see you," he says.

"I see you too," I say, and I do, and he does, and it's as if he has a microscope inside of me.

And then we are at three, and then we are at two, and then we are at one, and he is kissing me or maybe I am kissing him, but it doesn't matter because the old year is behind us and a new one lies in wait, and I don't worry about my mom and I don't worry about my next part or my next paycheck or my mom's next scan. Thousands of pieces of sparkling confetti rain down, mixing with the snow, and I feel like I'm caught in time, caught in a perfect moment inside a snow globe that maybe I'd beg my mom for at a gas station, and I can't find my breath, and my knees feel a little wobbly, and I try to remind myself to remember this moment, to hold on to it forever, to seal it up like we really are in that snow globe and to never let anything shatter the bubble that envelops us, that protects us from everything else around us in the outside world.

5

BEN

AUGUST 2014

Jesus, somehow I turned forty. Am turning forty. Tomorrow.

I let the hot water from the shower pulse against my face and neck for too long, and by the time I flip the shower handle to off, my skin is pink and a little angry. I grab one of the white towels hanging on the pewter hooks and knot it around my waist, then stare at the full-length mirror in the bathroom that is half packed because we're moving next week. Tatum needs a house with better security; Tatum needs a house that moves us one more step toward isolation. We're stuck in this bubble that is entirely our creation, and it feels as if there's no way out, no room to breathe.

I blame her for this.

I run my hand over my stubble, meet my eyes in the mirror. It's an unkind thought, and I chastise myself for it. She loves this house, loves the family we built here, though now that family is tenuous at best, though we are doing an excellent job at pretending that we're not falling apart—both to each other and to the various media outlets who occasionally sniff at some unhappiness but mostly paint her (and us) as something out of a blissful, stylized magazine spread.

We both—equally—loved this home in Holmby Hills that had seen us through so much. But a month ago we'd woken up to her stalker staring at our family photographs on our living room fireplace mantel, and after she hid in the closet and I called the police, we both knew that the house was just another thing we had to let go of, like anonymity, like a normal life where we (she) kept sane hours and caught up on our days over dinner and grew a vegetable patch out back and greeted tiny trick-or-treaters come Halloween. None of that is who we are anymore, not with Tatum's fame and the bubble that it's forced us into. The new place in Brentwood has a ten-foot wall in a gated community and is impenetrable, literally. A large Israeli man with a Bluetooth earpiece and a holster on his hip walked us through the security system and explained the ins and outs, explained how we were safer there than at the White House. (I was dubious, but we'd only been to the White House once—Tatum was invited for a press dinner. I was literally patted down in my tux twice and screened through four metal detectors, but what did I know?) We talk about getting a guard dog; Monster is old and slow, and besides, he'd befriend anyone who gave him a treat, threw him a literal bone. We talk about round-the-clock bodyguards, though I point out that the large Israeli man told us we were already safe.

"Hey." Tatum pops her head around the bathroom doorway. "You almost ready or are you too busy admiring yourself in the mirror? You're an old man now, come on."

"I'm looking good for forty." I grin, and suck in my stomach, show her my profile.

She sighs.

"Or not? I don't know." I let my stomach deflate.

"No, you do, you are. I just . . . I got my period. Maybe we're just too old."

"You're not forty, just me," I remind her.

We'd started trying for another child about nine months ago, last year, right around when Piper was pregnant. In fact, Tatum had sprung the news on me that she wanted another one when we were back in Ohio for Piper's baby shower. I figured it was the excitement and the nostalgia: the little onesies, the cute stuffed animals and music boxes. We'd always been fine with one, with Joey. We'd agreed on that—*one*. Tatum barely had time to fit Joey in her schedule, much less me. But she announced it with such authority and such conviction that I couldn't even question it: "I think we should have another baby, and I've already made time for it in my schedule, so I think it should work and let's just do it." I'd just gotten home from a run through her old neighborhood; I remember peeling off my shirt and Tatum lingering in the bathroom, as if she were issuing a press statement: *We're going to have another baby.* Not phrased as a question, not tossed out as a possibility.

I started to say, *You've already lost track of me. Will I be pushed out entirely when a new one comes along?* But it felt needy and jealous and a little childish too. Also, I had the weight of my guilt sinking me down, all of the ways, both big and small, I'd betrayed her over the past two years, so I nodded, flipped on the shower, and said: "OK."

I was happy with one, with Joey. Tatum needed more. I took it personally, until I remembered that I'd needed something more too, and Tatum had no idea. There are a lot of reasons that you say yes to something you don't really want. Guilt worked perfectly well for me. Besides, Leo had been everything to me; I could understand wanting to give Joey a sibling.

"We can try again next month," I say to her now, in the half-packed bathroom. Though the idea of rising with a screaming infant at three a.m. felt less palatable with every passing month. At forty, my own dad had a fifteen-year-old and an eight-year-old: he had the energy for us, but barely. A newborn? It sounds exhausting already. "Don't worry," I repeat. "We'll try again."

I don't know when I stopped telling Tatum my truths. She used to read everything about me, see through me. Maybe I stopped telling her my truths as a challenge, to see if she still could.

"I'm away next month. Vancouver, remember?"

I don't remember but I say: "Oh, right." I don't ask why or what for. There's a giant master calendar in the kitchen that I can consult if I need to know where to find her on a certain day. Her assistant uses color coding to make it easier: red for on set, blue for media, green for meetings, orange for Joey. I don't get a marker. It's assumed, I guess, that I can write in my own commitments to fit around hers. Actually, maybe that was when I stopped telling her my truths. When a giant master calendar went up, and there wasn't a marker for me.

"Then the following month," I offer.

She shrugs. "OK, hurry up. We have a reservation."

"Down in ten. When you're this good-looking, it doesn't take much." I wink, try to make her laugh.

"Ha," she says on her way out the door.

I reassess myself in the mirror. Though I don't want a newborn, I could manage. I am a younger forty than my dad was at the same age, though he rose most mornings to play racquetball, out the door before our nanny had even made us breakfast. I'm a more involved father too: a field trip in May to go berry picking (I was the only dad); coaching peewee soccer last fall; midnight trips into Joey's room when he has a bad dream.

For my dad's fortieth, we took a family trip to Paris. I remember it because he had just wrapped a monster trial, which meant that I saw him even less than usual, and my mom kept telling us: *We'll all have time together on this trip!* If she minded my dad's absence, she didn't complain; she doted on him when he was around, brought him tea, made his favorite dinners. When he wasn't, she was busy as the president of Dalton's PTA, as chair of one charity committee or the other. We flew to Paris first-class, and Leo, still cute and impish at eight, charmed the flight attendants into giving him all the leftover chocolate. My dad spent most of the flight quizzing me on my French (I was in honors) and then reading briefs for work upon his return. But Leo, hopped up on all the chocolate, was nearly vibrating, and he scaled the seat and somersaulted into the lap of the Frenchman behind him, who was none too pleased, and then quickly turned irate when Leo knocked the man's coffee into his lap.

My dad, who had just started wearing reading glasses, pushed them higher on his nose and said: "Ben, apologize in French to him. Make nice. Sort it out."

My mom was asleep from her two glasses of wine. My dad's own French had been honed at Yale; he could speak it better than I could, and after all, he *was* the parent. But I did as I was asked, partially because I wanted to impress him, partially because it wasn't phrased as a question.

Once I had apologized in my mostly fluent French and had Leo strapped back into his seat and had pulled out some crayons and a coloring book my mom had stowed in his backpack, my dad looked over from across the aisle and said, "Nice job, Ben," and then returned to his briefs.

It wasn't a big deal, it wasn't such a life-altering incident. But it was profound in its own way. That my dad sent the message that I was Leo's keeper just as much as he was. That he also conveyed that I was the responsible son, that I was literally there to clean up Leo's messes. I resented my dad for that. I remember stewing over it, staring out the window somewhere over the Atlantic and thinking: *Why did I have to talk down that French guy who was shouting about sending "enfants" to the back of the plane, while you acted like your briefs were more important?* But later in the trip, when we were touring the Louvre, I found myself showing off for my father, conversing with our tour guide as often as possible, asking questions I really didn't even care about because I wanted my father to look over once more and say simply: "Nice work."

I thought about that for a long time afterward. How complicated approval and resentment can be, how they can be tied together so closely that you might mistake one for the other if you're not careful.

My eyes falter in my bathroom mirror, as my phone buzzes on the vanity counter.

Happy birthday tomorrow. I wanted to be the first to wish you.

Then another buzz.

Sorry. Shit. I wish I hadn't sent that. You don't have to write me back. Or do if you want?

Instinctively, I grab my phone and start typing until my brain tells my fingers to slow down. They're shaking with adrenaline, so I'd have to delete most of what I wrote anyway. I delete it all. Rest my phone back on the marble, then swipe it back up and throw it into the bottom cabinet drawer. As if that can stop the temptation of starting back up with Amanda, when I'd been so resolute since I cut things off last December, eight months now.

I ended it only when I found a draft of an e-mail to Tatum's publicist, asking how she would plan a strategy for divorce. We were trying for the baby, but Tatum had always been one to have a backup plan. I read the e-mail to Luann—*How would you position this so people know I tried my hardest to make it work*—and something came undone in me: that while I'd been toying with Amanda, maybe seriously, but maybe not, Tatum was toying with a whole other life without me too. Amanda had been an escape. Tatum, it turned out, had one too. I'd closed out of her in-box and run to the bathroom and nearly shit myself. Literally. I'd been such a stupid, stupid fuck.

I have to remind myself of this every time Amanda texts, every time Tatum is dismissive of me, every time she doesn't even think to give me my own marker on our enormous calendar, or when she announces that we're going to try for another kid and doesn't expect to be challenged because she has a team of people who surround her now, wrap her in bubble wrap, to ensure that she is protected.

But after the e-mail calamity, I met Amanda in a Starbucks near Cedars. "We have to stop doing this," I said simply. "I'd rather cut off a limb, but I have to." Neither of us believed that to be true.

It was raining that day, and her flame-red hair was matted and damp, and she reminded me of how Monster sometimes looks: like he still needed to be rescued even after we took him in all those years ago. But as she batted her eyes, fighting back tears, it occurred to me that I'd misplaced my own rescue operation, that I'd been reckless and gotten high off the thrill of us, but I was the one who actually needed to be saved. There is nostalgia for an ex, and there is crossing a line to entertain that nostalgia. That's not love; that's not worth risking your life over.

Fuck.

I'd screwed things up so badly, and it was all I could do to try to right myself, ourselves, before Tatum ever caught wind of it. It was the first time it had occurred to me, not in an impish, thrilling way, but a deep-in-my-guts way, that Tatum could find out and leave me.

"I'm sorry," I'd said. "I'll miss you."

I drove home, my windshield wipers flapping too quickly, and realized I was no different from Walter, with his alcoholism and years of unkept promises, and no different from Leo, with all of his demons and screw-ups. We all have that shiny carrot we chase when we know it could be poisonous. We all step too close to the flame because we wonder how much it would hurt if we get burned.

I'd felt forgotten, overlooked by my own wife, when loyalty was what I'd always wanted. And so I found a way to be seen, found a way to trump her passive disloyalty with my own. That doesn't make it forgivable, it doesn't mean I excuse it. But that's what it was, is, all the same.

I reach for my phone from the bottom cabinet drawer. I knew it would do me no good, stuffing it there. Amanda had proven devoted, as if she'd learned a lesson from the years that separated us, and now she was mine if I wanted her.

It was more than that, of course, for me. It was the wistfulness, the pining for being young and unburdened, for a different partner, different breasts and legs and lips. She was an easy escape, a sure thing, when my wife was gone so often, returning home in mercurial moods, with mercurial haircuts, with mercurial wishes that I didn't often understand. Partially because I stopped asking. Partially because she stopped telling me.

I turn to the side and suck in my stomach again, watching it fall and rise in the mirror, amazed that this body of mine has been on this planet for forty years now, aware of how lucky I am to be alive. How fucking miraculous it is that any of us gets to be here another day.

I pick up my phone. Set it down. Pick it up again.

It's ok, I type. *I miss you too. But I still can't.*

All true.

"Ben!" Tatum's voice reverberates up the stairwell, echoes through the now mostly empty rooms, primed and ready for the movers. "My dad's here!"

Walter is babysitting, a concession that I've only recently grown comfortable with, but a small concession all the same. The first time I'd approved, agreed to let him stay home alone with Joey, Tatum had clutched my cheeks and kissed me, really kissed me, and God, it reminded me of how effervescent she was, not just compared to Amanda, but compared to what I'd grown used to now that I no longer really *saw* her every day, compared to what I'd taken for granted.

"Give me three minutes," I yell back to her, then scamper into my half-packed closet and retrieve a shirt from a suitcase. We're having dinner, just the two of us, for my birthday. We haven't been alone, on a date, since forever. Really, honestly, I can't even remember the last time we made this sort of time for each other. Tatum because she was so busy, me because I retreated to the writers' room for *Code Emergency* rather than face the massive calendar in the kitchen when I couldn't, literally, even be penciled in. It was easier to order in Chinese food with Eric and the writing staff than sit home alone in a quiet house surfing the cable channels (or sometimes porn) after Joey went down. Not unlike how I'd dumped Amanda before she could dump me all those years back when she applied to residencies three thousand miles away. Now I just stay busy so Tatum doesn't notice that her life is so much bigger than mine.

I fold my arms into the button-down, straighten up in front of the mirror, and meet my eyes again. I find the watch she gave me this morning (because she couldn't wait until tomorrow, and I'd laughed because impulse control was never her forte) from my top drawer, snap it on my wrist and feel its unfamiliar but not unwelcome heft.

Tomorrow, I tell myself, *I will start writing something for Tatum.* Something that will bring her back to me. Something that can make us whole again, after all the ways that life has sliced away tiny pieces of us. I want to be better—a better spouse, a more present husband, a more understanding partner. One who doesn't mind that she is lost for weeks on end in the mood of whatever role she is playing; one who doesn't begrudge her for the offers that pour in and take her away from me and from Joey, offers that she could say no to but does not. And of course, I want to make it up to her: for Amanda and my overt betrayals, though Tatum knows nothing of the tryst. I know how I failed her, and that's enough.

I find a tie—I almost never wear a tie, but I'm turning forty tomorrow, and a tie feels like the right way to commemorate it. Tatum will be in something gorgeous, and tonight I'd like to do right by her, be her equal. I knot it around my neck, run my fingers through my hair, and assess.

I gaze at my reflection. Yes, tonight I'm her equal.

Tatum used to tell me about how she and her mom collected snow globes, how they'd pull into a gas station or stop into the hospital gift shop and search for a new one, something unique to add to their collection. "It's always perfect inside a snow globe," Tatum once said. I always wondered why. And how. Because what it really seems to me is that you are trapped, stuck there in that fantasyland.

I wonder now if I can write something for her that isn't a bit like a snow globe: magical, self-preserving, romantic. I wonder, though, if staying in the bubble is really what's best. If that's what she wants, if that's what I want. And if we puncture it, if we'll still find a way to breathe.

6

TATUM

JULY 2001

It is too hot for a funeral. That is what I keep thinking. It is too hot for a funeral, and how am I expected to be burying my mom when it is 103 degrees, and I can't think straight because of the heat? I am sweating and clammy and red faced, and my hair is sticking to the back of my neck and my skirt is flush against the backs of my thighs, and the sun is so bright I wonder if I might go blind.

She wanted to be cremated, scattered in our garden. She told Piper as much when it became clear that this time the cancer was too furious to be beaten back.

"Just some of the gals from the hospital, you girls, and some cake afterward, OK?"

They hadn't told me it was as bad as it was until just a few days before she was gone.

And June, with Ben, had been blissful: he had found the money to turn the *Romanticah* short into a feature, and we'd celebrated his Tisch graduation with a real—if low-budget—shoot, spending the days tromping through Central Park with his small crew, his small cast, and me as his star, spending the evenings in his parents' sprawling uptown apartment. They were in Europe for June, so I could collapse in his childhood bed without shame, without the next-morning embarrassment of sneaking out. In our earlier days of dating we landed at my tiny apartment most nights, but its starkness compared to the luxury he'd grown up in was claustrophobic and a little horrifying.

When Piper called and told me that time was running out, I felt as if I were watching the conversation like a film: I was there but not really; distant but still engaged just enough. Maybe I hadn't been paying attention, or maybe I'd just been so lost in falling down the rabbit hole of this new life that Ben breathed into me—a nearly working actress, a woman worthy of being adored—that I hadn't wanted to believe the truth of Mom's diagnosis.

He'd told me he'd loved me right before I left to say good-bye to her. We'd been together six months, and I already knew in how he looked at me, by how he touched me. But I wasn't brave enough to say it first. As I was packing, grabbing whatever I could find that would be appropriate to wear to your mother's funeral, he sat on the bed and said simply:

"Hey, Tate, I love you."

And then I stopped grabbing whatever I could find and climbed back into bed with him and proved to him that I loved him too. Told him too. I'd told a million boys along the way that I loved them. This might have been the first time I understood what that meant, and even more so, how it felt to be loved back. To be seen. With my insecurities, with my bruises, with my baggage. It wasn't a coincidence that I'd done my best work with him on *Romanticah*. He was the first person who ever saw through me, but not because he wanted to expose me, but rather because I was willing to expose myself.

And now I am standing under the light of a thousand suns, and Piper is plunked down on a tree stump in our backyard, her shoulders trembling, her head low. She is weeping, and I need to move to comfort her, to place a reassuring palm on her back, because that's what older sisters do for their younger siblings when their mom has died. But I worry that if I move, I'll collapse, like I'm a pile of emotional dominos and a tiny reverberation will send it all to dirt on the ground where we are about to toss the fiery remains of my mother's broken body. Instead, Dot, my mother's best friend from nursing school and then the rest of her life, offers Piper a hand, pulls her to her feet and into a bear hug. Piper burrows into her shoulder and wails.

The doorbell rings inside the house, which brings me to.

"I'll get that," I say, right as Piper manages, "Leave it, don't."

The heels of my shoes slide off from my sweat, and I ditch them by the patio glass door and rush through the hallway to the door. I realize how hasty I am as soon as I've swung the door open. Everyone we needed to be here already is. Well, not Ben. But I told him not to come. He is racing to get *Romanticah* edited in time for film festival submissions, which I used as an excuse to tell him not to join me. But also, I didn't want him to see where I came from, didn't need him to know, unequivocally, that I didn't deserve him, even on my best days, even in our best life. My mother was a nurse and my dad sold life insurance, but not well and only when he was sober. It's not that I was ashamed, really, but it's not that I wasn't either. Our house needed a paint job, and the carpet was left over from the '80s. Ben grew up on an entire floor on Park Avenue, with a nanny and a housekeeper, and two parents who vacationed in Europe for the month of June. And even though he loves me, and even though he *sees* me, part of me (plenty of me) was still self-conscious: What if he saw how vast the divide was between us and decided that even when I put on my very best face, morphed into whatever role he needed from me, it still wasn't enough?

He wouldn't have been my first boyfriend to do that, and he was already miles ahead of them. Handsomer, more successful, better lineage. If all the rest of them could dump me, could deem me not worthy, what's to stop Ben when he uncovers the blights of my past? So I sat on the edge of his bed in his perfect childhood bedroom, with a signed Yankees poster from Reggie Jackson framed above his headboard, and I assured him I didn't need him to come. It was a masterful performance, really, convincing enough that he didn't even second-guess me. He kissed my tear-stained cheeks, and stripped my shirt off, and then the rest of my clothes too, and afterward held me against him until I stopped shaking and fell into a fitful sleep that offered no rest.

The doorbell chimes again as I wrap my sweaty palm around the knob and swing it open.

Shit, I think, as the bright light of day greets me.

"Shit," I actually say aloud when I see my dad standing on the precipice.

"Tate," he says, his voice breaking.

He is dressed in an ill-fitting brown suit with a loosely knotted tie. He's aged in the two years since I left the Canton outskirts, since I last saw him at my college graduation party, which my mom threw for me here in this very house. They were separated (again), and he got drunk (again), and she calmly asked him to leave and then he didn't, so I less calmly asked him to leave, and then he toppled my graduation cake onto the concrete of the back patio, where it smushed into a depressing pile of cooked egg and flour and green icing. Piper grabbed him by the elbow and called him a cab, and we all pretended that he hadn't just ruined the party like he had ruined a million things before. I'd gotten good at pretending by then: I'd graduated with honors from Ohio University, spent my summers in summer stock, where I'd met Daisy, been accepted to Tisch on grants and scholarships.

As Piper dragged him out, and just before he swiped a loose arm at the shelf with my mother's and my snow globe collection, sending glass and water and sparkles careening to the ground, I'd pressed my face into something of a blissful smile and made a passing joke about how my dad had celebrated a bit too much at getting his daughter out of the house. This was my mask. My act. I counted on both so easily that I wanted to make a career of it.

"Who invited you?" I say to him today.

"Piper." He flops his hands, which seem to want to reach for me, but don't move too far from his sides. He knows better by now.

"Piper!" I shout over my shoulder to the back of the house.

"I've been sober for a year," he says.

"Congratulations."

"That's the longest since—"

I wave a hand, cutting him off. I know it's the longest since high school. I don't need him to tell me. Like Piper and I didn't used to hang the moon around the times when he was clear and present, like we didn't shut the door to the bedroom we shared and turn up the radio and sing too loudly to drown out the times when he wasn't. He was never violent, never even particularly cruel, only destructive to himself and unreliable, which meant that the one thing a child needed—stability—was the one thing he could never provide. Some mornings, when my mom was sick, it meant he'd be too drunk to drive us to the school bus, and we'd end up walking the route to the stop, usually missing it, then trudging to school on foot; some afternoons, it meant asking the neighbors if Piper and I could join them for dinner, because our fridge was empty and Mom couldn't get out of bed and Dad was nowhere to be found. Well, he surely could be found, at A.J.'s, his bar of choice, but it's not like we were going to go down there and force him home.

"I'm here to bury Mom, to help Piper. I'm not here to deal with you," I say to him. The sun shifts from behind a cloud, and again it's too bright, blinding, melting. I narrow my eyes, squeeze them shut, then blink them wider like this is all a mirage. But he's still there when I open them.

"Dad," Piper says from behind me, then brushes past me into his arms. He emits a sob that sounds so guttural, I literally step back into the hallway.

We return to the garden, me unable to look at him.

"I couldn't not include him, Tate," Piper whispers. "He's our dad. He was her husband. He was here a lot these past few months."

I nod, pressing my lips tightly together so nothing slips out I'll regret. Piper was always more forgiving of him than I was. She doesn't remember when our mom was first diagnosed when I was twelve, and Dad coped by blacking out on the couch and getting fired from his job. She doesn't remember walking around the strip mall, going from store to store, asking if someone could give me a job, finally being granted a kind reprieve by Ralph at the pharmacy, who let me work as a bag girl. She doesn't remember him forgetting to pick me up from choir practice three times in a week, and how humiliated I was to slink back into school to ask Ms. Byrdwell if I could use a phone to try to call him . . . or someone.

He was sober again by the time I was fourteen, when my mother was in remission, then not when I was fifteen, and it stayed that way mostly until I graduated. I lived on campus at college, but was home enough to see the pattern of ruin he left, and my mom finally saw it too. She kicked him out, but she wasn't much better at sticking to her word than he was, and so their home became a revolving door for forgiveness. It wasn't any surprise that Piper learned the same lesson: *Come back to me, and I'll absolve you.*

Dot, my mom's oldest friend, asks for us to hold hands, to bow our heads in prayer that Mom is no longer in pain, that she isn't part of this physical world, that she is somewhere else, somewhere better. I don't know if I believe this; I don't know what I believe, really. But I dutifully drop my chin to my chest, and the sun is so very, very hot again, and I think of Ben and wish he were here but am also so relieved that he isn't. That he isn't seeing this mess of a life I've left behind; that he can't see my weeping, which is now coming in waves, that he can't see my father, who is clutching Piper's elbow.

I think of the last time I saw my mother. Jesus, it was Christmas. When we watched *It's a Wonderful Life*. She asked me if I was happy, as if I even knew what that meant.

I said: "I'm happy. But I'll be happier when I'm employed, you know, working as an actor."

She replied: "Don't define yourself by that, sweetheart, don't live a life marked by intangible achievements."

"That's not intangible; that's real."

She smiled at something I didn't understand.

"You're always saying, 'If you can dream it, you can be it,'" I said.

"Well, that's true." She nodded. My mom had always been a writer—well, she'd always been a nurse. But she'd also been a poet, *just for herself*, she said, *just because I can*. "I want you to be anything you dream of. But mostly I want you to be happy. Those things aren't always the same, you know."

"But what if they are?" I asked.

"That's why you're young; that's why you have the time to figure it all out," she said, before rising to go make herself some tea.

I feel dizzy under the sun's rays and worry I might pass out. Dot asks us all to step forward, to scoop my mother's ashes and to send them out into the air, over the garden, over our home, back into the ground where they'll bloom again in the form of flowers and snap peas and, if we're lucky, perfect strawberries in later summer. I squeeze Piper's hand tighter, unsure if I can do this, really let her go. But then I remind myself that I can do anything, be anyone. *That is what I dream.* I slip outside my grief, morph myself into someone else—someone who isn't here burying her mother—and I release Piper's grip and go.

7

BEN

APRIL 2013

I'm dreaming again, as I do so often now, have for the past year since everything turned bleak.

This time I know I am dreaming and yet I can't pull myself out of it. This time, as it has been recently, it's Leo. Always Leo, though it used to be my dad. Now it's a distorted version of something out of real life: that night on April Fool's Day when he ran away in seventh grade, when I was a senior in high school. He was pissed at my dad for something—in real life, it was that my dad threatened to pull him from the football team because his grades were so mediocre (for my dad, Cs and Bs), but in the dream, it's because my father drowned in the Atlantic Ocean off East Hampton Beach, and Leo was there, watching, unable to save him.

So Leo ran, and unlike how it really happened—where we thought it was a prank until one a.m. rolled around and my mom started crying and my dad started cursing, and I finally found him at his friend Nate's apartment, smoking cigarettes and skimming bourbon—in the dream I'm unable to trace him. I run down the emptied, littered streets of Manhattan, at night, at day, at dawn, at sunset, and Leo is simply gone. I shout down alleys; I scream around corners; and it starts raining, then hailing, and I am stuck in the middle of Times Square, unable to find any trace of my brother at all.

I startle awake, blinking too quickly, discombobulated in an unfamiliar bed, in an unfamiliar room.

A hand is laid across my chest, and a voice says: "I'm here," and my brain loops for a moment until I realize it's Amanda, not Tatum, and that we have spent the night at a room at the Standard after I'd e-mailed her, claiming we needed to end things, but agreeing to drinks all the same. One drink led to two drinks and then to a full bottle, and soon enough we were checking into a room, peeling our clothes off, doing the things to each other that I swore I would no longer do. My guilt was too heavy; the fear of being caught was consuming me—a tabloid had a small headline about Tatum's "unhappy marriage" and my "wandering eye" last week. Tatum never paid that stuff any mind, barring the scathing rumors after the Oscars, which I couldn't even begin to contemplate because of Leo. In another universe, another time, maybe it would have cut more deeply, but it was all I could do to *breathe* back then, much less contemplate what her behavior represented. It represented something, I knew, though. That much wasn't lost on me, even in my haze of grief and confusion. And maybe, yes, it served as a subconscious excuse for what I did next, with Amanda, with my self-destruction. I don't know.

But the headline about me, my affair, that one permeated. I'd been in the checkout line buying cereal at Gelson's and nearly had a panic attack worrying whether I'd closed out of my e-mail on my laptop, and if Tatum, who was sleeping in, would rise and see my glaring infidelity in my e-mails to Amanda over her breakfast of a hard-boiled egg and cappuccino.

I hadn't even meant for it to get this far, to go on for so long, but now we were eleven months, almost a year, deep. When I called her after the hospital, after Joey's broken arm, I'd only meant, theoretically, to meet for a catch-up coffee. But coffee led to drinks and drinks sometimes led to dinner. Dinner led to e-mails and texts and late-night phone calls when Joey was asleep. Tatum was working nights: she'd started (theoretically) getting choosier about the projects that wreaked havoc on our life. But *America*, a gritty drama about the LA riots and the ensuing fallout (the script was spectacular—Spencer, my agent, tried to get my name in for a polish, but this was before Tatum signed on, and it went to Landon Marks, Hollywood's new It boy, who got all the good polishes right now), kept us on opposite schedules. She'd come home in time to sit with Joey at breakfast, then collapse for the day before rising to sit with him again for an early dinner before her driver arrived for another day (and night) when we merely passed each other by. Coffee and dinners (and then much more) with Amanda really weren't all that hard to pull off, really weren't particularly sneaky, because Tatum wasn't logistically present for me to have to even sneak around.

"I'm here," Amanda says again, rustling the Standard bedding.

I inhale, and my undershirt, sticky with sweat, rises against her palm.

At home, when I burst from my nightmares, the bed is most often empty. In fact, just last night Tatum had taken Joey to Legoland as part of a thank-you to the *America* cast and crew: it had been a long, grueling shoot; she wanted to show her appreciation. I didn't want to go anyway, but she didn't offer. It was exclusively for the staff, the teamsters, the actors, who deserved some R and R with their kids, she'd said.

So instead I e-mailed Amanda to ostensibly break up—and then because she was there and loyal and sexy as fuck and made me feel *valued*, we ended up in six-hundred-thread-count sheets in a room at the Standard. I don't love her. She isn't my wife. But when our legs are intertwined at the bottom of the bed, and her hand is across my chest, and I am not *alone* as I so often am now, and Amanda *needs* me in ways that Tatum used to but no longer does, I tell myself that I just might. Maybe I love her? Maybe I could?

Being valued, being needed, being *seen* is an easy thing to underestimate. Like air. Like you don't realize that it's necessary to sustain you until it's suddenly gone.

Amanda feels like air. Not love. But somehow necessary all the same. Tatum used to say, and I used to believe, that I was the only one who could *see* her, and I could. I did. I felt the same: she inspired my directorial debut with *Romanticah*, she inspired everything in those early years. Now, who knows what we see? It's happened so gradually that I can't even say when things got so blurry: maybe as she found others who saw her as I did when it used to be only me; maybe as I chased success instead of chasing happiness. I don't know. If I did, I probably wouldn't be screwing my ex-girlfriend who plugs the hole in my heart but probably doesn't fill it.

"You OK?" Amanda says, her wide green eyes finding mine.

"Yes. No." I roll over, stare at the ceiling, then push myself up to my elbows. "I should go."

"You don't have to."

"Not because of you." *Yes, because of you!* my conscience corrects, but I lean over and peck her nose all the same, move down to graze her lips. "I want to work today. The house is quiet. I don't have to be in the writers' room. It's Eric's day there."

"I saw last week's episode," she says. "I think it was my favorite!"

I'm not working on *Code Emergency* today, but I don't tell her that. I just want to enjoy her adoration. Tatum tries to catch the show from time to time, and God, it's not a requirement to watch a network hospital drama that isn't even all that great, but it would be nice. It would be nice every once in a while to hear her say: "Last night's episode was my favorite."

I stare at Amanda for a beat, then another. I consider saying something cheesy like: *What have I done to deserve you?* or *Where have you been all my life?* But at the heart of it, neither of those things is true or worth asking. I'm cheating on my beloved wife, so I deserve nothing good, and Amanda hasn't been by my side all my life because our timing wasn't compatible in the way that you need it to be when you're looking for your soul mate. A few weeks ago, in another hotel room, in another hotel bed, I'd asked Amanda once why she chose a residency program over me back in 2000, back when I thought she'd be mine forever. She considered it for a long time, then said:

"I don't think I did it on purpose."

"But you had to know that it looked that way, felt that way to me."

She nodded. "I suppose, deep down, I wanted someone . . . stronger." She winced. "That sounds terrible. I don't know what the word is. I guess you were too nice."

I laughed at the irony. That I was now the least nice guy you could think of, screwing another woman instead of his wife, screwing another woman who he is pretending might be his soul mate, even though he doesn't believe in soul mates. I don't believe in that romantic crap that you pay twelve bucks to see on date night. Life is fucking hard, and life is fucking brutal—and maybe the most we can ask for is someone to get through it with us.

So for now, rather than soul mate, I accept her platitudes and ego stoking, and I let myself wonder about all of the what-ifs—what if I hadn't dumped her when she moved to Palo Alto; what if I'd stayed on the phone with her on New Year's Eve rather than run off to meet Tatum; what if my career had exploded and Tatum's hadn't . . . would I be happier, would I be more faithful? I do this partially because, at the heart of it, I miss my wife and partially because I'm angry with Tatum too. Angry that Amanda was the one who suggested I mend fences with Eric, whom last year I'd told to go fuck himself for insisting that I spend another year pounding out the drivel of a network hospital show, which felt so beneath me.

"Dude, don't do this," he'd said. "We've been best friends since freshman year. Don't detonate like this."

"College was a long time ago," I'd replied. If you lit a match near my mouth, my liquored breath would have caught fire. "Fuck this shit. I hate this show."

"I think you mean that you hate that Leo's gone." He'd said it kindly, but it was a bruise that shouldn't have been pressed.

"Fuck you, Eric, you don't know shit about me, about what I want, about what I hate." We'd met at a whiskey bar downtown, so I stumbled out to the valet, who refused to hand me my keys and instead stuffed me into a cab, where I nearly blew the contents of my stomach before making it home.

Eric and I didn't speak for seven months after that. But he'd accepted my recent apologies in the way that a best friend does when he knows you were self-destructing and now you're trying to piece together the wreckage. After Eric, I'd asked Spencer to coffee, and told him, with Amanda's praise still massaging my ego, that I was ready to work. Tatum had the luxury of soul nurturing; I just needed to work. Amanda kept saying that to me: "You need something that's your own, not hers."

Spencer nodded, called the network, and just like that I was back on *Code Emergency*, like the blight of the last seven months hadn't happened. Spencer made me pay the coffee bill, though, like a warning shot for being such an asshole.

"So what are you running off to work on in your quiet house?" Amanda asks while I dress. She stretches in bed, the duvet resting atop her taut stomach, her breasts exposed and calling me back beside her.

"*Reagan.*"

"Still? I thought you'd put that aside."

"It's going to be my one great thing, the script, the film, that will be my legacy or at least my new calling card." I heard Tatum's voice, not mine.

"Hmmm."

"Hmmm, what?" My voice is immediately too brittle.

"Don't be irritated with me," she says. "I'm not *her*."

"Habit," I say. "I'm sorry."

It is. Too often now, Tatum and I argue over misunderstandings and nuance: when she says she's being supportive of *Code Emergency*, and I take it as patronizing; when I tell her that I'm trying to trust Walter, despite his history of relapses and poor judgment, and she accuses me of being disingenuous.

"I only meant *hmmm* because I thought that Reagan was your dad's thing. God, I remember that his office or . . . library? Is that what you guys called his room?"

I nod. "His library. All alphabetized by author and then title. Leo once got so mad at him that he pulled every single book down into a huge heap in the middle of the rug." I laugh. "I think he blamed it on our dog, Bitsy."

Amanda smiles but I'm surprised that she doesn't laugh in the way that Tatum would at the memory of Leo and his impishness. Tatum would howl at the notion that my dad actually pretended to believe it was Bitsy, a thirty-pound poodle, his way of acknowledging that he could be a bit of a hard-ass on Leo, on me too. He was tough, my father, but he was also soft in unexpected ways, unexpected moments.

"Well, I remember that your dad had, like, two shelves of books on Reagan, biographies, presidential, historical stuff . . . I don't know." She cocks her head. "Maybe Reagan is his thing. Maybe it doesn't have to be yours?"

I inhale sharply when she says this: that it is so obvious, this script, this *thing* I've been chasing for half, no, more of my career. That it was nothing other than textbook psychology, some kid who was running around trying to impress his dad, whom he could no longer impress. I blink too quickly, wondering if I'm about to have some sort of emotional collapse right here in a Standard luxury room with a view of the pool.

"Oh, I didn't mean to upset you." She rises, naked, and moves to hug me.

"No, no." I wipe my cheeks. "You're right. I mean, you're probably right. I don't know how I didn't see this." I unwrap her arms from my neck, push her away too quickly, find that I can't meet her eyes.

"Ben."

"I should go, really. If it's not going to be *Reagan*, it should be something else. I have a quiet day. I shouldn't waste it."

"I wasn't being critical."

"I know." I exhale. "I know." I kiss her. "But Tatum will be home soon. I need to be there."

"Oh," she says flatly, and tries to wiggle her hands down my pants. "But what if you weren't?"

"I'll call you later," I say, stepping back and out the door.

I don't know if I will—call her—I keep meaning to end it, after all—but I promise that I will anyway.

Later, when Joey is asleep by six o'clock because they went to bed at midnight down at Legoland, and Tatum is reading a script on the couch, and I'm scrolling through my Twitter feed (and ostensibly rubbing her feet, but she keeps wiggling her toes to remind me to keep going), I say:

"Do you think I should keep trying on the *Reagan* script?"

It's a test, I know. It's actually more of a trap.

She rests the script in her lap, wrinkles her brow. "What brings this on?"

"I'm just thinking that maybe if it hasn't come together after all these years, maybe I should give it a rest."

She narrows her eyes, assesses, really takes me in. "I think you underestimate yourself."

I snort. "Well, then this town is right there with me."

"Ben . . ." It comes out as more of a sigh.

"Why didn't you tell me after so many years that this was really my dad's thing? That it was all some Freudian shit that I was chasing, like some textbook Psych 101 bullshit, and that no matter how good the script was, it wouldn't be good enough?"

She yanks her head back. "I . . . I never said that because I never saw it that way."

"Give me a break, Tatum."

"And even if I had, would you have listened to me? Maybe a while ago, but now? You would have just been pissed, told me I didn't believe in you, that *I* was underestimating *you*."

I start to say something snide, but stop myself. She's right, of course. I'd have blamed her for not being supportive enough.

I remove her feet from my lap, rise, and pad to the kitchen before she can read my body language, which is tense, taut, ready for a fight.

"Do I think you should write *Reagan*, even if, yeah, maybe it was at first something you wanted to do for your dad?" she calls to me.

I open the fridge door, find nothing of interest, close it too loudly. I turn and find her standing right behind me.

"Jesus!"

She rests her script and her bright pink highlighter atop the counter.

"I have a headache. I'm wiped from Legoland, and I don't want to turn this into something it's not."

"Like what?"

"Like a fight, because that's usually where this type of thing goes."

I try to relax my hunched shoulders. I don't want to fight either, and yet I'm on my heels, defensive.

Tatum sighs, rubs her eyes. Then: "But you asked me: do I think you should quit, and you already know my answer."

"You think I shouldn't quit," I say, a little too flatly. "I already know that the great Tatum Connelly never quits anything."

She stares at me in a way that makes me feel both transparent and invisible. Like she used to back in the early days; like I used to gaze at her too. Now, rather than making me feel supported, I feel exposed.

"I'm not here to tell you what to do. I just thought I was here to stand beside you. So quit. And see if that makes you happy."

8

TATUM

FEBRUARY 2002

The snow is piling up in Park City, but Ben and I are oblivious. I push him to the ground in the heap outside our hotel and fall on top of him.

"Oh my God, oh my God, oh my God," I say, before I press my lips to his.

He laughs so hard he can't keep kissing me, so I roll to his side, sinking into the eight inches of powder that fell overnight, and flap my arms and legs to create an angel. When he stops laughing, we each tilt our heads together and stare up at the gray sky, the flakes falling on top of our batting eyelashes.

It's been months since either of us has been able to entirely forget everything else: the horrors of New York on September 11; the grief we wear like our own shadows. I'm able to lose myself in my performances: since my mom died, my work has never been stronger. One professor pulled me aside just before Christmas and told me he'd be happy to recommend me personally to the best agency in the city if I pursue theater. "I don't know what happened between last year and this one, but you are truly extraordinary," he said, examining me like he wondered if I'd been possessed by someone else. "Off the record, you are the shining star of this year's class." I blushed because I still wasn't great at taking compliments, not as me, not Tatum the Great, and then thanked him and told him I'd take him up on that come graduation in June. I didn't say, *My mom died,* and that shifted something in me, unmoored new depths, allowed me to tap into new pain and emotion that might make me a wonderful actress but made me an open sore of a person.

Ben had his own grief, of course. With his dad. He focused on *Romanticah*, channeled his anguish into turning his once-small short film into the best little indie movie that he could, which is why we're in Sundance, why we're finally buoyant with joy, swooshing our limbs into snow angels as if our respective worlds hadn't fallen apart this past year. Sometimes I think that our grief bound us together tighter than if we hadn't faced loss within months of one another. Like he could know my insides how I knew his insides, and without that, maybe we'd have stumbled when we had stupid fights (usually when he was tired or I was feeling ungenerous). Or when I had days when I went to call my mom and wound up purging my guts over a toilet. Or he had moments when he disappeared so far into himself that he couldn't hear me, see me, listen to me, even if I was right there by his side on the couch: just staring at his hands without blinking, or staring at the ceiling without shifting his gaze, or grunting *uh-huh* when I know that he's not really listening to my chatter. We mourned differently: I wore it externally, grieved openly, then through my acting. He pushed deeper into himself, like a black hole swirled inside his guts.

But still, we were mourning together, and that was something. It was something we shared, something we saw in each other, like my scars were his and his were mine. Plenty of nights we found ourselves curled in bed, our heads intuitively touching, listening to the noise from the city and the sound of our breath and nothing else. We knew each other, we had each other, we saw each other, as if together we were whole, even if we weren't, of course.

He'd moved out of his parents' place in December. Well, his *mom's* place now. She insisted. He felt more than ever that he should stay, but instead Helen, his mom, nearly shoved him out the door, ensuring that he didn't have to take care of her forever. And besides, Leo was more shell-shocked than even Ben and was spending more nights at home with Helen, nursing a beer (or three) because he'd just turned twenty-one in November and could do that sort of thing legally now. Even if he hadn't been legal, at this point no one was going to stop him.

So Ben leased a one-bedroom in the Village with a big window overlooking the treetops of Horatio Street, and most nights we ordered in Chinese food or heated up macaroni and cheese, and I rehearsed lines for whatever scene I had due or hovered over his shoulder while he pieced together a rough cut of *Romanticah*. We talked about my mom; we talked about his dad. We knew neither of us would ever be the same, and that was OK. We learned that grief could be like glue, sticking us together, like veterans of war who understood only each other. Sometimes I'd read my scenes and linger in the accent, the mood of the character, long after we finished. And Ben would say some version of: "Tate, I don't want anyone other than you," and I'd rejigger my brain to bring me back to him. Without the pretense, without the act. Even though, way back at the bar—Dive Inn—that was exactly what I showed him. Tatum the actress. Now, he just wants me.

Today, in Park City, I roll toward him in the crevasse in the snow my body has made. His cell phone had rung thirty minutes ago. Because Ben didn't yet have an agent, one of the chairmen of the festival had called: Ben had won Best Newcomer at Sundance. It was beyond either of our wildest expectations.

"You are going to be the next big thing," I say, reaching a mittened hand over to clasp his gloved one, like I had when the snow started coming down on New Year's Eve a year and a few months ago, when we first realized that maybe this could be something real. "Award-winning filmmaker Ben Livingston. God, that sounds amazing." The swell of pride courses through me, as if his success is mine and mine is his, and together we're a double-helix, DNA.

His wind-chapped cheeks burn even redder.

"I feel like this was a mistake, like they're going to retract it."

"Nope." I squeeze his hand. "Not a mistake, no retraction. You gotta own this, right? How long have I been saying that?"

"Since we first met," he says, then inches forward to kiss my nose. "Since the very first day we met."

He kisses my nose again, and we right ourselves, sitting anchored in the snowdrift, absorbing how everything is about to change.

"I wish he were here," Ben says. *His dad.*

"I know," I reply.

"I think he'd be proud of me," he says, though it's a bit of a question too.

"I'm certain he would be."

He lets out his breath and mutters: "Fuck."

"Fuck what?"

"Fuck everything," he says, though there is so much to celebrate. "Fuck that he's not here; fuck that I want him to see my success; fuck that I care about his approval when now, I can't have it anyway."

"He would have been proud, Ben. *He would have.*"

He shrugs, blinks quickly.

"Don't be angry today, B. Not when today is a celebration." I've seen this recently: the start of his dark spiral. He tries to keep me out of it, steer me away from his moodiness, but I am trained—literally trained at Tisch—to read people, to know them. I have my own dark spirals, of course—my mom's childhood nickname for me, "Deflatum Tatum," granted because she claimed she could see the air sucked out of me along with my mood, nipping on all parts of me.

Today he seems to hear me, which he doesn't always.

"I'm sorry," he says. "It's just a lot."

"I know," I say, because I do. "Hey, I got you."

He blinks faster, then stares up at the sky and yells: "FUUUUUUUCK!" Then shakes his head and manages a smile.

I brush the snow off my pants, rise, and stretch out my hand, pulling him up, though he is weightier than I. But I am stronger in some ways, the ways that have proven important recently. We stumble back to the ski condo that his mom has paid for, because Ben's day job as a literary agent's assistant pays only enough to cover his rent, and my job at the bar pays even less. We peel our damp, freezing clothes off each other and step into the steaming shower until we are skin to skin with nothing in between. Afterward, Ben puts on a tie, and I slide into my customary black tight jeans and black fitted top, and he tells me that he couldn't have done this without me.

"Really," he says. "This film, this award, it's because of you."

"I can't take all the credit." I bat my eyelashes demurely.

He laughs. "Now, Tatum Connelly, don't you go and deflect when someone gives you praise."

I puff up my chest and slip into my role, the spitfire actress, the confident companion, and take a bow. "You're right. I'd like to thank the Academy, I'd like to thank my director Ben, but mostly, I'd like to thank myself because I'm really such a fucking genius."

He laughs harder, and so do I, both of us relieved to find a sliver of normalcy in a world that feels so upended.

Then quieter, more shyly, I say: "Don't forget to thank me up there. Please?" I elbow him, hoping I can play it off as a joke, that I'm not needy, that I don't really care. Though I do.

We'd watched the Oscars together last weekend and shrieked (in horror) when Suzanna Memphis (her real name) forgot to thank her husband. We then spent the next thirty minutes wondering if they were about to split, if the rumors were true.

It wasn't that it really mattered if Ben thanked me publicly, but what if it did? What if you had to proclaim your love aloud, onstage, to make it real?

"You'll be the first name I say." Ben kisses my neck, seeing through me.

When we get to the theater on Main Street, Ben is swarmed with executives and agents and important people who want to sign him as a client, who want to set up meetings in Los Angeles and New York about future projects. He grips my hand and holds on tight, but eventually, like we're caught in the undertow of the ocean, he's tugged away from me, even when we try our best to hold on.

I'll find you, he mouths over his shoulder as he goes.

I nod and think: *I hope so. Please don't forget me.*

The lights flicker at the awards ceremony, so I find a seat in the middle of the theater with a pulse of anxiety coursing through me, that minutes-earlier bravado already fading. I gaze at these unfamiliar faces, strangers who had suddenly seen the genius in my boyfriend, and something twitches deep inside, and I wonder if he'll want me as much as he always has, now that maybe he'll recognize how special he is, and that maybe I don't deserve to stand alongside his brightness. Just as I felt back when we buried my mother, just as I feel on my worst days when I can't beat back the throb of ever-present insecurity by disguising myself as someone else. *Please don't see me for what I really am. And if you do, please love me anyway.*

I glance around, wondering where he is in the auditorium, wishing I could see his face, find him, and beckon him to sit beside me. But it's just a swarm of Hollywood types and a few others like me: fazed, stunned, trying to pretend otherwise. I curl my fingers into a fist and press my nails into my palms, an old habit from middle school after my mom was first diagnosed, before her remission, when I'd feel myself start to cry and wouldn't want to come undone in the middle of Algebra or PE or the cafeteria at lunch. I remind myself that I'm an actress, a good one, and I can put on any face that I want to.

Someone is waving from the side of the aisle, and I turn to see Ben, flagging me over.

I excuse myself as I press past tilted knees and annoyed faces until I reach him.

"What are you doing? You have to be up there any second!"

"I know, I know. But I realized something . . ." he whispers.

"What?"

He leans closer, so only I can hear.

"Marry me."

"What?"

He is right by my ear now, his heat electrifying. "Marry me. I don't want to do any of this without you."

"What?" I can't have heard correctly, and yet my stomach leaps to my throat, my heartbeat detonating within my chest cavity. That he wants me, that he is choosing *me*.

He pulls back and stares at me with a hint of a smile, wordlessly, like I can read his mind. We'd discussed marriage in tangential terms, like maybe one day, like let's put it out there at some point, but nothing concrete, nothing that ever felt like it could be real.

"Marry me. Tomorrow. Next year. Whenever. Just say yes."

"OK," I say, because my mouth hasn't yet caught up with my brain, with its frenetic euphoria that wants to burst with a YES.

He raises his eyebrows. "OK?"

"OK, yes!" I giggle loudly enough that a few people hiss for me to pipe down. I clamp my hand over my mouth, but my smile is wider than the whole of it.

He removes his father's tarnished wedding band, which they miraculously recovered in the rubble, and which he's been wearing on his right index finger, and slides it over my thumb, the only finger it fits. "Can this do for now? We'll get you a real one when we're back."

"It's more than OK," I say. "It's perfect."

Later, when his name is called and he rises to accept his award, true to his word, the first person he thanks is me.

9

BEN

MAY 2012

I sink beneath the bubbles in the hot tub and wonder: If I stay under long enough, can I force myself to drown? Not that I want to drown, necessarily, but it's not that I don't either. I float my hands toward my face: my fingers and gold wedding band weave in front of me like an apparition. I count to twenty, holding my breath, swooshing my arms at my sides to keep me under the too-hot water, but as my lungs grow tighter I find that I don't have it in me to sink, to not stretch for a gasp of air. The flats of my feet find the bottom of the Jacuzzi, and I shoot upward, toward the open sky, toward the California sunshine.

Tatum appears on our back deck now, on the phone, pacing in a circle, her forehead knotted into something that signals a crisis. But what constitutes a crisis anyway? That the test screeners to *Army Women: 2.0* aren't positive? That her publicist has overbooked her interviews? Bad press for forgetting to thank me in speeches? I buckle my knees and head beneath the surface again. Even from my perch below the bubbles, I can see her scanning the pool for me, and I know I should reach out a hand, hold up a foot, to let her know that I am here and alive and breathing, but I don't. Instead, I count to thirty this time, until my lungs burn, and when I think that I absolutely can't take it for another second, I hold on, and I do.

Tatum's ankles draw me upward. She's standing on the ledge of the hot tub, and then she is crouched over, waving me north.

"It's Joey," she shouts, her face and voice and body language sharp like a blade's edge. "Get out. He's at Cedars. Broke his arm, hit his head." She stands abruptly. "Hurry up. I won't wait for you."

What she means is: *You spend half your time trying to drown yourself now, literally, metaphorically, whatever. I can't rescue someone who ties bricks to his ankles, who doesn't even attempt to swim.* She's not wrong— Tatum is rarely wrong. Since Leo, I sleep too long, though fitfully; I work too little, and not well; I pick fights with her and with Eric, who finally said, "Dude, maybe it's time you quit," and I did; I flip off drivers on the freeway for innocuous lane changes; I snap at the woman in Starbucks for taking forever to decide what to put in her stupid latte. Does it really matter? How much of this shit *really* matters?

I heave myself out of the hot tub, throw on my jeans, slide into my flip-flops. I feel myself moving through quicksand as everything else meteors past.

Tatum drives because she is better at outpacing the paparazzi who sit outside our house now, waiting for a wave or a glimpse or some interesting nugget about what makes this day any different from all the other days that they trail her, Oscar winner Tatum Connelly. I am an asterisk, an afterthought: her husband of nine years who used to be something great, but now, just look at his IMDB to see what he's done because no one could really tell you. One season of *Code Emergency*, that shitty NBC procedural which does OK in the ratings but isn't exactly mentally taxing, before he had some sort of breakdown in the writers' room one afternoon, in which he heaved the In and Out burgers (the writing staff's dinner) against the giant whiteboard that was littered with crappy plotlines, and then after the burgers, the milkshakes and some fries too, until the whiteboard was nothing but a smashed canvas of inedible garbage. At which Ben proclaimed: "Well, at least now the plotlines match the quality of the show." And Eric, his producing partner, said: "Dude, let's go to a bar and talk."

That's the sort of anecdote you might find on his IMDB page.

Joey is with his teacher, Ms. Ashley, when we arrive at the hospital. My hair is still damp, the water still floating through my ears. I handle the paperwork while Tatum rushes into the exam room. By the time I've filled out the insurance forms, Tatum has soothed him into a quiet whimper, and Ms. Ashley, after explaining he fell off the monkey bars at the playground and landed with his arm pinned beneath him, has returned to Windstream, the preschool of the Hollywood elite, amid multiple apologies and promises to call later this afternoon.

The nurses have checked his vitals, which seem stable, but they need to get him down to X-ray to check on the break, and they want to monitor him for a possible concussion since he's got a welt the size of the hard-boiled egg Tatum ate for breakfast on the back of his head. (She's eating only protein for two meals a day now.)

"We're going to wheel you down to Radiology, sweetie," the nurse says. "We're going to take a picture of your insides!"

"OK," Joey whispers. "Can I see them too?"

"You betcha." She smiles, then to us: "The doctor will be in to see you after she reviews everything."

"Can I go with him?" Tatum asks. "To the X-rays?"

"One parent can tag along," the nurse replies. "Though I promise he's in good hands."

"I know. My mom was a nurse." She loses herself to a memory that she doesn't share, which should make me bristle, but does not: I haven't earned her confidence recently. I don't deserve her secrets now. Shame rises through me at how unavailable I've been for her, but then drains just as quickly. Though she's been there, literally been there, for my harder moments, she hasn't been entirely present either. So maybe we deserve the half effort we get from one another in this pocket of time. Maybe this is the best we have.

"ER nurse?"

"Obstetrics," Tatum says. "I know the hospital runs on you guys. But . . . I'm his mom." I watch her, unable to read her in the way that I used to, unable to see exactly what she is thinking, where her actress persona ends and Tatum, my wife, begins.

"Mom always helps," the nurse says, smiling. "But no phones in that ward."

Tatum hands me her cell phone.

"I was supposed to do a call with everyone. If Luann texts, tell her I don't know when I'll be free."

"OK," I say. Luann is her publicist; her team is everyone. Tatum doesn't have to remind me that she plays the part of supermom well. That even if she is traveling for weeks on end—a press junket from London to Paris to Rome to Berlin—or even if she embodies people she is not, loses herself to accents and tics and character traits that unintentionally ebb into her own personality, she will show up and be accountable for Joey, be his backbone when he needs her. I will too. He's the one thing that we both do easily, equally, though to be fair to both of us, for the past six months, since Leo and the Oscars, I've spent a decent portion of my days wondering how much it will hurt if I drown myself.

The nurse and Tatum ease Joey into a wheelchair, and Tatum, not the nurse, steers him out of the room toward Radiology.

"Hang in there, kiddo," I say, before the door closes behind them. "You're going to be good as new."

I drop my head into my hands, sink my elbows atop my knees. Tears come almost immediately, which is no surprise. I'm stripped bare now, a walking open wound. How long does it take to mourn the person you swore you'd protect? Forever. It feels like I will mourn Leo forever. It's different from the grief with my dad, and it's different from the grief with Tatum's mom. She concedes this, even as she tries to be helpful: *Let's find a therapist, why won't you talk to me about it?* I should have done *something* to stop it, seen *something* to help my baby brother. I should have known. But I didn't, and now he's gone, and my son has a silly accident like slipping off the monkey bars and breaks his arm, and I am reduced to sobbing in a halogen-lit hospital room because I carry around my grief like a boulder, unable to ever find a resting place. Unable to forgive myself for not being a better, more present, more forgiving big brother.

My phone buzzes in my pocket, startling me. Spencer. Wondering when I'd like to start working again. I delete the e-mail, wipe my cheeks, try to compose myself. I close my eyes, drop my head back against the wall, and wait.

I'm nearly asleep when a knock rattles the door.

The doctor, with her red hair high in a ponytail and studious black glasses, is examining Joey's chart with a furrowed brow; then her eyes move up to mine.

"Oh my God," she says. "I thought the name . . ."

"Oh my God," I say. I knew the red hair looked too familiar, that her dancer's posture was like a shadow of an old friend. Something electric runs through me for the first time in so long. I don't pay close enough attention to examine it, what this feeling is, what it means, if I should lean in and touch the live wire, if I should instead run.

She laughs and shakes her head in disbelief.

"Ben, Jesus. I haven't seen you since—"

"The Plaza Athénée," we say in unison.

Then: "Amanda." It's recklessness, that feeling. Now it comes alive. "God, it's been forever."

❦

"Joey's still getting his X-rays," I say, after we've stumbled over our hellos.

71

"Sorry about that: he was supposed to be back by now," she says, tilting her glasses to rest atop her head, so she looks no older than when we loved each other a million years ago. But we split, and now here I am, married with a kid. In a gasp of a moment, a prolonged heartbeat. "Today is a mess here. I'm covering for two other pediatricians who couldn't make it in. The timing's off all over the place."

"Timing never was our forte," I say, more boldly than I meant to, but then maybe exactly the amount of boldness that I intended. I haven't felt something like this in too long. A spark, a fire, so while I might tell myself that I don't mean to flirt with my old girlfriend who left me for a residency in San Francisco, I know that plenty of things we tell ourselves are untrue. Like that I'm not responsible for Leo's death. Like I haven't intentionally cratered my career because nothing felt important after Leo. Like Tatum might be growing weary of me. Like I have stopped trying to read her—in small ways, like if her smile for the nurse today was genuine, and in larger ways too—and I haven't done anything to change it. I tell myself all sorts of lies every day, so this one—that I don't mean to overstep with Amanda—is just another on my list, another way I betray myself. Another way that I test Tatum too: Would she notice that I spent the afternoon flirting with my old girlfriend? Would she sense it on me, like a dog smells fetid garbage, like she once would have?

Amanda grins. "I always wondered if I'd run into you here. Not *here* here. At Cedars. But LA." She shrugs. "I guess it's a big city. And you're married now. To Tatum Connelly. My God. I never had a chance."

"Hey," I say. "You're the one who broke my heart."

"If I recall, you broke up with me."

"Oh, you know. Beating you to the punch and all of that. It's not like I didn't sit and cry myself to sleep that whole first summer. Also: lots of alcohol was involved."

"But then you got over me." She smiles.

"Only because my endless weeping was seriously crimping my rebound sex."

She laughs, and I do too. A dormant staccato rising up from my chest, bouncing off the beige exam room walls.

"How about you?" I ask. "Where are you on the scale of single to rebound to commitment?" Jesus, a loaded question if there ever was one. I'm shocked at my brazenness, more shocked at how easily it comes.

"Oh, well, still single. Engaged once but that didn't stick." She glances to the floor. "I don't know. I guess being a doctor pretty much takes up most of my life. And I have all these kids . . . my patients."

"Oh," I reply because I'm suddenly nervous. Not that I've exposed too much or that she has, but that just as quickly, there is an unexpected tension—the tension of possibility—between us.

"Don't feel sorry for me. There are little frozen Amandas sitting in a laboratory not far from here, ready and waiting for that perfect specimen of sperm!" She blushes and holds a hand to her face. "Shit, sorry. I always overshare when I'm uncomfortable."

"I remember." I smile. "And I don't mean to make you uncomfortable. God, not at all. Sorry, that's on me. I've been a bit of an emotional sieve recently." I flop my arm. "I apologize."

"You *were* always such a fucking nice guy." She sighs. "I thought that would bore me, but it turns out that nice guys are harder to find than I thought. More valuable, I mean."

"I'm really not that nice." I should say: *Just ask my wife.* I turn the light out before she can come to bed; I ignore her requests to write a script just for her; I leave the room when my mom calls and Tatum holds the receiver out to me because I am petty and childish now that my mom has a new husband, Ron, and a new life where they take cruises in the Mediterranean, and have a membership to the tennis club near the summer home they're renting in Connecticut. I'm still here. I'm still stuck.

Leo is gone, and I have lost myself with him.

"Well, Tatum's lucky. That's all I mean. I'm sure she knows that." Amanda exhales and seems to consider something.

I fiddle with my wedding band and worry what else she'll say, what else she has heard, what will break me from this foreign bubble of happiness. As if she can read my cues as well as Tatum can (or used to), she says: "Well, this is a happy accident. I mean, not that I wanted your son to break his arm! Just . . . you know . . . anyway, I think he's going to be OK. I'll check his X-rays, of course, but these things on kids manage to heal faster than you'd think." She slows her rambling. Inhales, smiles. "Wow, your son. That kind of blows my mind."

"Trust me, me too." I smile back, working muscles that have nearly atrophied.

"Anyway, they'll bring him back from Radiology, and I'll let you know. We may need to keep him here overnight to rule out a concussion."

"OK," I say. "I'll stay as long as it takes."

She grabs the door handle to leave, then hesitates. "Look, I don't know." She pulls a card from the front pocket of her lab coat. "Take this. If you ever want to, like, catch up, give me a call."

I stare at the card for a second too long. It feels like a dare; it feels like an alarm that I should run from.

"Or don't," she says, blood rising to her cheeks again. "God, this is unprofessional. Sorry."

"Don't be sorry," I say.

"OK," she replies. "Then I'm not."

10

TATUM

MARCH 2003

We marry in Santa Barbara in March. Neither of us wanted much of a to-do; I'd have been happy at City Hall, and Ben is so busy now that he is Hollywood's It boy that, through no fault of his own, he couldn't involve himself in more than showing up. "I will show up *very* enthusiastically," he says, before throwing me atop the duvet and kissing my neck. "But the flowers, the cake? I don't care. Only care about the woman waiting for me at the end of the aisle."

But after the wreckage of the previous year—his dad, my mom—it felt like we owed something more to our families, well, to his mom, Helen, and to Leo and to Piper, my sister, and if giving them a wedding also gave them something to be happy about, it was a small concession. Not a concession. It was a celebration. But the typical trappings of a formal wedding weren't for me. Not without my mom here, anyway, and maybe even if she'd been here, not then either.

I take a week off work: I'm the Tuesday–Saturday bartender at P. F. Chang's on Wilshire, and Ben shutters his laptop and his trips back and forth to the studio where they are finalizing the reshoots for *All the Men*, with the hopes of having it prepped for the Toronto Film Festival this fall. Since landing in LA nine months ago, our lives, well, Ben's life, has spun into a whirlwind—mine mostly consists of pouring cosmos for tourists and snacking on bar nuts with Mariana, my bartending cohort and also an aspiring actress. Ben and I promise ourselves that we can press Pause for a five-day sliver of time to marry. Though P. F. Chang's is my paycheck, I am stuffed with classes, workshops, mailings to agents and managers and anyone who will have me. I went to goddamn Tisch, but no one out here seems to notice all that much. Maybe if my breasts were bigger or my vibe more available. I don't know. Mariana says the only people who make it in their first year are the rich kids with connections, "like the Spielberg kids or whatever," so I don't tell her that my fiancé is making it in his first year, because I'm not sure that I want her to point out that he's "a rich kid with connections," or maybe I'm not sure that I want to believe that Ben wouldn't have made it regardless.

"It's not that I don't dream of becoming P. F. Chang's employee of the month," I said to her a few weeks ago.

"Oh babe, I hear you. I was Ms. January, and let me tell you, it's the stuff dreams are made of." She laughed.

Daisy, my best friend from Tisch, flies in from New York for the wedding, packing in a few auditions for the week (rich kid with connections), and a hodgepodge of Ben's high school friends jet out too, landing in LA, but then driving to Santa Barbara to stay at the Biltmore or the swanky boutique hotels tucked into the sides of mountains where celebrities unwind for the weekend. In the nine months since we left New York, Ben and I have planted roots in a rental bungalow on Ocean Avenue in Santa Monica, and Piper heads out three days before the wedding to stay in the guest room (Ben's office) and help me prepare, though there isn't too much to do. Helen found a woman in Santa Barbara who coordinates beach weddings for a living, and I've merely had to reply to e-mails with things like "full bar," "lilies not roses," "salmon sounds fine," and that's that.

"You seem so unexcited," Piper said the morning before we were set to drive north for the event. We were walking along the beach, just a stone's throw from the condo complex. From my bedroom window I could see the horizon, the towering palm trees, the stairway leading downward to the path on which we now walked. "You're happy, right?"

"Of course I'm happy," I said, sliding off my flip-flops, stepping from the concrete boardwalk onto the cold sand. It was a gloomy morning, the skies overcast and low.

"Like, if it were my wedding, I'd be way more into it."

"I just feel like the wedding stuff is stupid. I just want to get going, live my life."

She plopped onto the sand, reminding me of how gangly she was as a toddler, always tumbling down, scraping her knees, skinning her palms. Maybe it's no surprise that she's a nurse now, just like my mom was.

"Do you think Mom and Dad were happy?" She craned her neck toward me.

I was startled by the question, felt a hiccup in my heart.

"Dad was a drunk," I said. "I don't know how you live with that."

She shook her head. "Before that. Like, now, when they were just about to get married, like you. She must have loved him as much as you love Ben, right?"

I scanned the ocean, the waves riotous and angry. I didn't want to think about how my marriage could be like my parents' or how Ben could be like my dad. Not that he was. Not that they were anything close.

"I don't know, Pipes. I guess. Maybe."

"I think every marriage must start off hopeful, right? You know she forgave him for everything at the end." Her voice caught. "You know he was back home with her, I mean, with us, by then."

What she meant was: *We all forgave him, can't you?* Or maybe what she meant was: *Everyone screws up, in marriage too.*

It felt important to Piper that I believed my parents were happy, so I said: "They must have loved each other as much as they thought they could. I guess that's all you can know, right? I can't measure my love for Ben against Mom's love for Dad because it's not like you can quantify these things. It's not like I can pour them into a cup and see which one measures more."

"Remember all those snow globes you and Mom collected?"

"Of course," I said.

"It feels like marriage should be like that: trapped inside but in a good way. With sparkles raining down and protecting you."

"I don't think that marriage is really anything like that."

She sighed. "It would be nice if it could be, though. Just all that time together, knowing each other inside and out."

I wanted to say: *I don't know that you can ever know somebody inside and out, and I certainly don't want Ben to know all of my ugly insides.* Nearly all of them, yes, but every last ugliness? Probably not. Would he love me enough then? Would I love him? He tells me: *You don't have to be a role* or *Stop pretending* when he catches me slipping into someone who I'm not, and I do. Or at least I try to. Because Ben wants to *see* me, the whole of me, and when he does, he still loves me. But it's not like there isn't still wiggle room to fall into a cloudier place wearing my masks, not like old habits can be shed in a single moment.

I said to Piper: "Sure, that does sound nice."

I'm quiet on the drive up to Santa Barbara. Ben and Piper play I Spy, even though no one has played it since we were children, but they are silly and bored, and we hit a bad patch of traffic that grates on my nerves but doesn't faze Ben, because he's not mired in the question *Does he love me enough?* I know I do him. And inherently, I know that he does me too: he doesn't string me along like Eddie from college, who constantly dumped me for his girlfriend back home and then offered vague platitudes that made me forgive him; doesn't invalidate my sexuality or feelings like Aaron in high school, who stripped me of my virginity. He is respectful, he is kind, he is loving, he is smart, he is everything I could have envisioned for myself and more. But what if, like my own parents, something changes, we change? Then, will he still love me enough?

The car creeps forward in the traffic, and Piper's voice grates on me, as if I am physically bristling at her for even planting this notion, this seed of insecurity in me. Will he love me forever? Love me like he does now, when he thinks he sees everything about me, but maybe he hasn't?

I see you, he says to me all the time. What he means is: *I love you.* But what happens when it gets uglier? Will I still look the same, my insides, my outsides?

"I spy with my little eye a fiancée who is looking like she sucked on a lemon," I hear Ben say, and Piper's piercing laughter rings out from the back seat. He brings me to, brings me back, like only he can.

I turn and roll my eyes at him.

"Sometimes my mom used to call her 'Deflatum Tatum,'" Piper laughs. "Because her mood would just go . . . poof."

"'Deflatum Tatum!'" Ben howls.

"Excuse me," I say. "It is this ability to tap into all sorts of emotions that will one day win me an Oscar."

"Now, *that* I believe," Ben says, still grinning. He eases his hand off the wheel and squeezes my thigh. "But no bad moods allowed in this car."

"It's the traffic."

"You live in LA now, baby!" He says this in his slickest, slimiest producer voice, and I descend into my own fit of laughter. He glances from the road toward me and winks. *I see you.* I exhale. Of course we love each other enough. How could I even doubt that for a moment? We are not my parents. There isn't a measuring cup for our love.

Helen has rented us a suite at the Biltmore and, though I asked her not to, paid for Piper and my father as well. I told Ben how uncomfortable this made me, and he said, "Babe, I know, you've worked since you were twelve. But it's just a weekend, and it's just to make it go smoother for all of us, so let's let it go for now, and this will be the last time we accept such a thing, OK?"

And because he is pragmatic and kind, I, of course, let it go. He likes taking care of me, being my alpha. I'm the one who isn't used to being taken care of.

My dad is shuffling around the lobby when we pull up in Ben's Toyota, and Piper says: "Be nice, Tate. Please, just be nice."

So I kiss his cheek and try to pretend that when I get close, I'm not sniffing for alcohol. He looks sober, though, clean. He reaches for me and pulls me tighter than I'd like, and says: "I wish so much she were here. She'd want to be here so badly."

He is crying already, so I press myself back from him. "Dad, please, come on. No tears today."

And he nods and sniffles, and then Piper is at his elbow, asking brightly if he's already checked in, and maybe he wants to take a walk?

Ben rolls our bags to our suite, which is covered in rose petals and makes us both sigh, because I hate roses (as did my mom), and then giggle because Helen has tried so hard, and it's a little funny that our bed has been showered in something I loathe so deeply. Ben whisks them off the bed with a sweep of his arms, then tugs his clothes off nearly as quickly, jumps on top stark naked, and says: "Now, *this* is a better view, am I right?"

I sleep fitfully that night until he presses himself next to me, nearly swallowing me against him, and then, when I can hear his heartbeat in my ear, I tumble toward sleep, as if his pulse is soothing mine, as if his heart is also assuring mine. We *don't* need to measure our love, not when our hearts can beat in rhythm, not when they can beat in tandem, as if they are one and the same.

It is unusually sunny the next day. You never know what you will get by the ocean in March, but for us, it is cloudless. Sky-blue.

I take this as a sign.

I wear my mother's veil.

My dad behaves himself, though I opt to walk down the aisle alone.

Piper, as my maid of honor, holds my bouquet of lilies (Mom's favorite) and passes me a tissue when I find myself weeping when Ben says his vows.

Leo, as Ben's best man, winks at me when I try to gather myself together, which makes me choke, then laugh, then cry harder, and so then Leo starts laughing, and Ben turns toward him, and Ben starts laughing, and soon all of us together have broken down into uncontrollable gales that echo over the beach waves just yards away.

Though it is not the wedding I planned—Helen took care of all the details—it is perfect. We are perfect. Ben's cheeks are sun-kissed and his eyes aglow, and he cries when he kisses me, and lofts our hands joyfully when the officiant declares us husband and wife, and I gaze at my *husband* and this menagerie of people who have stood up to celebrate us, and I realize that if we did measure our happiness, our love for each other, we would be full.

⌒

Daisy finds me by the bar after the ceremony.

"Please tell me you're at least taking a few days for a honeymoon."

I stir my martini. "Ben has to work. They're aiming for Toronto."

"He should just cast you. Like you're not the best actress he could find."

I shake my head. "I want to do this on my own merits, not because I'm Ben Livingston's wife."

"Everyone in this town uses their connections. Christ, look at me."

"It would be different if he wrote something just for me or whatever. I don't want him wedging me into a project just because. I'll pass."

"Your call," she says. "But there are easier paths to becoming a star."

I shrug as if to say: *Let's talk about something else.* Not that there is much to discuss anyway. Though we've been in Los Angeles for only nine months, I can barely muster commercial auditions, and even those haven't gone well. (I am never pretty, only "cute," or I am too pretty but they want "cuter," or I am too tall or too short or too flat-chested or too brunette. I am "too" much of everything but what they want, it seems.) But I meant it: It wasn't Ben's job to find me work. It was mine. Had been since I was twelve, and it isn't any different now.

"Jesus, Tate, come on, what happened to that fire from back in the bar, the girl who wouldn't turn down a bet?" Daisy says.

I poke at an olive and pop it in my mouth.

"That girl was a role, Daisy—give me a break, like you don't know that. Also, LA is fucking hard. Everyone out there is beautiful and aspiring."

"But you have more talent in your pinky than they do."

I shrug again.

"Tatum, you were the best one in our graduating class. You were the one who won raves in *Romanticah*. None of the rest of us."

"Only because you got sick."

She shakes her head. "No. *No.* Professor Sherman always gave you the harder work, always handed you the trickier parts."

"Because he was a hard-ass."

"No," she says, squeezing my shoulders. "Because you were the best. How did you not know that?"

"Easy for you to say." Praise was never my strong suit, perhaps because my dad gave me so little of it, perhaps because my mom was so overly effusive that her endless compliments came to mean nothing, were just jumbles of words. "You're already, like, taking Broadway by storm."

"Off-Broadway," she says. "And by the way, it's basically for minimum wage."

"It's gotta beat the tip jar at P. F. Chang's," I say.

"Well, I still think he owes you a honeymoon. It's the least he could do for making you lose that bet." She winks, then dips her fingers into my drink and pulls out the remaining olive. "Also, to bring this back to yours truly, I think you have me to thank for this: (a) the bet, (b) getting the chicken pox."

"I'll be sure to thank you in my acceptance speech," I say with a grin.

"Assholes who don't give credit to the people who get them there are the worst." Daisy sticks out her tongue. "Blech." She makes a retching noise. "Ooh, so you'll also have to thank that ex-girlfriend. If she had stuck around New York, who knows what would have happened?"

"Amanda." I make my own retching sound. "But no talk of ex-girlfriends tonight."

"You're right." She nods and pulls me closer for a hug. "You guys were meant for each other. No one is more meant for each other than you and Ben."

"My cup runneth over," I say.

Daisy motions for the bartender, and we toast to my good fortune.

11

BEN

FEBRUARY 2011

My face hurts from smiling, and I hate that I'm aware of this. I'm happy for Tatum. But the press line on the red carpet is endless, and her publicity team keeps shuttling me to the side for each interview, escorting me to the back when the photographers call out for a "single." *Single* meaning just her. *Single* meaning all the ways she outshines me.

I'm not throwing a pity party; it's simply true. Tatum has ascended above me in all the ways that matter to this town.

"I'm sorry," she'll say each time as she's swept off into that photographer sea. "It doesn't mean anything other than they want a shot of my dress"—but it's hard not to feel like she's splintering off from me, leaving me behind.

I wave to Eric, who is on the arm of a producer he's been dating, as I wait for her to wrap another interview. Ryan Seacrest now, fawning, making her spin in a circle. The racket on the carpet is too loud to hear the two of them, but I see Tatum throw her head back into a completely realistic cackle, and I wonder if I'm the only person out here who knows that she's faking it. I still know her, still love her, still see her, which I think she both values and demands.

"This is nuts," Eric says as he weaves his way toward me. He's grown a goatee in the two weeks since I've seen him; I've had no time for my own friends or my own work since I've been out with Tatum at industry events each night.

"Nice goatee," I say.

"All the A-listers are doing it." He grins.

"Which makes us A-list adjacent, I guess?"

"On our best days." He laughs. "On our best days, dude."

I shrug. "No room for the plebian TV folks here."

"(A) we're not plebian TV folks: *Code Emergency* is going to kill it, and (b) you're with the night's only sure thing, so take up a little more space."

Tatum's publicist waves me onward.

"Gotta hop, duty calls. Find me at a party later. Save me, more like."

"I expect you to be working the room," he says. "Selling the shit out of *Code*."

"Noted." I nod, losing him as the crowd folds behind me.

Of course, I have no intention of talking up our new network deal at Fox, the one that guarantees us a full season of *Code Emergency* (set to air this coming March!). TV is not film, even when Tatum says that she's proud of me, even when the paycheck is lucrative. *Code Emergency* is formulaic hospital stuff, not what I had envisioned when I was hailed as Hollywood's It boy, not the stuff I had imagined when I pieced together *Romanticah* or when I was wooed to LA, riding on my carpet of fairy dust, and penned *All the Men* or *One Day in Dallas*. Some days, when I'm feeling even less generous with myself, I wonder what my father would say. Not that I'm not a grown-up, not that I should still heave around daddy issues, much less dead-daddy issues. But still, yes, some-times I hear his voice rattling around, wondering why I'm marooned in the middle instead of scrambling toward the top. Other than Tatum, my ambition has been the only thing I've held steady since film school. To abandon that means, essentially, that I have failed. Tatum would tell me this is crazy, that I am echoing my father, but Tatum is ambitious in her own ways, so to tell me to quell my own lust for success is senseless, hypocritical.

I've tried to get back into film; it's not as if I haven't. But you can only have so many flops in this town, or so many scripts put into turn-around before you're relegated elsewhere. TV. Network TV if you're really hurting. "If you can dream it, you can be it," Tatum tells me, which, years ago, she used as her own mantra, and it used to be kind of cute, the kind of thing that I'd tease her about and then throw her over my shoulder and cart her to the bedroom, but now it just makes me bristle.

"It's not as if I *don't* want it," I say. "It's not like I'm not trying."

"I didn't mean it that way," she'll say. "You're misinterpreting."

On the carpet, Tatum wraps the interview and glides toward me, blowing out her cheeks, widening her eyes. "God, I have twenty more of these, and I've already run out of ways to be charming. Save me."

"You're much more charming than I am, so I wouldn't know how if I could." I kiss her forehead. A photographer will snap us in this pose, and we'll appear to be the picture of happiness. Sometimes we are.

Lily Marple taps her shoulder before we can be herded to the next talking head.

"Darling," Lily says, tilting forward to air-kiss both of Tatum's cheeks. "Ben." She raises her eyebrows, which I know Tatum sees, and which I also know will irk her the evening through, even though her life is about to change times infinity. "I just wanted to wish you luck," Lily says.

"Thank you." Every one of Tatum's muscles is frozen except for the ones squeezing my hand. She hasn't forgotten, all these years later, how Lily shoved her hands down my pants on *One Day in Dallas*, how Lily thought she could take what she wanted because she was a star, and how what Lily wanted was me. I didn't bite, of course. Which is why it was easy to laugh about it when I told Tatum, until I realized she wasn't laughing.

"I mean it," Lily says, lowering her eyes. "I know we're not friendly, and I know that our rivalry sells a lot of magazines, but I wish you luck. I wish you success. I wish you only good things."

"Thank you," Tatum says again.

"We should put this behind us," Lily offers, and she strikes me as genuine, like a once-young upstart who learned that being an asshole gets you nowhere. Or at least makes you no friends. Since Lily and I worked together, she has gone just about everywhere a career can go, trailed only by Tatum. I watch Lily now, debating how honest she's being with her truce offering: she is also an excellent actress, and with excellent actresses you never can tell. It occurs to me that perhaps I should start to wonder as much about Tatum.

"OK," Tatum says, not at all genuine, like someone who can hold a grudge forever. My gut relaxes just a bit: I can still read her; she is not as foreign to me as Lily.

Lily grasps her free hand. "I voted for you, doll."

The photographers sniff out their union from behind their press barricade and start shouting their names. "Lily and Tatum, give us a smile! Show us some leg! Just you two, ladies, just you two!" The publicity team yanks me out of the shots, tucks me back into the corners where the plus-ones belong.

I admire Tatum from my perch to the side. Tonight she is almost too beautiful to look at, even though I've looked at her for years now. She is in a beaded, strapless gold gown that somehow turns her green eyes almost violet and her skin iridescent. Still, she is too skinny, as she always is now ("skinny photographs better," she says), her collarbone protruding, her back a string of knife edges, but I've also grown used to the way that her hip bones jut out when I reach for them, how the curve of her belly is nearly concave such that you'd never know it was once swollen with Joey and beautiful. Tonight, even beside Lily, who is alluring and sensuous in her own way (though I am certain to never breathe a word of this aloud), Tatum is a star in every context of the word: glittering, golden, ethereal.

Finally, her publicist barks, "Enough," and whisks her to the next interview, then the one after that, and then after an endless ocean of sycophantic reporters and executives and hangers-on, we wade toward the lobby of the theater.

"You ready?" I whisper in her ear. Her lips find mine in reply, lingering for a beat as she calms herself. I linger for a beat too. My wife isn't Lily Marple: she is still transparent to me, regardless of the masks she puts on for her roles, for the lavishing press, for her adoring fans.

"I'm so fucking nervous," she says, pulling back. "You would think I could get a grip."

"I see you," I say, like I used to all the time. "I'm here." Which surprises me as much as it may surprise her. I know that I have dragged my feet to some of these parties, that I have let my ego too easily be bruised when an exec brushes past me for someone more important. That this is her moment, and while most of me has championed her, perhaps the whole of me hasn't because I've been too stupid and too insecure not to be a small bit competitive. I know that she can see me calculating—*Why her, not me*—as if there is only so much success to go around. I tell myself it's not about *her*, I'm not that guy who cares that his wife lives larger than he does. It's about my missed potential, about half-realized dreams that remind me of all the ways my cup can still be filled; it's about watching Tatum live up to all of her potential while realizing how much of mine I've wasted. About landing in LA as Hollywood's next great thing and now penning a shitty network hospital drama.

Some of that wasn't my fault: scripts were put in turnaround; finished cuts weren't as well received as we'd hoped they'd be. Some of it was on me, though: how personally I took the rejection and the poor reviews; how much my work suffered after my dad died, as if I kept trying harder and harder to please him, and it was only backfiring with all the effort; how I was still the kid showing off his French at the Louvre to get his dad's approval, only now that was impossible. How I never could get *Reagan* right, though not for lack of trying.

I didn't used to be this way, at least I don't think so. Or maybe it's just that as a rich kid out of Dalton and then Williams for college, everything was realized for me, because that's the sort of path that's paved for you when you're a rich kid out of Dalton and Williams. Sometimes I'll find myself watching Tatum at one of these endless industry parties where she kisses cheeks and laughs in that way that only I know is fake and hugs acquaintances like they're best friends, and I'll resent her for all of it, and then I'll rewind and try to pinpoint when I became so cynical, when I became such a dick. It's not like I don't know what I am.

But I'll forgive myself for that too. Because how can I not still be a little angry over the way he died, what the nineteen men on those planes took from me, the way it left us? How it wrecked Leo, how it unmoored me, how my mom found someone new and moved on as if this weren't the ultimate blight on my hope of normalcy? How I'd never write a script that was good enough for him or win me the Oscar like I promised him because he wouldn't be around anyway? How I'd never have the chance to forgive him for the way he pushed me, for the way he goaded me, and yes, for the way he inspired me too? To be the best, to expect the best. Now I was simply left with a void of that: of the best. And in this void, all of my best had suffered. It was years back now, and not something I dwell on, but the wreckage of his death ruined me maybe more than it should have and ruined my work along with it.

None of that is Tatum's fault. That dark seed inside of me has nothing to do with her. But still, when I watch her glide through a room as if she's lit by a spotlight and wonder, *Why her, not me*—just like I've wondered a million times in the shadowy corners of my grief about my dad, and how these seeds flare up with Ron and Walter now too: *Why my dad, not someone else?*—it's hard not to be resentful all the same.

Tonight, I try harder. I kiss her again and say: "You're going to be great. You have your speech?"

She nods, and then exhales and reaches for my hand, and we sail through the lobby toward Tatum's destiny, and I remind myself to enjoy it, to savor it, to champion it, because this is the stuff that dreams are made of, if we open up wide enough to let those dreams in.

~⊘

My phone starts vibrating on the commercial break before Tatum's category. I check it: my mom. I drop it back in my tux pocket.

While others are flitting about the theater, clutching hands, making deals, Tatum is sitting stone still, trying to compose herself.

"Almost there," I say. "Try to enjoy it."

Tatum had won every major award leading up to this; there would be no upset, no surprise. In exactly three minutes she'll float up to the stage and accept her Oscar. My phone buzzes again, then quiets, then buzzes again.

"Shit, my mom won't stop calling."

"It's OK, you have a minute, you can take it."

"I'm sure she wants to wish you luck."

Tatum turns to me and offers a lopsided smile, which reminds me of why she slayed me way back during the *Romanticah* shoot and then made it official when she kissed me (or I kissed her?) on New Year's Eve.

"I'm about to puke, so just thank her for me, and I'll call her later," she says.

I stand, press the phone to my ear.

"Mom, I have about thirty seconds. What's up?"

I expect her to say: *Oh, just wanted to be the first to congratulate Tatum,* or *Kiss your fabulous wife for me before she wins.*

Instead she shrieks like I have heard her only once before in her life.

And in an instant, it's ten years ago; it's horror and death and the fallout that is destined to come.

"It's Leo," she yells. "My God, Ben, it's Leo."

I run up the aisle and out to the lobby, just as the lights flicker to return us to our seats.

I miss Tatum's category, but then nothing that happens after this moment matters. And I miss Tatum's speech too, but later I'll learn that she forgot to thank me anyway.

12

TATUM

JULY 2004

My "big" break comes fifteen months of slinging cosmos and sex on the beaches and chardonnays for tourists at P. F. Chang's. I don't mind the work so much. It keeps me busy, though the children are often ill-behaved and whiny, and the tourists are loud and don't tip well. But Mariana, who logs most shifts with me, has become a good friend, and with Ben still working unending hours, this time prepping for *One Day in Dallas*, a Kennedy biopic set to shoot next spring, the stint gives me structure, fills my days with something other than scanning the trades for shitty auditions, staring at my cell phone in case my (relatively dodgy) agent calls, running on the beach to lose a few pounds which will take me from girl-next-door to girl-someone-wants-to-fuck. (In Hollywood terms.) I'm contemplating adopting a dog for the companionship, but Ben isn't home often enough for me to get an affirmative. "I might just do it without you," I said to him one night while he was nose-deep in a revision. "You'll just come home to a strange animal in the kitchen!"

"I prefer strange animals in the bedroom," he said, and I laughed, so he pushed his luck and teased: "See, I'm listening to you, even when you think I'm not."

So a dog is a possibility, a positive on the potential horizon.

Still, in the months that have passed between landing in LA and now, my ambition has gone from hopeful to desperate; my attitude has devolved from optimistic to jaded. There's a reason you see aspiring starlets hopping off the bus in movies full of sunshine that turn pale and gray as the scenes roll past. How many doors can one knock on before the rejection starts to sting? Ben tells me to keep my chin up, but Ben is working on his third feature, which I am happy for (of course). It fills our bank account, offers us stability. His success makes him happier than ever, as if each chit, each accolade, brings him closer to God. A self-anointed Hollywood God, but God all the same. He tells me sometimes that he's chasing the ghost of his dad, and I tell him that he now has to satisfy only himself, and he nods and sometimes seems to believe this and sometimes he doesn't. I don't try to talk him out of it too much, though; I understand the weight of parental baggage. It's not as if I'm not heaving my own shit around too. It's not as if I'm not wandering about, trying to find my own way too.

What I'm trying to find is what I embraced at Tisch, and what I discovered as a senior in high school after my rocky earlier years, and after my dad was absent and my mom was present but also on one of her holistic jags where she was more focused on the soothing nature of lavender or why we should ban dairy from our home than noticing that her teenage daughter was flailing about with a broken heart (and a lost virginity), and with no one around to guide her. At the time, I was taking drama because it fulfilled my arts requirement, and we were staging a modern rendition of *Romeo and Juliet*. Our teacher allowed us to adapt it for the modern era—think more Leonardo DiCaprio and Claire Danes than Shakespeare—and when he cast me as the lead,

I had to read the call sheet three times because I was sure he'd gotten it wrong. He hadn't, and to my surprise, I held the audience rapt, silent, almost reverent. The school newspaper had given the production a mixed review but handed me a rave. My mom, an amateur poet who never had loftier aspirations, attended the performance and wept afterward.

"If you can dream it, you can be it, baby," she said on the drive home.

"So why didn't you ever try to get published?"

"The art is sometimes enough," she said, squinting against the headlights of an oncoming car. "The art sometimes just has to be enough."

But the art wasn't just enough for me. I knew that immediately when they dropped the curtain on *Romeo and Juliet*; I knew it all through college, through the slog of hailed shows with great performances (*Hamlet*, *The Heidi Chronicles*), and less successful shows with still great performances (*The Importance of Being Earnest* and a particularly jarring *Lost in Yonkers*, where I was the only one who could pull off the accent). Daisy wasn't wrong back at my wedding: I probably *had* been the best one in our class at Tisch, but out here in LA, Tisch didn't mean much. Out here, big boobs and a small waist and, sometimes, a suggestive nod to a producer who may or may not want to undress you in his office after a meeting meant much more.

Daisy moves out the weekend of July 4th and crashes in our spare bedroom in our small bungalow. Though it's theoretically Ben's office, he's gone so often that it's mostly empty space where I sometimes unroll my yoga mat or find an exercise show on TV and run through a series of squats and lunges that make me hate myself, or when I'm feeling more generous, hate this town for making me care about the circumference of my thighs. Daisy is tiny and oozes all-American, so it's no shock that she has a slew of auditions at the ready. Also Daisy is connected in ways that I'm not, in ways that Ben is. I try not to begrudge them this: Hollywood never promised to be a level playing field, but when her brother's friend casts at ABC, and when her dad's college roommate runs Paramount, it's hard not to feel the nick against my skin. I want to call my mother, want to complain about the inequity of it, not because it means I won't work hard—harder—but because sometimes the complaining is the solution in and of itself. But my mother is no longer here to listen.

Sometimes I call Piper. But she's an obstetrics nurse (like my mom) who works nights and sleeps days, and I hate waking her with my burdens. Sometimes I'll complain to Leo, who himself calls more often, needier now that his own dad is gone, though I never had the impression that he dumped his inner life on his dad in the first place. But grief and death can do that to you—slice open a place that is vulnerable and wanting—so he leans on me like a big sister, and in return I lean on him because he makes it easy to. He listens to my grievances about my humiliating auditions or the way I collided with a waiter carrying a full plate of hot fried rice, and how even half a day later, I found charred peas in my hair and plenty down my bra too, and also how I'm just a girl from Canton who can't call in favors. (There's Ben, yes, who floated my name to casting with *One Day in Dallas*, but I wasn't the right "type," as is too often the case out here.) Leo may be a rich kid with a trader job he hates, but he listens, and because he wants so desperately to shed the burdens of his own background (the job he loathes, the expectations of a dead father he can now never outrun), he understands.

Now, Daisy has rented a convertible until she leases a car of her own, but insists that I drive.

"I'm hopeless with maps," she says. "Besides, it will be more fun if you come."

So three days after she lands in LA, I chauffeur her from audition to audition. Daisy is naturally skinny with just the right amount of curves, and she is very blond, like she was bred on the farmlands of Kansas, a look that happens to be in high demand right now at castings. (Well, really, it's always in high demand.) She goes out for guest spots on two teen shows, a small read for Quentin Tarantino's newest, and more commercials than I've auditioned for all year. If it were anyone else, I'd hate her. Actually, it occurs to me, as I sit in the car at an expired meter so I can argue with the meter maid if she circles around, that I *do* hate her a little bit, but she's Daisy, and one day, if asked, she'll drive me around to my own set of auditions. I try to meditate as I wait: I'd attended a freebie class on the beach last week run by a celeb guru. I was kind of hoping to meet someone famous who might decide to be my best friend and help me forge connections of my own, but also I thought maybe I'd learn something too. To help me quiet my mind, to still my unfulfilled ambition. In the car, I breathe in and count to seven, then breathe out and count to seven over and over and over again, but then Daisy raps on my window, and my eyes fly open, and I'm as I was before: listless, annoyed. Jealous, if I'm really being honest with myself.

"You OK?" she asks, sliding on her seat belt, undoing her rubber band so her hair spills effortlessly over her shoulders like in a shampoo commercial.

"Yeah." I put on my blinker to head up Sepulveda to take the back roads toward the Valley, hoping to beat traffic. "All good. All fine. Just tired."

"Hey, I'm not getting any of these, you know that, right?"

"Of course you are," I say. "And I want you to."

"Well, I'm not. I mean, I've sucked it big all day."

"You don't have to say that. You don't have to make me feel better." I fiddle with the dial on the radio.

"I thought that you were fine."

I sigh. "It's not you. It's me."

"You were the best one of us at school, Tate."

"That doesn't matter out here."

She quiets, losing herself to the view out the window.

"Were you meditating just now?"

"I refuse to answer on the grounds it might incriminate me," I say.

She chokes on her laugh. "What the fuck? You've been out here for, like, a year, and you're meditating? Whatever happened to the fuck-all bartender from NYU I knew and loved?"

"That fuck-all bartender was just an act, you know that. When have I ever been fuck-all anything in my life?" I come to a stop at a light. "Also, I took a class with Lily Marple's guru. And you know that she's nearly the highest-paid actress right now? I mean, it must be working."

"Eh, I know someone who knows Lily Marple's agent. Said she'd give a blow job to anyone who asks."

"Shut up."

She shrugs. "It's true."

"Jesus, I'm so fucked."

"No, dear, not that, just a blow job or two." She starts to giggle, which spirals into an uncontrollable fit of howling, crying laughter, and soon I'm laughing so hard I can barely keep the car in my lane.

"Hello, Hollywood! Daisy is here and she is prepared to give blow jobs!" I scream out the open air of the convertible until I realize that we're actually in front of the audition building, and I jolt into a parking spot. "I take that back!" I shout. "Daisy is here, and she is the most professional, qualified actress I know!"

Daisy reins in her laugh until it sputters to a slow chuckle, takes three deep breaths, and then flips open her compact mirror. Her eyeliner has smeared, her cheeks are blotchy from the hysterics.

"God, I look like hell. Also, I'm wiped; I don't think I can deal."

"Come *on*, Daisy, get out. Don't be late."

"Can't. Don't make me."

I put the car in park. "Daisy, seriously, this is for *The O.C.* That's, like, real shit, real exposure. You can't be too tired for that."

"I am. Jet lag." She groans, then tilts her head toward me and smiles. "Besides, I'll never get the part. It's for a bad girl with, like, tattoos. Not the blond all-American."

"Well, they wanted to see you."

"Oh God, you know as well as I do that they have no idea what they want to see. And I'm pretty sure they only agreed to this because my dad made some calls." She shoves the sides—the audition dialogue—at me. "You go. Tell them you're me."

"I can't tell them I'm you! I don't even have my headshots on me."

Daisy pops open the glove compartment and pulls out a stack. "Please, if I know anything about Tatum Connelly, it's that she's always prepared. Sign in with my name, then give them your real stuff when you get in the room. They won't say no."

"They'll say no."

"Then so what? I'm not getting this part anyway."

I glance at the sides. She's right: this role was practically written for me. Not *me*, Tatum, but the version of me I so easily inhabited at the bar, the one who threw shots down her throat, dismissed the tarty undergrads, picked up men for the sport of it. That version of me could play this role as if I were someone else entirely.

"They're going to say no," I repeat.

"So make them say yes," she answers and shifts her seat back to take a nap, as if she's put the question to bed.

᎐

They ask me to read three times through, then whisper among themselves, conferring in a tight little huddle behind a table littered with scattered headshots, discards of actors who are disposable and unwanted, not right for the part. The director, Seth, a guy about thirty, give or take a few years, with a scraggly goatee and a worn Red Sox hat, flips my résumé over and rereads it.

"So," he says.

"So," I reply.

"I could be blind here, but I'm pretty sure you are *not* Daisy Alexander, now, are you?"

I stutter, feel my composure ebbing out of me. I remind myself to play the part, to be anyone they want me to be, to be anyone I need to be. I tilt my chin higher, puff out my chest.

"Listen. I just thought . . ."

He waves a hand, indicating for me to be quiet. I turn to go.

"Wait, it's OK, it's OK." His eyes narrow on my résumé again. "Ah, *Romanticah*. I knew I knew you from somewhere." He smiles. "Ben and I grew up together."

"Ben grew up with everyone, it seems like."

"I know, right?" He laughs. "You from the city too?"

He means: *Are you part of our circle? Shouldn't we have met? Are you someone from whom I should curry favor?*

"Sort of," I say.

"I'm intrigued," he says, raising an eyebrow.

"Give me the part, and I'll tell you anything you want to know."

His raucous laugh shocks his associates into laughing too. I smile, though I think: *You are all such fucking lemmings.* I put my hand on my hip, jut it outward, flip my hair in a display of attitude. It's not so hard, this bravado. It's what I practiced for at the bar with Daisy, it's what I trained for practically since *Romeo and Juliet*. Being someone other than me. I slip into it like a second skin, like if I try a little harder, soon I won't even notice the difference.

"I like it," Seth says, nodding.

Me too, I think.

They call the next morning with an offer for a three-episode arc, tell me to have my agent reach out to go over the details. I only have my dubious commercial agent, with his dreary office in Van Nuys and who mostly got castings for non-union local commercials (and possibly soft-core porn), so Daisy calls her own agent, and just like that I have real representation and am a working actress. Daisy had booked two of her commercials and the spot in the Tarantino movie. *The O.C.* was small potatoes compared to that, but I didn't have a dad who knew people who knew people; I didn't have a high school network to call in favors. Not that Daisy wasn't talented; not that Ben wasn't either.

Also, not that I wasn't indebted to Daisy for giving me the audition in the first place.

I was. I am.

I love them both.

But even with them in my army, it had been fifteen months without as much as a nibble, without as much as a solitary yes.

I was the most talented one at Tisch.

Ben ditches the office early, and he, Daisy, Eric (his writing buddy from Williams), and I toast to our successes at Nobu off the Pacific Coast Highway in Malibu as the sun blazes out into darkness, painting the sky in oranges and pinks and yellows that seem unimaginable if not for viewing them with our naked eyes. Ben snakes his arm around my waist and tugs me in for a kiss, while Daisy and Eric flirt over the bottle of champagne that Ben ordered, and we drink too quickly.

"You didn't have to do all this for me," I say, waving my hand, still clutching a mostly empty flute of champagne. "It's just a guest part on *The O.C.*"

"It's the start of something; it's the beginning of a snowball." He tilts forward and touches his forehead to mine.

"So we can snowball together," I say.

"Let's snowball together," he repeats.

"OK," I say.

"I see you," he whispers in my ear.

I close my eyes and kiss him because we see each other so easily, we can do so even with our eyes pressed shut.

13

BEN

MAY 2010

My mom has asked me to give a toast, which should be easy, which should be cake. I'm a writer, after all.

Tatum leans over, kisses my cheek, adjusts my tie, and says, "Breathe." I rise with a flute of champagne held aloft, though if anyone were to look closely enough, they'd see a tiny tremor, a small betrayal of my feelings. I want to be happy for her, for her new life, but I'm trapped in this bubble of melancholy, of what-ifs. *What if he hadn't been on the plane that day? What if he'd been around to see my success? What if he'd been around to see that success falter? How would I be changed? How would I be unchanged too?*

We've spent the month in New York for Tatum's shoot, so I've gotten to know Ron a bit better, broken down some of my walls. We've gone to the movies, drunk wine, taken in a Yankees game; he even joined me for Joey's music class, which was filled with mothers and nannies, and made a pretty funny wisecrack about our levels of estrogen rising just by crossing the threshold. He asked me about my work: if I'm relieved to be moving on from *Alcatraz*, the TV stint that Eric and I embarked on but that never really caught fire in the ratings; if I have anything new in the hopper. Ron told me how much he loved the new Reagan biography, and that he knows my dad revered him, and recounted a story of how he once met him at a Hollywood party in the '70s. "I was so far out of my element," Ron laughed. "Not made for it like you and Tatum."

This isn't true—that I'm made for it—and this assertion rankles me, even though, ostensibly, he's taking an interest, getting to know me. I'm not at all made for Hollywood the way that Tatum seems to be now: her A-list mommy-and-me group; her trainer and chef who appear in our kitchen at seven a.m.; her newly hired assistant, Stephanie, to oversee all the details that she no longer has time for. I'm part of all of this, true, but it's as if I'm standing on the outside of a glass door looking in. I can hear the clatter, but I'm one degree removed. We used to tell each other all the time that we could each *see* the other; it was our code, our something private.

But now I see her less and less. Not just literally, because she is gone on set or on location, but metaphorically too. And not in how she is ambitious—I understand ambition—but in how she doesn't let me in like she once did. Or maybe it's that I don't try as hard to gain entry, because there is so much other stuff—her career, mine, Joey, miscommunications, exhaustion, grief, Walter—standing between us. What I have always loved the most about Tatum, her transparency, is slowly fading. I don't know how to get that back; I don't know what sort of work I have to put in to get that back, when she is the one who is always leaving. How do you tell your wife that you want her more to yourself, that you wished she worked less, without sounding like a jealous, emasculated asshole?

"I still want you to write something for me," she says from time to time, just like she used to say before she had more offers piling in than she can handle, before she could be choosy about awards bait and commercial success, before beauty companies dangled lucrative contracts, before *People* and *Us Weekly* and TMZ took an interest. I usually nod and say, "I know," and yet I never start that script, the one just for her. Not because she wouldn't be luminous (to be clear, Tatum is luminous in everything—just read her reviews), but because I wonder if maybe I can no longer match her brilliance. *Alcatraz* getting canceled stings. Your wife recognizing that your talent isn't what she always believed it to be would go way past that—it would be decimating.

Breathe, Tatum mouths to me at my mother's wedding to her new husband, our eyes locking as I weave to the front of the garden. Tatum called in a favor and reserved the private townhouse of Mitch Sterling, the producer on her new project, *Fallen Manhattan*, in which she saves Manhattan (and the world) from alien invasion. (It's penned by Alan Frank, the Pulitzer Prize–winning author, so her team thought it was a smart play: turn on the teenage and young twentysomething guys while still reaping critical acclaim.) Mitch's townhouse is largely unoccupied while he spends his time in LA, so he happily opened it up to us for the occasion. My mom hadn't wanted much of a to-do, but she'd wanted something.

"That we found each other through this tragedy is really something to be celebrated," she'd said. And it was, it is. I bristle at Ron but not because he is Ron. I bristle, as Tatum points out when we argue about my distaste for her own father, because I have "issues" with paternal figures. That I have unresolved feelings toward my dad. "It's textbook," Tatum says, and I'm sure it is. But that doesn't change the bitterness I swallow, mostly about Walter, but sometimes about Ron too.

Leo is sitting at the table with my new stepdad and his daughter, Veronica. Leo winks at me as I pass by, reaches out and squeezes my leg. "Yo, bro. Love ya."

"Daddy!" Joey shouts from his perch on Tatum's lap. "That's my daddy!"

Everyone laughs and turns to gaze at him, in his tiny Brooks Brothers suit, with his curly blond hair that resembles neither mine nor Tatum's.

"That's your daddy!" Tatum says, and everyone laughs again, not really because it's nearly as cute or funny as when Joey said it but because people laugh and fawn when Tatum says just about anything these days. It's not her fault; I know this. It's simply inevitable, the way that fame shifts everyone else's perception of you while you've done nothing to ask for it. Been in a few good movies, locked in a few excellent performances. That's not nothing, but it's not everything, either, in the way that fame can masquerade that it is.

Tatum would say this too. But she'd tell you that the fame part of it, that's just someone else's expectations and has nothing to do with her or the work or our day-to-day lives. Still, it's an amorphous mass, a cancerous blob that has taken root, and though she tries to ignore it, tries to pretend that nothing has changed—that her being asked for autographs in the airport on our way here, that her being comped a ridiculous bottle of wine when we snuck out to a small Italian joint around the corner is all status quo—in truth, her fame has shifted nearly everything.

Maybe *everything* is me being ungenerous. I hate this side of me, but like that cancerous blob, I don't know how to simply cut my pettiness out of me. Its toxicity is everywhere. Also, Tatum is so often not present that she hasn't felt the mass, hasn't noticed what's festering. Maybe that's what keeps it alive in me: that like a child, I want her to give me attention, stand up and say, *I still see you.* Sometimes she does. I don't mean that she doesn't. And I know that I am thirty-five and no longer able to excuse juvenile behavior away.

It's textbook.

So why isn't there an easier fix? For me to find? For her to suggest? Therapy, sure. But I don't want to be one of those LA types who sits on a couch and moans about the inadequacies of his cushy life. I want my wife. I want to see my wife. I want her to see me. Then maybe I won't be so brittle, maybe I won't be so easily broken.

Tatum sees me today, though, meeting my eyes again. Wishing me on. I clear my throat, gaze at my mom and Ron, who seems to wholly love her, and whom she appears to love wholly in return. I'm not eight or ten or twelve years old; I know that he is not taking my dad's place; I know that my mom should be happy. My eyes move to Leo, and I wonder if this isn't a bit how he felt over this past decade, how I tried to be his father without him asking for it. It's different, of course. I'm his blood; I promised my dad I'd look out for him. But this notion that someone can be taken from you, disappear into a void in a matter of literal seconds, and then you have to live in the vacuum of that void? It hasn't gotten easier. So maybe that was why I tried to put my foot down with Leo, tried to guide him in the way that I thought my father would think best. Maybe that's why I'm pricklier with Ron, even when I know better.

I raise my flute toward the open sky in the back of Mitch Sterling's garden, which has been lavished in yellow roses, my mother's favorites. "Lub you!" Joey calls to me before I can start speaking.

"Love you, buddy," I say back.

Love you, Tatum mouths to me.

Love you, I mouth back.

"Love you," Leo shouts, which makes everyone giggle again.

"Love you," I say sincerely back to him.

Leo rises and wraps me in a hug, slapping my back, holding me for a beat longer than the pre-rehab Leo would have. He's been clean for almost a year now. He calls me on Sundays to check in, he is rededicated to his job, he left the nightclub business, and he never told my mom about any of it. His skin is shiny, his eyes well rested, his muscles strong when my hands press against his shoulder blades on the other end of the embrace. It wasn't a seamless process, my tough love, my insistence that he finally grow up and grow a backbone and accept responsibility for the roads he'd put himself on. Tatum wanted to do it differently, and Walter, her dad, told me I was mistaken, that I needed to offer support, not just firmness. But here we are, and he is thriving, and Leo and I proved them wrong.

"I know I'm a writer," I begin. "But that doesn't make me an expert in the ways of love."

"Bullshit!" Leo calls out. "You married Tatum Connelly, so you must be doing something right!"

"That's true!" Tatum shouts from a couple of tables behind him.

"Well, marrying my wife was the one smart thing I've done in the name of love my whole life. Though that just makes me lucky; that doesn't really make me smart." I don't know why I'm announcing this, my most neurotic insecurity, to the crowd of my mother's and new stepdad's friends, and I don't know when I started to think that this might be true. But it comes off as self-deprecating, and everyone grins, then turns to gaze at my wife in the back of the room.

"Don't sell yourself short," Tatum calls out, playing to the audience, and everyone laughs. She says this a lot to me now—*Don't sell yourself short, dream it, be it!*—and I know she's not trying to be patronizing, but it is. It's fucking patronizing and demeaning, and even now I feel a red flare of anger rush through me. Like if she still *saw* me, she'd know that I don't need uplifting quips to get me back on track; she'd know that I'm already trying to right my train.

"OK, well, with that established," I say, "I just want to say that I'm not necessarily wise in the ways of love. I don't know why our dad was taken from us, and Ron, I can't say why your wife was either. But I can only say life sometimes grants us second chances, and if they should fall upon you, if you should be lucky enough to be offered another chance at happiness, then you'd be a fool not to seize it."

I look at Leo, with his own second chance, and he nods, grateful. I look at my mom and Ron, who are genuinely overcome with emotion: her with tears on her cheeks, him wiping them away.

"And so, I'll ask all of you today to raise your glass to second chances. May we all be lucky enough in our lives to be granted the opportunity for love and joy and family, and when that opportunity presents itself, may we all be as smart as my mom and Ron, who refused to let life slay them when life sure as hell tried."

Everyone raises their glasses.

"To second chances," they all say, as Ron leans close to my mom and kisses her. Tatum meets my eyes and blinks, our old code, our old signal. She still *sees* me now, like she used to, like we both used to.

"To second chances," I say again, telling myself I won't squander my own, whenever the opportunity arises.

14

TATUM

MARCH 2005

Piper calls with the news while I'm in hair and makeup for *Scrubs*. It's nothing glamorous, a guest star as a college student who comes down with shingles, but the exposure is good, and it's another line for my résumé. Since *The O.C.*, the work has been steady, though not swift, nothing so lucrative and assuring that I've wanted to quit P. F. Chang's. Well, I always want to quit P. F. Chang's, but I still take a shift now and then, and I still stop in on Thursdays to keep Mariana company or sometimes jump in for her hours if she has an audition of her own or a gig that's come up. None of the customers recognize me, no one thinks I'm anything to double-take at. I'm not. Half the waiters have booked guest spots of their own or have made it all the way to testing for pilots. At Tisch, I was something special; in LA, I'm a slash—a bartender/actress. I have an audition next week—a period piece called *On the Highlands* that would shoot later in the year in Scotland—that would launch me out of the slash category, propel me into the full-time actor mode, but I've stopped pinning all my aspirations on every audition. There are too many nos to get invested each time.

"Pipes," I say into my cell, holding it an inch from my cheek so I don't mess up the shingles makeup that took two hours to perfect at six o'clock this morning. "Not the best time."

I can tell that something's awry before she even speaks. Maybe it's in the way she inhales or the way that she hiccups or just the way that sisters who have been through so much together can intuit one another, even when thousands of miles apart.

"Piper," I say. "What's wrong?"

"I know you don't want to hear about this," she says, her voice breaking, then dropping into a whisper. "But I don't know who else to call."

"You call me," I say. "You can tell me anything." I forget about the painstaking makeup and press the phone to my ear, like that somehow brings us closer.

"It's Dad."

I already know, once she has said this, why I was the one she didn't want to call. Other children might worry about car accidents or heart attacks or some sort of unfortunate accident befalling their solitary living parent, but not me, not us. We've lived through this too many times.

"What did he do?" I ask. I don't want to hear this, I don't want to pick up more pieces. I want a mother who is alive and a father who is sober, and if I had to swap one for the other, my mom should be here, not him. It's a horrible thought. I stare into the illuminated mirror in the makeup trailer and actually think this—*That is a horrible thought*—but it's true, and it's not like I haven't thought it before. When she was going through chemo, and he coped with whiskey: *It should be you, not her.* When we buried her, and he showed up at our childhood home's door, sober but not exactly put together: *Why her, not you?*

And now again.

"Scooter found him passed out on the side of the road last night. Held him for the night, called me this morning when Dad had woken up."

Scooter Smith was Piper's high school boyfriend. They'd split just before college—she'd gone to Ohio University, and he headed to Wisconsin for football—but they were still friendly, the types who sometimes had a beer together if they'd run into each other earlier in the day, sometimes slept with each other if one beer turned into four. He was a deputy sheriff, thought about being mayor someday, which you'd really never, ever expect if you'd known him back in high school. Still kind of didn't expect now. But I was sitting in a makeup chair playing a college junior with shingles, so what did I know?

"Bail?" I say. "Do you need bail money?"

"Tatum!" she snaps. "No, Scooter let him out, but I mean, we need to get him help."

"Again. We need to get him help *again*," I say, just as a production assistant hustles into the trailer and barks: "Tatum Connelly, you're up in five. Tatum Connelly, five minutes."

"Don't say 'again' like we've had to do this a million times," Piper says.

"How many times then?" I nod to the PA, and mouth *Wrapping this up,* and he answers me by marching out and slamming the door.

"Three," she sighs. "OK? Three times. Does that make you happy?"

"Of course it doesn't make me happy, Piper!"

"Well, it doesn't make me happy either. But you're out there in fancy Los Angeles; I'm here sitting in the shit trying to clean it up. So please stop giving me a hard time and help."

"Fine. How can I help?" I say, kinder now. "Is it money?" I don't really have any money but Ben has plenty, and what's his is mine. Theoretically. We didn't sign a prenup; he didn't even mention a prenup, and he takes care of me in the ways he expects a husband to provide for his wife. But I still haven't quite adjusted to having a safety net. Thus, the Thursday shifts at the bar. Also, the (modest) checking account I opened shortly after I landed *The O.C.* gig last year, splitting my paycheck between our savings and, well, now my savings. Ben wouldn't have cared if I'd told him. But I didn't. I'd planned to, the night that I went to the bank, and now I can't even remember why I didn't; maybe I'd fallen asleep while he was working late or maybe he'd done something that irritated me, or maybe I'd just wanted something for myself when my husband seemingly had everything else. Either way, my checking account won't fund my dad's rehab, but Ben could. Ben would. Happily.

"Not money," Piper says. "Well, I mean, maybe some money. But I want him at an in-patient facility. No more do-it-yourself patchwork sobriety."

Do-it-yourself patchwork sobriety was my dad's specialty.

"I'll ask around, Pipes, OK?"

The makeup artist's walkie springs to life. I'm needed on set.

"Why don't you come home?" Piper asks, her voice shaking.

"I can't just come home."

"Because you're a big, important person now?"

"Hardly. But I'm working. And we adopted the dog, and Ben is out of town half the time, and Monster weighs a hundred pounds and isn't exactly well trained, and I can't just take him on the plane with me."

The makeup artist says: "Tatum, they're ready for you."

Also, there is nothing I'd rather do less than go home. Home is cobwebs and ghosts and memories of my mother, who should be here. Home is discomfort and high school awkwardness and working at the pharmacy or at Albertsons while other girls were cheerleaders and going to homecoming dances. Home is my dad drinking a case of Coors Light in one sitting and us tiptoeing in the kitchen the mornings of his hangovers so we don't wake him and have to smell his puke. Home is our back garden, which my mom nurtured once my dad left but now holds her ashes. So even that had turned to literal dust. I'd do just about anything other than return home.

"Bring him here, Piper," I say rashly, without thinking it through, my mind already on the set, on to nailing the role so I'll get something better, something bigger, something that will take me further from who I used to be. "Just . . . get on a plane and bring him here. We'll figure it out together."

⁓

We drive him down to a thirty-day dry-out clinic that weekend. Ben has made some calls, asked for favors, and we found him a bed at Commitments, a no-nonsense facility whose motto is *Commit to Yourself, Commit to Life, Commit to Your Sobriety.* Piper and my dad sit in the back, Ben drives with his knuckles turning white against the steering wheel, and I stare out the window at the rush of palm trees and desert that whips by.

"You won't have to do this again," my dad says as we flank him in the lobby, as a kind nurse with huge fake breasts and adhesive eyelashes pats him on the shoulder and prepares to walk him to his room.

I chew on my lip and say nothing.

"I know I have failed you," he says, crying now. "It's not like I don't know it. It's not like I'm not ashamed."

Piper hugs him. "We're all fallible, Dad, it's OK."

I want to scream: *We are not all fallible, not in the ways that he is.* But I do not.

He says: "I just miss her so much, your mom. And I shouldn't have found the answer in the bottle, I know that. I'm stupid. It was stupid, I hate myself."

Piper takes his hand. "We'll get you through this, Dad. I'm sure you can stay here as long as you need. Can he take your guest room after?"

"Our guest room?" I repeat. We hadn't discussed plans after this, but this certainly was not part of it. No, my dad would return home with Piper, get back to work, get back to his own life. But I can't say this now, as we're checking him in to dry out. I can't set him up for failure before he's even started. "We'll see. OK? Let's just see."

"It would help him recalibrate, get away from his triggers," she says. "I said we'll see."

She nods. Ben narrows his eyes, starts to say something, then does not. It occurs to me that it's his guest room too, that he'll want a say. But Ben is always benevolent; of course he'll offer for him to stay.

The nice nurse with enormous breasts says, "OK, well, family is welcome next weekend, in seven days. If you head to the desk around the corner, they'll give you all the information."

And then she nods to my father, who is so defeated and looks so much like a broken little child, and ushers him through the swinging door, which eases back into the frame and latches.

Piper starts crying, and I stand there, my hands flanking my hips, my brain drifting to all the ways I want this moment to be different, like I'm in a movie and writing my own script. Like I'm a daughter with a mom who is alive and a daughter with a father who hasn't been a terrible disappointment. In my mind, in my new role, I'm anyone I want to be, anyone I dare to dream.

"Let's go," I say, unable to stand there a second longer in the muddle of the real moment. "Please, can we just get out of here?"

I spin quickly and head for the exit. They linger for a moment before following, because they are better equipped for this reality; they don't need to write themselves into a world of make-believe to get by.

15

BEN

JUNE 2009

The doorbell rings early, too early. The sun has barely risen, and I can't imagine who could possibly be at the front door before seven a.m. I roll to my left but Tatum's side of the bed is empty. She must have gotten up for a crack-of-dawn run on the beach. She's been doing that lately to lean down to ensure that she fits back into the corsets for *As You Like It* after gaining fifteen pounds (all muscle) for *Army Women* (a break from the awards-bait films in an attempt to go commercial and expand her fan base).

The doorbell rings again.

Shit. This had better be an emergency. And whoever it is had better not wake the baby. I push myself to my elbows, then flop my feet to the carpet. Then I remember the last real emergency from eight years ago, when my dad—when three thousand people—died, and chide myself for ever wishing for something so stupid. *The best you can hope for is that there's never an emergency again, you dumb fuck!*

I haven't slept well, and the left side of my neck aches. I woke at three thirty, as I do most nights now worrying about *Alcatraz*'s dismal ratings—how Eric and I had spent the better part of two years committed to this TV project, how after a hot start it's become creatively wretched—you can only have so many shankings before the audience yells *jumped the shark!*—and how I didn't even want to do network TV in the first place, and now even that is going south.

My dad used to say that if you aim for the middle, you shouldn't expect to come out on top: when I came home with a B in English sophomore year, when I told him I was content on the JV squash squad, when I announced that I didn't care if I were named editor of the school paper, as long as I got to write.

He'd push his glasses up on his nose, sip his scotch in his library amid biographies of great men throughout history—Washington and Churchill and Babe Ruth (and eventually plenty of Reagan biographies too; Reagan was only a few years out of office when I was in high school)—and remind me that I'd get lost in the middle, that my potential would seep out of me like water through a drain.

Shortly after our trip to Paris for his fortieth, my dad was hospitalized for what they thought was an early heart attack. He'd been in court that day and seized, then fainted. Leo and I were pulled early from school by our nanny, and a waiting town car raced us to Mount Sinai Hospital, a straight shot up Madison Avenue. My mother was there, hysterical, though the nurses were trying to calm her. I remember trying to make myself as still as possible in the waiting room; our nanny had taken Leo to the cafeteria for a snack, and my mom was still weeping, and there was nothing to be done other than wait. And to still myself. Like a superstition: if I could hold myself as if I weren't breathing, prove to God that I could do it, maybe He would save my dad. I never lasted very long—I'd count to forty in my head, maybe forty-five, and then I'd fidget or get distracted by the nurses' station. Finally, I heard my dad in my brain telling me that if I was going to do something, I'd better do it right. So I did: I stared at the floor and held myself still until I reached six hundred and thirty-seven, and just as I was at six hundred and thirty-eight, a doctor emerged and said:

"It was a cardiac incident, not a full-blown attack. He's going to be OK."

And I exhaled and felt something come unpinned inside of me, something crazy, something that thought: *Maybe I just had to prove to him that I could do it* right, *and he felt that and came back to us.*

Now, so many years later, I can see this as literal wishful thinking, but at fifteen, it felt almost prophetic. That I could be named editor of the paper and be granted a seat at the chessboard with my dad. That I could win an Oscar and, like a piece on a chessboard, move closer to my father, the king. And even if I resented it back then, even if it rankled me, I understood it as I got older. I admire it now, in fact. That if you aspire for mediocrity, that's what you will get. But if you hold your breath for the world record, you'll get your name written up in a book.

Alcatraz is mediocrity, and not even good mediocrity at that.

So I lie awake every night, staring at the ceiling, wrapped in my embarrassment and disappointment. That Tatum is coasting toward the stars doesn't help alleviate my shame of knowing that I have settled. That's not her fault. Of course it's not. But it does shine a mirror on my own inadequacy when what I'd like to do is look away.

The doorbell clangs.

I wipe the sleep out of my eyes and pad down the hall in my underwear. I stick my head into Joey's room, watch his chest rise and fall for a beat. Tatum's been doing breakfast so I can sleep late, before she heads to the set. Joe murmurs something in his sleep, then falls quiet, a small victory.

"I'm coming," I whisper to the door. "I'm coming."

The doorbell chimes again.

"Jesus! I'm coming," I call louder.

"It's me," I hear from the outside.

I click the latch, swing the door open wide.

"Jesus Christ," I say, my hand covering my mouth instinctively. He is wan and disheveled and appears to have puke on his dirty jeans.

It's Leo. He sees me, and he starts to cry.

⌒

He tells me the drugs started out just for fun.

"Those lines in Toronto, remember?"

I shake my head. "No."

"When I met you at the film festival. That was the first time: that coke—that party the first night?"

I remember then. I flew him up to meet me. I wanted to watch out for him, said I *would* watch out for him. I'd do better, be better, with my dad gone.

Leo drops his head into his hands, then folds himself atop the kitchen table. I brew some black coffee, pour us both too much, and it spills on the counter, where I leave the mess and hand him a mug.

I do the math. "I don't understand . . . this has been going on, you've been using for six years?"

Where have I been? How did I miss this?

"I called you once," he says, his eyes filling again. "A few years back . . . I think . . . you were in Dallas? On a shoot? That Kennedy thing? I don't know. Anyway. I called you to tell you that I thought I needed . . . help. But then I lost my nerve. Thought I could do it on my own. Then, I mean, obviously, this nightclub investment thing was not the best move."

"Nightclub thing?"

"I invested, remember?"

I shake my head. It sounds familiar, but I often only hear Leo through a tunnel: I pay close enough attention to ensure that he's checking off the boxes, then tune out the rest of the clatter because there is so much clatter. Everywhere he goes, there is noise. Tatum would probably say I do much the same with her.

He sighs. "I went in with some buddies on a place in Miami. Disposable income isn't my problem, thought I could invest it and have fun at the same time."

I nod. I have no recollection of a nightclub in Miami. I chastise myself. "So you've tried to stop?"

He shrugs, something small and pathetic, which is to say no, he really hasn't tried all that hard to stop. Even though one look at him—dirty, disheveled, bruises beneath his eyes, cracks along the edges of his lips—informs us both that he is teetering on the edge, close enough to stumble off it and maybe never come back. He tells me that he hasn't slept in three nights, that he was downtown partying and a girl he was with OD'd, that he knew if he didn't get on a plane and tell me now in person, ask for help, he'd be next.

"So you haven't tried to stop?" I hear my voice, the judgment. I hate myself for it but it's there all the same. Tatum hears this all the time with Walter; this is the first time I've really heard it for myself.

"It could have been me, Ben. *Shit.* It could have been me."

"Have you told the people at work? Because if you haven't, then you shouldn't. They can fire you."

He slaps both palms against the table. "This isn't fucking about work, Ben!"

"It's not, I know." I sit beside him, rest both of my hands on his knees. I have to do better at this. If Tatum were here, she'd be better. I try to intuit what she'd say. "I just meant . . . Look, we've been through this with Walter, Tatum's dad. We'll get through it, but you'll need the month. Thirty days to get straight."

He nods. "I'm their best trader. They'll give it to me." He pauses. "Ironic, isn't it? How good I am at something I hate?"

He loathes me when he says this. I know it; I can feel it cutting through my soul. As if the words are fingers pointing at me saying:

You made me stick with it; you tried to be my father when I just needed a brother.

"I just tried to do what I thought was right," I say, sliding my hands back into my own lap. "I thought it was time for you to be a grown-up."

"Whoever gave you the right to tell me how to be a grown-up?"

"Dad did," I say, and regret it immediately.

"You're not Dad," he says, intuiting my thoughts. He rises and heads toward the bathroom. I hear him vomiting for a good five minutes. And I know I should go in there, rub his back, offer some comfort, but I find that I'm unable to, unable to stand and do what's best for him, when what's best for me is to stay here, stuck in my chair, without having to confront the reality of all the ways I have failed him.

Tatum handles all the things that I cannot. Her tank top is still sweat-pocked, her cheeks still pink by the time she has called Commitments, spoken to the staff as if they are old friends, secured Leo a bed. She phones her agent, tells her she'll make it to set that day—she's a pro, after all—but will be leaving immediately after the crew breaks for the union-mandated lunch. She often lingers around to shadow the director, to play scenes with her costars off camera, a benevolence the pros afford their peers when they all get along.

"Family emergency," she says to Jocelyn, her agent. "I'll tell them when I get there, but FYI. This comes first for me today. In case you get any gripes. Or, whatever, in case anyone calls me a bitch to TMZ."

Only recently has the tabloid industry started to take interest in Tatum. Every once in a while I'll be in the checkout line at CVS and catch a small snippet about a usually made-up bit in *Us Weekly*, or I'll lose myself to the Internet by googling her name when I should be writing, only to find a handful of stories about on-set behavior (or romances) which surely aren't true. Tatum pays them little mind. Sometimes they'll print a quick bit about her rivalry with Lily Marple, and she'll scan the copy and mutter something like: "God, she's such a bitch."

That one they get right.

"I'm only doing one shot today," she says fifteen minutes after hanging up with Jocelyn, bounding down the steps, wrapping her just-showered hair into a bun. She's gotten more beautiful as she's gotten more famous. And it's not that her beauty is tied to her fame; rather, she's grown more confident, more comfortable in her skin, like she's finally living her best life (I was watching *Oprah* recently and heard that phrase, in case you're wondering). "I'll be home just after noon. We'll head down then. I called my dad to come by in the meantime."

I steel my jaw. She notices.

"Don't even start with me," she says, throwing her script and phone into her bag. "He's been through it. He'll help."

Joey starts to wail from his room.

"Shit," she says. "Jocelyn is asking them to push everything up for me today. Can you handle breakfast?"

I nod.

"It's not like I want to miss his breakfast," she snaps. "It's my favorite part of my day."

"I didn't say that you wanted to."

She sighs. "Constance will be here in thirty minutes. If you don't want to do breakfast, she'll handle it."

The truth is that Joey doesn't like me feeding him. He greedily laps up whatever Tatum and Constance, our nanny, put in front of him, but with me, no, it's on the floor or against the wall or sometimes in his mouth, then dribbled right out. Tatum says it's because he can sense that he's pushing my buttons, so he keeps going. I suspect that she knows a thing or two about this because she does the same thing. It's not that we want to fight or snip at each other. But we find ourselves doing so more often now: she's working too much; I'm working on something I have no interest in (*Alcatraz*!)—and which is doing poorly anyway. Neither of us is sleeping in the way that you need to not to take a small injustice and spiral it into something that suddenly feels like you'd stake your life on it.

Also, of course, there's her father. How forgiving she has been of him; how unforgiving I have been. That he is alive and has abused so many of his years here is too much for me to ignore, even if he has rehabilitated himself, even if he is now clear-headed and present. I recognize that this is petty and also small-minded. Addiction is not a character flaw you hold against someone forever. And yet, I do. Fair or not, rational or not. He is here and has been given so many second chances, and my father had been given none.

"I'll do breakfast," I say. "It's not a problem. Maybe he'll finally agree to eat on my watch." I make a face that signals, *No way in hell will that happen*—and it's meant to make her laugh, but she misses it as her phone buzzes in her bag, and then she runs to the town car the studio sends each morning.

"Yes, yes, thanks, Dad. I'll be back in a few hours. He's here. I'm sure that would be great."

She is sending Walter, knowing how much it will annoy me, knowing that she didn't even ask me if I'll mind. She's been doing that more often now: making executive decisions, both big and small, without asking. Usually I don't mind. Today I do.

The door shuts behind her, and the house is quiet once more—Leo is sleeping out back in the guesthouse—so I plod up the stairs to retrieve my crying son, who will fight me over his oatmeal because he can sense that I'm weak. Survival of the fittest. Human instinct.

∞

Walter rings the doorbell right as I open my laptop.

Of course I can't work today, can't focus, and besides, Eric is overseeing this week's script, which may be our last, as we await our inevitable cancellation. But I'd promised myself that I'd revisit *Reagan*, figure out what exactly I could tweak to lure Spencer back in to shopping it around, to reengage the studios, get me back into the good graces of the film world, not this shitty network TV world.

In the doorway, Walter shakes my hand because we're not the type to hug.

"We'll get him through this," he says, as if I've asked or said anything contrary.

I check my watch; Tatum will still be gone for a few hours. "I just have to make a quick call," I say before ducking into my office. There's no phone call to make, but Walter probably knows this; it's easier than standing around making small talk. "Thanks for coming. Leo's sleeping for now. There's coffee."

"No problem, no problem. I'll wait until he's up, and then I'll talk to him." Then, "Joey?"

"Oh, out with the nanny, you just missed him."

I slip into my office, shut the door, then lock it.

Walter has done everything a reasonable person could ask to rehabilitate himself. He's been clean since we brought him to Commitments. Yet I lock my door anyway, a quiet *Fuck you for being here when my father is not. Fuck you for being fine with mediocrity, for not wanting more.* Yes, his sobriety is perhaps "more"; yes, he is trying. But I find that I am my father's son, unwilling to make accommodations for a lifetime of mistakes, even when Walter's mistakes weren't my own, weren't even Tatum's.

There's a knock from outside of my office, and I steel myself.

"Ben?"

I startle and race to unlock it. Leo.

"I'm up," he says, the back of his hair matted upward, the exact way it used to when we were younger and he'd wake after falling asleep in my bed even though I'd try to kick him out. I was a teenager by then and wanted my privacy, and he, just seven or eight, tried to cling on for as long as he could.

He flops on the loveseat across from my desk. Tatum's awards (SAG, Golden Globe, Critics' Choice, all of them) line my top shelf, my Sundance newcomer award front and center on my desk, a reminder of the potential of what once was. *Is.* What still is.

"Please don't tell Mom." It's more of a sob.

"She doesn't know?"

"It would kill her. So please."

"We won't say a word," Walter says from the hallway before I can even think to offer my reassurance. "The only thing you worry about now is getting better. Your sobriety comes first."

Leo nods, meets his eyes. "Thank you."

I want to say to Walter: *Don't speak for me, don't go around making promises on my behalf.* But Leo looks both so broken and so grateful in this moment for Walter and his comfort that instead I fold my hands in my lap, wait for Tatum to come clean this up, and I say nothing at all.

16

TATUM

OCTOBER 2006

The fact is this: nothing is done for you in this life if you don't do it for yourself. I don't care how many people claim they are "on your team"; the only person who can *helm* your team is you. We talk a lot about "teams" in our family therapy sessions, which I now do every month with my dad. It's part of the outplacement of Commitments. "We are committed to a life of recovery," they say in their brochures and in their e-mails and in real life. Also, when we checked my father out after his thirty days, and every single time we have revisited since. Not that my father has needed to revisit for drinking. Rather, we drive down once a month for family therapy. Well, for father-daughter therapy. Or: Dad-and-me therapy.

Piper is back in Ohio, back to her life of nursing and living in our childhood home and back to dating Scooter Smith, who, she has confided, might propose soon.

We brought my dad home after his month at Commitments, and he hasn't left, which was not my choice, but I couldn't just stuff him on the first plane back. The counselors told us that he needed to be away from his triggers, and that he needed a stable, supportive environment. What was I going to do? Prove that I was no better than he had been for his erratic, unreliable years and kick him out? He was trying, and so he stayed.

Ben was doing well with no signs of slowing down—there was early awards buzz on *One Day in Dallas*, and he was turning down offers by the bucketload. So we boxed up the Santa Monica bungalow, which was our first home together, and took out a mortgage on a house in Holmby Hills. There was a small guesthouse in the back, nothing fancy, just a one-bedroom with a kitchenette and a bathroom with cotton candy tiles that needed updating. But my dad moved in without complaint—not that he had much to complain about: the guesthouse, with its dated decor, more closely resembled our childhood home than the main house, which had soaring beamed ceilings and a kitchen larger than my entire New York apartment. It took me weeks to get used to not being able to shout to Ben and have him hear me from anywhere in the house. Daisy swung by and said, "Yup, this'll do," and I didn't say a word about how Ben had covered the entire down payment because I was earning a little more than zero, but nothing substantial.

There had been four sitcom guest parts, and an arc on *CSI*, and, of course, *On the Highlands*, but it wasn't "down payment in Holmby Hills" sort of money. Ben didn't care. Ben didn't even think twice. "What's mine is yours," he said. "We're a team," he said. Which we were, but we still weren't entirely because he had this big, looming life, and I was still stuck in mine. The best actress at Tisch who just got shot down for the girlfriend part on *Two and a Half Men* because, my agent tells me, I wasn't blond enough. (I am not blond at all, in fact.)

My dad had celebrated one year of sobriety in March. Our deal was: as long as he stayed sober, he had a place in our home. Ben didn't like it; he bristled about the loss of privacy and he worried about my dad relapsing and letting me down, but he lived with it all the same, which I appreciated. Piper flew out to celebrate the one-year anniversary. We went for a hike in the Santa Monica Mountains at dawn, and he hugged me and told me he was proud of me, grateful for sticking with him. He went back to night school to re-earn his accounting certificate, which had lapsed, "something I've thought of doing for a long time." We aren't fixed, we aren't even close to perfect, but we are better, we are healing.

Each time we drive south to our therapy sessions, Dr. Wallis, our therapist, reminds me: "Don't be afraid to let your dad know when you feel like he's not on your team."

I do tell him, which is something I'd learned to avoid in my childhood, an avoidance that made me a better actress, and, frankly, freed me from the burden of my past. When I became somebody else, I no longer had a father who was an alcoholic and also negligent. But now, as myself, I am a sieve with my father: *I am angry that you used Mom's death as an excuse to fall off the wagon. I am angry that she was sick and I had to hold the house together. I am angry that I never knew if you'd be sober enough to take us to school or there to pick us up afterward. I am angry.*

I am still angry some days. But every once in a while I'll forget to be mad, and those will be the better days too.

Like when I landed a coveted role in *On the Highlands*, which took me to Scotland to be directed by Sir Edmund Wolfe and was filled with a cast of British acting royalty. And me. And my dad drove me to the airport because he knew he'd missed so many other chances to take me to choir or practices or just show up. And when he picked me up at the airport upon landing too, because Ben was in San Francisco for a scouting trip, and my dad knew that after a difficult, wet, lonely shoot (surrounded by British acting royalty who didn't warm to the young American upstart), I could use a friendly face.

Or when I lost the lead in three pilots that my agent all but assured me were locks, and he came home to me eating a peach pie straight from the pan, though he also knew that I was on a strict diet because each role—covert double-agent spy, sexy teacher-by-day-detective-by-night, and NASA engineer who discovers a plot against America—required me to lose at least seven pounds. ("Ten would really be ideal," my agent said just before my screen test for the NASA role.) Rather than say a word about the nearly eaten entire pie, he spun out the door and returned fifteen minutes later with Entenmann's doughnuts. Because Entenmann's had always been my favorite for Sunday morning breakfasts before our household fell apart.

So it's not that my dad isn't on my team. And it's not that Ben isn't either.

"When I slow down, when I have the time, I want to write something for you, like how we did *Romanticah*, and how that was perfect."

"I don't need you to," I'll say, but I'll crawl atop his lap anyway. "This *CSI* gig is really fulfilling."

"Hardy har." He'll kiss my nose. "But you are brilliant, and *I* am brilliant, so let me write something for our brilliance together." He'll meet my eyes, see right into me. "It's OK to let me take care of you."

My skin will prickle when he says this, because I am so used to solely taking care of myself, but Dr. Wallis tells me I need a team, that we are all a team, so I kiss him and say, "Thank you." And I believe that Ben *will* write something great for me, and I hold on to that because he knows me as I know myself, and so of course he can write me the role of a lifetime. He won't write it because I need him to, and he won't write it out of obligation; he'll write it as a testament to how we are whole together.

Still the truth is, no matter what Dr. Wallis says, no matter what Ben says, what I have learned about this town and this industry is that most days you are a team in and of yourself. I don't have the connections of Ben and Daisy; I don't have the network that offers ties to prevent a hard landing. I have lost role after role, and true, gotten a few too, but Daisy knew a girl from high school on *New York Cops*, who set up drinks with the producer, and now Daisy's a regular. Next year her name will be in the opening credits. And Ben is back and forth to San Francisco working with Eric Johannsen—his old writing buddy from Williams, who happens to be related to *the* Johannsens, who run JH Films, the hottest independent studio in town—on a new spin on Alcatraz.

I only have me.

So when Daisy e-mails this morning that she'd run into BAFTA winner David Frears's partner, Franklin, a costumer on *New York Cops*, at Runyon Canyon, and that he'd mentioned they were headed to the Brentwood Farmers Market later in the day, I scramble into my most flattering yoga gear and click on Monster's leash. And then I drive directly to Gretna Green Way, finding a parking space less than a quarter mile away (no small miracle). Monster and I loiter by the strawberry stand until I see them.

Variety had reported that David was remaking *Pride and Prejudice*, and that he was looking for someone experienced but not too well-known whom he could turn into a star.

"I mean, that is pretty much me," I said to Ben over our morning coffee earlier in the week. "I'm vetted, but not exactly well-known."

He looked up from his mug and the Reagan biography he was nose-deep into, and said: "Yes, that does sound like you."

"Wait, you agree that absolutely no one knows who I am?"

His forehead wrinkled. "Oh, I don't think I heard you correctly. Sorry." He recalibrated, rewound. "I think you are the town's undiscovered diamond." Then he grinned. "Better?"

He ran his hand through his hair, which needed a trim, but he hadn't found the time for one. He hadn't been sleeping well, I knew: the buzz on *One Day in Dallas* (out next month!) was all positive, but even positive buzz meant new hurdles—PR folks who were lining up the awards push, media days that sucked up what little time he already had, less focus on the Alcatraz project, which was gunning for a season-long pickup at HBO, the only place to be in TV. (And even then, Ben remained slightly unconvinced that TV was the right next move, but the lure of the network that aired *The Sopranos* proved too much.) Of course, it also meant more time away from me.

"I was only saying—they want someone seemingly kind of famous but not so famous it's distracting. Do you think that's me? You know I've been honing my accent." It was an insecure, needy question, and in a different lifetime I might have fronted more bravado. But Ben meant that I didn't have to.

His attention had drifted back toward his book. "Yes?" He rubbed his eyes, confused at the question. Then: "I don't know?"

"I bet they're looking at Lily Marple," I said.

"Lily Marple has nothing on you. Besides, she actually *is* superfamous."

My face slackened. "Thanks."

He laughed, extended a hand across the table to reach mine. "I meant that you are so much better for the part. Lily Marple in *Pride and Prejudice*? No thanks."

"You're just saying that because I hate her for sticking her hands down your pants."

"I may just be saying that because you hate her for sticking her hands down my pants, but I don't need any excuse beyond that anyway." He stood to kiss me, then disappeared into his office with the biography.

At the farmers market, Monster keeps trying to eat the strawberries off the table, and the vendor barks: "No dogs allowed! Can't you read the signs?" So I buy three pints from her and plop on the sidewalk, feeding them to Monster from the palm of my hand, which I surely regret later when he poops them all over our backyard. I'll pick them up before the gardener comes on Tuesday, though Ben tells me to leave it, but I can't fathom the thought of paying the gardener to pick up our dog's shit.

The vendor keeps staring, and I wonder, fleetingly, if she recognizes me from something I've done, maybe *The O.C.*, maybe *CSI*?

"These are really delicious," I say to her. She cocks an eyebrow and turns toward other customers. Monster pants happily, his tail beating against my back, his drool spilling onto my yoga capris, when I see David and Franklin strolling into the top of the market. They appear to be midargument—David's face is a wash of downward-pointing lines and Franklin's hands are fluttering—and I start, then stop, then start toward them.

"Franklin, Franklin!" I wave, and skitter up to him.

His angry face turns surprised, and he pastes on a grin.

"Doll! Tatum!" He grasps both my shoulders and double-kisses me. David chews on his lip and stares at the ground, saying nothing. Franklin rolls his eyes. "Don't be rude," he says to him. "Don't be pissy because you lost the argument."

"I did not . . ." David starts, then huffs. "I did not lose the argument. You are wrong, and you just can't accept that." At this exact moment, Monster chooses to jump atop David's chest and run his strawberry-covered tongue across his cheeks.

"Monster! Monster, stop, *off*!" I yank his leash, and Monster reluctantly drops to all four paws, still wagging his tail enthusiastically, as if he hasn't just physically accosted one of Hollywood's most beloved directors.

"Tatum Connelly, meet David Frears," Franklin says. "And Monster." He claps his palms together. "Oh, you're the perfect person to resolve this argument."

"Oh," I say, "I don't know that I should get in the middle of an argument."

"No, listen." Franklin waves a hand, then scratches behind Monster's ears absentmindedly. Monster repays him by leaving a large swath of drool across the left leg of his shorts. "David is currently angry with yours truly because one of *our* dogs pooped on our white living room rug this morning, and he believes that it's my job to wake up early and let the little shitter out."

"Oh," I say. "Yikes."

"I was in the edit bay until two a.m.," David snaps. "Of course it's your job, since you were asleep by ten!"

"I do need my beauty sleep." Franklin winks.

"Who's responsible for *your* dog?" David says to me.

"Uh . . ." Well, technically, I am. That was the pitch when I brought him home two years back. *I'll take care of everything, I promise! I know how busy you are, Ben, and this will be great practice for kids!* Not that we were discussing kids, not that I was anywhere near kids, since they'll wreck my body and my body is fighting a battle against twenty-two-year-olds now, when I'm twenty-nine, nearly thirty. But still, a dog seemed like a good warm-up. Also, he'd keep me company, so I vowed to Ben that I'd do the heavy lifting. The reality of it was that . . . it hadn't quite worked out that way. I liked to sleep late, so Ben walked him at dawn, and though I did pick up the shit from the backyard, I wasn't exactly meticulous about enforcing the no-couch rule or not feeding him from the dinner table, which was too tempting *not* to do, but which admittedly did not foster the best manners from our behemoth animal. Still, I say: "Mostly me, I do most of the work, so yeah, Franklin, not to be a bitch, but I kind of have to take *his* side. Late-night work means the buck falls to the other person." Forget that Ben wakes early to deal with Monster regardless of what time he's gotten home.

Franklin frowns, and David seems to notice me for the first time.

"Exactly! Exactly. And now that rug, which if you recall, we had shipped in from Italy"—he says *Italy* in three slow, drawn-out syllables—"has a giant brown shit stain right in the middle, and I can't exactly cover it up with a piece of furniture!" He widens his eyes. "He actually proposed that we just stick a coffee table over it."

"Like that is the worst suggestion in the world!" Franklin says.

"I mean, I guess . . ." I stutter, trying to recalculate. On the one hand, Franklin is my entry point to David; on the other hand, David is the money grab.

"Look, fine," Franklin interrupts. "I should have woken up and let him out. OK, are we happy?"

"I'm happy," David says, though he does not look happy at all.

"Jeeeesus," Franklin says. "These fucking dogs. They're basically going to be the death of our marriage." Then: "They were his idea."

At this, Monster jumps atop David again, who rather than recoil says, "Ooh, your mama is very smart. She got Franklin to admit that he was wrong." He purses his lips and kisses Monster on his black, wet nose. I mask my embarrassment with a too-aggressive laugh.

"I'm sorry, Tatum?" David asks, when Monster has finally jumped down and is seated, looking on expectantly. "It's Tatum, right?"

"She's Daisy's best friend," Franklin says. "You know *On the Highlands*? She's in that."

"Aah, we just watched a rough cut the other day. I knew I knew you from somewhere."

I haven't yet seen a rough cut, and my anxiety spikes in the form of an accelerated pulse, a jumbled tongue.

"Oh, gosh, I haven't yet seen it . . . I hope I was OK . . . I was kind of out of my . . ." I stop. *No. Play the part, pull it together, don't give them something to find fault with.* I've almost gotten rusty at this, complacent because I am so disarmed with Ben. I refocus. "Anyway, what I mean is: I haven't seen the rough cut yet, but I'm hearing good things."

"You should be hearing good things," David concurs. "It was excellent. You are excellent."

"Oh, thank you." I shake my head like it's nothing. "I did love the shoot, though. I'm completely obsessed with period pieces. It's amazing to me how the literature holds up even a hundred years later."

"I just . . . I literally just said the same thing to Franklin, didn't I?" He turns to Franklin, their skirmish entirely behind them now.

"He did."

"I'm dying for another one," I add, then immediately want to retract it. I've fallen out of the role I'm playing, and I know better than that. I *am* better than that. The point here is to be spontaneous, not pushy, and it's a fine line to walk. Pushy means desperate, and any actress can tell you that desperation can be smelled across the farmers market by a mile, maybe even over the shit-stained white rug that they have to throw out.

The scent goes undetected by David.

"I'm about to do *Pride and Prejudice*. Early prep work now, shooting next spring. I know, I know, remaking a classic, but I think I can bring something new to it, you know? I wouldn't have accepted the job if I didn't think so."

"You don't have to justify it to me!" I laugh. "God, who wouldn't want to try their hand at Austen?"

"An actress who reads!" David claps his hands together. "And whose dog is impossibly adorable and who takes my side in an argument with Franklin. I think I love you, darling."

"Well." I grin. "I won't tell Franklin if you don't."

17

BEN

JUNE 2008

It's raining in Los Angeles, and no one knows what to do about it. People are scattering around, hovering in Whole Foods, tweeting with panicked abandon: *It's raining! It might be the apocalypse!*

I'm set to meet Spencer for lunch to discuss my next steps in my career: *One Day in Dallas* hadn't blown up like we'd all thought, and for the first time I have to consider strategy; I have to "take a meeting" with my agent to ensure that I don't, as my dad would say, slide into a wasteland of mediocrity. It's happened to plenty of other golden boys. It can't happen to me.

Tatum is in majestic Hawaii while I am here on daddy duty for the next ten days. It's longer than she wanted to be away from the baby, but she'd been back at work since he was four weeks old, the necessary requirements of capitalizing on Oscar-nomination heat, and thus when production on *Shipwreck* called for nearly two weeks in Hawaii, she packed her breast pump and was flown first class to the Big Island. She calls on her breaks, asks for me to put Joey on the phone, though he doesn't seem to understand that his mom's voice is being beamed in across an ocean, and he usually just wiggles around in his crib. Eventually I put the phone back to my ear and assure her that we're doing fine. That I am defrosting her frozen breast milk, that the night nurse is cutting his fingernails and minding his diaper rash, that we can survive a week and change without her.

I can. We can. We can survive ten days without her. I don't want to think of myself as one of those guys whose wife does everything better than he does simply because she has a uterus. That guy was my dad. That guy was my grandfather, who showed up from time to time in a three-piece suit to hand us a hundred-dollar bill and then shooed us out of the room because he didn't like to hear children playing. I'm fucking capable.

But . . . I'm also completely inadequate. The house is a disaster; I badly need a shower; I've eaten stale Cheerios for more than a handful of meals. And also, though I would never say this to Tatum, I'd rather be working. I'm envious that she gets to jet to Hawaii and sleep in a quiet hotel room with a view of the ocean, while I rise to quell whatever Joey is screaming about in his crib and then stare at my laptop for the afternoon, trying to muster inspiration but mostly dawdling back to lackluster plotlines for *Alcatraz*'s next season—the writers' room starts back up at summer's end.

Neither one of us was quite ready for the baby—we'd figured Monster was our biggest responsibility for the foreseeable future—and Joey was an accident ("a happy accident," we've gotten used to saying). I was more panicked than she: I had never quite hit my stride in toeing the line between being brotherly and fatherly to Leo now—sometimes I was too stern, sometimes I was too distracted, sometimes I just didn't want the responsibility of picking up where our dad had left off. And there were plenty of nights while Tatum was pregnant when I'd wake up damp from sweat, pulse racing, the fragments of a frantic dream reverberating in my consciousness until dawn broke. I've been surprised, to be honest, that I'm not worse at parenthood now that he's here.

Joey, named for Tatum's mom—Josephine—and I were supposed to go with her to Hawaii. But then he got an ear infection two days before we were set to fly, and it wasn't like we could ask production to delay on our account. So Tatum asked our night nurse to stay around for a few hours during the day to lend a hand (Tatum had been interviewing nannies endlessly but had not yet found someone she thought was suitable, even though Joey is nearly six months by now, and even though I thought they were all mostly suitable) and left for LAX. I called my mom to see if she could fly out and pitch in, but she and Ron were headed for a cruise around Turkey and Greece. I picked up the phone to call Leo, but he'd have been no help. I'd seen him back in New York shortly before the mayhem of the baby and the Oscars, and he was working too hard, juggling crazy banking hours. He was looking too ragged and thin, and I implored him, for once, to ease up just a bit.

He laughed and said it wasn't work that kept him out so late.

"You're twenty-seven, Lee," I said. "Aren't you over that shit?"

"Over beautiful women?" he howled. "God, I hope the answer to that is never."

"Settling down can be a good thing." I thought of our impending arrival, how the baby would solidify Tatum and me after months of feeling like we were slipping away from each other in the whirlwind of the awards season, as the snowball of her career picked up speed, and I stood at the top of the hill and watched. "Don't you want kids?"

"I have time," he said. "Who's in a rush? Besides"—he swatted my leg, then rose with a groan to pour himself a beer—"I'm gonna live forever."

So mostly, with Tatum in Hawaii, it was Joey and me. And Kendra, the night nurse, while I slept. Walter and Cheryl, his girlfriend, promised to stop in and relieve me, but Cheryl's real estate business was booming, and even three years sober, Walter wasn't someone I was entirely comfortable leaving alone with the baby. It wasn't fair, it was a weird grudge of distrust that I couldn't move past, and

Tatum and I argued about it whenever I was stupid enough to let my biases slip into a conversation.

Today, I wrestle with Joey's car seat and buckle him in. I'm due at Barneys in thirty minutes, where lithe fortysomething women resemble lithe thirtysomething women, and men in suits huddle around tables, forking their salads, discussing box office returns, summer blockbusters, under-twenty-one actresses they'd like to screw. I told Spencer I have the baby, that Kendra had another client she couldn't cancel (I suspect she really just wanted to go home and sleep, and I didn't blame her), and I asked to reschedule. He insisted I *bring* the baby because his lunches were booked for the next month. Surely he could have pushed another client, but he doesn't. If *One Day in Dallas* had made the Oscar cuts, then he'd have cleared his day. If *Reagan* had a start date, hadn't been delayed first by the director dropping out then by the studio hedging over the budget, then he'd have brought me breakfast in bed.

Instead, I sling Joey's diaper bag over my shoulder, push the stroller onto the elevator at Barneys, and pray that he doesn't shit himself in the middle of lunch.

Spencer greets me at the hostess station with a slap on the back and feigns delight at the baby.

"The cutest," he says. "That is the cutest fucking baby I have ever seen. No surprise given how hot your wife is, am I right?"

He laughs, so I laugh, as if half of my conversations these days, after her Oscar nomination, don't revolve around Tatum. (A percentage that surely would have skyrocketed even higher if she had won rather than Lily Marple, a victory that left Tatum nearly apoplectic and certainly contributed to her unending willpower to get back to pre-baby weight within three weeks of delivery. "I will absolutely demolish it in *Shipwreck*," she announced before going out for a run that the doctors had not yet cleared her for. "I will absolutely look like a goddamn goddess on film, and Lily Marple is going to weep and wish she had my abs.")

"We're going to walk the room right now," Spencer says. "We're going to introduce you to everyone you need to know to get this little project of yours off the ground."

I pushed the stroller and trailed him. "*Reagan* isn't a little project. It's my best work yet."

"I know, I know," he says, like he doesn't really know at all, doesn't know how much it fucking means to me.

He glides me through the tables like a prize pony, stopping every now and then to shake hands, introduce me, show me off.

"You've met Ben Livingston, right?" he'll say, slapping me on the back.

Or:

"If you don't know Ben Livingston yet, you gotta know him now," slapping the other person on the back. "Remember *All the Men*? Did you ever see that little indie that could, *Romanticah*?"

Most times, they rise enthusiastically, their chairs shooting behind them, their napkins dropping to the floor, and they grasp my hand, gripping tight. They'll congratulate me on Tatum's nomination or mention that they've heard great things about *Shipwreck*. Some of them tell me how much they're enjoying *Alcatraz*, Fox's new midseason show with decent ratings; some of them raise an eyebrow at Joey and offer a bland compliment about his chubby cheeks.

We sit and Spencer orders a Diet Coke, tells the waiter not to bring us any bread.

"Ben, let's relight your fire."

"My fire is pretty well lit, at least on my end," I say. "Talk to the studio about green-lighting *Reagan*; then we won't have to have this conversation."

"I'm talking to the studio every day. Every fucking day. We're close. We're very, very close. But you gotta do something else too, take more meetings, give me some pitches to work with if you want to stay in film.

The TV gig is great, fucking fantastic, but it's not film. And we wanted HBO. We got Fox."

I cut him off. "I haven't been sleeping, Spencer."

This isn't true. We have Kendra. I've been sleeping as well as I ever did, at least as far as Joey is concerned. Occasionally I'll wake and watch the alarm clock tick down until it blares, wondering how to tweak *Reagan*, wondering when I got such a grown-up life, with a mortgage and a child. Joey is an easy baby: he gurgles and grins and though he prefers Tatum to me, he is healthy and cherubic, and my anxious, sleepless nights from Tatum's pregnancy are gone. But mostly I sleep just fine.

"Do you need a nanny?" He punches something into his phone. "There, I e-mailed Diana, she'll have you seven nannies by the time I pay the bill."

"I can't hire a nanny without Tatum. Why do you think the baby is with me today?"

Joey gurgles in his stroller and starts to fidget and fuss. I gave him a bottle before we got here, so I can't imagine what he wants. Tatum can tell these things on instinct. Like, she'll be in our garage (newly converted to a gym) on the Pilates reformer, hear his cry, and run out and say: *Diaper!* Or be nose-deep in one of the half-dozen scripts she has piled high on our kitchen counter, listen to a wail over the baby monitor, and pull out her boob on the way to his room. Today, I pop a pacifier into his mouth and hope it holds.

Spencer leans closer. "I hope your balls haven't been cut off now that your wife is a big shot."

I laugh because I don't know what else to do.

"I assure you, I still very much have my balls, Spencer. Big balls. Huge balls."

I've been with Spencer since *Romanticah*, but he is oily, in his expensive suit, with his whitened teeth, with his slicked-back hair, with his pores practically oozing ambition. It occurs to me, as the waiter brings us Diet Cokes and forgets about Spencer's no-bread missive until Spencer nearly snaps his hand off when he offers it, that I don't particularly like the man in charge of the trajectory of my career.

"I want *Reagan* to go, Spencer. I believe in it. It's the project of a lifetime."

He ignores me. "*Alcatraz* is a hit or at least enough of one. They're gonna give you two more seasons at least. You can count on that. For sure."

Joey's pacifier has fallen on the floor, and a waitress with ample cleavage stoops to grab it, then cleans it with a napkin.

"He's adorable," she says.

When she heads back to the kitchen, Spencer whispers, "You should totally tap that ass."

"OK, I'll get right on that."

"Hey," he says louder. "This is Hollywood. What do you think your wife is doing right now?"

"I'm pretty sure she's not screwing the waitress."

This makes Spencer honest-to-God cackle, and, as if I've earned his respect, he says: "Fine, Ben, I'll cut you a deal: you sign the two years to *Alcatraz*, and I'll squeeze the shit out of the studio to get *Reagan* back on the table."

"I think it could win me *my* Oscar," I say.

"Got a taste of it with the wife's nomination?"

"No," I say. "I mean, *yes*. I am proud of her, and she deserves it. She should have won."

"I know. I saw you there that night," he says. "You were basically weeping with pride. I almost wondered if you still had a ball sack."

"Fuck you, Spencer."

He laughs. "I'm just messing with you, dickhead. Please? Like my wife doesn't have me wrapped around all ten of her fingers. Good for you, seriously. Being on her arm, telling everyone how proud you were. Takes a real man."

"I was proud, am proud."

"But you want an Oscar nomination of your own."

"Not just a nomination. A win. I just really think *Reagan* can be incredible, the best thing I've ever done."

"Ambition," Spencer says, easing back his lips into his smarmy Cheshire smile. "I can smell that from a mile away."

I start to apologize, just as Joey starts to cry, but Spencer waves a hand, which is covered in a ring too many. "Don't say you're sorry for that, man, don't ever apologize for going after what you want. That's the mark of winners; that's what separates you from the rest of the pack."

I blink a few times to clear the thought: he sounds so much like my dad, I forget for a moment that he's no longer here.

18

TATUM

MAY 2007

I can put it off no longer: I have to go home to Ohio for Piper's wedding. David Frears has given me loads of advice on "going home again." All through the media push for *Pride and Prejudice* leading up to the June release, he's assured me that you just put on a face like you're putting on a role.

"Darling, if a gay can survive a weekend visit to bumblefuck Nebraska, where, when I was in high school, a city councilman tried to tell my parents that I could get electroshock therapy to deal with my homo-ness, you can endure your little sister's wedding."

David's taken me under his wing, told me I'm the best Elizabeth Bennet in the history of Elizabeth Bennets, of which there have been many. He's protected me through the slow but ever-present bleat of tabloid coverage (rumors of sleeping with Colin Farrell on the set), the mounting tide of whispers of an Academy Award, the connection with a stylist so I'm not caught looking like a general garbage dump when I'm out in public. "Darling, I'm sorry, but this?" David once said, waving his hand at my brunch getup of Nike running pants and an Ohio University hoodie. "This will not do, not for a future star."

Ben calls David my "gay husband," and Daisy tells me that anyone whom he deems the next big thing really *is* the next big thing. Of course, I dedicated myself to the shoot: British accent at all times, delicate mannerisms, headstrong attitude. Ben flew over for a month of the two-month ordeal while he was on a break between his own projects, and he said it was like dating a total stranger.

"Sorry," I said. "It's for the part. Full method."

"Don't apologize," he said before grabbing my waistband and pulling me into the bedroom of the suite I'd been put up in. "I like it."

"So you get to cheat on me without really cheating on me?" I laughed.

"Bingo," he said, kissing me and shutting the door with his foot.

Still, all the method preparation, all of David's advice, hasn't calmed my nerves, settled my butterflies about heading back for Piper's wedding.

Now, in my childhood home, Ben flops on my childhood bed. "So this is where the magic happened."

"Ha," I say, thinking of Aaron Johnson, the football player, and how I'd lost my virginity to him in the back seat of his car in the deserted parking lot of the grocery store where I worked on the weekends. Then we did it exclusively in his car for a few weeks until he dumped me. "There was no magic happening here."

I haven't been back since my mother's funeral, and I run my fingers over my dresser, which is covered in stickers. When I was ten, my parents were fighting about something, so I locked Piper in my room with me, and we pasted our sticker collection all over my furniture. I remember hearing my dad's truck engine start, then my mom knocking on my door, and her exhausted face absorbing the stuck-on damage.

"Well." She shrugged. "I hope you like it, it's not like I can buy you new furniture. Enjoy." Then she closed the door quietly and retreated to her room for the rest of the night. Piper and I tried to peel off our favorites, put them back in our sticker books for trading in the future, but most of them were too stubborn. Now, twenty years later, my faded Boynton collection stares back at me, a half-ripped-up memory of another life.

Ben bounces off my bed. "Want to go grab something to eat? What is there around here?"

I shrug. Denny's. IHOP. Probably an Outback Steakhouse, which I remember seeing the last time I was here. Nothing that I'd want to take Ben to, nothing that has anything to do with who I've become since I left the Canton outskirts, tackled New York, wooed David Frears, and slayed Elizabeth Bennet and anointed myself the next big thing. That he is even here with me is a leap forward, an acknowledgment that I've let him see my insides, that he knows everything about me. But still. You can peel back an onion only so far before your eyes start to sting.

"There's not much to eat here in the way of fine dining."

"I don't need fine dining," he says. "I just need sustenance." He grabs the keys to the rental car. "Come on, we'll find something."

Downstairs, my dad is circling the kitchen while Piper brews a pot of coffee.

"It feels strange," he says. "Being back here without her. I mean, being sober back here without her."

He steps closer to me and wraps me in a tight embrace, close enough so I can feel his stubble and his wiry gray hair against my neck. I stiffen but then remember Dr. Wallis, whom we still see from time to time at Commitments, just for check-ins, and also to celebrate two years of sobriety, and how he urged my dad (and me) to bridge the physical divide. Not to violate personal space, not to tilt anyone toward discomfort, rather to move past words and, well, reach out and touch someone. My dad has thus become a hugger. I soften and my arms link around his back, which has lost its doughiness, as he took up hiking when he met Cheryl, an age-appropriate real estate broker, who has a one-bedroom condo in Westwood, which is now more or less his second home.

"It's strange being back here in general," I say. "Isn't it?"

He wipes his damp eyes, and I see Piper drying off her own cheeks with a dishrag.

"I was such a terrible father to you."

"Dad, we've been over this—"

"I know, I know. You forgive me. It's just . . . being here." He shakes his head.

I swipe my wallet from the counter. "Well, Ben and I are not going to be here. We're heading to IHOP."

"She's giving me the grand tour!" Ben pipes in, averting his eyes from my dad. He is still jumpy around him, edgier than when my dad is out of the picture. I ask him about it, and he tells me it's a work in progress, and because I trust him, I believe him.

"Ooh, take him by the high school," Piper says. "They've totally redone it."

"Why would I want to relive the worst years of my life?" I say.

My dad sighs audibly.

"Dad." My hand finds his shoulder—*reach out and touch someone!*—and I let it linger there for a beat. "I wasn't referring to you. I was referring to all those dickwads I dated and all the asshole girls who thought I was a piece of trash for working at Albertsons."

"If they could see you now!" Piper calls after me, as we head through the foyer and out to the rented Ford Explorer.

I drive through the streets of my childhood city, my hands tight around the steering wheel, my knuckles pale. Ben's head is turned, his eyes out the passenger window, and I can almost hear his thoughts, calculating how vast the divide is between who he thinks I am and where I once came from.

"I know," I say. "It's depressing."

"What?" He looks toward me. "What's depressing?"

I slow to a stop at a red light, next to a strip of stores where two of the letters droop in the mall sign, where a liquor store abuts a ninety-nine-cent store.

"This place. This town. It's not like I'm exactly proud of it."

He shrugs. "I don't think it's depressing. It's just . . . part of you. So what?"

The light flips to green, and the car in front of us loiters, so I press the horn too firmly, and the car jolts, the driver flipping me off, and Ben jumps in his seat.

"Jesus, calm down, Tate. Come on, we're here for a *good* thing, your sister."

"Marrying her high school boyfriend. Straight out of a clichéd script. Nothing you'd ever write."

"I like Scooter. I like this place. It's where you came from, and if you want to talk scripts, you should know that background matters."

I want to say: *Of course background matters!* That's why I morph into whatever role I need to be for however long I need to be it. That's why I'm only purely myself with Ben, no one else. That's why I was the best at Tisch. That's why there is Oscar buzz building around Elizabeth Bennet. You don't so desperately try to escape your childhood without becoming an expert at pretending you're someone else, someplace else.

Instead I say: "I just miss my mom. She'd like to be here for Piper, help with the wedding. And, I mean, you know, to see my success."

He rests his hand on my leg. I reach down to grasp it. It's not like I don't know that he doesn't feel the same about his father; it's not like we're each not operating with a phantom limb. But Ben loses himself in his writing, where he can exorcise his pain. Not that Ben writes about his father, but even in the new *Reagan* script, there is messy family interaction, there is catharsis between fathers and children, and there is room for grief at the end. These aren't Ben's stories but in some ways they are.

But Elizabeth Bennet is Elizabeth Bennet. I find ways to relate, I find ways to turn her into a bit of my own, but it's not the same: creating and inhabiting. It's why, despite not wanting to take advantage, despite never resting on my laurels, I ask him to write something for me, *just me*. Not any actress, not any hot young thing. Ben knows my story. Ben knows my soul. I want him to write for that, to that, to me. Because when he taps into *me*, and I braid myself to him, we are a galaxy unto and of ourselves.

He tells me he will, as soon as he's done polishing *Reagan*. Or maybe the next one after that. He's promised, and though he promised two years ago, I believe him. Still.

I turn into IHOP, which is across the street from Albertsons.

"I used to come here after my shifts," I say to Ben. "They had an all-you-could-eat thing after nine p.m., so it was like I could tackle dinner and breakfast all in one sitting."

He laughs. "I find that hard to believe, knowing what I know now. Fifteen hundred calories and not a bit more."

"Not funny," I say, though I'm blushing because he's not wrong. I've become rigidly inflexible with my diet, weighing my chicken breasts, dicing my broccoli, measuring my protein powder for my morning smoothie. I'm never skinny enough, never lithe enough. There is always another pound to lose for the camera, always a side note that Jocelyn, my agent, passes on: "Be sure that she doesn't gain anything," or "She works for the time being, but anything more, and we'll hire a trainer." Sometimes they just say: "Too heavy. Pass." So I weigh and I dice and I measure, and I put a supersensitive digital scale in our bathroom, and I pee each morning and tiptoe onto it, and if I'm good and it's steady, I grant myself three Hershey's kisses for the day, and if I'm less good and it's less steady, I do not.

The IHOP is mostly empty, since it's four p.m., and not quite dinner, not quite lunch, so we seat ourselves. It hasn't been updated since I left: orange and brown and Formica, with a '90s station playing overhead and oversized foldable plastic menus.

Ben flips the menu from front to back to front again. "Well, I am getting the never-ending stack of silver dollars. This I have to see."

I roll my eyes, feel the blush rise to my cheeks again. "There's nothing better around here. Sorry."

"I'm being serious!" he says. "Stop apologizing. God, Tate, you know I don't care about this stuff."

I flop a hand, but he grabs it and steadies it.

"Listen," he says. "You don't think that when I was being dragged out for, like, raw sushi to impress one of my dad's clients as a kid that I wouldn't have done anything just to plop down in an IHOP?"

Before I can answer, a shrill "Oh. My. God!" bleats out from the hostess station. We turn and my pink cheeks turn magenta.

Julie Seymour, the field hockey player Aaron Johnson dumped me for, is barreling over, arms outstretched, face contorted with a look I normally see on rabid Lily Marple fans.

"Tatum Connelly!! Oh. My. God!" Her hot pink lipstick is smudged against her front teeth, her thick mascara flaking on the side of her left cheek. "I cannot believe that I am seeing you! You are, like, the biggest thing to happen to this town in, like, forever!" She folds herself atop of me in the booth.

I've never been recognized before. No autograph seekers at LAX, no drinks on the house at swanky restaurants in West Hollywood. (Admittedly, I don't go to many swanky restaurants in West Hollywood.) But no one double-takes when I hike in Runyon Canyon, no photographers trail me when I grocery-shop at Gelson's. Not that Julie Seymour counts as true recognition, since my face is already familiar, but she has already spoken more words to me now in IHOP, at which she is apparently the hostess, than in the entirety of our high school careers.

I start to talk but she cuts me off. "Oh. My. God! I mean, I knew your sister was getting married; she helped with the delivery of both my babies." She pauses and slides a photo out of her front shirt pocket and shoves it toward me. Two cherubic boys. "But I didn't imagine that you would come back! And come into our little restaurant in our little corner of the world!" Now she turns to Ben, who is beaming, loving every second of this. "Oh, gosh, excuse me, where are my manners? I'm Julie, and oh my gosh, this is so exciting! You must be so excited to be here with Tatum!"

Ben's grin grows wider, and he shakes Julie's hand vigorously.

"We always knew she'd be something big in high school!" she practically shrieks. I roll my eyes, but then she turns back to me. "Oh God, what if I got everyone back together? Like, so many of us are still here! We could throw you a party! I don't have my kids tomorrow night—"

I wave a hand. "Oh, that's really great of you, Julie. But we're just here for the wedding. And we have the rehearsal dinner tomorrow—"

Now she interrupts me. "Oh, right, right. You must be so busy. Being a big-time star and all of that." She looks genuinely forlorn.

"Could I trouble you for a coffee?" Ben asks. "Tatum keeps me up all hours, working, reading scripts, fielding her media calls. I'm the hardest-working assistant in Hollywood."

Julie's eyes grow to the size of IHOP's silver-dollar pancakes. "Oh, right away!" She scampers off, and Ben bites his bottom lip to abate his machine-gun laughter.

I watch her disappear behind the kitchen door.

"In case it wasn't obvious, I hated her in high school."

"In case it wasn't obvious, you're a pretty big deal here," he says.

My eyes nearly disappear to the back of their sockets.

"So after you binged on IHOP, what did you do? Where did the high school Tatum Connelly spend her evenings? Gallivanting about town? Getting wasted and passing out in alleyways, giving herself to men left and right?"

This makes me honest-to-God belly laugh. "No. Usually, I just went home and minded my mom, when she was sick, or helped Piper with her homework or cleaned up the kitchen."

Ben's look of solemnity breaks my heart.

"I mean, sometimes, I *did* screw Aaron Johnson in the grocery store parking lot."

His face lights up. "Well," he says, "you'll have to give me *that* part of the tour next."

19

BEN

DECEMBER 2007

I am being polite to Ron; I can feel myself being polite, trying too hard. He is perfectly nice, perfectly innocuous. I realize that I'm thirty-three years old, and stewing over my mother's new relationship puts me at the emotional maturity of about, say, a nine-year-old. Also, it has been six years since my dad died. She's had her time to mourn. So have I.

"He's so nice," Tatum said in the car last night after we met for dinner at the Beverly Wilshire Hotel, where they were staying for the visit. "And your mom seems really smitten."

I cornered too sharply around a turn on Sunset.

"Hey, Jesus, Ben!" Tatum's hand flew to her belly, the way that a mother's arm would fly toward the back seat if the car stopped too abruptly.

"Sorry, sorry." I slowed and put my own palm atop her stomach, which has the perfect curvature of a beach ball. The baby wasn't exactly planned, and its inception wasn't exactly the stuff of true romance, maybe a romantic comedy if I were to write that type of thing. While back in Ohio for Piper's wedding, and after a stop at IHOP for a pancake special, Tatum and I got busy in the back seat of our rental Ford Explorer (sorry, Hertz) like we were high schoolers. Afterward, she said: "Yeah, I think we've pretty much re-created my stellar high school sexual experience." And then, as I climbed into the front, she said: "Oh shit," upon realizing she had left her pills at home. Then a few weeks later, from behind our bathroom door, she said, "Oh shit" again. I sat at the foot of the bed and shouted back, "Really? Oh my God, really?" and hoped that I sounded at least 50 percent less terrified than I was. When she emerged from the bathroom, I swept her into a hug so high her feet left the ground, and I wondered if she could feel my hands shaking as I did.

God knows I haven't yet found the right tenor for fatherhood with Leo: I've been too steely and too hard-nosed, much like my own dad had been, and though I want to let down my guard, just be his brother, I know that boundaries are there for a reason. My dad was never my *friend* (I can envision him cringing at the notion), and now, with Leo, I can't quite find the balance either. Who knows what sort of dad I'll be? How I'll manage?

"Daddy issues," Tatum says from time to time. When I fall silent in Walter's presence, when I grimace in Ron's. But is it so wrong to mourn the man my dad could have been—he was only fifty-two when he died—the relationship we could have had, the ways I could have proven myself to be the son he knew I was capable of, and not wanting to open myself up to the men who could replace him? Not Walter. He doesn't try to replace him. He just inserts himself into our lives, into our business, without ever really asking. So him I resent for plenty of other reasons too.

Tonight, Ron finds me in the kitchen, where I am attempting to carve a turkey for Christmas dinner because Tatum is off other forms of meat/protein, partially because the scent makes her queasy from the hormones, partially because she is on some new "diet" (though she assures me it is not a "diet" because she is pregnant) that promises less heartburn, better skin, and sinewy muscles. Or something. "You try being a whale during awards season," she'd snapped at me a few days ago. "Really. Just try it. Then tell me that you wouldn't go on a diet too."

"You're beautiful," I'd said. Because she was, as she always was, had been.

"Tell that to the designers who might have to make a dress to fit a blue whale."

"Need some help with that?" Ron asks. "I know a thing or two about carving. Though I try not to carve out a heart on the OR table."

Ron is a cardiac surgeon at New York Presbyterian, and he is obviously joking, so I force a smile but doubt it comes off as particularly genuine. I wish I could like him more, but I don't. *Probably,* Tatum once said, *because he's not your dad.* Also, probably, both literally and metaphorically, because he can carve a turkey way better than I can.

"All good," I say, waving a knife. "Almost there."

I am nowhere near almost there. In fact, the turkey looks like it's been run through a paper shredder.

I wait for Ron to point out how far from "almost there" I am, as my dad would have. Instead, he reaches for a wineglass.

"Oh, there you are, Ron," my mom says, her heels echoing on the tile kitchen floor. As if our house is so cavernous that he'd be anywhere else, as if she were utterly lost without him.

"I'm starving," Leo says, coming up behind her. "Can you hurry the fuck up with that thing?" He steps closer and surveys my damage. "Dude, let Ron take it from here. He chops up people's hearts for a living. You type on a keyboard."

"He was doing all right," Ron says, and this is a kindness that I accept but also cringe at. That he's ignoring my mediocrity, that he accepts it. I sigh and pass the tools to Ron, who wields them while my mother rolls up his sleeves, then drops an apron around his neck and ties it around his waist, while Piper loops into the kitchen and out to the dining table to place the rest of the meal. Scooter, her new husband, follows dutifully, his hands steadying platter after platter that Tatum had catered and delivered, since, as she said: "I'm way too huge to cook." Also, cooking isn't her forte, but I'm not about to point that out with her current moodiness and temperament. (And, in fact, I never point that out even when she serves a dinner of burned roasted chicken or eggplant parmesan that's chewy enough to make your jaw cramp. I grab my fork and knife, and dig in with more enthusiasm than is required.)

I find Tatum moored on the living room couch, with Cheryl, her dad's girlfriend of nearly a year, massaging her feet. Tatum has had no quandaries about Cheryl, no qualms with her dad moving on and falling in love with someone who is not her mom. Which I find wholly ironic, since she's had qualms with her dad her whole life until now, a change brought on by their therapy sessions and his sobriety. I watch them for a beat from the corner: Cheryl, with whom Walter now lives in a one-bedroom condo in Westwood, my pregnant wife with her eyes squeezed shut in utter delight, and her sober dad reading the new issue of *Variety*, which features a roundtable of this season's most buzzed-about actresses on the cover, including Tatum.

Three people whose lives have utterly diverged in the past few years, who have taken totally unexpected paths to lead them to here. And yet, they're all relaxing, accepting, enjoying the comforts of my living room, while I linger in the doorway like an observer to someone else's life. Not that it's not *my* life, not that I'm unhappy. But the way it has veered left when I thought it would turn right, the way I haven't adapted to the roadblocks as adeptly as I always assumed I would. That's on me, I know: with my surprise at how quickly this town knocked me off my pedestal when a few projects like *One Day in Dallas* or *All the Men* didn't hit as we thought they would; with how I've watched Tatum ascend the Hollywood ladder as if I'm standing below her; even with how I have seen my mom fall in love again and change with that love—she's more open, more flexible, more honest, and vulnerable too. And yet I keep waiting for my dad to walk through the door and snap her out of it. Maybe I keep waiting for my dad to walk through the door and snap me out of it as well, remind me that I'm floating in the middle, that I should be shooting for the top. If he weren't dead, if he were to walk through the door and tell me that, I'd probably resent him for it, though I'd heed him all the same. But because he can't walk in and chide me, I chide myself. Plenty, too much, always.

Success alone doesn't make you happy, he once said. *But it sure does help.*

No shit.

Tatum opens her eyes. "Hey, come sit," she says, when she sees me.

"Ron relieved me of my carving duties."

Cheryl stands and grants me the couch, then hovers behind Walter and massages his shoulders.

"Babe, relax, please," Tatum says, plopping her feet atop my lap. "Also, please rub."

Walter rests the *Variety* on the coffee table, his eyes misting.

"I can't believe that my baby is going to win an Oscar."

"I'm not going to *win* an Oscar, Dad. Please don't say that. You're cursing me."

"Yes, shhh, Walt!" Cheryl coos. "We'll have to cleanse this room from your juju if you keep it up."

He stands, his knees creaking, though he's lost twenty pounds since drying out, and now, as a regular hiker (he and Cheryl are contemplating two weeks away in the Argentinian mountains), he is in better shape than I am.

"Let's help in the kitchen," he says. "Let Tatum get a little rest."

"I'm fine, Dad!"

"You have big things on your plate," he says.

"Just as long as the plate is under fifteen hundred calories," I joke, but no one finds this very funny.

"You can put the *Variety* at the bottom of the pile," Tatum says once they're gone. "We don't have to have my face peering up at us from the coffee table."

"Why would I do that? I'm proud of you."

She wiggles her foot in my lap, as if to say, *More please.* Then she says aloud, "Next year you're going to rack up the Emmys."

"Maybe." I smile. "An Oscar for you, an Emmy for me. I'll take it."

Eric and I had a buzzy show launching in March: *Alcatraz*. It's true that we'd landed the deal because Eric's uncle ran JH Films, one of the biggest production companies in town, but he and I were the ones who had put in the elbow grease, taken a standard prison drama and elevated it with smart, sharp writing. We wanted HBO. I'd balked at network TV, but Fox had promised us the moon, made it impossible to believe that it wouldn't be a monster hit. It wasn't film, true, but it was going to be great television. It was going to be my ticket *back* to film as well. I was banking on it.

"Tate, you know how much I love you, even when I'm being an asshole, right?"

She grins. "I do."

Ron emerges from the kitchen. "Dinner is served!"

"Moo," Tatum moans from the couch, which is something she's started doing, first as a joke, then, as she grew, more seriously.

"You are not a cow." I smile and offer a hand to haul her up. Then, to her belly: "Hey kid, your mom is the sexiest bovine I've ever seen."

Tatum swats my butt, and I skitter.

"Can we go out later?" Leo pops his head into the living room.

"It's Christmas Eve, Leo. Chill."

"Dude, I have to check out the competition. See what's hot here that can translate to the city."

"Competition for what?" I shake my head.

"The nightclub he invested in, babe," Tatum says as she hoists herself to her feet. "His outlet from that dreary job at Merrill Lynch." She winks at him.

I vaguely remember the details he'd shared last night as I was drifting to sleep on the couch, and as he whisked out the door to a waiting cab. Something about a club in Florida—Miami, maybe?—that he and his friends had gone in on.

"Nothing's open tonight," I say to him, as Piper emerges from the kitchen with her hands in oven mitts and a steaming plate of green beans between them. Scooter tails her with a final casserole dish.

"We used to always watch a movie Christmas Eve, remember that, Piper?" Tatum calls to her sister. "Remember how Mom would let us choose?"

"You always got to pick," Piper says. Then, to Scooter: "She was always Mom's favorite."

"Well, how could I not be?" Tatum says. "I mean, look at me." She moos again.

"Stop, Tate. You're beautiful," I say, and I wink. *I see you.*

"OK." She nods as if she knows that if I believe it, then it must be true.

I raise my glass. "To my beautiful wife. To . . . family. To all of us being together here to celebrate."

I put aside my baggage, and I stare at Tatum, my glowing wife ascending a meteoric star, and for the moment, I mean it.

20

TATUM

FEBRUARY 2008

The baby has been kicking me all night, and when I do manage to sleep, my heartburn roars up my esophagus and shakes me awake.

"I'm sorry, I'm a mess," I say to Hailey, the makeup artist the studio sends.

"I'm sorry, I'm a whale," I say to the seamstress who lets out my gown (more of a tent) another half inch.

"Don't be silly," they both say, because I'm now an Oscar-nominated actress who is due any day now, and they are effectively on my payroll and are told to say reassuring things like this to a hormonal tank several hours before she may lumber onstage to accept the award.

It's a relief to be done with it all tonight. To be done with the air kisses on the red carpet, with the cocktail hours and dinners and Q and As and interviews, even though some of those interviews have granted me covers like *Variety*. But my ankles are swollen, and my fatigue is drowning me, and I can't possibly imagine how I could take one more week of the pomp and circumstance, of faking nice with Lily Marple in front of the cameras or at sit-down roundtables like with *Variety*, where she smiles at me but mostly just exposes her teeth. When we took a bathroom break before the photo shoot, she leaned close (too close) and said:

"How's Ben?"

And I rubbed my belly and said: "We couldn't be better."

She raised her eyebrows. "I remember him being pretty good on the set of that little movie we shot too."

And it was her implication—*He was pretty good*—that made me curl my fingers so tightly into little balls that my red manicured nails practically sliced my palms. He hadn't slept with her; he'd spurned her, and he told me, immediately. But the way it rolled off her tongue—*He was pretty good*—she made me doubt him, not that he had slept with her. Of course not that, but that maybe he'd been tempted. My dad had never been much of a partner to my mom until the end; Piper told me that was when he dug in and committed. I sat in the stall in the bathroom until it emptied, reminding myself over and again that we weren't my parents, that I wasn't my mom, and Ben wasn't my dad, and I steeled myself for the rest of the day with Lily, and the rest of the awards season with her too. And I transformed myself into someone I wasn't: a woman who believed that she'd left her old self behind, a woman who wasn't still chased by the ghosts of her childhood.

Now, on the last night of awards season, I swallow four Tums and hope that they fight back my braying, ever-present heartburn.

"You OK?" Ben says in the limo.

"Fucking heartburn," I say, and burp. Most of the time, in the press, at the endless awards dinners, I try to play the role of a glowing, cherubic mom-to-be, but with Ben, there's no need.

"It's almost over," he says.

"The baby or the awards?" I laugh.

"Both." He swings one of my waxed and faux-tanned legs atop his lap and massages my elephant-sized ankle.

"You've kept me sane," I say, easing my head against the leather seat, emitting a groan. I meet his eyes. "You know that, you've kept me sane, right?"

"Ah, every actress says that right before she goes batshit." He laughs.

"I make no promises," I say with a grin, then close my eyes once more.

But he has, it's true, and I probably haven't been gracious enough, thanked him enough. It's admittedly a quieter time for him as he waits for *Alcatraz* to go in March, and then hopefully gets *Reagan* out of turnaround. But he dutifully shows up as my plus-one, sings my praises to the likes of anyone who will listen, rubs my belly with cocoa butter to prevent stretch marks, heads to the guest room to sleep on nights when I am sweaty and restless and need the entire bed to myself.

"My hands are shaking," I say, as the limo rounds the bend to a line of other black cars, all carrying anointed Hollywood types. "Jesus, I guess this is really real."

His hands move from my ankles to my fingers, where he weaves his own into mine.

I blow my breath out.

"You have your speech?" he asks, moving both of our hands to my belly, stopping expectantly to wait for the baby's kick.

"I'm not going to need it. Lily's gonna win."

"But do you have it? Because you never know."

"Yes." I exhale again, crane my neck to see how far we are from the entrance, then, as Ben checks his phone, I rehearse my speech one last time. *I'd like to thank my agents, my publicist, my amazing team, David Frears for seeing the sliver of potential in my terrible audition, for dreaming that I could ever inhabit this beloved role of Elizabeth Bennet! Colin Farrell, oh thank you so much, dear, you know how much you mean to me. My dad, who is a fighter! My sister, love you, Pipes!! I can't forget my husband and, well, let's be honest, there's no denying it now, this baby who might come out of me at any moment . . .*

My publicist had tweaked the speech for me, felt that a dose of humor and heart were the perfect way to introduce myself to the world on a larger scale. *Pride and Prejudice* had given me industry cred, like *Romanticah* had done for Ben, but I wasn't yet a household name, wasn't yet commercial. It wasn't like I didn't have practice delivering a speech, though. It was my favorite way of disappearing when my mom first got sick, my favorite way of imagining a road out. From my suburb in Ohio, it's not as if there had been a streamlined path. Nina Blackwood, whom I watched every afternoon on MTV in fourth grade, was from Cleveland, and Teri Garr, who was in *Tootsie*, my mom's favorite movie and thus my favorite movie for all of seventh grade, was from Lakewood, but there wasn't a brick path paved with gold from our state borders to Hollywood. But still. I'd stand in front of the mirror, with a hairbrush or a flashlight in my hand, and I'd thank all the little people: *I'd like to thank Mr. Lawrence, my sixth-grade PE teacher, for announcing my mile time as the worst of the grade; I'd like to thank Philip Paulson for pointing out that my training bra was, in fact, too large.* I'd bow, and I'd spin, and I'd swirl, and sometimes Piper would come in and sit on my bed and applaud and ask me to do it again and again. *I'd like to thank Jessica Johnson for telling Philip Paulson that I just got my period. I'd like to thank Aaron Johnson for taking my virginity and then dumping me for Julie Seymour. Thank you, thank you! Look at me now! Ha ha ha ha ha!*

But when I flitted about in the mirror or for Piper, mostly, it was just fantasy, a dream of a dream of a dream.

Now, the dream of a dream of a dream seems tangible; my team is already strategizing my next move: how to leverage this to catapult me to A-list. Offers rush in at a dizzying pace; roles I'd never have had access to prior to *Pride and Prejudice*, as if I somehow became a better actor overnight. I've done magazine covers, I've done *Ellen*. I've been asked for pregnancy advice, I've been asked for marital advice. I've been asked how I stay grounded and how it feels to be vaulted into the Hollywood stratosphere. Everything has shifted.

The baby kicks against my taut stomach just as the limo edges up to the red carpet at the Dolby Theatre.

"I think I might puke," I say to Ben.

"You look perfect. Nowhere close to green," he replies, though he's actually looking a little peaked himself.

"It's all this makeup, you can't see anything close to what's going on beneath the makeup." That was the point, Hailey explained. To cover up my dark circles, the hormonal acne that had flared along my left jawbone (despite the weekly facials since the nominations), my splotchy T-zone.

"You're going to be great," Ben says, leaning his forehead to mine.

"Thank you for doing this all with me, beside me. I couldn't be here without you."

"Not true," he says, pulling back, waving a hand, averting his eyes. I wonder, for a beat before I lose track of it, why he does that. "You would have done it on your own. It was just my privilege to watch you."

"I don't believe that. That's not true."

He stiffens his spine and turns his attention to the window, to the roar of the crowd that is greeting whichever star just made her own grand entrance.

"Hey," I say. "I mean that. You get that right? That I couldn't have done it without you?"

He looks back toward me. "Yes."

"What's wrong?"

"What? Nothing's wrong. We're at the Academy Awards, and you have a fairly decent shot at winning. What can possibly be wrong?"

"I feel like you think I haven't appreciated you."

"I didn't say anything like that." His eyes return to the window.

"But I *feel* that way."

"How did we just take this turn?" he asks. "I told you a minute ago that you could have done all of this on your own—*you are that good*—and now I feel like we're about to fight about something I don't understand."

"I just got the sense that you were tired of all this, that I haven't appreciated you enough."

"You got that sense from me telling you that you deserve this?"

I chew my (perfectly lipsticked) lip, narrow my eyes, and feel like I walked into a trap.

"I'm just suddenly realizing that this was a bit of a chore for you."

"It has not been a chore for me, OK? I've done everything you've asked of me, and I've done it with a smile. More than that. I've been genuinely enthusiastic. I've gone to industry parties and put my ego aside when I have to say I'm working in TV. Do you know how some of these assholes look at me? Poor little Ben Livingston: we thought he had something special, but I guess not." He squeezes the bridge of his nose. "I've sucked up your dad living in our guesthouse for almost a year, I've grown used to you urging me to therapy to deal with my own 'daddy issues,' though I'm working stuff out in my own way. I've done it all, Tate. All of it. Not complaining, not taking anything away from you. But please don't tell me that I can't be a little exhausted."

"I don't even know what to say to all of that," I snap. Because I don't. Because I had no idea that any of this lived inside of him, not when I thought that we were so transparent with each other that his insides could be seen from the outside, at least to me.

"There's nothing to say to it," he says plainly. "I want to celebrate tonight and make this special, and I don't mean this rudely, but you are stressed and hormonal, and can we not make a mountain out of a molehill right now?"

"So now I'm being too emotional?" I *am* being too emotional. I can feel my floodgates open, the tide of hormonally fueled hysteria washing in. This tide is exactly what I need when I'm in front of the camera; it serves me less well with Ben. My cheeks flush, my heart races, white noise fills my ears so I can't even talk myself down if I wanted to.

"Please," he says. "Can we drop it?"

"I'm sorry that I'm up for an Oscar when you're not, when both of us always assumed that it would be you," I say, and it is immediately too cruel, too dismissive. I am drowning under my emotional tsunami, and I regret it at once.

He blinks and stares out the window.

"Shit," I say. "Shit, shit. I didn't mean that. I'm sorry." I rest my palm on his leg. "I just . . . shit. I didn't realize all of this was going on with you. I wish you'd told me."

"There's nothing to tell," he says. "Besides, you have your own stuff."

"My stuff is your stuff," I say. *What's mine is yours and yours is mine, and we are braided together, remember?*

The limo glides to a stop.

"OK," he says.

"We're OK?"

"Sure." He kisses me, just as our chauffeur opens the back door and the roar of the waiting crowd ushers itself into our private bubble.

"Hey," I say, reaching for his hand.

But he's already stepping out to the pavement, squinting his eyes against the glare of the bright sun. He turns to help me ease my pregnant body out of the limo, and I breathe it all in: the adoration, the success, the Academy Awards that are terrifying and exhilarating and everything I thought they would be when I was standing in front of my mirror with Piper on my bed, when my mom was still alive, and my dad was still drinking, and Ben wasn't even a speck in my imagination.

Everything has shifted, it's true.

Then the baby kicks again, hard this time, and I reach again for Ben's hand and find it, and he steadies me as I glide, as gracefully as one can when labor is imminent, out to the carpet.

The cheers are near deafening now, the blur of the camera flashes, the electricity palpable.

The photographers shout, "Give us a single, Tatum, give us a single!" Meaning: *Leave Ben behind, give us a shot of just you.*

"Go," he says. "You look great."

And so I do. I inhale and exhale and try to transform myself as the actress who is owning her first Academy Award nomination. And then I move into the glittering lights and the catcalls, and I step into my future.

21

BEN

SEPTEMBER 2006

The sky is robin's-egg blue, just as it was five years ago.

I stare upward for a beat too long and am blinded for a moment, hazy yellow orbs obscuring my vision, despite my sunglasses. Leo stands ramrod straight next to me, his shoulders pinned as if literally stapled back, but his toes jigger up and down, his fingers twitch in nonstop motion. My mom is weeping silently to my other side, staring out at the vast wasteland of a construction pit at Ground Zero, staring farther to the two reflection pools she says will bring her a bit of solace, but I can't see how. Tatum had planned to come, but then the roof to the new house in Holmby Hills cratered in, and I told her she should stay behind to deal with it. She assured me that her dad could manage on his own—he was living in the guesthouse and taking classes at UCLA for accounting—but I didn't mind. Really. I wasn't interested in delving too deeply back into my grief, and if Tatum had been along, she'd have poked and prodded and asked me over and over and over again if I'm OK, if I shouldn't see a therapist—when really, I just wanted to be done with it.

I don't need a therapist when I have learned how to soothe myself on my own: I avoid New York unless mandated here for work (or family, but it's easy to lure them out west instead); I flip the channel when newsreels and talking heads pontificate about the horrors of the day, one dimension removed from those of us who live it, dream it, breathe it, in order to (almost) forget about it. Sometimes I start to call my dad to share some tidbit about my career—the acclaim for *One Day in Dallas* or the *Reagan* biopic I'm drafting that he would have been so proud of because Reagan was his hero. Or even something ridiculous, like the fact that I taught Monster to wake Tatum up by licking her face. Of course those moments sting; of course they raise it all up for me again.

But mostly I just want to ignore it. Mostly, I don't want to be standing here, listening to Mayor Bloomberg speak at the site of my father's death. It shouldn't seem like that much to ask.

A town car retrieves us after the ceremony, and I uncoil as we head uptown.

"Brunch now," my mom announces.

"I'm not hungry," Leo says.

"You're never hungry these days," she says, squeezing his leg, staring out the window at the rush of Eighth Avenue traffic.

"Occupational hazard."

"Work makes you lose your appetite?" I ask.

"I made associate," he says flatly. "All I do is work."

My mom laughs at this. "Leo, sweetheart, I'm sure the women of New York would disagree."

The town car deposits us outside the Plaza Athénée, where my mom has evidently arranged for a grief brunch with friends she has met through fundraising, which is how she has channeled her own pain. We all have our outlets. I bury mine. Leo works through his. And my mom raises money for the widows of firefighters. It's admirable how she has forged on, her chin up, her cause determined. I consider, as we shake hands and make introductions in the marble lobby of the hotel, how I would cope if I lost Tatum. My mother introduces me to a man, Ron, whom she looks at with affection and who, she tells me, also lost his wife—this is simply how they introduce themselves here, in this committee of battle-wounded survivors—and I barely hear her, barely pay attention, because I'm absorbed in the question of what I would do without Tatum.

I simply don't know. It is an unimaginable question with no answer.

I duck to the bathroom to call her, to tell her I miss her, which I don't do often enough. In fact, I'd promised I'd call last night, but Leo and I had gone out for beers (too many beers), and I'd passed out before I could remember that I'd forgotten. That she'd be sitting by the phone, waiting to hear from me. It wasn't intentional, my neglect. Tatum was just needier than I was; she needed more reassurance, more connection, more of *us*.

She picks up on the first ring.

"Is everything OK?" She is talking in a British accent.

"Tate?"

"Are you OK?" she says again, still in the accent. I sigh. I'd forgotten that she'd caught wind that they were beginning to cast for *Pride and Prejudice*, and she was honing her accent in the hopes of wedging herself into an audition.

"Is my wife around?"

"I'm here." She drops the pretense.

I don't normally mind—the masks that she wears. Sometimes it's exhilarating, like when I flew out to Scotland and visited her on *On the Highlands*, and we pretended we weren't married and didn't already know each other's secrets. But today, when we mourned my dad all over again, I can't stand it for a second; I don't want to have to expend any more emotional effort than I've already put forth, talking to a woman who doesn't feel like my wife.

"Hey," I say. "Thanks."

"So you're OK?"

"Yeah, I mean. The day has been shit, but yeah."

"I didn't hear from you last night. I stayed up until two, worried."

The words are concerned but her tone is sharp. So what she means is: *Why didn't you call because I hate it when you don't call and I feel forgotten.* We argue about this sometimes now: that I grow absentminded when I'm in the middle of a project, that the world I'm inhabiting on set or in my mind takes me from the world in which I'm actually living. I'll unlatch the door late at night, and she'll be sitting on the couch with folded arms, or I'll get three voicemails, each with increasing annoyance. *Hey, where are you? Hey, can you call me so I know if you're home for dinner? Hey, did you die on the 405 on the way to work, and if not can you please call me back to reassure me that you haven't?*

"I'm sorry," I say, a little bit because I am, a little bit because we've had this conversation before, and there's no point in doing anything other than smoothing the waters. Tatum is independent to a fault until she's not, until she's territorial and a little bit clingy, which is part of the bass note of who she is, and I don't mind all that much unless she escalates it into something it doesn't need to be. "Leo and I went out drinking . . . I lost track of time."

"It's OK," she says, because she knows I mean it sincerely. "I was just worried. How was today?"

"Horrible." I tug the knot of my tie looser. "But over."

"Your mom?"

"We're brunching," I say. "So I guess as well as I'd expect, better, maybe?"

"And Leo?" She asks right before she shouts: "Monster, get down! Shit, hang on, Ben. Monster, *get off the counter.*" There's a clatter behind her, and she yelps. "Goddamn it! Ben, can I call you back in a second?"

She clicks off before I can tell her that I wish she were here, that I don't know what I would do without her, which is why I was calling in the first place. *I should have led with that,* I think. *I need to lead with that more often.*

I splash water on my face, pat it dry, then readjust my tie. I meet my eyes in the mirror and remind myself to tell Tatum this as soon as she calls back. My stomach growls, and I spin back toward the dining room. As I turn the corner from the restroom, I collide with a woman emerging from the ladies' room.

My brain does this thing where it takes a minute to catch up with my breath, with my adrenaline, which is flying through my limbs.

She gapes. "Oh my gosh!"

"Oh my God," I say. Then manage: "Hey."

"I didn't . . . what are you doing here? I mean, this is so random." She blinks quickly, which she always used to do when she was frazzled.

Her red hair falls atop her shoulders like it always did; her cheeks are pink and spotted with freckles, like they always were. She looks exactly the same as the last time I saw her seven years ago. I broke up with her in the kitchenette of her Greenwich Village apartment when she was leaving for San Francisco, when she made it clear that she could dive into *her* new reality without me.

I lean in and kiss Amanda's cheek. She smells like that honey perfume that she wore way back when too.

"I'm in for a conference," she says, swatting her bangs, which are new, from her eyes. "I didn't . . . I mean . . ." She laughs, then exhales deeply. "Let's start over. Hey."

"Hey. You look great," I say. Because she does. My phone buzzes in my palm. Tatum calling me back. I start to raise it to my ear, but then, without thinking, drop it into my pocket. I'll call her back in a minute.

"You need to get that?" she asks. I shake my head. "Well you look great too. God, it's been forever. You're married now."

I nod, wave my ring finger. "Off the market for good."

I say it in this deep superhero voice, which I don't think I've ever used before. I don't know why I do. Maybe because I'm standing in front of the last woman I loved before Tatum, and even though I'd never betray Tate, I still want Amanda to find me fuckable; I still want her to consider what she could have had if she hadn't accepted her residency in Palo Alto and left me behind. It's not that I want Amanda—I don't. But it's not as if I don't want her to want *me*. Those are two separate things, after all. Like my dad said when I was applying to college: you want them to *offer*; that doesn't mean that you have to accept. (He was, however, deeply disappointed in me when I got waitlisted at Yale.)

"Married to an actress, right?" Amanda says. "I mean, I'm not keeping tabs." She laughs self-consciously. "Maybe a little."

"Yep," I affirm and feel my shoulders relax back, my chin raise higher. *She keeps tabs. She might kind of want me.* I make a note to mentally record this to tell Leo as soon as I get back to the table. "She's about to audition for Jane Austen. She's amazing." *Tell Tatum this more often,* I remind myself.

"I get that. You always needed someone who could keep up with you creatively."

My forehead furrows. "I don't know about that. I think I just needed someone who didn't ditch me for a residency in San Francisco."

She laughs again, this time with genuine humor. "Touché. Well." She shrugs. "You know you broke my heart."

"I find that impossible to believe." And I do, though the signals she is sending—and the words she is using—tell me otherwise.

"I work too much now to meet someone." She blinks again rapid-fire. Then, as if just realizing: "Oh my God, your dad. Today . . ." She trails off, her hand covering her mouth. "I e-mailed you a few years ago . . ." She stares at her feet.

"It's OK," I say. "I'm actually here with my mom and Leo. Just came from the memorial."

"I should get out of your hair," she says, though she doesn't move, doesn't look like she wants to get out of my hair at all. I remember this about her: that she'd frequently say the opposite of what she meant, that she was often a code in need of breaking. The opposite of Tatum in some ways. Tatum, whose emotions and vulnerabilities are always ripe and available and fully in view. It's not that Tatum is any less complicated, just complicated in different ways, complicated in ways that allow me to read her, allow me to know her.

I size Amanda up and realize that she is wrong in her comment from just a moment ago: it's not that I needed an actress or someone who could keep up with me "creatively"; it's that I needed someone who let me in. Even when Tatum is needy and irritated because I've misplaced my priorities—work first, her second—she lets me in; she tells me; she speaks plainly, and I *see* her.

My phone vibrates again against my hip.

"I should be getting back," I say. "My mom is with her foundation co-chairs. They'll want to say some words. I should be there."

She nods, drops her chin. "You always were the good guy. The nice one who got away." She tilts forward, kisses my cheek.

"Good to see you, Amanda."

"Don't be a stranger," she says, then shakes her head. "Forget it. I don't even know what I meant by that."

I grin, and she grins, and then she kisses me again and offers a little wave and is gone. I watch her all the way until she spins through the revolving glass door, out into the street, out under the perfect blue sky which is little more than an illusion of happiness.

My phone is still buzzing, and I reach for it on the last ring before it would shoot to voicemail. "Hey," I say.

"Hey," Tatum says. "Sorry about before. Your dog just ransacked the bread bin."

I inhale and smell the scent of Amanda's honey perfume, which is still thick in the air. It's familiar and alluring but dissipating quickly, like if I stand there for another few seconds, I won't be able to recollect the smell at all. But rather than linger and let it fade on me, I stride through the lobby and leave it behind.

"That dog," I say. "He is such an asshole."

Tatum cackles on the other end of the line. "Well, he's *your* son."

"Takes one to know one," I say. I think of my own dad, whom I wouldn't call an asshole, at least not today, but who was prickly in ways that I'd never now grow to understand, not with him gone.

She laughs harder.

"Guess it sucks to be on cleanup duty, right?" I say. Tatum had promised that she'd do all the work with Monster when she brought him home. Mostly, I walk him, clean up, pick up the figurative shit. I don't mind, but I don't *not* mind that she's getting a taste of it today.

"I don't even want to know what's going to come out of him later."

"I can tell you exactly what will come out of him," I say. "Do you want all the disgusting details, such as what happened when he ate the whole lasagna off the table or when he dug up the garbage and ate the remains of our burritos, and I had to take him out all night, every hour on the hour?"

"Ugh," she groans. "I *don't* want any of the details."

"Works of art," I laugh. "Those craps were works of art."

"Monster!" she says to him. "Why are you such a little asshole? I love you! I love you so much, but you are such an asshole!"

Leo waves to me from inside the dining room, and I'm beckoned back to my current responsibilities. Tatum can handle the dog's digestive system for one day.

"Tell my asshole son to behave himself," I say. "Tell him his dad will be home soon."

22

TATUM

AUGUST 2009

The lobby of Commitments is hushed, with a waterfall fountain nearly the only noise, the receptionist and intake nurse working soundlessly behind the desk. Sunlight from the skylight on the ceiling illuminates the eggshell walls, photographs of the ocean and landscapes adorning them. Fresh flowers spill atop the side tables next to the cozy couches where only a solitary family sits, looking both gray and grave, clutching the arm of a young man who is obviously on his way in.

Dr. Wallis greets us with a firm handshake that evolves into a bear hug.

"One of my best success stories," he says, grabbing my dad's hand, wrapping him in his arms as well.

"You guys saved my life," my dad says, his eyes tearing as they always do now. Some people drink and get emotional. My dad got sober and now has never been more in touch with his softer side.

"How's he doing?" I ask.

"Good, good." Dr. Wallis nods, ushering us through the glass door, out of the lobby into the facility. "We are making real progress. This extra time was a gift for him."

We point ourselves down the silent hall, our heels clicking against the hard wood, toward his office, where my father and I have spent so many hours rehabilitating ourselves, our relationship too. We're here for Leo today, but when you return to a place that, well, "saved your life," it's hard not to be awash in gratitude for much more. My dad wipes his cheeks and shakes his head as Dr. Wallis guides us into the family meeting area.

Ben doesn't know we've come. His last time down here, two weeks ago, hadn't gone well, and Leo had requested just me this time. Leo's thirty days had evolved into sixty, and Ben hadn't understood why he wasn't just . . . *better*. It was surprising coming from my husband, whom I'd fallen in love with at least in part because of his kindness, his expansive heart: his devotion to Monster, his patience with Joey, who favors me. Yet Ben still tries to feed Joey most nights, though the boy mostly throws the food against the wall. Ben doesn't get angry; he doesn't flip the high chair tray in frustration like I might. He just points to the wall and tells Monster to start licking, to enjoy the buffet, and then he kisses Joey's forehead and says: "I get it, Joe. Dads are complicated. We'll try again tomorrow."

But with Leo, he is different, clinical. There is none of the patience I'd expect, little of the compassion. Not brotherly like he used to be, but paternal in the way that I imagine his own dad was. Namely, cooler, less affectionate, less tolerant of speed bumps too. We argued about it when Dr. Wallis had first called, explaining that Leo felt too fragile to leave after just a month, explaining that another few weeks would make him less likely to relapse.

Of course Ben understood *that*. That we wanted to do everything we could to ensure Leo would stay clean. It wasn't like Ben was unfeeling, but he seemed to think that you could work your way out of addiction, that if you put in enough effort, like maybe you would on a script, then you'd get the end result you desired. And if you didn't—if you didn't commit yourself in the way that was necessary, then of course you'd fail, and you'd have only yourself to blame.

"He's been clean, he's been through the program," Ben said when he hung up with Dr. Wallis last month. "He should get back to the stability of his life, the structure. It's what my dad was always saying about him: Leo had too much freedom, too much time on his hands, which never led to anything good."

"That's not how it works," I said. "He needs to feel ready. They're giving him the tools there. And you're selling him short, Ben. He's done well with his life—it's not like he's destitute."

Ben sighed, and though his back was to me while he chopped a pepper, I could almost sense him rolling his eyes. I retrieved the chicken breasts from the fridge, dropped them on the counter, grabbed a mallet to pound them. This was our new ritual—cooking dinner together, our way to spend time together. Between my time on set and the time at home when I had to read scripts or run to a junket or prep for a photo shoot, we were losing track of each other. On the rare days I had off, Ben was either in the *Alcatraz* writers' room or tweaking *Reagan*, which he had once asked me to read—I used to read all of his early work—but now said wasn't ready for review. I knew it was: I knew he'd shown it to Eric, had a draft out to Spencer, and I wondered if, with my success, he somehow wanted something just for himself. But I didn't ask, I didn't press him. It was easier not to point out the growing divergence in our power and acclaim, as if not illuminating it meant it wasn't there in the first place.

I unwrapped the chicken, laid it on the cutting board. "God, you work in this industry, Ben, you've met a million people in recovery, how are you not at least a little more sympathetic?"

"I *am* sympathetic, Tatum." The knife rattled against the counter. "I just think . . . listen, Leo's never wanted to do the work with anything, and I just think it's probably the same here."

"Do you hear what an asshole you sound like?"

Ben squeezed the rim of the counter until his knuckles turned white; then he faced me.

"Yes, I hear what an asshole I sound like, OK? But you didn't grow up with him, you weren't there when he was busted for cheating his junior year or when I found his pot stash and covered for him with my parents." He waved a hand. "I just think he needs to take responsibility for himself. And when he's in there, he's not."

"You don't get this at all."

"Don't patronize me," he snapped. "I don't 'get it' because you and your dad are like, the gurus? I'm not saying it's a fucking vacation in there, Tatum. I'm just saying that you don't know my brother like I know my brother, and if he can get a helping hand so he doesn't have to do the really gut-wrenching difficult work, he will." He shook his head. "And if my dad were here, he'd say the exact same fucking thing."

"Ben, your dad's *not* here, and you don't have to act like you are somehow his replacement."

He stared at me for too long a beat, and I wasn't sure if he was going to explode or weep. He did neither.

"Listen," he said, his voice rising only to a low tremor because neither one of us wanted to wake Joey. I had an early call time, and Ben wanted to use the evening to write, so these child-free hours were precious, too valuable to wreck even for a fight. "In fact, I *did* promise my dad that I'd look after him, and God knows even as an adult, Leo needs a minder, a keeper. And my mom has been through e-fucking-nough, so even if I don't want to be a hard-ass with him, even if I didn't exactly ask for this, that's what I'm doing."

"Ben—" I interrupted.

He kept on. "Leo's not your dad, Tatum, and Leo's not your blood, and it's not your responsibility to look after him. It's mine. So with all due respect, you can't, like, therapy your way to happiness in this one."

"What does that even mean? What are you even talking about?"

"That you and your dad seem to think that you know everything here, that I can't do what's best for my own brother. You go down there, to Commitments, have this cozy relationship with the staff, hell, your dad is practically on their brochures . . ."

"And that's a problem for you?"

He turned back toward the stove, clicked on the burner, rattled the pan on top.

"No," he said. "It's only a problem for me when you try to tell me how to deal with my own brother, when I've let you deal with your own father without butting in."

"I didn't realize that you wanted to butt in," I said.

"I don't. But it was never discussed with me: him living in our guesthouse for a year, him being such a new and heavy influence in our marriage."

"He's my father, Ben!"

"And he's my brother, Tatum. Don't you see how you can't have it both ways: make these decisions without me for your dad, and yet insist that you know best with Leo?"

Ben sliced off an enormous pat of butter, though he knew I was on a rigid diet for *As You Like It*, and plopped it in the pan. He stood there frozen, waiting for this to drive the wedge further into our evening.

Finally he said: "Tate, you know me. You think I want to be like this? You think I am the type of guy to *not* give him the benefit of the doubt if it was at all reasonable?"

I considered this, and it was true. If anyone could make room for empathy, it had always been Ben. But before I could reply, he said:

"So you have to do this my way. That's it. I'm not negotiating on my own brother."

And so I swung up the cutting board, dumped the peppers onto the pan, and said: "Since we're doing everything your way, I'm going to read my lines. Just leave me dinner in the fridge."

Our child-free evening turned into an adult-free evening as well.

Today, at Commitments, Leo greets us with a hug that is tighter than the one from Dr. Wallis. He is skinny and disheveled, but his skin glows and his smile fans all the way to his eyes. He sinks into the white couch in the family meeting area.

"Thanks for coming all this way," he says. Then: "Does Ben know you're here?"

I shake my head.

"Thanks for that too. I don't want to fight with him." He rubs his eyes, and it occurs to me that Ben is fighting so many of us these days. I think of my husband, alone in the kitchen chopping peppers, and part of me wants to race home, lean in and listen, try to figure out what's ailing him too. It's not like I wasn't angry with my father for a long time, it's not like I can't remember what it feels like to be furious at someone for wrecking their life. It's just that giving in, being less obstinate, was probably easier for me because I was always more malleable than Ben, like I have an emotional spigot that I turn on and access. I'm an actor, after all. Being malleable is my calling card.

"I should probably tell him when we get back," I say. "I don't want him to think that I'm keeping things from him."

"OK," Leo says, nodding.

"But we'll do what's best for you," my dad says in his best sober coach voice.

"I don't want him to be angry with me," Leo says. "It's not helping. Like, he comes down here, and it's just all *You need to get back to work,* or *Take responsibility for this.* It stresses me out. Like he can't understand that he's not my dad."

A small voice in me wants to say, *Stop blaming your brother for your own choices,* but I'm pretty sure that's Ben's voice from a few nights ago, so I say instead:

"It's fine, Lee, don't worry. I won't tell him anything you don't want me to. What matters is getting you better."

"Thanks, Tate. *Thank you.*" He eases back into the couch. "Then let's keep this between us right now. I hate to ask, but maybe it can just be our secret?"

I nod. "Sure, OK."

And with that, I learn how easy it is to betray my husband.

23

BEN

JULY 2005

Our car sputters to a stop in the middle of nowhere Arizona. I'm right, of course, we should have stopped for gas, but Tatum insisted, *No, no, that's BS, they just* say *the tank is almost empty, but it's not.*

The tank is empty. Tatum squeezes the wheel and grits her teeth and looks toward me, batting her lashes. "Don't be mad."

"Tatum!"

"OK, so I should have listened to you. But . . . you know . . ."

"No, I don't."

"Well, you're just *usually* a little melodramatic about the tank running low, so I figured—"

"That I couldn't possibly be right when the orange light is flashing frantically to alert you that we're about to run out of gas?"

From the back seat, Monster yawns loudly, then rises—he's tall enough to hit the ceiling on the SUV—and pokes his head between us.

"Monster doesn't like it when Mommy and Daddy fight," Tatum says.

"Tatum!"

I pull out my cell phone and stick my hand out the window, desperate for a signal, which we haven't gotten for miles since we dipped into the Arizona canyons. This road trip was supposed to be fun, a vacation of sorts. A break from babysitting her father and his new, tenuous sobriety, a time-out from her down-on-her-luck series of auditions. Not that she's not landing a punch every now and then, but her career is not lighting up the way she expected. Not like mine, anyway, which she doesn't say explicitly but also doesn't have to. I'm due in Texas in three days for a week of reshoots for *One Day in Dallas*. We figured we'd hit up kitschy hotels (that accept dogs), stop at Southwestern diners, carve out time for each other the way we haven't been able to lately, mostly because of my schedule, but also because of her dad and all the energy that has sucked from her.

She's changed because of him. Hardened and softened in ways that I'd write, if I were writing a character—which, I've told her, I'd like to do for her one day. Because, as she says, together we're unstoppable. And we are. I believe that too. I've never been better than I was on *Romanticah*, though I'm chasing that greatness on *One Day in Dallas*, been told that the script has heat, has all the markings of an award winner.

Tatum seems to be chasing something too now. With Walter back in her (our) life, she is more fragile, as if her father's reentrance has turned her to glass, but she's also more open, as if the valve she'd shut off to her empathy has spun open. This means she sometimes cries at inexplicable moments (when she found me sleeping on the couch with Monster's head resting atop my chest—I'd been up most of the night because Monster had eaten burritos out of the garbage and had endless diarrhea), and also bristles at things that I'd never expect to rattle her. A couple weeks ago a waitress at the sushi restaurant overheard me talking about *One Day in Dallas* and pushed up her cleavage and batted her eyes at me in an attempt to get a shot at a bit part. Tatum fumed about it the entire ride home: how suggestive the waitress was, how disrespectful she found her. I wouldn't have even given it a second thought if Tate hadn't blown it up so disproportionately.

So we embarked on a road trip to leave all that behind for a few days, and now we are out of gas in the canyons of Arizona. The sun is tucking itself behind a mountain peak, which grants us reprieve from its blistering rays, but it will be dark within hours, and then we're really fucked.

"I can't get a signal," she says. Monster licks her cheeks as if this is good news.

"I can't either."

She shrugs. "I guess we walk?"

"We walk where?"

"To the next town?"

"Tatum! We have no fucking idea where we are! We have no idea where the next town is! It's ninety degrees outside, and then it will be dark, and it'll be, like, forty, so then what?"

She frowns. "Well, do you think your attitude is helpful, like, at all?"

"I think what would have been helpful is if we stopped for gas the last time I suggested it!"

This is one of our things, one of the few quirks I cannot stand about her, and likely, she about me. Something as inane as the gas gauge, and yet symbolic too. How she pushes it to its limits; how I pull into a station as soon as the alert light goes on.

She grips the wheel and stares ahead.

"Don't blame me."

"Don't *blame* you?" I shove my phone out the window again, stare at the signal indicator, get nothing, shove it back in. "Who am I supposed to blame? *Monster?*"

"I was distracted," she pouts. "Thinking of what I was going to say to Lily Marple when I finally see her."

"You are actually coming up with a monologue of what to say to Lily? I've told you: say nothing, forget it. It wasn't a big deal."

I'd made the mistake of telling Tatum that Lily Marple, who plays Jackie Kennedy in *One Day in Dallas*, had tried to sleep with me on the shoot. I mean, I can't be sure, but she tucked her hands down my waistband at the craft service table, and said, "I think you're going to win lots of awards one day. And I'm thinking I could be your muse. Want to meet me in my trailer?"

I thought it was funny, not *ha-ha* funny, but amusing enough: that she'd be so desperate when she was already a lead, that she thought I'd take the bait when I was clearly committed and, also, not a total dick. Plenty of this sort of favor swapping went down on sets, to be sure, but usually the writer—who was not exactly high on the totem pole of power—was not part of the sexual favor hierarchy.

Tatum did not find it funny, not even in a *ha-ha* way.

"First she gets, like, a dream part, then she tries to screw you?" she'd yelled. Tatum wasn't up for the part of Jackie; she didn't wield that kind of consideration among casting directors and producers. Not that she wasn't good enough for the role, but casting was about power, and Tatum simply didn't have a power hand to play.

"She wasn't, like, trying to *screw* me," I said, even though that was exactly what she was doing.

Tatum suddenly shifted to tears. "*I* want to be your muse. Not her, not anyone."

"Babe, *babe*," I said and ran my hands down her shoulders. "I'll write you something great, something brilliant. Let me just get through this first. But then I promise."

She wiped her cheeks and apologized, and I told her not to. Part of loving Tatum was loving the tempestuous actress, the version of her that held me riveted behind the lens on *Romanticah*, the version of her that I can't imagine I'll ever grow bored with, ever outgrow. Sometimes she's like a firework, explosive but still mesmerizing, and it's not like I don't want to sit back and watch the show.

"Tate," I'd said then. "I see you. I have you."

I hadn't realized she'd dwelled on it—Lily's overt pass at me, but now, here we are, in the middle of the Arizona desert, and somehow her refusing to fill up the gas tank has morphed into raising the issue all over again.

I wave my phone out the window again, still nothing. "I think we might die here," I say. "Like, in the middle of the desert with our dog. This is how I'm actually going to fucking die."

I open the car door and Monster scrambles into the front seat, across my lap, and out to the shoulder of the deserted highway.

"FUCK!!" I scream into the canyons. My voice bounces off the rocks and back to us. *Fuck-fuck-fuck-fuck,* until it fades. Monster cocks his head and looks at me curiously.

Tatum slams her own door, marches around the Jeep, and says: "Jesus, you're acting like I did this intentionally!"

"I don't think you did this intentionally, Tate. But I asked you three times to pull over, and you kept saying we were fine."

"I thought we were!"

"So as I said—maybe not part of a Machiavellian master plan, but I *do* think that sometimes you get off on the drama without thinking through the consequences."

"Like when?"

I jerk my thumb toward Monster. "Like that impulse acquisition? Like the very first time we met, at the bar, with the bet?"

"It's not like any of those things ended badly," she says.

"It's a metaphor."

"So this is my fault." She clenches her fists and rams them into her hips.

"Well, technically, yes."

Monster wanders over to a bush and lifts his leg.

"We can hitchhike," she says.

"We haven't passed a car in hours."

Monster spins over a spot next to the bush and poops. If we were in Santa Monica, this is when I'd walk over and scoop it up with a little baggie while Tatum watches. Because we are in the middle of nowhere, I leave it be. I check my phone again. No bars. I am due in Dallas in two days. Even if we lose these hours and these miles, I'll still make it. That's not a concern. Freezing to death in the middle of the desert tops my list right now; not throttling my wife who was too stubborn to stop for gas isn't far behind it.

Tatum's eyes well up, almost as if she's been given a director's cue, but I know that this is genuine, not some emotion she's aiming for in her close-up.

"I'm sorry, OK, I'm sorry! I thought I was being spontaneous, and I thought I was, like, I don't know, living on the edge or something, and now we're fucking stranded here in the middle of the desert, and I don't have any idea where the next town is—you're right—and I was impetuous and dumb!" She pops the trunk to the Jeep and sinks into the open space, her shoulders heaving under the weight of her tears. Monster senses her despair and leaps into the trunk, sitting next to her as if on guard.

"OK, listen," I exhale. "It's just one night. And I don't want to fight."

"It's just one night!" she wails. "We're going to be, like, eaten by coyotes!"

"Monster will protect us," I say.

She momentarily slows her cries to gape at Monster, as if considering this, as if, were we to be attacked by coyotes, this goofy lump of a dog could do anything other than take a giant crap on them to scare them away. Then she rubs behind his ears absentmindedly, then gazes back toward me, her eyes still swimming pools. Though she is the best actress I know, I also can see that she is sincerely sorry for this. And because she is so transparent with me, here, now, and because this is a reminder that she is nearly always transparent and that we trust each other and we are each other's best allies, I feel myself softening.

I shove my hands into my pockets, teeter back on my heels, stare up at the wide-open pink and orange and still blue landscape above us. The stars are beginning to poke their heads out of the dusk sky, announcing night's arrival.

"Did I ever tell you how once Leo and I got lost in the woods one night in Vermont?"

"No," she hiccups. Monster settles in, nestling into her lap, and she pats the top of his head, then leans down and kisses him.

"Well, anyway, my parents used to have a house up there. Good for skiing, good in the summer for hiking and getting bitten by ticks. They sold it after Leo got Lyme disease one year."

"Oh," she says.

"Anyway, we were pretty much given free rein to romp around the woods, do whatever, you know. That's how kids grew up back then, like, no one watching, no responsibilities." I pause because it occurs to me that Tatum grew up with nothing but responsibilities. But I press on. "I was always super careful to mark our trail: I carried different colored chalk in my pockets to clip the trees so we could make our way back. Once I forgot about it, and it went through the wash . . ." I laugh. "Oh my God, my mom, just . . ."

She bites her lip, waiting for more, her eyes round and hopeful that this is leading to forgiveness.

"Anyway, we set out one afternoon, I must have been . . . fifteen, so I guess Leo was eight, maybe nine. And he insisted he was old enough to mark the trees, to take the lead and ensure that we could find our way back."

She nudges her head up just a little, like she already knows what's coming next. "Oh boy," she whispers.

"Yeah." I raise my eyebrows. "Exactly. Needless to say, Leo was never a Boy Scout—"

"In any sense of the word," she says.

"And we got completely turned around. Couldn't find our way back; it was just a total disaster. We fell asleep under a tree, and then it started to rain, like the way that it rains in Vermont in the summer, so Leo took off all his clothes and I was screaming at him about how we were going to die, and he started dancing like he was on fire, shouting at the sky about it being a rain dance and how he was beckoning the gods to send down more."

At this, she manages a laugh. "That does sound like Leo."

"Anyway, it turned out that we didn't die—"

"Obviously."

"And we hiked back in the morning. We used *my* old markings to figure it out." I grin. "And my mom was in a complete panic—my dad had already left to go back to the city, but my mom was flipping out, and all night, I had planned to sell Leo out, but once we got home, I realized that this was like, the best story ever. That we got lost and did a rain dance and camped out and made it back on our own, and that I wouldn't have traded it for the world." I consider it and snort. "It's something that when he ever gets married, I'm gonna use in my toast."

"Something about a metaphor about getting lost in the forest but finding the trees?"

I laugh now too. "Something like that." I slide next to her in the trunk.

"So one day, you'll use this in a speech about how much you had to learn from your wonderful wife?"

"Or one day, maybe you'll use it to remember to fill up the tank when I tell you?" I kiss her nose.

"And maybe on that same day, you'll acknowledge that a little adventure never killed anyone?"

I grin. "We haven't made it through the night."

I lower the back seat, and she finds a blanket that we bought at a swap exchange in Sedona. We rest our heads on our duffel bags, and Monster snores and keeps us warm. We sleep. We survive. No coyotes eat us after all.

When we wake in the morning, a truck slows and offers to double back with gas—it turns out the next town is only three miles east, and we fill our tank, and we leave this hiccup by the side of the road where it belongs.

We find a diner for a breakfast of eggs and bacon, which she eats only because our dinner was dry cereal found in our bag of snacks.

"Maybe one day you'll write this into your script for me," she says, breaking off a piece of the strip of bacon, savoring it under her tongue. "Not that dreadful Lily Marple."

She means this as a rib, as something we've wrestled and can now leave behind, just like last night's fight.

I sip my coffee and nod. I'd like that. To slow down, to create something just for my beautiful wife who is so stubborn that she doesn't fill the gas tank but also allows us to sleep under the stars, to outstretch our hands and feel like we can nearly reach the Big Dipper.

"Yes," I say. "Maybe one day I will."

24

TATUM

OCTOBER 2010

I'm in New York only for the weekend and a day. A quick in and out to do a junket for *As You Like It*, which is on all the awards lists, though no one has actually seen anything other than rough-cut footage, some scenes here and there. But the industry is abuzz with a David Frears–Tatum Connelly reunion, after all the awards heat with *Pride and Prejudice*, and buzz in Hollywood is just about all you need to convince people that something is real.

Daisy convinces me to meet her for a drink downtown at Harbor, the hottest, newest nightclub with a rotation of celebrity guest DJs. She's back in the city for the month—*New York Cops* is shooting on location to attempt to capture the grit that they have lost over the years by filming on a soundstage in Burbank, and she texts me relentlessly until I agree to venture south of Bowery to meet her.

I call Ben before I pull myself from the bedding at the Four Seasons. It sounds like I've woken him, though he's three hours earlier.

"Asleep?" I ask when he picks up on the third ring.

"Mmmmm," he replies. "Whiskey at dinner." I hear him rustle and rise.

"I thought this was a working weekend." I say it lightly, though I worry it comes out too brittle, too judgmental.

Ben had holed up at a writer's retreat for the weekend, trying to finesse the pilot of a hospital drama—*Code Emergency*—that he and Eric are bringing to the networks. I think he's better than that, better than an average hospital drama that he could write on his worst days, much less on his best ones. But I don't want to have that argument again, the one in which he tells me that I don't need to remind him of his own mediocrity, which is never my intention, but we've been out of sync lately, and so he takes my suggestions as criticisms, and now I just try to avoid suggestions entirely.

"Whiskey goes perfectly well with working," he says.

"OK."

"Oh God, Tatum," he groans. "Give me a break."

"I didn't say anything."

"You said everything."

"Ben, I asked if you were working, that was the whole point of this retreat!"

"And I did—I worked for eight hours, OK? Not on my earth-shattering masterpiece, OK? On *Code Emergency*, which I know you think is beneath me."

"I don't think that." I do, but there is no point in getting into it now, when I already know how this discussion is going to go. This TV stint is fine, it's *fine*. But Ben's potential is stratospheric; it's so far beyond this that it almost literally pains me. But to say that to him— which I have mistakenly from time to time—is condescending, patronizing. And I know that. I do. But sometimes I can't help myself anyway. He is *brilliant*, and I only want him to know that he doesn't have to sell himself short. When I say this, he replies that I sound more and more like his father every day. So I try to censor myself now, something that I never thought I'd have to do with him.

"Well, I worked all day. My shoulder hurts from hunching over my laptop. And then, at dinner, a couple of guys and I had some whiskey. So what?"

"So nothing. I'm glad. It sounds great."

It's too late to backtrack from my passive-aggressiveness, and we both know it.

"OK," he says.

"I just—"

"Here we go," he says.

I stop myself. It's easier to say these things—*You can do better*—over the phone when I don't have to look him in the eye and see how much my disappointment guts him. It's a cheap betrayal, saying the hard things when you don't have to witness their recourse. So I don't tonight. Besides, Hollywood is mercurial, and plenty of Ben's stumbles have been no fault of his own. It's not like he's not out there trying.

"Home tomorrow to see Joey?" I ask.

"Yeah."

"Give him a kiss for me."

"I will. I promised him ice cream. We'll go to the beach," he says.

"Give him an extra scoop, tell him it's from me."

"I will," he says.

"Love you," I say.

"You too," he answers.

But each of us sounds empty, as if the words can't transcend the divide of the three thousand miles between us.

❧

Daisy texts me as soon as I hang up. *GET YOUR ASS DOWN HERE.*

"Aren't we too old for this? Clubbing somewhere after midnight on the Lower East Side?" I say to her, after the bouncer has slipped me past the velvet rope without even glancing at the guest list, after the hostess has fawned and ushered me back to the VIP room, after the owner has said personal hellos and sent over a bottle of Veuve Clicquot.

"You're never too old to be clubbing at midnight somewhere on the Lower East Side." She refills her flute with the Veuve Clicquot. "Besides, look at all the beautiful men." She fans her arms wide, her champagne spilling over the lip of her glass. "There are so, so many beautiful men."

"I have a beautiful man."

"I know." She pats my leg. "I meant for me. Also: you can look but not touch, you know."

"If I even look in the wrong direction, it will be on Twitter in five seconds."

This is true. It's also a new adjustment for me, being endlessly scrutinized in public. I can't wait on line with Joey for ice cream without noticing stares; I can't grab apples at Gelson's without someone posting a photo on Twitter. Now I'll just send my assistant out for those mundane errands: tampons, tomato sauce, toilet paper, which isn't how I want to live my life—Ben rolls his eyes in mock horror that I actually say things like *Just ask my assistant to do it*—but that's my new reality, that's the price of my fame. It's not by choice, certainly not by my choice. I love getting lost in the wide aisles of a grocery store, filtering through bruised fruit to find the perfect peach, gazing at my endless options in the cereal aisle. I started doing this when my mom was sick and our pantry went barren because my dad was no use. I'd hop a ride with a neighbor to the store, fill the cart until it was towering so high that I couldn't see past it, and lose myself in the simple utopia of the cereal aisle.

At Harbor, Daisy rises to greet an impossibly handsome man whom I vaguely recognize from a show I've flipped past. My phone vibrates, and Piper's text illuminates the screen in the otherwise mostly shadowy club lighting, which flares every few seconds in time with the pulsing beat.

Piper and her husband are babysitting for the weekend—my dad and Cheryl had already planned a golf trip, and Constance had given up enough of her weekends to need a break to see her own family. Not that Ben would have wanted my dad to watch Joe; he'd have just canceled his retreat instead. But I bought Piper and Scooter first-class plane tickets and promised them a suite at the Beverly Hills Hotel for a night when I returned. They would have come anyway; they were trying for a baby of their own, and they considered this excellent practice, though Piper was already exasperated that Scooter mostly wanted to watch the World Series rather than lend a hand at bath time. I laughed when she told me this, but it wasn't like I could join in on the complaints.

Ben had plenty of faults, but he pulled his parenting weight, more even than I did, not because I didn't want to, but because my time was no longer my own. My heart was probably in it more than Ben's. Joey still fought with him over meals, as if challenging his dad was a sport in and of itself ("God, this kid is like Leo," he said to me one night after a bath where more water had ended up on the floor than down the drain); and Joey was in this interminable phase when he never wanted to wear clothing, especially when Ben tried to dress him. But still, Ben had more hours with Joey, simply because he had more time. With *Alcatraz* canceled, Ben had open days, empty nights. There is *Code Emergency*, but a pilot script isn't a full-time job. I did breakfast and took him to an occasional birthday party and sometimes gym class too, when my stardom didn't make me too self-conscious, but still, if you were to graph who put in more hours, it was Ben.

Piper texts me a picture of Joey sleeping in his toddler bed, and something comes untangled in me. *What am I doing here?* At Leonardo DiCaprio's favorite new club, in a throbbing scene of lithe limbs, skinny models, vaguely recognizable faces of people I saw once on a TV rerun in the late-night hours when I couldn't sleep? Daisy has moved to another couch, pressed close to the guy she knows from somewhere, and I rise to go. I'm bone weary from the flight and from the day of press, and I have another round tomorrow. Also, this has never interested me, this scene of too-beautiful strangers who pretend to enjoy each other's company for the evening. Not when I was putting myself through Tisch by working at the bar, not in my early days in LA when this type of evening would have been so easy to stumble into.

I spin my wedding band on my finger, glance again at the picture of my sleeping child, and stand to leave.

It's then that I see him.

Not clearly at first because of the lights and the bass from the song, which is nearly literally warping the walls and the dance floor.

I see him in staccato beats, in and out of the glare, in and out of my brain, like I'm not quite sure he's in front of me. I push past the VIP hostess until I'm right in front of him, right by his side. His eyes are closed as he skitters to the beat of this song, which has suddenly become unbearable to my early-thirties ears. I jab his chest, jab it again, and his eyes fly open, and I know right away. He is not clean, not in any way sober.

"Leo," I shout.

"Heeyyyyyy!" he shouts back, wrapping his arms over my shoulders, still bouncing to the music, like I'm now part of his groove.

I push him off me, lean closer into his ear. "*Leo*, what the hell?"

He slows the pulse of his legs, his arms dropping to his sides. I yank his elbow and wade through the crowd toward the bathrooms, where it is only marginally quieter, so I stick my head into the women's room, which is empty, and pull him in, locking the door behind us.

"Talk to me," I say. "What happened?"

He meets my eyes, and his pupils are wide and dilated. His hands jigger by his sides, so I take them in mine, hold them together, and say, "Breathe."

He does. He inhales and exhales, and inhales once more, then says, "I fucked up. Three weeks ago. I don't know what happened."

"Have you been going to meetings? Lee, you were clean for over a year." And he had been. After his sixty days at Commitments, he'd been a model of sobriety, at least as far as I could tell. And I'd gotten to be a pretty good judge with my father.

He shrugs. "Work has been crazy, and then I got invited to this weekend in Key West, so I thought . . . blow off steam . . ." His shoulders flop again. "Relapsing happens, you know? So fucking what? I'm not that bad, I can stop."

"Leo . . ." I release his hands but he can't still himself. He paces back and forth in front of the vanity, just as someone knocks on the door and yells: "What the fuck? I have to pee. Open up!"

"Don't tell Ben, OK? Please just don't tell Ben." His eyes are wild and terrified.

"Let me call my dad; he'll know how to help."

"I'll start going to meetings again, one every day." He is taking the floor in two steps now, spinning around, two steps more, spinning again, two steps more.

"Come back to LA with me; we'll get you back into Commitments. My dad is there every weekend as a sponsor."

"No, no." He shakes his head. "I can do this, I'm not so bad. Just . . ." He stops finally. Stares at me, pleading. "Please don't say anything to Ben. I can't take his disappointment, I don't want to hear his judgment of my failure."

"He won't judge you," I say quietly.

"He will," he says back, and I know that he's right. Ben will give you a second chance, but a third? It's part of his hang-up with my dad: how many times he hurt me, how many ways I had to forgive him. He does this to protect me, I know, but mostly it comes off as a rigidity that makes him seem unkind, even when he is not.

"Shit, Leo. That's a big ask. A big thing to keep from him."

"I'll get clean," he begs. "But please. It makes it so much harder if I have to do it to please him."

"You're not doing it to please him."

His eyes are so frantic, so desperate. "Please, Tate."

I don't know what to do other than to promise him, because if I don't he won't come with me. Not because it's the right thing, though maybe it is. But I consider how tightly wound Ben has become—how he has been unwilling to embrace Ron, how he has been slow to warm to my father, how I've gradually grown aware that my success outpacing his own has become a weed that has planted roots and is rising between us. For reasons that I can't explain, I remember that drive through Arizona and Texas, the one where I pushed the gas tank to zero, and Ben was so angry, if only for a few moments. But the rage was there, the irritation that I should have done things *his* way, even if we spent a nice night underneath the stars. He's angry like this more often now; he's drinking whiskey to chase that anger too. I consider all of this as Leo's eyes pool and he pleads with me. He's not wrong, I realize: Ben won't easily forgive this, and God, their family—our family—has been through enough. Isn't it easier to tuck this away, get Leo healthy, and move on as if I weren't at Harbor, as if Leo hadn't relapsed?

Maybe I tell myself that this is a kindness I offer my husband, to relieve him of more anger, to relieve him of more pain. But maybe I also know, even as I make my decision, that it's a betrayal too.

"OK," I concede. "But you'll go to meetings, you'll leave with me right now, and you'll sleep in my hotel suite—and first thing tomorrow, you will go to a meeting."

"All right," he says. "Thank you."

I unlock the bathroom, and we file out past three irritated girls whose dresses barely cover their breasts. Tomorrow, the *Post* will run a story about how Tatum Connelly locked herself in a bathroom with an unnamed but very attractive man, and Ben will see it, and I'll laugh and tell him that, as always, they have it wrong. And he'll believe me, because we tell each other the truth. Most times. Not always. Like tonight on the phone, or in plenty of our arguments about his potential and my schedule or simply in how we fill our time when the other isn't there: he drinks whiskey rather than write; I go to Harbor rather than sleep. Besides, I lie for a living now. This one isn't any easier; this isn't any harder either.

25

BEN

AUGUST 2004

I wake to Tatum on top of me. She leans close to my neck, then to my ear:

"Happy birthday, baby."

"Holy shit," I groan. "I'm fucking old."

"Shhh," she whispers. "I'm about to make you feel very, very young."

"But Leo . . ." Leo is in the next room, crashing on the pullout in my office.

"Leo didn't come home until three a.m.; he's not going to hear a thing."

"OK," I say.

"OK," she says, easing her way lower.

After a few minutes, I forget that I'm now thirty and that my brother is fifteen feet away, and that I have a deadline for a script that's a mess but that I will somehow wrangle into greatness. I forget everything except my wife on top of me and her ability to make me feel like I could live forever.

Leo is here for the week. It's a terrible week with my schedule: *One Day in Dallas* is due to the studio on September 1, so we can shoot just at the start of the new year, but Leo insisted, and Tatum thought we should make a big to-do, have a party for my birthday, so of course I said yes.

We'd spent yesterday at the beach, and admittedly it had been perfect. Leo surfed, and I dove in and out of the waves, and Tatum read a book from the sand—she never loved going in—and we bought lunch and beers from the vendor on the boardwalk. Just before sunset, we'd asked a jogger to snap a photo. "So we remember that time you turned thirty, and Leo crashed on our couch," Tatum said. We grinned and said: *Cheese!* And Leo shouted: "My brother is so fucking ancient, man!"

I slip into the living room, then the kitchen, for coffee; Leo hasn't even made it to the pullout in my office. He's splayed on the couch, breathing through his mouth, one hand down his pants. Monster, the part-Lab, part-who-knows-what rescue dog whom Tatum had taken pity on outside of Whole Foods in July, is curled up by Leo's head, snoring to his own beat, and they sleep in tandem. I lean over and kiss the top of Monster's head, and he opens an eye, cocks an eyebrow, and falls back to sleep. It's fitting, I think, these two lost boys who have made their way onto my couch, neither at my behest.

Tatum thought Monster would be an excellent warm-up for parenting; not that parenting was on the table, not that I had time to walk a dog or pick up his shit or run him to the vet when he swallowed a chicken whole. (Which he did the first night he was with us: we left the rotisserie chicken on the counter, went to open a bottle of wine, and returned to find our dinner missing and Monster's tongue swirling across his black lips. We were going to change his name, but it was so fitting—with his jowly drool and mismatched eyes, one gray, one green—that it stuck.) Tatum adopted him on a lark—she'd tried to call me but I was in pitches all day and not answering, so she took him anyway, and when I finally trudged through the door after an exhausting afternoon of meeting after meeting after meeting with executives who wanted me to write things that neither interested me (*I'm thinking space: 2070, and all the aliens have eaten the humans but now want to regenerate them!*), nor seemed like particularly brilliant ideas (*Stick with me here: a remake of the knockoff of* Cocoon, *but for teen boys!*), I was greeted by a hundred-pound nearly feral beast jumping on my chest.

"Meet Monster!" Tatum sang out. She was wearing an apron, as if she had actually been cooking. She pulled that (soon ill-fated) chicken from the Whole Foods bag.

"Who is Monster?"

Monster was sitting at my feet, wagging his tail aggressively.

"Our new dog!"

Monster jumped on my chest.

"Sit, Monster," she said. He did not sit. "Sit, Monster!"

He pushed off me and raced around the living room, panting.

Tatum shrugged. "I'll do everything, I promise. Take him to obedience class, take him on walks . . ."

Monster was now humping our couch.

"Monster!" Tatum barked. "No!"

"Tate! Jesus, you couldn't have waited to consult me?"

"It had to be then or he was going to a kill shelter."

I sighed. "I'm guessing it's too late to return him?"

She put on her sheepish fake grin that I was usually immune to. "I always wanted a dog, so please?"

"Don't give me that grin. It might work on casting directors, but it does not make me weak in the knees."

She stuck out her bottom lip in her best actress pout.

"Oh God," I groaned. "Well, that, how can I say no to that?" Then: "You'll do the work?"

"I'll do the work." She held her hand to her heart.

I kissed her on the nose. "Monster stays."

Then we went to open the wine, and Monster ate our dinner.

This morning, the morning that I'm thirty, Leo stirs and opens an eye, then reaches his arms overhead, nudging Monster awake too. Monster stretches his Jurassic jaws wide open and yawns, then looks at me expectantly. I trudge to the bowl by the back door and scoop in his food from the locked bin. (It had to be locked: we learned this lesson the first week when he tipped over the bag we had lazily leaning against the wall and ate the entire contents, which resulted in yet another emergency trip to the vet, which I absolutely did not have time for, but what was I going to do? Fail at this early test of canine parenting?) Monster bolts from the couch, his back paws stepping on Leo's face, and gallops toward his food.

"Your dog is a disaster," Leo says.

"Funny, I was just thinking how he's kind of exactly like you."

"Low blow." Leo pushes himself upright, his hair wild, his eyes bloodshot. "Happy birthday, old man."

"One day you'll be thirty, baby brother; don't knock it."

"Thirty," he says, flopping back against the couch, scratching his navel. "Shit, dude, that's like real adulthood."

Monster has finished inhaling his food and is back at my feet, spinning his electric tail in quick-fire circles.

"I gotta take him out; want to come?"

Leo shrugs. "Not really."

"I thought you came out here for the fresh air, for a break from the New York summer. Come on, a beach walk."

In truth, I know he came out here for more: for permission to ditch his job, to become that surf instructor he's wanted to be since graduation, for me to ease up and say, *Make yourself happy, don't live in Dad's shadow.* Tatum keeps telling me to say this. *Jesus, Ben, he's had a shitty few years. Let him just be happy.* And part of her is right, but we've all had a shitty few years—her with her mom, us with my dad, and that's not an excuse not to grow up, to shirk your responsibilities. God help me, even if that makes me sound like my dad. That doesn't make it less true.

If I pay for graduate school, Benjamin, I expect an Oscar. I can still hear my dad, as if getting an Oscar were the easiest fucking thing in the world. It wasn't; in fact, he didn't even mean that it was. He meant that even if it were the hardest fucking thing in the world, he still expected it. That was probably *why* he expected it. It rankled me so much back then—his rigidity, his expectations, and yet, how can I point fingers now and say that he was wrong? Not when he pushed me to the success that I've become—not an Oscar winner, sure, but on my way, hitching a ride to the next strata in the industry. My dad isn't around now to do the same for Leo. Whether I wanted to or not, whether I begrudged my dad all those years ago or not, it was up to me now to pass along the message, to ensure that Leo understood that the journey matters just as much as the destination. *Go work hard, Leo. Go do your job. Go be an adult.* It's what my dad would have insisted on, so it's what I insist upon too.

Leo wiggles into his flip-flops, and while he brushes his teeth at the kitchen sink because that's where he left his toothbrush last night, I check my e-mail. Monster is panting in my lap, his drool running down my thigh.

"Buddy, hold on, hold on, I'm coming." I pat his head absentmindedly.

I'm about to click out of my in-box and heed Monster's unrelenting demands when I see a name that jolts me.

Amanda Paulson.

Jesus.

I haven't thought much about Amanda since Tatum and I married. Sometimes, yes. I mean, in the way that anyone remembers an ex and tries to reconcile how they spent years with someone who is now a stranger. Like maybe it happened to someone else. Like maybe her fiery red hair and her fiery self-determination were something I created like a dream, because now that I'm with Tatum it feels so very far away.

But seeing her name in my in-box reminds me that she wasn't a mirage, wasn't a memory that happened to someone else, like my images of her are a movie that someone showed me once.

I loved her once, I think. *Now she's just a minefield in my in-box.* She writes:

> B—I know it's been a few years, and I should have been in touch sooner. I mean, not sooner. I know you're married. I know you're the toast of Hollywood. (I'm not stalking you, I swear. You just hear things, you know?) Anyway, I never worked up the nerve to call you after your dad, and I should have. So when I woke up today and remembered that it was your birthday, I wanted to write and say how sorry I am. How sorry I was. I think of you often and wish you only good things. Happy birthday, Ben.—A

I reread the e-mail, then delete it. Then go into my deleted files folder and trash it forever. *It is so typical,* I think, *offering condolences three years later, offering them when only convenient for her.* I shut my laptop quickly and stand so abruptly that Monster's head, still in my lap, jolts back with surprise.

"You OK?" Leo asks.

"Fine, yeah, fine. Let's take this dog out before he craps on the floor."

"Do I really have to leave here on Sunday?" Leo whines, as I clip on Monster's leash.

"It's my birthday, Leo, do me a favor and don't give me a hard time for one day. Besides, surfing and hanging out at the beach all day are not exactly résumé building."

"Noted." He swings the front door open and eyes me, reviewing me in the way that only a sibling can. "You sure you're OK? You don't look right."

"I'm fine," I say, stepping out into the California sun. "It must be my old age. Maybe it's just how you look when you're thirty."

He laughs, and Monster wags his tail at Leo's glee.

"But you're living the dream," he says, slugging my shoulder.

I think of my dad and how this is what he'd want: me pushing my brother into responsibility, me ascending the ladder of Hollywood, ready to reach for everything this town has to offer.

"I am," I say, and we point ourselves toward the sea and the horizon that lies behind it.

26

TATUM

MARCH 2011

Leo dies four days after I win the Academy Award.

We linger by his hospital bed, where he is unable to be revived, and then finally Helen agrees to remove the ventilator, and his chest rises almost undetectably until it rises no more. I'm supposed to be in Panama; I was scheduled to start principal photography on *Army Women: 2.0* just after the awards season ended, but they rejigger the schedule and give me an extra week to allow me another handful of days off for the funeral. A handful of days feels unbearably unjust, though I understand the overtime and the budget and the payroll and the crew; this movie isn't just about me, though I'm its star. A handful of days to grieve with my husband feels like a bomb that could explode between us—among everything else, I'd forgotten to thank him in my acceptance speech.

It was a humiliating oversight. I literally blanked out; I was so stunned to be onstage that I forgot my speech nearly entirely. But it shouldn't have been hard to remember to thank the one person who mattered the most. The gossip blogs have been all over it, the tabloids too. Rumors about what it means, rumors that we are coming undone. I don't want to think that it means anything, though if I pay close enough attention, maybe it does: maybe it was my way of letting Ben know that I've felt him pull away, that we no longer see each other, that he could be more supportive, even when dealing with his own shit. None of this was conscious that night, at least not that I contemplated anyway, and I'd give just about anything to go back and do it over.

I've apologized to Ben relentlessly, but he waves me off. Not because he doesn't forgive me but because, with Leo in the ICU, it feels inconsequential. That I am so caught up in my Academy Awards mistake feels even more shameful; that I worry about my Panama scheduling too only piles on. I could drop out. They'd recast and move on without me, but Ben insists that I don't. He practically pushes me to stick with it, as if sticking with it will ensure normalcy, and normalcy might mean that Leo hasn't died.

It was an overdose. Of course it was. I'd tried to keep tabs since I'd run into him at Harbor five months back; I'd check in once a week, at least through the new year, and he always assured me, promised me, that he was going to meetings, walking the straight line. He'd say, "Tater-tot, don't worry. I'm as clean as a whistle. And . . . nothing's been said to Ben, right?"

"Nothing," I'd say, half-listening for the intonation in his voice, a sign of a lie. But I was admittedly distracted, with the awards rush, with Joey's occupational therapy (evidently he did not hold a pencil correctly for a three-year-old, and this set off all sorts of alarm bells with his preschool teachers), with training for *Army Women: 2.0*.

Of course I thought about telling Ben. Of course I didn't want to bear the weight of a secret between us. But Ben was finally finding new footing: he and Eric were moving into preproduction on

Code Emergency, which had been picked up for the fall season, and he seemed encouraged about its potential. Why drag him down with Leo's drama when Leo was assuring me he was fine? At least, that was what I told myself; that's how I rationalized it. Now, though, those are the what-ifs you live with. What if I'd told Ben, and he'd kept better track of Leo's sobriety? What if I'd told Ben and he'd found a way to keep him alive?

I fidget with my dress, readjust Joey's tie in the town car on the way to the funeral, consider telling Ben today.

"Hey," I say and rest my hand atop his. He doesn't move, doesn't intertwine his fingers with mine. *If he turns to look at me, I will tell him. If I can make him see me, make him understand that my mountain of regret is enormous, I will tell him.*

"Ben," I say again. He blinks quickly, his gaze out to the dreary grayness of the Long Island Expressway.

"Daddy," Joey says, and finally Ben refocuses, sliding his hand from under mine, and tousles Joe's hair. *Look at me, Ben, look at me!*

"Sorry, Joe. Dad's just having a tough one today."

Joey nods, his face solemn. "Sometimes when I have bad days, a nap helps."

Ben manages a smile, though it is pained and drawn. He turns back to the window.

"Ben," I say. "What can I do?"

Look at me so I can tell you the truth, so I don't have to wade around the what-ifs, so I can deal with your justifiable anger, and you can forgive me.

His shoulders flop, and he says, eyes still toward the bleak freeway landscape: "Nothing, there's nothing you can do, Tate."

I watch him for a moment and then glance away, kissing the top of Joey's head, clutching him tighter to me. I will tell him one day but not now.

Not yet.

We bury Leo in a cemetery outside the city, next to Paul, his father. There are hundreds of mourners: beautiful, lanky women who likely once loved him, clean-cut men in well-fitting suits who were coworkers or teammates from Dalton or old college buddies who heard about this on Facebook. I think of my mother's own quiet service, of us in the garden of my childhood home, where Piper now lives, where she and Scooter are trying for a baby and trying to build their own family under the roof that had plenty of sad memories, but some happy ones too. I think of my dad knocking on the door that day we spread her ashes, how unforgiving I was, how much he hurt me for so long, and that, over time, I'd forgotten all of this because he'd earned my forgiveness. Somehow I'd blurred the lines between the work my dad put in and the work Leo had. I'd assumed that because my dad had found a way to rehabilitate himself, that Leo could—or would—too. Blood rushes to my cheeks, just as Ben rises to speak at the service. At my shame for not being more watchful over Leo, at my shame for blurring the two of them together, thinking that Leo's wounds would heal as completely as my dad's.

I should have told Ben when I knew, after that night at Harbor. I should have told him, and maybe everything would be different.

Shit, I think now, when it's all so clear and yet also all too late. Maybe Ben could have saved him. Part of me knows this isn't true. No more so than the ways I used to play *what if* with my mom: What if she'd been diagnosed earlier? What if she hadn't had to take care of the two of us and had paid better attention to her health? What if she'd had better doctors? Would it have changed anything? Everything? How am I supposed to know? How am I supposed to live with that?

My dad drank because he couldn't live with it. Or kept drinking because of this, I suppose. It would be unfair to blame my mom's cancer for his devotion to booze. It started before she got sick, and it spiraled from there. I dealt with it by losing myself to people who aren't me, people who are written on a page, people who put a wide swath of emotional space between my reality and who I was for those minutes onstage. Eventually, just like my dad, the habit stuck.

If you can dream it, you can be it, she used to say, shaking one of her beloved snow globes or tucking me into bed at night when she was still healthy. I suppose I took this further than she imagined, in ways both big and small.

I watch Ben stumble to the pulpit, and I wonder if she would be proud of me, how she'd define success. An Oscar, sure, well, yes, though she wrote poetry quietly and only for herself, and found that perfectly satisfying. This secret looming in my marriage? Maybe not that. But then again, she and my dad weren't a fairy tale, so maybe she wouldn't judge. Maybe she'd just say, *You tried the best with what you had.* How was I expected to know that Leo was lying to me on our phone calls, in the e-mails I deleted as soon as they hit my in-box so Ben wouldn't see them and ask questions? Maybe my mom would wonder why my loyalty was to Leo, not to Ben on this, and maybe I'd question that too. I know that it's about my father, about my absolution of him, how far he had come since that day my mother's ashes blew from her garden into the cloudless June sky, and that I wanted absolution for Leo too. I thought I was doing Leo a kindness, and maybe doing Ben one too: letting him off the hook from being the father figure after Paul died. But yes, it's possible, maybe I wanted Leo to rehabilitate himself in the ways that my father did—not just get sober but genuinely reinvent himself—to prove to Ben that I was right about my dad, right about reinvention.

Ben clears his throat and clutches the podium next to the coffin at the cemetery on this dreary day in March.

He hasn't shared what he plans to say. He hasn't shared much since he ran up the aisle at the Academy Awards, out of the Dolby, just as the lights were dimming on my category. I reached for him as he bolted, but then production rushed a seat filler into place next to me, and I sat obediently (and expectantly), because how was I in any way to know of the news he was receiving on the line? He still wasn't back by the time they called my name, and as I traveled up the steps to claim my gilded honor, part of me cursed him for missing it. And maybe omitting his name wasn't as unintentional as I've told him it was, through all of my apologies. Maybe I thought I was settling a score. I don't know. I wept up there, wept for my mom, wept for me, wept for my triumph and determination and for the fact that a girl from outside Canton can work hard enough, roll up her sleeves and dig deep enough, to make something from nothing.

I was whisked backstage for press immediately following—that was when they peppered me with questions about forgetting to thank him. I cried apologetic and honest tears, and I spoke of how grateful I was to him, how he saw the best of me when I wasn't famous and has lived with the worst of me now that I was. All of it was true, even if there were things I omitted too.

We weren't reunited until after the ceremony: he staggered toward me in the valet line, with a cigarette in hand. I couldn't remember ever seeing Ben smoke, and I began to panic, thinking he'd heard my gaffe, thinking he was disgusted that I'd become that self-involved star who forgets to thank the people who matter most. His pallor was the exact opposite of my own glow, as if the universe has only so much goodwill to dole out, and sucked it all from him and dumped it out onto me. I started to apologize for my mistake, but he cocked his head and squinted, and it was clear he had no idea what I was talking about, the way that I'd publicly cut him down, if only by omission. Selfishly, I wondered how long I could play that out, how long it could be before he realized that I'd become the type of celebrity we used to mock.

And then he told me: overdose, coma, no brain activity, and the universe sucked everything from each of us, and there was nothing to celebrate at all.

At the funeral, Ben begins to speak now, so quietly that I shift forward, willing him to lean closer to the microphone too. As if he can intuit me the way that people say twins can, or spouses who are so connected that they can read the other's thoughts from across the room, from across an ocean. But Ben does not lean forward. He pinches his nose and starts again, however, this time, a little louder, though no stronger in tenor than before.

"To know my brother was to love my brother," he says, then stops. He winces, shakes his head. I know he is criticizing himself, telling himself that if there were ever a time for him to display his command of words, of language, it is now. Or at least I think he is doing this. He looks so different from the man I've grown older with that it's hard to even say what is running through his mind. If I could reach him, speak to him, though, I'd tell him that his words could start to heal us, heal him; his words, like many of the brilliant ones he's penned before this, can help someone see something in a whole new light. Not that Leo's death should be seen in a whole new light. Not now. Not yet. Maybe not ever. But Ben will have to try to see it in a different light, or else the weight of his grief will bog him down forever.

"Come on, baby," I whisper under my breath, and Joey looks at me and says, loudly, "What, Mama?"

Ben's eyes move from the dirt at our feet toward me, then toward Joey, and something steadies in him. I think something steadies in him at least, but then his gaze is back at our feet, then toward the deep hole in which Leo will be lowered, where he'll rest next to Paul, his father, forever.

"I should have saved him," Ben says to the mourners. "I always worried that in the end, we could save only ourselves. But that's not true. Because I could have saved him. I didn't. And I don't know how you ever let go of something like that."

I want to race to Ben, I want to tell him that he's not alone up there, that we can save each other, that this is the entire point of everything we've done, everything we'll do. But I find that I'm unable to move, weighed down by what—my shame? my guilt? the crevasse that is growing between us?—and instead, I lower my head to my chest, and I weep.

27

BEN

SEPTEMBER 2003

I am greeted like Moses at the Red Sea at Toronto, the figurative waters parting in front of me. We are here to screen *All the Men*, my follow-up to *Romanticah*, and the studio has sent early clips and bits and pieces to all the important press: *Variety*, the *Hollywood Reporter*, all the papers whose reviews can launch a career into the stratosphere. The early buzz is hot—Spencer, my agent, calls it "so fucking hot it's like an all-ten stripper joint," and I'm swept up in the wave of accolades, despite knowing better. Despite the fact that what matters most to me is Tatum and our life back home, well, fuck, who wouldn't want the praise and the heralding and the calls that I might be the once-in-a-lifetime voice of my generation? I never thought this mattered, the fawning attention, the over-the-top praise, but it turns out that I was wrong about parts of myself, that it's more than a little bit gratifying to be told that you're "the fucking shit, man."

The studio flies us out to Toronto first class, and Spencer and I each drink four Bloody Marys and don't notice the turbulence or the bump on the landing. I invited Tatum to come, but she'd snagged a few decent auditions this same week, and given how hard she'd fought to even be seen by casting directors, I wasn't about to tell her to abandon it for a few days in Toronto. And I don't think that she would have wanted to anyway: that's not who Tatum is, and that's not what I'd want from her, to ask her to set her aspirations aside for mine.

Instead, I sent Leo a ticket for the long weekend. That the dates coincided with the second anniversary of our father's death wasn't coincidental. I mean, coincidental on the part of the festival, but not on my part. I didn't want to jet to New York to wallow in grief that only makes me angry. I'm still grieving, of course, but I take it out on my early morning runs with metal rock playing too loudly in my ears or by racing down the 405 too quickly, jutting in and out of traffic, like my grief has made me more dangerous, like it cuts through me like a knife's edge, and if I move quickly enough, furiously enough, I won't feel the pain.

Tatum will ask me about it on those mornings when I come home, my T-shirt clinging to my chest, the music still blaring in the head-phones around my neck.

"Your dad?" she'll say, and curl up on the couch and wait for me to answer however I need to.

Sometimes just that she is asking, absorbing my rage, is enough. The grief quiets itself for the moment.

Other times I'll sink next to her and talk about how angry I am that he isn't here to see my success, how angry I am that he was such an unforgiving bastard, and yet also, how much I miss him because it's not like he was like that always—how goofy he was in the way he loved our dog, Bitsy, how he'd insist on buying my mom flowers every Friday, delighting in how he could surprise her with a new type each week. And it's not like he wasn't right most of the time too. About what it took to drive me, about the motivation and work ethic that I needed to succeed.

"It's OK that it's complicated," Tatum will say. "God knows that nothing about my own parents was uncomplicated."

"So why aren't you as angry as I am?"

She'll rest her head on my shoulder and consider this, and I can hear her breathing, her chest rising and falling, and then she'll say something luminous like: "I had a long time to mourn that my mom was sick, so it's easier to get past the injustice of it, you know?" She doesn't mention her dad, the injustice of his alcoholism and how it stripped so much of her adolescent innocence.

We'll sit that way until my rage has subsided, as if she can soak up my angst just by proximity, and then I'll rise and shower and go to work and pretend, for the moment, that my grief isn't still there, as present as my heartbeat.

So no, now, come September on the two-year anniversary of his death, I was not going back to New York for the anniversary, to stew in the injustice of it all.

I tell myself that, instead, I grieve for him by honoring his work ethic, by being my best, by being *the* best and not accepting anything less, by steering Leo toward the same.

Leo's already in the room when Spencer and I coast up to the arching hotel driveway in the town car arranged by the studio.

"Hey, big bro," he says, slapping my back after I slide my keycard into the hotel room door. He surprises me by pulling me into a hug. I'm still a little tipsy from the flight. "Let's party."

"I gotta nap," I say. "Then I have to work." I face-plant on the bed.

"Whoa, dude. What's my responsible big brother doing drunk in the middle of the afternoon?"

"Tired," I say into the pillow. "So, so tired."

"I'll occupy myself, no worries."

"Call me," I mumble, and then the Bloody Marys take hold, and I sleep.

I wake to the darkness. Leo must have pulled the blackout shades, which is so endearing it slays me. That kid trying to take care of me. That's supposed to be my job. Taking care of him.

I push myself up to my elbows, then gingerly swing my feet over to the floor. This hangover, though. My head is beating like a marching band. I never day-drink, and even when I night-drink, it's not usually four or five in a sitting, like on the flight. A glass of wine or two, maybe two martinis to take the edge off, kick back at the end of the day. Over the summer, when I had the time, Tatum and I would grill fresh fish on the tiny patio in the back of the bungalow, and then, yes, a cold beer with a lime wedged down the neck was perfect. But I've never done well with waking to regret, never been the type to be OK vomiting into a toilet at all hours. (Not that anyone is really OK with this, but some of us choose it more often than others.)

I check the nightstand clock. I'm due at a dinner in forty-five minutes; then I have three party invites. The thought of eating and/or partying is enough to raise a small burst of bile, but I swallow it down and reach for my phone in my back pocket. I debate whom to call first: Tatum or Leo. I settle on Tatum but I'm shot to her voicemail. It's almost four o'clock in LA; she'd be leaving one of her auditions.

"Hey, babe, hope you slayed it. I must have missed you but let me know how it went. Love you."

I buzz Leo but he's also not answering. I shoot him a quick e-mail:

Dinner until prob 10pm. Meet me at the Sony party after?

I stand up in the darkened hotel room, arch my back, groan, then peel off the dank airplane clothes and head toward the shower.

Spencer wants me to handshake with Marvin and Steven Feinberg. ("Marv" and "Steve" if you know them.) Tatum had told me insider stories about Marvin that would curl your hair (involving but not limited to casting couches, bribery, blackmail, and some vague, potential felonies), but there is no one hotter right now, and if Marvin fucking Feinberg wants to shake my hand and butter my bread, I'm certainly not going to spurn him. Welcome to Hollywood, baby, where half your job is deciding how to shave slivers off your moral compass while still keeping it just enough in check for it to guide you toward superstardom.

∾

Spencer put Leo's name on the guest list, so the bouncer informs me that he's already arrived when we roll in around eleven p.m.

I wade through a sea of half-dressed starlets who look both angular and bored, shake hands with a few executives who assure me of my greatness, stop for a quick catch-up with James Austin, inarguably the hottest actor around right now. I'm considering penning a Kennedy biopic that focuses on his assassination—*One Day in Dallas* is my working title. He tells me he might be game, to send it to him when it's done. When he meanders off to fawn over a girl who looks no more than eighteen, it's hard not to puff out my chest, feel the rush of confidence that comes from playing in the big leagues, of orbiting in this kind of stratosphere. I'm Hollywood's It boy. Fuck it, I enjoy it.

I find Leo in the corner, lounging on a purple velvet couch, his arm draped on an actress who won a Golden Globe a few years back. Tatum and I had watched the show together, and I remember Tatum saying: "Good for her. She's so untalented, this is a real coup." I laughed so hard at the backhanded compliment that I had to run to the sink and spit out my drink.

"Dude," he shouts, leaping to his feet. "Where have you been? Have you met Mina?"

"No." I extend my hand. "Nice to meet you, Mina."

She curls her face into something like a constipated smile, then removes a vial from her purse and eyeballs my brother.

"Be right back," he says. "Don't move. I'll never find you again."

"Leo . . ." I feel the blood flush my cheeks. Too much booze I can ignore, I can even indulge in; drugs are a more dangerous territory for a mostly buttoned-up me.

"Don't be a prude, man. It's coke. Big fucking deal."

"Since when do you do coke?"

He shrugs. "I don't. No time like the present."

"Come on," I say. "Let's get a drink. Don't start with this shit."

"Just a line or two."

"How the fuck do you know what just a line or two is or will do?"

He shrugs again. "I'm not a kid anymore, Ben. I get to make my own choices." He brushes past me, then turns. "Don't look at me like that."

"Like what?" I ask.

"Like Dad," he says. "Right now, you look exactly fucking like Dad. So don't."

I want to say a million things, like: *He wasn't perfect, but he actually knew a thing or two, and if I could look or act even fractionally like him, it would be a blessing,* or, *Don't shit on his grave by being an asshole tonight and snorting away his memory,* or, *Come on, Leo, I love you, man.*

But I say none of this. I'm not my dad, and even if I were anything close, he mostly parented with tough love that I don't have in me at eleven p.m. at a Hollywood party in Toronto where everyone is singing of my genius. Leo detects this momentary weakness and salutes me, and then disappears into a crowd of people who aren't too different from me: along for the ride, unsure where they're going, unsure of where they'll land when the carousel stops but willing to take the chance anyway.

28

TATUM

SEPTEMBER 2012

The road trip seemed like a good idea when I proposed it. *Let's drive to Texas like we did years ago! Bring Joey! It will be the perfect way to spend Labor Day weekend, the last gasp of vacation before I have to report to work.*

I was due in Austin the first week of September, not ideal timing because Joey was starting a new school for pre-K, and I'd have to fly to LA for the morning drop-off, then fly right back to Texas to make the day on set. But the Oscar win had given me all sorts of clout, and when the studio told me I could direct the little project I'd agreed to star in—nothing big, just a fifteen-million-dollar gimme about *Roe v. Wade* that won't generate a huge box office but will generate some critical praise (if I direct it correctly, as I intend to, of course)—I wasn't about to turn it down because I'd be jetting back and forth for day one of school.

I've forgotten how hot it is, in these canyons through Arizona, how boring hours on end trapped in the back seat can be for a four-year old.

Ben is driving because I am returning e-mails on my phone, when Joey starts whining again that he's hungry. I hand him a granola bar, which he throws on the floor. I hand him a ziplock bag of Cheerios, which he whips open and dumps on the floor. I pass him an apple juice, which seems to placate him for a hot second, and then he squeezes the box and turns the straw into a fountain, which sprays Ben on the back of his neck. He's been going through this phase—we call it the terrible fours—where he pushes our buttons to see whom he can set off first. It's always Ben, who tells me I try to be too much of Joey's friend, while he's left playing the heavy, the bad cop, the enforcer, which just makes Joey press his buttons all over again.

"Jesus Christ!" Ben barks, swerving momentarily across the yellow line of the mostly deserted highway.

I place a hand on his leg, try to calm him. He's been this way for the full year and ensuing months since Leo died: like a live grenade that, if touched the wrong way, could detonate without warning.

"I want French fries!" Joey shrieks. "French fries!"

I type "McDonald's" into the map on my phone, but service is terrible, and my in-box tells me that e-mails from the past hour have not gone through. Locating a McDonald's isn't happening for the foreseeable future.

"We'll find you McDonald's, Jojo," I say. "But you have to hang in there."

Ben sighs audibly, as if he can't believe I'm placating this shit. I shouldn't be. Probably. But we're in the middle of nowhere, and the kid wants McDonald's, so this doesn't feel like the hill (or mountain canyon) I want to die on.

"How long?" Joey crosses his arms. With his angry red cheeks brought on by repeatedly lowering the window, gasping at the whoosh of heat, then raising it again, he looks just like my father used to when he'd come home drunk.

"I don't know, buddy, but try to go to sleep. That will make it go by faster."

He narrows his eyes at me, suspicious. Like time can't go by faster than time can go by. He's not wrong. Like Ben and I wouldn't will this horrific year to fast-forward until his grief has abated, until we've recalibrated and found our way back to normal.

"Remember when we did this?" I say to Ben, who has turned the radio up too loud in an effort to signal to Joey that we won't be held hostage to his complaining, that we can possibly drown it out. I notch the dial down again, and Ben glances toward me as if to say: *I don't want to hear his whining, so please don't give him a voice.* "Remember how we ran out of gas?"

"How *you* ran out of gas," he says, without the humor to match my own.

"It was fun!" I poke his side, and he adjusts just a tiny flicker of a movement away from me. He's doing this more often now, pulling away, flinching as if he were in pain. He *is* in pain, though, so I try not to take it personally. Even though, of course, it is personal. Our greatest strength had always been that we saw in each other exactly what the other needed, that we could intuit it without words, without anything other than being in the other's presence. Now, who knows what Ben needs? Not me. Because he won't let me see him, because he doesn't try to see me. I tell myself that maybe I brought this on us: like he senses that I deceived him with Leo, and this is my just reward.

I pull my hand away from him now, rest it back in my lap. Maybe I deserve his coolness; I could have done better by him, could have told him the truth, even if he's not aware of my deception. Maybe he is, in the way that we always understood each other. Maybe now he knows, without even knowing it, that I have done him wrong.

"I seem to remember that I reminded you about ten times to fill up the tank," he says, as we curve around a bend.

"But if we had, I'd never have given you such a perfect story for the script you'll write for me one day." My voice is too light. I can hear myself trying too hard.

I see something clench in his jaw. This is a sticking point between us—how many times I've asked; how many times he's deflected. I probably should have just let it rest since we're trapped in a car together until we reach McDonald's or wherever we pull off because Joey can't take it for another second. Ben dropped out of *Code Emergency* in the spring, despite its huge ratings for Fox, despite its multiyear pickup, which was almost unprecedented. He didn't want to write "some bullshit hospital garbage," he said. He didn't want to waste the best years of his life on "fucking shitty TV." I'd said fine. I'd said, "Do whatever you have to in order to be happy," but Ben was like a weathervane on a windy day, spinning back and forth with no direction at all, no idea whatsoever what *would* make him happy. So I'd propose writing something for *me*, and unlike when we used to banter about how it could be our *something great* we'd do together, now he just tells me that he doesn't want to ride on my coattails, that he doesn't want people to think that I'm the only reason the project had wings. If I argue, he'll remind me that I once said the very same thing to him back in my early years. And then he usually leaves the room to pour himself a drink.

So now he's not writing; he's not doing much of anything that I'm aware of.

"Are you thinking of sending *Reagan* back out again?" I asked one night a few weeks ago while we were in bed, each reading our own material. Him: yet another book recounting the Reagan-Bush years; me: the *Roe v. Wade* script I was highlighting and annotating for prep work.

"No one wants it." He shrugged, his eyes not leaving the page. "Spencer said that: 'It's dead, for fuck's sake, Ben, it's fucking dead.'"

"Maybe this new bio will give you fresh material, a new angle?"

He stopped then and looked at me. "It's dead, Tatum, OK? Let it go."

I wanted to say: *I have, but what about you?*

But we don't have these discussions anymore, not when my suggestions seem like an affront to him, not when my success has outpaced his to the point where neither one of us can ignore it. I've never thought that Ben has begrudged my ambition, but maybe he's begrudged how I have gotten lucky when he hasn't, when each of us worked as hard as the other, and yet I was the one who got the accolades in the end; I was the one who has been anointed with the Oscar. I don't say this to minimize my acclaim, but luck is some of it, to be sure, and in that respect, surprisingly, after so many years of a bad streak, mine broke the other way. Ben's did not.

But rather than spiral into another argument, I eased out from under the duvet to check on Joey, then to e-mail my assistant about my schedule for the next day: whom I had to meet for lunch, whom I had to e-mail and in what order of importance, where I could steal time to shop online for new school clothes for Joey. I still liked to maintain some sense of normalcy, be a mom like every other mom preparing for her child to start pre-K.

And then, because we can all be our own worst enemies, I'd google my name and remind myself of all the things that people hated about me and all the rumors that were nothing more than fiction but flamed my cheeks and accelerated my pulse all the same. You'd think I'd have more armor now, less insecurity. Sometimes I do. Sometimes, though, because my vulnerability is a requirement for my craft, I'm exactly who I was at sixteen, with my drunk father and sick mother and lonely nights working the register at the pharmacy.

On the web, there were rumors of me engaged in a texting romance with Colin Farrell (whom I viscerally loathed when we worked together on *Pride and Prejudice*), rumors of Ben canoodling with an ex-girlfriend. I lingered on that one for more than a beat, but though Ben may have been discontent over the past year—his middling career, the catastrophe with Leo—he wasn't disloyal. Also, it wasn't like he had the energy or the will to canoodle anyway. I clicked the *X* on the tab and forgot about it: another made-up story about a life that had nothing to do with mine.

I sat in the darkness of my office, illuminated by the glow of my desktop, and told myself to go talk to him. Go tell him that I understood that *Reagan* was really a love letter to his dad; I understood that Reagan had been Paul's hero. That Paul had a signed, framed letter from the president expressing admiration of a case that he had won, and that the signed, framed letter was now collecting dust in Ben's own office. I understood that Ben couldn't move past this script until he moved past the fact that he wasn't going to bring the film to life and that his dad really had no ownership over him, especially a decade after he died.

But none of this felt kind to say to Ben now. Maybe before Leo I'd have spoken up, told him that he wasn't any type of failure, not to his dad, not to me. But now I simply slipped out of bed to hide in my own office. My own secret built a wall between us, and only in my honesty—telling him that *he couldn't have known about Leo because Leo worked so hard to deceive him*—would I free him. But then I also knew that my honesty would undo us; he wouldn't forgive me just as he hadn't forgiven himself.

Today in the car in the canyons of Arizona, Joey is still whimpering, so I pass him a coloring book and crayons, urging him to hold the crayon as I've taught him, as Constance has shown him. He grabs at it with his full fist and scribbles.

"The school isn't going to be happy." I sigh, turning back to Ben. "He's still going to need OT."

He snorts, shakes his head. "Our not-even-five-year-old is in therapy because he doesn't hold his crayon properly. Welcome to LA, man."

"Well, I mean, breaking that arm didn't help. Set him back, those muscles all regressing." I stare ahead at the wide expanse of rock ahead. "I'll just tell them that. Say he was in a cast for two months."

"Tatum," Ben says. "Seriously, who gives a fuck?"

I glance to Joey, who is rapt in his coloring and hasn't picked up on Ben's use of "fuck," which I have repeatedly implored him to tamp down on in front of the baby, as Joey is prone to repeating it at the top of his voice in the most public of places. Which lends to excellent tabloid fodder. *What Sort of Mom Is Tatum Connelly? Her Son Yells "F*ck" in Gelson's!*

But Ben has said it intentionally, to pick a fight, and though I feel myself bristle at his churlishness, I don't want to take his bait. I want to cruise around the winding corners of the Arizona landscape and remember how we tucked ourselves under the blankets in the back seat of our SUV and watched all the stars light up the blackened sky. And that he promised, one day, he'd write about it for me.

I look at Ben, and he sighs remorsefully. We're not so disconnected, he and I. Not yet, not ever.

"I'm sorry," he says. "I don't mean to take it out on you."

"I know," I say. I reach over and squeeze his shoulder, let my hand linger there, as if I can heal him with my touch. He doesn't pull back this time, rather angles his head closer to me. I smile and breathe that in.

"That was a nice night," he says. "When you were so stubborn that we ran out of gas."

I laugh, and it feels good in my belly, feels like it echoes and reverberates all the way to my soul.

"Jojo," Ben says, looking in the rearview mirror. "Let's go find a McDonald's. You want a Happy Meal?"

"Daddy!" he exclaims. "I *always* want a Happy Meal!"

"Me too," I say to Joey. "I *always* want a Happy Meal too."

I wait for Ben to reply, to join in on the momentary joy. He is lost again somewhere, gone for the moment, tucked into his head where he scurries more often now, where I have to reach further in to pull him back to me.

"Ben," I say. "You want a Happy Meal too, right?"

"What?" His eyes find mine. "Oh, of course, buddy. Happy Meals for happy campers."

Then he turns the radio back up, and we lose ourselves under the shadow of the red rock mountains.

29

BEN

JUNE 2002

Leo is his best self at his college graduation. Sober, shining, electric. After my dad, Leo's had his good days, and his less good days, but he was a senior and allowed to get wasted and wake up with a wicked, gut-churning hangover, so I didn't hover, and my mom was busy with her new charity, dedicated to raising funds for the families of 9/11 victims, so neither of us judged his bad days. Or, maybe more accurately, neither of us was present enough to judge them. You could see them in bruises under his eyes, in his half smile when recounting a memory of some stupid story or antic that he wasn't sure he was getting quite right because he couldn't remember it fully, or the way that he sometimes really needed a shower. But Leo was Leo, born with an impish streak, and he showed up at Sunday family dinners—a tradition Tatum had suggested in January when it was clear we all needed a bit of glue—cogent, present, hilarious. He could make my mom drop her head back and cackle, and we didn't get that too often these days, so we let him go on being whoever he was.

Today, he is the brightest star in a sea of blue gowns washing over the Columbia campus. It's an overcast June day, sticky with threatening clouds, which is just as well. Every crisp spring and summer day reminds me of that crisp day in September—the air smells the same, the sun shines the same, and I'm happy for the gray skies whenever they present themselves. My leg is jittery, more out of habit than because I feel on edge. It started after that day: a tic, I guess, like my body is out of my mind's control. Tatum rests her palm on my thigh, as if she can absorb some of its fire.

"Well, this is a lot of pomp and circumstance," she whispers into my ear.

"To be fair, no one really knew if he was going to graduate," I reply, and she laughs, and my mom glances over and smiles like she is glad we are laughing but not quite sure of the joke. She looks that way often these days.

"No one made this much of a fuss for me last week," Tatum says.

"I did," I whisper back and kiss her forehead.

She nods because she knows I did, in my own way.

Tatum had her own graduation from Tisch just eight days ago. She hadn't wanted a to-do, didn't invite her dad, didn't want Piper to spend the money on a plane ticket. I wondered if it wasn't about her mom not being there to celebrate, but she said, "I have to get used to celebrating a lot of things without her, Ben. I just want to get this over with, move to LA, start our new lives."

She wasn't being a martyr or anything. She was just being practical, pragmatic. An oxymoron for an actress, but that was Tatum all the same. Able to compartmentalize her grief while also recognizing how much it shaped her, shifted her insides. So Leo and I sat through the graduation ceremony and whooped when her name was called, and afterward we went to the Corner Bistro and ate hamburgers, and then we boxed up her kitchenware and a few more items from her student apartment, and Leo jetted uptown. We were dusty and achy by the time we climbed into bed, and Tatum said: "This was perfect. I just want to get busy living life." But she was jittery in the way that my leg was, figuratively staring at the horizon, awaiting whatever comes next, tucking our respective blights behind us.

Now Leo is called onstage to collect his diploma, and my mom weeps, though she would have wept with or without my dad here, so I ease my arm around her and squeeze her shoulder.

"He would have been so proud of Leo," she says, wiping her nose with a tissue.

"Yes," I say, because that's all I can manage.

Leo has a job lined up after graduation as a trader at Merrill Lynch, exactly as my dad wanted. He starts in July, so he wants to come bum around California with us before his training, though I haven't acquiesced. It will be chaos, for one thing: the move, the unpacking, the settling down. I don't need my tornado of a brother there stirring up the winds. He tells me he'll be on his best behavior, but I'd cleaned up enough of Leo's messes over the years—the pot in high school, phone calls to me at college to ask how to cajole money out of my mom or appease my dad's temper when Leo had been busted again for drinking at some kid's house, the summer camp he got kicked out of after my parents tired of him starting figurative and literal fires at the house in Vermont—to know that while Leo might promise the moon, he'll often never even glance up at the sky. And my dad wouldn't want me to let him off the hook with all his shit, wouldn't want him to come out to LA and sleep with beautiful women and drink too many vodka shots and act like he could be careless and not face consequences. I was never careless, because it was clear to me that carelessness was unacceptable. Leo nearly always was because he didn't care how angry it made my dad.

Also, I'll be busy, too busy, to entertain him. Actually to mind him, since Leo always manages to plant his nose in trouble. He's grown now, and it's not my job to keep him out of it, but I also don't need him sleeping on my couch while stirring it up either. *Romanticah* propelled me into studio meetings, executive handshakes. I've already finished the working draft of my next script, *All the Men*, and it's been green-lit in a hurry to capitalize on the hottest, latest thing bursting on the Hollywood scene. We shoot in September, which means there is a frantic rush for rewrites, tweaks, notes from the studio that aren't smart or particularly savvy but which I have learned to say yes to because arguing only sucks up time and energy that I don't have, between Tatum and Leo and my dad.

It's exhilarating, this validation. It's moving so furiously that I can barely process it. And all the trappings of Hollywood's approval are not unwelcome. My father had long told me that being the best was the only goal to reach for, and now that I'm here, anointed and on top, I can understand exactly what he meant, why he pushed me. The success feels addictive, like a high of a drug I've never taken, so I work harder, longer, more, chasing it even as it chases me.

Also, we are getting married. There is a wedding to plan.

I explain all of this to Tatum, that Leo in California will be one more thing I'll have to monitor, and I simply can't. My insides are dry and barren and a bit of a wasteland.

"I don't mind," she says. "He can keep me company."

"I don't think you get it—Leo is a handful."

"He's not a toddler," she laughs.

"Worse. He's an adult with toddler instincts."

"Like he's not potty-trained?"

"Like, hide the matches because he might burn the house down," I say. "Besides, you'll be busy on your own, setting the town on fire."

"True," she says. "True. I guess we'll just have to wear fire-retardant clothes at all times."

Today Leo wants to walk home from Columbia, though it's at least two and a half miles to my mom's, and the clouds are drizzling thick, pregnant drops. A plane roars over us, too close, and I jolt, and he does too, but then it coasts past, and we shake our heads and keep going.

"You do that too," he says. "I don't know how to get used to it."

"I think with time."

"I hate this city," he says.

"Leo . . ." We've had this discussion a million times. He has to work, he has a job, he needs to show up and be accountable. College is over; it's time to embrace real life.

"I know," he says, batting a hand. "Don't start in with me. I know, OK? I can't quit on Merrill before I've even started. I get it. I'm a big kid now, time to cut the purse chains."

We amble in silence for a while after that, then stop in a bar, Westside Tavern, on Amsterdam Avenue.

Leo primarily wants to get drunk, and that sounds like as good a plan as any.

The place is mostly empty. A European soccer game is muted on the TV above the bar, and we pull up stools, then I order two beers, then Leo says: "Also, four shots of tequila."

"Leo, it's three o'clock in the afternoon."

"And your point is?"

I don't really have a point, so I do both shots and chase it with the beer.

"Maybe I'll just stay in California," he says, as he motions to the bartender for two more. I wave to the bartender to stop, to please cut me off, but he shrugs and slides the shot glasses our way. "I can still be a grown-up in California." But he wants to surf in the mornings and sleep on our couch in the afternoons. He explains this when he's actually being honest, which we are about two shots away from.

"Don't you have a graduation party later?" I shift the subject.

"Yeah, and?"

"You're going to show up wasted?"

"Yeah, and?" He laughs. "God, when did you become Dad?"

He stops laughing abruptly, and both of us reach for the shots, since the alternative is weeping or picking a fight or pounding our fists into the wall, which feels like it would help with the rage, but mostly also seems like it would just fill one form of pain with another. Drinking is the right solution.

"You can't skip out on your job, Leo," I say, as the tequila burns the back of my throat, the pulp of the lime fleshy on my tongue.

"Why not? Who gives a fuck?"

"I guess I do?" I say it as a question because it is, and also because I'm drunk, but mostly because I've never had to care one way or the other about my brother's irresponsibility. But now, with my dad gone, it occurs to me that I do.

"Ugh," he says. "So you're the new Leo police."

"Come on, Dad never busted your ass the way he busted mine."

He snorts. "You were the prodigal son, give me a break. Bust your ass! Like he ever did that a day in your life."

I pick up the rind of the lime and chew on it. I haven't eaten anything since breakfast, and I'm newly aware that I'm as hungry as I am inebriated.

"It's funny," I say. "I think we both thought that. I always thought the same about you. That he was easier on you because you didn't give a shit."

Leo gulps in too much air.

"I fucking miss him." He drops his forehead to the bar, and his shoulders start shaking, and it takes my woozy mind a moment to catch up and realize that he is crying. *No no, let's go punch a wall. Let's not feel this pain as we need to feel it. It's too acute. It will gut us, spill too much blood for us to recover. My dried-up insides can't bleed another ounce.*

I put a hand on his back until his jagged breathing becomes more steady, and then he wipes his nose on the sleeve of his gown, which is exactly what he'd do when he was little and my parents would make me babysit for him, and we'd watch TV while he wiped boogers on himself. Not so much has changed in the span of a decade or so, I realize. Leo still needs someone to look out for him: rub his back, wipe his nose.

I ask for the check and resolve right then that it will be me.

30

TATUM

JULY 2013

From: Ben Livingston
To: Amanda Paulson
Re: things
Date: April 10, 2013

A—listen, god, this is probably the hardest thing I've ever written. But, well, you know that I've been struggling lately, I just, ok, here goes: I think we should probably take a break. I'm typing that and it doesn't seem right or maybe none of this seems real. I don't know. I'm so fucked up now, and I want you. You know how much I want you. But there are all these stories in the press now, and if Tatum finds out . . .
I don't know what I want yet, and if this explodes before I've figured it out . . .

Jesus, this is the most inarticulate thing I've ever written, and that's saying a lot.
I want you. I need you. I just don't know what to do about it.
What do you think?
—B

From: Amanda Paulson
To: Ben Livingston
Re: re: things
Date: April 10, 2013

B—I understand. You know I do. But I do have to be honest and say that being with you again, well, it made me realize what an idiot I was back in New York, and if there's any way that I can keep you in my life, selfishly, I want that. I need that. I don't know how to undo this past year. I don't know how to turn this off. Does that sound overdramatic? I don't mean it to be. I only mean that you're so easy to love, and I can't help but feel like the only thing we've had wrong is our timing, our chronology.
—A

From: Ben Livingston
To: Amanda Paulson
Re: re: re: things
Date: April 10, 2013

A—want to meet for a drink tonight at Sunset Tower and discuss? Maybe it will feel better if we do it in person.
—B

I am only on Ben's laptop because I forgot my charger in LA, and Ben's is fully juiced and open and available, and Stephanie, my assistant, can't FedEx me the charger until tomorrow because FedEx doesn't make Sunday deliveries, and there is not an Apple store anywhere near Canton, and the electronics store at the mall is out of stock. So, all of this to say that I'm not even supposed to be on Ben's laptop.

We're back home for Piper's baby shower, and I was looking forward to a weekend of just being Piper's big sister, not Tatum the movie star, not Tatum the Great. Everything was so much more complicated now, with this big life up for public consumption. Ben has left his computer atop our bed when he went for a run, and it doesn't even occur to me that I shouldn't log on, that there is anything illicit to be found, that Ben might have a secret just as I do. Though a different one, of course. He has been writing again (sprawled all morning on the bed, pecking away, occasionally glancing toward me when I pop my head in and say, "How's it going?" and giving me a thumbs-up); he's been exercising again. We've been making love from time to time. He's even willing to read a script or two for me when I'm deciding what to tackle for my winter projects.

I'm in the thick of an HBO miniseries right now—a modern take on Agatha Christie (TV is suddenly hot, even for an Oscar winner), and then perhaps another directorial project, *Love Runs Through It*, to follow up *Roe v. Wade*, which I haven't even officially put to bed. I've been offered Broadway, but with Joey in school, I can't uproot him to New York, and who wants to be in New York for the winter anyway? Maybe over the summer. I'd proposed that to Ben: *New York over the summer, and we can revisit all the old haunts? Do you think that Dive Inn is even still there? What about that cream puff store we used to love?* He hesitated, said it depended on his own work, and I nodded and said, *Of course,* and then chastised myself because I was trying to remind myself, or at least remind Ben, that my work didn't trump his, even when part of me thought that it did. Even when, intentionally or not, I did put my work first; I did forget him in my Oscar speech. Daisy had suggested that maybe he just felt emasculated, maybe that was the reason for his funk, and I'd figured if I danced around my own successes, downplayed them enough, massaged his brilliance enough, I could reverse that.

"You shouldn't have to apologize for your success," she'd said. "I mean, you haven't been perfect about all of it, but success, nope, you can't begrudge yourself that."

We were out power walking in the hills behind our house, my hat pulled low so no one would recognize me, her huge black sunglasses imploring someone to recognize her. My weight these days was a constant battle; you'd think that industry acclaim meant that five or ten pounds was forgivable, but if anything it only got worse. There was constant scrutiny, not just with the gossip on my life and the candids in the tabloids, but nearly everywhere I went now. Going out to dinner was a chore: there were eyeballs and stares, and inevitably, someone stopped by the table for an autograph. There'd been a stalker concern recently, a lanky oddball in his twenties who loitered outside the house and yelled lewd things at my car window every time I came and went. Finally, I hired security, who had him arrested. Dropping Joey at school was a dance with the other mothers, who pretended they hadn't just seen my face on some blog like Dlisted, and I pretended that they weren't pretending. I was sized up in the line at Starbucks, sized up in wardrobe on sets. Even Luann, my publicist, would look me up and down and raise her eyebrows and say, "Darling, I love you, but no one loves a chubby girl." I almost fired her right then, but she'd just booked me the *Vogue* cover, which I needed to starve myself for anyway.

"I'm not apologizing for my success," I said to Daisy between breaths. "I just think . . . Ben's had a shitty time, you know? With Leo, with his dad, all of that."

"I don't mean to sound like a bitch, but his dad was a decade ago. And the Oscar thing? Two years ago."

"I didn't say anything about the Oscar thing. Ben never even mentioned it."

"Listen, I get it, it's terrible. Terrible things happen all the time. When does he stop carrying that around?"

"He's been so much better recently." I stopped and flopped over, touched my toes. "He's back on *Code Emergency* . . . he even went birdwatching with my dad last weekend."

Daisy considers this. "Well, I gotta give anyone points who is willing to go birdwatching with anyone."

I right myself, aim my arms toward the sky, arch my back, and groan. Then softly: "I never told him about that night at Harbor. I mean . . . I never told him that Leo had relapsed."

"So that's what this is about. This guilt, your apologies."

"Leo asked me not to, and Ben had been so unkind toward my dad, and I just . . . I just wanted to prove Ben wrong, that people *can* get better and change. If Ben had known . . . I just felt like he would somehow be vindicated. Not that he wanted Leo to relapse. But just that . . . I don't know . . ." I sigh, turn my face toward the breeze blowing in from the west. "I guess I was certain Leo would clean up, and then what harm did it do, not telling Ben?"

"You couldn't get Leo better any more than you can heal Ben," she says. "That's not your responsibility. You've gotten used to doing things your way, Tate. But this isn't one of those things. This was Leo's thing."

But what if it were my thing, what if it were Ben's too? I wanted to say, but she had already loped ahead of me.

240

Today, in my old bedroom in my old home, where I entertained plenty of what-ifs when my childhood took turn after turn, I wonder if Daisy wasn't right, and I wonder how I can possibly change, let go, if she is. In fact, I'd opened Ben's laptop to search his e-mail for Dr. Paulson's follow-up report on how long Joey might have residual arm pain: he'd stumbled on a rock and fallen in my mom's garden and was whining about his wrist now. Piper had assured me that he was fine—she's a nurse, after all—but I couldn't take her advice; I had to solve it for myself.

But I don't find that e-mail. What I find is something so unexpected that it's literally as if my heart is seizing. I read and reread the e-mail, then all of the e-mails with the name "Paulson" that litter his deleted files folder. They date back to last May. And that's when I fit the puzzle pieces together: Ben didn't even tell me she was *that* Amanda. Not at the hospital, not after.

I check and recheck the dates of the exchange when he says he wants to end it: three months ago. Where was I three months ago? I scroll through the calendar on my phone because I need a calendar on my phone to keep track of my life now. At Legoland. At goddamn Legoland for the evening with the crew of *America*, a reward for those grueling night shoots, for enduring the lecherous looks of the director, Ronnie Slater, who liked to finish a take by yelling something like: *That was so good that my dick got hard just watching,* or *Tatum, you're so fucking hot that it's all I can do not to beat off right here behind the monitor.* I'd told Ben that the event was just for cast and crew, spouses weren't coming. But that wasn't true. A handful of wives and husbands caravanned down with us to San Diego for the festivities. But I had lied to Ben because it was the easier thing to do. Tote him along, watch him fumble with small talk, worry if he was having fun, worry if I were giving him enough attention. I just wanted this to be *mine*, as small and as insignificant as one stupid night at Legoland was.

It occurs to me that I probably just could have said that: *Do you mind if I do this last thing with the crew without you? You can come, but would it be OK if I went on my own?*

Ben has never begrudged me my independence, because he knew I'd show up when he needed me, and he probably would have just shrugged and said, *Sure.* He hated theme parks anyway. And yet I lied, maybe to be a little spiteful, maybe because he'd been distant enough that it was a test—to see if he'd notice, to see if he was paying close enough attention.

I close his e-mail quickly, and then I race to the bathroom where I spent hours examining my face as a teenager, trying to line my eyes just so to make them alluring, trying to scrub my skin so it shined like those Noxzema ads I saw. I heave over the toilet, purging what little I'd allowed myself for breakfast. A wisp of a memory makes its way in, as I ease down to the floor, trying to catch my breath.

IHOP. The endless silver dollar pancakes and the look of surprise on Julie Seymour's face when she recognized me.

Back here, so many years ago. God, we'd been so happy then. How do you go from there to here? How does one moment in a lifetime of moments completely detonate the foundation you'd rested your existence on? Not that we hadn't been better recently. We had been. He was writing more; I was around more often. We had dinners with Joey and sometimes evening walks too. We weren't all sharp edges about my dad or misinterpreted words about his career or my time commitments or whatever it was that we found to argue about.

I hear Ben in the bedroom and shut the bathroom door quickly with my foot.

"Tate?" he calls. "Back from my run."

"OK."

"I was gonna shower, you almost done in there?"

"Almost," I say. If this had been years back, if this had been IHOP, when we were so hot for each other that we screwed in the rental car's back seat in the grocery store parking lot, like I had in high school, a random moment in time that had granted us Jocy, I'd have ushered him into the bathroom with me, slipped into the shower with him to feel his skin pressed against mine.

Now, I try to slow my racing heart and say, "Give me another minute. Then I'll be done."

I pull myself up, meet my own eyes in the mirror that has reflected my face back a million times, and tell myself that I already harbor one secret. Maybe if I keep this to myself, I can make it right, I can fix it on my own. We were doing better now; who we used to be half a decade ago at that IHOP didn't feel so far, too far, in the distance that we couldn't get it back. Ben was coming back to me, or maybe I was moving back to him, but we were starting to *see* each other again in ways that were ephemeral but tangible too.

Or maybe that was me misreading the script.

Still, I'm not willing to abandon us yet, not when I can envision how we can get it all back. So yes, I will tuck this away, right the ship, bring Ben back to me, bring me back to Ben. This is just one more secret between us. One more role I will myself to play.

31

BEN

SEPTEMBER 2001

The only reason I'm awake is because Tatum had an early class and set off the fire alarm when she tried to fry bacon before leaving.

"Shit, shit, sorry," she said, scrambling around her tiny studio, flopping an oven mitt toward the smoke, batting down the alarm with a broom handle. The plastic cover popped off and crashed to the floor, where it promptly split in two. Tatum jumped like she hadn't expected that, for gravity to work, and then her apartment was silent again, other than the sizzle of the torched bacon.

"Shit," she said again. "Go back to sleep. I didn't mean to wake you."

I'd been up too late in the edit bay, splicing together the final cut of *Romanticah* before I sent it out into the festival world, praying someone will take notice and give me my shot.

"It's fine," I said, rubbing my eyes, waving her closer. "I promised Tom I'd read two manuscripts today anyway."

"You're seriously the best assistant agent he could hope for. Two books in a day?" She shook her head and kissed me, hovering over the bed so her tank top fell low and offered me a view.

"Now how am I supposed to concentrate with *that* on my mind?"

She straightened and laughed, low and husky, and I leaned back against her headboard, my arms folded behind my head, and matched her grin. The first two months since her mom died were a spiral of gray, everything muted, everything numb. She kissed me because she loved me, and she sometimes (not as often as before) slept with me because that's what you do, but she wasn't *here* here. She didn't eat enough, and she nearly got fired from the bar because she kept mouthing off to customers, but slowly she'd come back. I didn't know if she would, though I never dared say that. Those words were never worth the damage they would have inflicted. I'd give her space, and she'd tell me I didn't care. I'd try to talk to her, and she'd tell me I was hovering. Then she'd cry and say it wasn't me, it was her fucking grief, and that I was the best thing about her life, and to please forgive her for being such a bitch. And of course I was going to forgive her for that.

I didn't understand it, though, her moodiness, her push/pull. Daisy explained that all actresses (herself included) are basically nuts, so get used to it. But that was too easy, too pat an explanation. So Daisy said that Tatum must trust me in order to show me all her ugliness, to not try to dress up her grief into something rosier or shinier or easier, and then I understood: she was letting me inside her, and for me to stand by her, to sit with her, was enough.

But now she is coming back to me. Her classes help, I know. The structure of having a planned day, the lightness of becoming someone else for a few hours. Someone whose mom hadn't died. Someone whose dad wasn't a fucking mess. And time too, though it had been only three months.

This morning she'd said, "If you keep this in mind long enough, I'll be back from class, and then—"

"Then what?" I laughed.

"Then it will just be your lucky day, I guess," she said, her hand on the front door. Then she was gone.

By the time I shower and scrub the burned pot she'd abandoned on the stove, it's nearly nine a.m. Her coffeemaker is broken, like many other things in the apartment, so I slide on my flip-flops, thump down the building's concrete stairwell to the cart on the corner. It's a perfect, cloudless September day. Crisp breezes. Powder blue skies. As if this is our reward for suffering through the sweltering days of August. It does kind of feel like my lucky day, actually. My editing session had gone well; I'm getting paid by a top literary agent to read early manuscripts. My girlfriend is smiling again and wants to screw me tonight.

I pay for the coffee, slide my headphones into my ears, and decide to take a walk. Stretch my legs. Enjoy the fall air. The caffeine electrifies my blood, and I resolve to do this every day. *Self*, I say, *do this every day! Rise early. Kiss your sexy girlfriend good-bye. Start the day with some exercise to pump some energy into your veins! You are young! You are virile! It is going to be your goddamn lucky day!*

Three police cars race by me so quickly that I can literally feel the wind off their wake. Two fire engines roar to life behind me, flying around the corner, startling a woman next to me such that she jumps and slaps her hand to her heart. I fiddle with my Walkman radio where the DJs are talking about a small plane that has hit the World Trade Center. I halt quickly at that, peer around to see if anyone else is hearing what I'm hearing, but the morning rush hour keeps passing by. A Cessna, they're saying. Must have been a total fluke.

I adjust my headphones and start up again. My dad works in the World Trade Center, but what are the odds? These guys probably don't even have it right. A small plane hitting a building?

I shake my head. That can't be.

Through the foam of my earbuds, I can hear sirens suddenly burst from all corners of the city, and this time people around me do stop, their faces registering alarm, like we were all listening to these same radio stations and all thinking *bullshit* but now perhaps realizing that this is not a joke. Not at all funny. The DJs shout in my ear, "There's another plane! Another plane has hit the Towers. Folks, this appears not to be an accident. We can only speculate, of course . . ."

A woman stops next to me, her headphones plugged into her own radio, and grabs my arm.

"Holy shit," she says.

"Oh my God," I reply. Then: "My dad!"

I turn and start running back to Tatum's apartment, my flip-flops not able to match my pace, and I stumble when all I want to do is move faster than I've ever moved in my life. I take the steps two by two, jiggle the shaking key in her lock, and flip on her TV, which, thank God, is working today (it isn't always). I grab the phone and dial my mom.

"Benjamin," she says, out of breath. "He's not there. It's OK. He's on a flight today. Going to San Francisco for a deposition."

I can feel myself uncurl, like the cells in my body had been magnetically bonded together and have been granted release.

"Jesus, Mom, thank God."

"I know, I know, but those poor people," she says, as I find CNN on the dial, the reality of the images worse than I could have imagined even when the DJs were shouting in their mics. "Oh, Ben, call waiting. Let me take this."

I can see a monstrous, foreboding plume of smoke rising from each tower, like a death knell, like the black plague. My dad's firm is on the ninety-ninth floor. I lean over and squint, trying to assess where the planes hit, if he'd know anyone inside.

The commentators are saying things like *intentional* and *terrorist*, and they already have a reporter on the ground. There is debris flying and terrified New Yorkers running, and though the reporter is trying to stay calm, her voice is quavering, and she is coughing into her elbow.

"Get out of there!" I shout to the screen, as if I know her, as if she can hear me. Then I remember: Tatum. She's downtown in class, not too far from the Towers. She doesn't have a cell phone because she is foolish (and tells me she doesn't want another bill to pay). I call her beeper number. I call it again. I try Daisy, but they're not sharing a course load this semester: Daisy is focusing on stage, Tatum on film, and their schedules rarely overlap now.

The CNN anchors press their fingers to their ears. "We are hearing that these were not small planes," one of them says. "They were major airliners. We are talking about a possible hijacking situation."

I feel my stomach rise to my throat, my pulse quickening in my neck.

My dad is on a major airliner.

No. No, no, no, no, no. I just spoke to my mom, and she said he was fine.

I call Tatum's paging service again. *Where is she?*

I rise and open the front door, poke my head out, looking for . . . I don't know, someone, Tatum, a neighbor, to confirm that this is real, this is actually happening, and I'm not completely losing my shit. I should call Leo. I close the door. I should call Leo, and he will tell me that I am being overdramatic and paranoid, because Leo is never overdramatic and paranoid, and he'll make me laugh because I'm such a worrywart of a baby. I'll probably wake him. Fucking college students and their ability to sleep until noon. But I'd promised my dad over the weekend that I'd call him anyway, have a heart-to-heart about his future, try to "get his head on straight."

"He's barely pulling Cs; Bs if he's lucky," my dad said. "Forget about the LSAT, a decent law school."

"That's just Leo," I replied. "Don't worry."

"I'm trying to get him an interview on the trading floor at Merrill." He sighed. "Calling in some favors. He needs to have a plan. He's graduating in nine months. He can't live on our dime forever."

"No law school at all?" I asked. My dad had always wanted him to come on board his firm, especially when it became clear that I wouldn't.

"Maybe a year or two as a trader, then he can transition. He needs to grow up, Ben." I could picture my dad shaking his head like he couldn't imagine how Leo had gotten this far in life without being drafted into clown school.

"He's all right, Dad."

He was silent for a beat. "I know," he said finally. "Of course I know that." He didn't sound like he did, though. "I know I push you hard, Ben, and I know you don't always appreciate it . . ."

I laughed, but not really in a joyful way.

"Anyway, you're making something of yourself," he said. "That's why I do it. And now it's time for your brother to do the same. He's slid by for too long."

"It's because he's so fucking charming," I said.

My dad laughed at that, but this time with true glee, because it was the truth.

I grab the phone now, sink back onto the couch. Just as I start to punch in Leo's number, the CNN reporter starts shouting, running; then a black cloud like nothing I have ever seen rushes toward the camera and overwhelms it. I drop the phone, cover my mouth, let out a scream that bounces off Tatum's small studio walls.

No.

The first tower falls, crumbling like a fragile set of pick-up sticks. I sit there, paralyzed, completely disbelieving what my brain is attempting to register.

Tatum. I need Tatum so very much right now.

The door unlatches behind me, and she steps over the threshold, as if she could hear my spirit calling out.

"Jesus," she says, which comes out more like a wail. "Jesus," she says again, this time crying for real.

The phone rings on the couch where I'd left it. I look at her, she looks at me.

"I don't know who it is," I say. "I'd only been trying to reach you."

I free it from the cradle.

"Ben," my mom shrieks. "Ben! It was his plane! It was his flight!"

"What?" I say, my mouth dry, my stomach already lurching through my throat. *What?*

"Your dad," she screams, a piercing pitch that I'll dream about for years into the future. She breaks down into unintelligible sobs. "He was here this morning. And now he is gone."

32

TATUM

NOVEMBER 2014

Ben wants to spend the day at the beach, Leo's favorite spot, a little north of the lifeguard stand that's just below the drop-off of the cliff near our very first place together. That one-bedroom bungalow on Ocean Avenue.

It's a Thursday, so Joey is at school, and I'm due in the edit bay in the afternoon, tweaking and honing the footage we shot in September and October for *Love Runs Through*, my second directorial feature. Directing means endless hours of prep, of hand holding, of decision making, of administration, of imagination. It distracts me from Ben and Joe, and I know it makes me less of a partner, but the studio offered, and I couldn't say no. Didn't want to say no; I accepted as soon as they called, *on* the call, in fact. Only later that night, when I shared it with Ben—uncorking a bottle of Bordeaux that the agency sent over—did I realize I'd said yes before asking him. He paused, and his jaw flexed in a way that signaled his displeasure, but he raised his glass all the same and said:

"To Tatum. Who always said she would light the world on fire."

He waited until the next morning to ask me how, logistically, this was all going to work, that he knew—and thought I did too—that directing again was going to turn our schedule on its head and that he didn't think it was too much to consult him first.

He was right. Of course he was right, and I was stupid and impulsive and selfish and caught up in the moment with the offer. But part of me was also still angry about the affair with Amanda, though it had been a year, and I checked his e-mails from time to time, and it really did seem to be over. And yet, I bruised him in ways that I knew I could, when I could.

"I'm sorry," I said.

"This isn't the sort of decision you get to make unilaterally."

"I know." I thought of Amanda, and how he had made that decision unilaterally, without me.

"Directing is such a bigger commitment than acting, Tate, and I'm working now too." On *Code Emergency*, which he doesn't care about, not in the way I care about making an impact as a female director in a male-driven industry.

This was an unkind thought, truly unkind, and I blinked, literally blinked, to usher it away.

"I'm sorry," I said, and moved to him. "I got caught up in the moment, and I screwed up."

But today I have my morning, something that I've tried to hold sacred even as the days and years mounted into chaos. Just like all those years ago when Joey was a baby, and I was shooting nights or rushing to a fitting or an audition or a meeting to charm a director into giving me a part, I still did the mornings. Breakfast with Joe, then, when the paparazzi aren't swarming outside the driveway, a drop-off at school.

I hadn't forgotten it was Leo's birthday, and I hadn't forgotten that this was Ben's ritual, and I wanted to be there to support him. Show up. That's what he always needed from me. And I'd failed him in ways both big and small, but we're trying again, because if I dig through our chaos, I find that I still love him. Want to keep building a life with him. Love at this stage of marriage is less concrete, more routine. Not the heady stuff of constant humping and platitudes. It's a pulse inside of me that quickens if I think of being without him, not day to day, but in the grand scope. Of passing Joey off on weekends, of returning to an empty house, of not sharing my joy of landing a gig, of not reading the drafts of his work.

And Ben seems happier too, like sleeping with Amanda exorcised his anger at all the ways his life had diverted from his plan. I'd made a concession to myself that if this is the worst of our betrayals of each other, I could live with it. I'd betrayed Ben in my own way too: by accepting jobs without considering his needs, by stowing the secret of Leo's relapse, by contemplating (albeit briefly) leaving him without ever confronting him about Amanda. I already know why he did it; I understand probably better than most given my profession, given my rocky teen years with my mother's cancer: I understand how healing it can be to slip into another life, another reality, and Ben slipped into his by screwing Amanda.

Piper, whom I told at her baby shower when she caught me crying in the bathroom, couldn't forgive him. Daisy, whom I told when we landed back in LA, suggested that I ride it out, wait for Ben to return to me. "No one can get through life without vices," she'd said as if that made perfect sense, which, to me, it had.

"So don't confront him?" I'd said.

"I'm not married, Tate, I don't know what line I'd draw."

I thought about that long afterward, the lines we all draw in all of our relationships, not just our marriages. How I'd drawn a firm line with my dad and how we'd redrawn it over the years, expanding our boundaries until the original line had all but disappeared. How I'd drawn firm lines with my career and how I'd had to redraw plenty of those too: flirting with scummy directors for parts, appearing on shitty TV shows just to launch myself out of P. F. Chang's. How my mother had drawn and redrawn her line with my father until she finally ran out of ink. Who's to say that my own pen had to be dry simply for Ben's one indiscretion? Who's to say that my own line with Ben wasn't pliable too? I hadn't screwed around with anyone on set, but I hadn't confessed about Leo, and I hadn't explained why I'd pressed Ben for a second baby, though we'd been unable to conceive. I said it was because Piper's ebullience at her shower was infectious, that I wouldn't mind some downtime as a family. But it had really been because of Amanda, because I thought that another baby could bring Ben back to me. So it wasn't like I hadn't shifted my own lines; it wasn't like they weren't plenty malleable too.

Today I let Ben drive because the photographers don't follow his car like they always do mine, and we find a spot not too far from the steps that cross the Pacific Coast Highway and take us right to the sand's edge.

"I just like coming here to remember him," he says. "I want to do it every year."

"OK," I say. "We will."

I think: *I like the sound of that, every year. Our future.*

He hands me his keys, then his phone, and strides ahead of me and reaches the water first. The waves are choppy and bleak, uninviting, which is maybe how it should be, though I think Leo, who was brighter than the shiniest star in the galaxy, would want it some other way. Ben wades in, to his ankles, to his knees, then all the way to his chest. Everyone else out here is in a wetsuit, if they're brave enough to venture in at all.

"Ben!" I shout, though I can hear my voice dissipate in the whoosh of the sea winds. "Ben, come on!"

He arcs his hands above his head and dives under. If he hears me, he doesn't flinch.

I let him sink for as long as he needs to. He'll return to me when he's ready.

჻

He's been out there for fifteen minutes and must be half frozen when his phone buzzes. On instinct, I glance at the screen. Not because I mean to, not because I'm snooping. It simply vibrates in my palm, and I uncurl my hand, and there it is.

Thinking of you today.

Then:

I'm here if you need me.

Blood floods my heart and everything speeds up: the rush of the waves, the sound of the ocean, the footsteps of the jogger behind me, the sway of the palm trees that lurch as I spin around and race to the concrete boardwalk, which may provide surer footing. It can only be one person; this can only mean one thing. I fold myself in half, trying to abort the crest of nausea, the dizziness in my brain.

Ben didn't come back to me like I thought. I inhale and exhale and try to stop the vertigo.

I right myself and draw a line in the sand with my toe. And then I kick it away, gently at first, then angrily, furiously. When I calm myself, I'm surprised to discover that, upon further examination, there is no trace of the line at all.

჻

He heads straight to a warm shower when we get home. Into the cavernous white bathroom that is just off our cavernous white bedroom of the new house we moved into three months ago that was supposed to be our enclave, our safe haven to protect me from that stalker and from the rest of the outside world too. I sit outside the closed door in the nook where he usually writes—his laptop is open, and I consider checking to see what he's been drafting, if he ever got around to writing that bullshit script for me, if he ever even was honest about that. But instead, I simply sit, and I wait. If I don't say something now, even on Leo's birthday, I worry that it will get swallowed up like Ben might have underneath the waves today.

I curl my hands into balls, a familiar release from way back when— from my mom, and Aaron, and my drunk dad, and all the failed auditions and paltry tips at P. F. Chang's and everything in between—and I squeeze my eyes shut just as tightly. I can become anyone I need to be, just like I do in front of the camera, though my pulse beats loudly in my neck and a thin film of sweat forms underneath my armpits, in the crooks of my elbows. Despite my expertise, however, I find I cannot become a woman hiding all these secrets any longer.

He stays in the shower for minutes on end, and it's gotten so late that I nearly run out of time. I won't be late for the edit bay; my work won't suffer for this. It never has. It simply won't. I will tell him. I will compartmentalize this. And then I will go about my day because that is what I've trained myself to do.

"Shit!" Ben yelps, when he opens the bathroom door and sees me on the loveseat. An oversized white towel is knotted around his waist. He's still in shape for forty, still built like he was a decade ago, though everything beneath that exterior has changed. It's a startling realization for me. Every actress constructs her career on matching her insides to her outsides: play a kind prostitute and you wear trashy makeup, ask wardrobe for an extra push-up bra, ensure that your pink manicure is chipping, which might make viewers empathize with your heart of gold. Play a hardened lieutenant but still-loving mom in *Army Women*, and you train until your body fat is down to 8 percent and you dangle a gold necklace with your kids' initials atop your army fatigues.

What we see is always about telling a story until one day you realize that it's not.

"Sorry, shit." Ben holds up a hand. "You just startled me."

"I know about Amanda," I say, quickly, tersely, like it is just another fact that belongs to someone else's life.

"What?"

"I know about her." I stand. "I have since Piper's shower. Back in Ohio. She texted you today, and well . . ." My hands find my hips. "I thought you should know."

"I don't . . ." He opens his mouth, then closes it. "It's over. I mean, it's been over since . . ." He shakes his head. "It's been over since May."

"Don't lie to me after all of this, Ben, please, just don't."

Ben sinks onto the loveseat, the towel splitting into a V atop his legs. He drops his head in his hands. "No, I'm not . . ." He raises his head, his tearful eyes finding mine. "Sometimes she texts me. That's it. It's *over*, Tate. I . . . I don't even know why I did it." His head returns to his palms.

I want to say: *I do. I get why you did it, and it's for all the reasons my own lines got blurry with you and everything else.* Instead, without thinking it through, I say:

"I knew Leo had relapsed. I ran into him in New York, and he was high, and he promised me he'd get better."

Ben's face flies up, the rest of his body following.

"What? Wait, you what?"

"I knew Leo had relapsed." I press my lips together, offer a small, defiant shrug. "I guess we both had our secrets."

"You *what*? I could have fucking helped him, Tatum!"

"You couldn't have."

His face morphs from angry to astonished and back to angry again.

"How could you know that? How the hell could you know what I could and couldn't have done?"

"You don't get it," I say. "We can't save other people. They can only save themselves, *we* can only save ourselves."

I turn to go.

"You are *not* just leaving now," he yells. "After dropping this bomb on me."

I glance back, and see him frozen in rage. My hand mimics dropping a grenade.

"Boom."

33

BEN

DECEMBER 2000

Amanda calls just before I slide on my coat to leave for New Year's Eve. Caller ID alerts me to the 415 area code, and I check my watch because I don't want to be late. I can spare three, maybe four minutes. Despite my better instincts, I press the Talk button.

"Hey," I say.

"It's me," she replies.

"I know."

The clock on the microwave in my parents' kitchen tells me it's 8:23. I told Tatum I'd pick her up by nine, so we could wedge our way into Times Square by midnight, which I still can't believe I've agreed to.

"This is practically highway robbery," I'd said when she proposed it. I'd stopped at the bar to thank her for her work on *Romanticah*, and she'd said: "Well, as payback, you have to come to Times Square with me for New Year's."

"Like a date?" I'd grinned.

"I might let you kiss me if you're lucky," she said, then her eyes widened, and she laughed her machine-gun staccato and slapped her hand over her mouth. "Oh my God, sorry, I don't even know where that came from."

I sip a lukewarm beer abandoned on the kitchen counter. Leo must have opened it as part of his pre-party celebration.

Three minutes, I tell myself. *Then you hang up and are gone.*

Leo wanders in, his coat zippered, his gloves already on, and swipes the beer from my hands and chugs it. Then notices I'm on the phone and shoots me a quizzical look.

A-man-da, I mouth.

He rolls his eyes and slits his throat with his gloved finger.

I flip him off, then shoo him out of the room.

He turns and whispers: "Hurry up, dude, we gotta stop and get Caroline."

He says this as if I have any idea who Caroline is, one of the ever-revolving lithe young women from high school or now, his dorm or fraternity house up at Columbia.

"I just . . ." Amanda starts on the other end of the line, three thousand miles away; then she falls silent. We haven't spoken since she left for California in June. Technically, we broke up—I broke up with her—in February, but I did it solely to get out in front of it: the fact that she was leaving, the fact that she chose a residency over me. It didn't feel real back then—we still occasionally slept together, still sometimes found ourselves crying to each other in the dark hours of the night when one of us couldn't sleep, and the permanence of her move or my decision (or hers) would set in.

"I just wanted to call to wish you a Happy New Year," she says finally.

"Thanks. You too."

Leo circles back and whispers, "Hang up, dude. This isn't just some casual call, like girls don't call on New Year's Eve to say 'hey.'"

I press my finger into my other ear to ignore him, listen to Amanda's quiet crying through the line. I think she's crying, anyway, but I don't want to ask because now I have two minutes before I'm pulled toward someone new, toward Tatum, and I'm not sure I want to get sidetracked.

But we'd dated for three years, a lifetime in your early twenties. We'd made plans for this millennium; we were supposed to be in Cancún right now, not on separate coasts making lonely phone calls that wouldn't change anything. I was going to be the next Scorsese: write from New York, tell New York stories, build a family here, invite Leo over on the weekends to play the part of overly indulgent uncle to our 2.5 children. She was going to work at NYU or Mount Sinai, eventually shifting to private pediatrics so she'd have more time for all things that mattered.

But then she applied exclusively to schools out west and it became clear, then clearer, that maybe the story I'd spun about the two of us wasn't much more than something akin to the scripts that I'd dreamed up too.

She said she just needed some time to live on her own.

I broke up with her and gave her that.

Though it didn't make it easier, of course. Didn't mean that you stop loving someone just because you've split and said good-bye. She left in June, and I refocused on my work: drafting, then redrafting *Romanticah*, writing it *for* her, no, writing it *about* her. Those were two different things. About all the ways that love goes wrong, then all the ways that it corrects itself. When I really thought about it, maybe I was writing it about me. About how love disappoints you but also finds its way back to you.

"I keep thinking about Cancún," Amanda says, gathering her breath and composure. "That would have been fun."

"Yeah," I say. "It's freezing here."

One minute on the clock. Then I have to get to Tatum.

"You going out? Big plans? A wild party?" She laughs, though it rings hollow.

"Times Square."

"Shut up." She laughs for real now.

"I swear. Don't ask."

"You'd never be caught dead in Times Square. You always wanted to stay in, fall asleep on the couch."

"I guess things change." *You and me. Times Square. Cancún. Everything.*

"Wow," she says. "It must be for something special."

I want to correct her—*someone* special who might want to kiss me and who announces such things like she's surprising herself for doing so, which surprises me—and I'm learning I like that in a partner. But I don't correct her, don't say anything because it's Amanda, and my stomach is churning and my brain is jumbled and my adrenaline is sending me uncertain signs.

"I miss you," she says. "I guess that's what I was really calling to say."

I chew on my lip. I miss her too, but now there is Tatum. And if Amanda had called a few weeks ago, before Tatum starred in *Romanticah* and before I stopped by the bar to thank her, and before . . . whatever else, I don't know. Maybe things would have been different. Maybe I'd be willing to forgive her or move to San Francisco or just have flown out for the holidays and slept with her again just because. But she didn't call a few weeks ago, and now Tatum is waiting for me to take her to Times Square and kiss her.

"I should go," I say.

"OK."

"Happy New Year, Amanda."

She's silent, and so am I. It's been six months, and my foot is out the door to Tatum. But that doesn't change the swell of sickly nostalgia for what you once had, how easy it is to revisit those softer spots in your heart for someone who once occupied it.

"I wish we were in Cancún, Ben," she says after my final minute has expired.

"But we're not," I say.

"That doesn't make me not wish it anyway."

"I know."

Leo reappears in the kitchen and signals for me to hang the fuck up.

"I guess our timing was wrong," she says.

"Something like that," I reply, just before I click off for real.

34

TATUM

DECEMBER 2015

How do you divide a lifetime?

Where do you begin? With the items that don't matter to each of you or the ones that matter most? If we can agree on the tangential things—the lamps in the bedroom, the treadmill in the gym, will we agree on the bigger stuff—the painting we bought from that artist in Austin on the road trip, the necklace you got me after *Pride and Prejudice*, the watch I bought you for your fortieth birthday, Joey's schedule, our sanity?

The moving trucks came on a dreary day in February. I was scheduled to be in the edit bay that day but canceled at the last minute. For Joey's sake, though he was at school, and for the sake of not making us hate each other more than we already did, I stayed home, then shuffled around the house, trying to remain out of the way of the movers (and Ben), but there all the same.

It felt like I had to show up for that, for Ben, for us.

He was moving to an apartment only two miles away, but it might as well have been across the ocean.

When the truck pulled away, Ben stood in the doorway, his hands tucked into his pockets, the lines on his face pointing downward. The rain fell behind him, clattering off the roof of his Prius. He started to say something but then stopped, so I started to say something and also stopped.

Neither of us met the other's eyes, and he stared at the doormat, and then, wordlessly, spun around and left. I watched him go, and once he had, I crawled into bed with Monster and wept like I hadn't since my mom died. It was bad enough we were broken; it was even worse that we couldn't look at each other, could no longer see anything about the other that we understood or thought was worth preserving.

Now, ten months later, Susan McMahon, my lawyer, insists that I be unemotional. Or, if I can't, to let her handle the details. But how can a divorce be anything other than emotional? I ask her that, clutching the Perrier her assistant has brought, and she shakes her head and says: "Actors are particularly terrible at divorce. There's an irony there."

"What's the irony?" I ask.

"That all the reasons your marriage was great are also all the reasons it goes to shit." She says this with a little shrug, like it's just business, which to her it is—she handles dozens of these high-profile catastrophes a year. The *Hollywood Reporter* just ran a piece on her: she owns a home in Cabo, an apartment in St. Moritz. It's good to be Susan McMahon. It's less good to be sitting across the desk from her.

"Ben and I were different."

She raises her eyebrows as if to say: *That's what everyone thinks; that's the lie we tell ourselves in order to survive.*

$\backsim$

Piper, Scooter, and Emily, their daughter, fly out to stay with me for the holiday. Helen, Ben's mom, and Ron are also in town to see Ben and Joey. Because Ben and I are trying to be civil, even kind, I invite them over to the house for Christmas dinner. Joey had been with Ben the few days prior; then Constance retrieved him from Ben's apartment and returned him to me for Christmas Eve before she and her kids left for the week to visit her own extended family, a three-hour drive north.

U don't have to send nanny. I'll drop him, he'd texted me.

Please don't. I'd typed it quickly and realized, only after I hit Send, that he'd misinterpret my intention. It wasn't that I couldn't bear to see him. It was just easier this way. With the paparazzi's long lenses hovering in trees to spy over our wall, with the mixed messages it sent my emotional system when he loitered in the foyer, attempting small talk.

OK, he replied.

My dad, Scooter, and Joey watch football in the screening room upstairs, which I almost never use, and Piper sits on the living room floor with Emily, reminding her to be gentle with Monster, who is old now and worries me constantly: how long he has left, how I'll ever make the decision to say good-bye. The good-bye with Ben took all the stoicism out of me; I already know that I won't have it in me to sit with Monster, rubbing his ears, while he is lulled into a permanent sleep. Maybe I will ask Ben to come with me, but that is part of my old life, when I felt like I could lean into him, and I try not to remember much of that old life anymore. I'm too busy mourning it to allow much of it back in.

I find that I have forgiven him for Amanda, which surprises me. When he insisted, back when I was electrified with the discovery, that she'd texted him but he hadn't reciprocated, I'd spurned his apologies. But over time I replay his words, and I believe them, and they've appeased me. But he was equally angry with me: for not having faith in him to do right by Leo, for thinking that I knew better because of my dad and all that we'd been through. I suppose that he has forgiven me my own mistakes now too—I see it in the way he sometimes starts to make overtures but then falters—and since neither one of us has built a bridge back to the other, I meet with Susan McMahon, I contemplate how you divide a lifetime, I worry about taking Monster to the vet on my own. Someone from my team would come, surely, but those are not the people I want to call family, even if I'm forced to by default now.

The doorbell rings today, and I jump, worried that it is Ben, worried that though I invited him, I'm unprepared as always to face him with our newly redrawn lines. But it's only Daisy, with a poinsettia in one arm, a Bundt cake in another.

"I told you not to bring anything," I say, kissing her hello. I've seen more of her since Ben and I split. She, Mariana, my old friend from P. F. Chang's, and I will elude the photographers and, at sunset, sneak into a quiet restaurant with a view of the horizon; or she and I will power walk into the hills of Malibu or Bel Air or wherever we can go unrecognized. We'll pretend that things were like they used to be back when we did these things all the time because we didn't have other obligations, because we didn't have broken hearts. (Mariana had eloped in Vegas last year, and the marriage spiraled south six months afterward.)

"I never show up for a party empty-handed." She glances up the staircase. "Is Ben here yet?"

I shake my head. "No."

"Breathe," she says, her hand lingering on my shoulder. I nod, blinking back a surprising burst of tears.

The caterer I've hired is in the kitchen, so Piper delivers Emily to my dad in the screening room, and she, Daisy, and I pour ourselves too-full glasses of mulled (and spiked) cider and wind our way to the patio. It's Christmas, but in Los Angeles it's seventy-three and clear, like any other day, like every other day. I've had the gardeners braid white lights around the trees in the back and the frame of the entire house, and as the sun sinks lower, they begin to glow like a parade of fireflies throughout the yard.

"It's like it's not real here," Piper says. "This is so far removed from any aspect of real life."

Daisy shrugs. "That's the irony of this town: you come for the glitter, you really get the gritty underbelly."

"It doesn't look like there's much grit around here," Piper laughs, waving an arm toward our massive backyard, the tennis court, the heated pool, the guesthouse.

"You don't see the sacrifice," Daisy says. "You don't see that we open up our guts to get where we are. The lecherous directors, the constant rejection—"

"I'm sorry," I say to Piper, interrupting her because I'm suddenly embarrassed for all this excess and for Daisy making it appear as if this is a hardship.

"Don't apologize," Piper says. "I love it here, don't get me wrong. It's just that it feels like something from a movie set, that's all. But if you asked me to move in, I wouldn't say no." She leans over and squeezes my knee. "You've just come a long way from Canton, Tate."

"I guess I always wanted to get as far away as I could."

She makes a face like I've hurt her.

"Not from you, Pipes, from there."

"If you can dream it, you can be it," she says in a faraway voice that reminds me of home. She laughs, shakes her head. "Mom."

I gaze up to the white lights and wonder if maybe I hadn't been clear on what I dreamed.

⁓

Ben lets himself in and finds us on the patio. It was part of our mediation, the custody: he can have a key, though he can't come and go as he pleases as if he still lives here. But it's a sign of good faith, and it's intended to be a symbolic gesture so Joey doesn't feel like his parents are at war.

"Hey," he says, and we all tilt our heads toward him as if he is a familiar stranger. "I'm . . . just here. Just . . . letting you know."

"Joey's with my dad in the screening room."

He nods. "My mom went to find them."

He plunges his hands into his pockets, as Piper stands too quickly and kisses his cheek hello, reaches for an awkward hug. She's forgiven Ben for Amanda too, and now she's encouraged me to take a breath, to slow down the divorce papers, but Piper relies on Scooter in ways that I never did with Ben, and I tell myself that this makes her more vulnerable, more romantic in her worldview. Piper excuses herself to the kitchen, and Daisy scampers out behind her.

"You OK?" Ben asks when we're alone.

"I'm worried about Monster," I say. "His back legs aren't doing well; he can't do the stairs . . ." I don't tell him about how he pees on the rug involuntarily; how I sometimes have to bring his food to him because he's too listless to rise.

"Have you spoken with the vet?"

"Of course I've spoken with the vet," I say, then chide myself. I'm not trying to be shrill, it's just the easiest way, the default between us now. "Yes," I say more gently. "I mean, he's fine for now, but . . ."

"Listen." Ben steps closer. "I'll come with you, we'll do it together."

"It's OK," I say. "I mean, I'm fine."

"Tate, he's *ours*."

I want to say, *I've spent so much time dividing our life together that I don't know what that means anymore.*

Instead, I head toward the kitchen. I head toward safety.

35

BEN

OCTOBER 1999

Daisy put me up to it. I'd run into her at Ray's Pizza earlier in the night, and she told me she was working a shift that night at a bar off Fourth—Dive Inn—and told me to swing by for a beer. Amanda was at the hospital until eleven o'clock, so I figured what the hell. I buzzed Amanda, who said she'd stop over when she got off, then we could go crash at her place, which wasn't too far, just a couple blocks over on Astor. Easier than me shooting uptown to my parents' on the subway, which was unreliable at night, and besides, it was my parents'. Not exactly living the dream. But that had been part of the deal with my dad: he'd wanted me to be a banker or a lawyer or head to business school after Williams. Like the writing was on the wall with my liberal arts education, my major in English: that I wasn't going to amount to much, at least by my father's definition. My mom convinced him: pay for grad school, at least most of it, but don't subsidize my lifestyle. I took out a small loan and landed at my parents' doorstep, the ink on my diploma barely dry.

Leo still lived at home back then too, so it was like old times, only now he reeked of weed and had beer on his breath, but my mom pretended not to notice because he got by at Dalton and played on the football team, and also, he was the baby, and we loved him for it. *That's just Leo,* we'd grown used to saying with a shrug. My dad indulged him because Leo did well enough to likely matriculate to Columbia, where my dad was occasionally a guest lecturer and had connections, and because Leo had a slight inkling of maybe becoming the banker my father had hoped I'd become, or maybe a lawyer at my dad's firm.

"God help us if Leo's ever the one to have to bail someone out," I said to my mom one night last year, after Leo had swung down from campus to have her do his laundry.

"Benjamin, stop it," she'd replied, folding his T-shirts. "Your brother has so much untapped potential . . ." She shook her head, pressed her hands on the cotton to smooth out the wrinkles. "He can do anything one day." Then she added: "You too, Benny. You too."

Daisy's shift is ending, and my beer is getting warm, and Amanda hasn't shown. There's a pay phone in the back of the bar, and I debate trying the hospital but I know what she'll say: *Something came up. They needed me. I couldn't help it.* I'll say, *OK, I get it.* I try not to take it personally, like my mom's backhanded compliments.

"You look like you need to have some fun," Daisy had said when she proposed the plan. "I'm running a bet with my friend. Stay until midnight, and when she asks for your phone number, refuse to give it to her."

"Weird bet," I said.

"Part of our acting process." She scooped up a handful of pretzels and popped them in her mouth. "Helps us pretend we're anyone but ourselves."

"Actresses are very strange." I laughed.

"You don't know the half of it." She untied her apron from her waist, waved over her friend, then passed the apron to her.

I spend the better part of the hour checking the door, swiveling my neck so often a muscle pinches. I should say something to Amanda, tell her how much it annoys me when she just goes AWOL, but I hate getting into it, the confrontation, the fights.

We met through mutual friends at a Yankees game two summers ago: a Goldman analyst buddy had been released into the wild for the night and his partner had given him the Goldman box—fifteen of us were invited. Amanda and I hit it off immediately: we were all hot dogs and kettle corn and cold beer for the three-hour stretch of the game. Every once in a while, she'd stop to look out on the field and yell: "Jeter, you're such a little bitch!" but she was from Boston and a Red Sox fan, so I forgave this. Besides, her fiery attitude was perfectly in line with her red hair, her zeal. She was passionate about her med school, she was passionate about politics (we were in the midterm election cycle that year); it was only surprising that she was just as passionate about me. We took the subway home together, with everyone really, and when I went to exit at my parents' stop, she said: "No, you're not getting off here. Astor Place is your stop." And so I abided.

But now it's nearly midnight, and my neck hurts and my beer is flat and warm. I have promised Daisy that I'd stay until her friend, Tatum, who is wiping down the bar and shutting down some girl I recognize as the sister of an asshole I went to high school with, loses the bet.

"Bitch!" the girl yells at Tatum, who looks on with mild interest, the epitome of cool, not rattled in any way. I watch her for a beat, as that asshole's sister falls off her stool and to the ground, and am struck by the fact that Tatum's face doesn't flinch for even the tiniest of seconds. I remember that asshole, how I'd be reading in the library and he'd come by and shove my book to the floor, and how I was dating Paige Brewer and he wanted to sleep with her, so he told me that she left her underwear in his locker. He'd taunt me, cajole me, and never once did my face *not* flinch, never did I shake him off so completely, like Tatum is able to shake off his sister now. She grabs her towel and wipes down the bar, and I wonder what I could learn from her, what she could teach me.

"I hope you don't take her personally," I say. "I went to high school with her older brother. I think being an asshole is genetic."

She laughs at this, throws her head back like it's the funniest thing she's ever heard. I'm great at writing drama, milking emotion out of real life, but I've never been a comedian. Amanda never finds me gut-busting hilarious. Something needy swells in me. *More.*

"Free refill for you," she says.

I wave her off, though not because I want to. I'm just trying to be responsible. I have an early shoot, and also she makes me uneasy, like I'm sitting here waiting for Amanda but want to be sitting here talking to her. I've never been disloyal, never even considered being unfaithful. I make a mental leap—to me unbuttoning Tatum's shirt, kissing the nape of her neck—and then press it to the back of my brain. *No.*

"I don't need another," I say. "I'm on my way out."

"You turn into a pumpkin before midnight?"

She's closer now, and I can see how beautiful she is. Long brown hair tied up in a bun, sharp green eyes that probably veer toward hazel when the sky is overcast. She has a dimple on one cheek, a fan of freckles on her nose, not dark enough that she couldn't cover them up, but tonight, she lets them breathe. I imagine, again, taking off her shirt.

"Nah, just . . . I have an early shoot tomorrow and the person I was meeting tonight never showed."

"A shoot? I'm intrigued," she says.

"Grad student."

"Are you at Tisch? I've never seen you before; I'm there for theater."

"I'm there for writing, MFA. You know, about to set the world on fire as the next big screenwriter."

Shit. What a stupid fucking thing to say. Selling myself short, listening to the voice of my dad in my ear.

I add, "Or something like that. I don't know, talk to my parents and they'll tell you I gave up my very lucrative analyst position at Morgan Stanley for a graduate degree in film."

"Banking boys are so boring. No wonder you quit." She smiles and her dimple craters, and now I'm on to removing everything she has on, stripping her naked. "Eh, tell your parents to screw themselves."

"I'm still living with them, so that's a little hard." *Fuck, fuck, fuck, fuck. Why am I saying all this?* I play this off like I'm joking. Like I'm not sitting here exposing all of my shortcomings to the most intoxicating woman I've met since, well, since that Yankees game with Amanda.

"Yikes," she says.

"Tell me about it." I laugh, wave a hand, recover.

"Tatum Connelly." She extends a hand, and I clasp it, don't want to let go.

"Ben Livingston." She winces when I do indeed hold on for a moment too long. "Sorry. Habit. Trained that way by my dad since I was six."

"Fun childhood."

"My dad's only paying for grad school on the promise that I win an Oscar," I offer, surprised to hear how quickly I share this confession.

But she grins and says: "So win an Oscar." Like it's nothing, like it's not the finish line, the nearly unattainable triumph my father expects.

"Uh . . . OK." I grin back because I like her breeziness, her candor. "Now you sound like him: 'If you're going to do something, Benjamin, you'd better at least be the best!'"

"There are worse role models," she says, and something like sadness washes over her for a beat before she sheds it.

"I'm probably making it sound worse than it was." I am. Mostly I love my parents, loved my childhood. No one is perfect; we all did our best. "You know, to make you feel sorry for me or something."

"Fun childhoods are overrated," she says, but then chews on her lip, lost in that same trail of thought that she doesn't give me access to. "But why would you want me to feel sorry for you?"

"Oh, I don't know, so when you get my phone number, you might take pity on me and actually call," I say. Daisy kicks me from underneath my side of the bar.

"Come on," she says, incredulous.

"Come on what?" I know I'm flirting now, in spite of Amanda, in spite of my previously unwavering loyalty. To Paige Brewer, to Melissa Thompson (college), to Felicia Hollis (also college), to Amanda.

"What makes you think I want your phone number?" she asks. "And even if I *did* want your phone number, why then wouldn't I call? For your information, as a female bartender, I get numbers thrown at me all the time." She's rattled. *I've* been the one to rattle her. I picture her naked now, me beside her.

"Well, good, because I don't hand out my number to strangers." I grin. Daisy told me to drag this out for as long as possible, until after midnight.

"I'm not a stranger," she says. "I'm Tatum."

I want to say: *I know. Now tell me everything about yourself because that won't be enough. I want to consume you, breathe you, explore every inch of you.*

Instead, I say, "But you don't want my number, Tatum, so we don't have anything to worry about it."

"Well, I don't want your number, in fact."

"Perfect," I reply.

"Great," she says. Then: "Well what if I do want your number?"

"I already told you: I don't give my number out to strangers who scare me."

God, do I want to give her my number.

"Something else you learned in your childhood?"

"They trained me well."

"What if I'm not a stranger?" she says. "What if I tell you something about my own less than fun childhood that assures that I'm just Tatum, your local friendly bartender!"

"I'll consider it."

"I started working when I was twelve, have had a job ever since," she says. "So, no fun for me."

"Hmmm. Nope." I try to shut that down quickly, worried she'll ask me about my own work experience, which is shamefully lacking. A camp counselor for a summer, teaching racquetball for another. I've never callused my hands, never worried about a paycheck. Certainly never slung drinks for assholish NYU trust fund brats.

"Oh, come on," she says. "Are you going to make me beg?"

"Yes," I say. *Please beg, please ask me to do whatever you want me to do. I'm sold.* "I am going to make you beg. Very much so. Come on, give me your best begging face."

Daisy clutches my shin, then pulls herself up to eye level, tears building, then spilling down her cheeks. She grabs my arm to steady herself against the onslaught of her laughter.

"What?" Tatum looks from her to me then back to her. "Were you, like, crouching underneath the bar? Listening to this the whole time? I don't . . . what the hell, Daisy?"

Daisy catches her breath in sputters. Then finally: "Tatum, Ben, Ben, Tatum. And just so you know, you lost."

They both look at the clock on the back wall.

"I'm aware," Tatum snaps. "And he and I met. As, evidently, you did too." Then to me: "I take it you know her?"

"Ben wrote a short about dating I did a few months ago," she says. "I told him about our ongoing contest to get numbers at the bar, and he wrote it into the script."

"That *Women Are from Mars* short?" Tatum asks, her eyes wider. "That won an award last semester, didn't it?"

"I just wrote the script," I say. "She starred. And the dude who directed it, another guy I grew up with, actually got the award." More deflection, more slighting myself though I know better. *Shut. Up. Ben.*

"All you fancy Manhattan kids," she says. "The next Scorseses. But you, don't do that." She squeezes my shoulder and a jolt of adrenaline rushes to my heart.

"Do what?"

"Dismiss any notions of greatness, act like you're not worthy of winning some award."

The adrenaline shoots all the way through me, straight to my cheeks. She's read me so well, like I'm transparent, like she can see right into my guts.

"I'm serious," she says. "Like, if that had been my film, I'd be standing on top of this bar, screaming about it with a microphone."

I debate telling her to prove it, that if she's so chock-full of bravado, she should jump up on the bar and *prove it.* But I don't need her to; I don't want her to. I want to savor this moment, her having my back, just for us. Our eyes linger for a beat, and then I remember: *Shit. Amanda.* I stand abruptly, fishing my wallet from my back pocket, sliding forty dollars her way.

"I should go; looks like I'm getting stood up."

"Well, that sucks. And you don't owe me forty bucks."

"It's midnight, and you lost the bet," I say, suddenly embarrassed, like she thinks I'm some rich kid who is trying to do her a favor. I clarify: "A big tip—an actual tip, not a wise-ass tip from that girl whose brother I knew—is the least I could do. And anyway, I actually feel kind of bad about setting you up to lose. I really never do things like that." I point toward Daisy. "She begged me. So I apologize, and please, take the tip."

Daisy nods. "I did. It was too perfect not to. But yes"—she holds up her right hand—"I can attest that Ben is the rare breed of actually decent man who is not a total asshole. I've known him since we were kids."

"Nice," I say, hoping that Tatum will recognize the truth behind Daisy's sarcasm, then hoping she won't, because she doesn't seem like the type who goes for nice guys.

"She's not from here," Daisy interrupts. "She's only very recently become acquainted with New York men."

"Ohio," Tatum says with a shrug. "We breed only nice men in Ohio. Nice men who don't trick us into losing."

"Thus, the forty dollars."

"Well, I *don't* like losing." She frowns, and the freckles on her nose shift into a new constellation, and I'm back to wanting to remove all of her clothes. "And I do like big tips."

"No one really likes losing. And I think everyone likes good tips."

"Are you making fun of me?"

"No," I say, shaking my head. God, that is the last thing I intended. I'm like the five-year-old on the playground, poking fun at the girl he likes. *But I don't like her. I'm with Amanda.* I try to recenter. "I swear, I am not making fun of you. And I have Daisy to testify that I am indeed a non-asshole New York guy who wouldn't do that sort of thing."

"We went to Dalton together," Daisy says. "I've known him since forever."

"I suppose that losing a bet and getting forty bucks is better than getting stood up, so my night is not quite as bad as yours." Tatum shrugs again. "So fine, I will see your forty bucks and raise you a tequila shot. On the house."

"I'm not sure if I'm quite being stood up . . . it's complicated. My girlfriend's in her third year of med school. I mean, I think she's still my girlfriend. I can't quite pinpoint when I last saw her, so . . ." I watch Tatum, wondering if she'll betray any interest. She raises her eyebrows for just a glimmer of a second, and I tell myself that's enough. It's enough to hold on to for now.

"So I couldn't have gotten your number even if I hadn't been set up by my so-called best friend?" She smiles, and her whole face opens into something radiant.

"Hey, Daisy put me up to it."

She downs her shot, so I do too. "Well, I guess you owe me one."

"Well," I say. "I guess I do."

2016 (NOW)

36

TATUM

NOVEMBER

I see Ben as he leans over the white fencing that separates the path from the cliff down to the beach. He tilts over and assesses, then rights himself and starts toward the steps to the ocean. I sink lower in the driver's seat, though I'm a block away and the SUV has tinted windows, which usually guard against the prying eyes of fans who recognize me or paparazzi who need a slice of me whenever they manage to track me down. I've gotten better at evading them; figured out how to leave early before they plant themselves outside my gate, or how to barter for a good shot if they agree to give me freedom for the rest of the day. So for now, I'm alone, something I rarely am anymore, an irony that isn't lost on me now that Ben doesn't sleep on his side of the bed.

I'd realized I'd forgiven him a few weeks ago. He'd shown up to get Joey for the weekend, and rather than abruptly stand by the door and make courteous small talk (or have Constance do it and skip it altogether), I surprised myself by inviting him in.

"Really?" His brow wrinkled and the corners of his lips curled into a smile. "Well, sure, OK!"

I poured him a coffee—all black like he always took it—and he pulled up a stool at the kitchen island, wrapping his hands around his mug like it was warming him from within.

Neither of us quite knew where to start.

"So," Ben said.

"So," I replied.

There were so many things I wanted to ask, mostly *How are you* and *Do you miss me?* Which I hadn't even realized were on my mind or were something resonating within me until he was there, clutching his coffee like he'd done a thousand times in front of me before.

But before either of us could find anything important or even casual to say, Joey came rushing down the steps and threw himself on Ben's leg.

"Daddy! You're here in the kitchen! Does this mean you guys are getting back together?"

We both cleared our throats, and Ben set his mostly full mug in the sink, and they were gone before I could ask Ben to stay longer, which I'd found myself rehearsing in my head while he sipped his coffee, the silence hovering between us, the bubble of so much unsaid hovering too. I washed the mug afterward, staring out the window above the kitchen sink, wondering how that can happen: how in an instant you can forgive someone without consciously doing so, how you can miss someone without recognizing how lonely you were without them.

It had been well over a year since we blew up, almost two, if you start with that day when I told him about Leo, when I admitted I knew about the affair. So long that it was hard to remember who had wronged whom. There was Amanda, of course, his infidelity. But I'd wronged him in plenty of ways too: Leo, yes, but also in the smaller ways that I chose my career over him, put him second. It wasn't that I apologized for my ambition, but I'd come to recognize that ambition and thoughtfulness are not incompatible.

A year or two is a long time to hold on to bruises that you're partially responsible for making.

This morning, near the Santa Monica beach, I watch Ben disappear over the crest of the horizon down the steps to the sand, and then he's gone. I adjust my sunglasses and an old Tisch hat that I used to wear when Daisy and I went power walking, when I had all that baby weight to lose.

I knew he'd be here, though we haven't spoken in four days. But we still know each other well, or I like to think that I still know him—love him—well enough to know that he'd be here, remembering Leo on his birthday, that time when Ben told me it felt like the world stopped, and it was just the two of them and the waves on the ocean.

I glance up and down Ocean Avenue to ensure that no one has tailed me here, that I haven't been followed by the long lens of a prying camera. But the street is empty on this sunless Sunday morning. Joey is at a school retreat for the weekend. The isolation, which I've grown used to, built around myself like armor, feels lonelier, cooler today, and I want to reach for Ben to warm me, like the Tin Man who was looking for a heart and needed to be loved.

I slam the car door and jog to the spot Ben just vacated, only a block or two away from our first place together, where we lived when he was something brilliant with *Romanticah*, and I was something less so. I squint against the glare that permeates through the heavy veil of clouds, looking for him. No, it wasn't that I was less than he, it was just that this town told me as much, valued me as lesser. Now I'm the most valuable player. Like anything as ephemeral as fame should define you. Like it says anything real about who you are, whom you love, what you have to offer.

I thought about this more these days, called Piper—who had a new baby at home—sometimes drove down to Commitments with my dad for refresher therapy sessions, sometimes booked a therapy session just for me. But I thought about all the things we choose to let into our lives and how much of a choice that really is, how much ownership we need to take, how much responsibility. Ben made his choice with

Amanda; I made mine with my loyalty to Leo, with my unwillingness to assume Ben could forgive him, like he had stubbornly refused to forgive my dad.

I think we'd both choose differently if we could do it all over, and I tell my therapist this, I talk about my regret, I talk about my responsibility. That it was easier to dive into my work than come home and confront him about his affair; that it was easier to lose myself in a role than ask Ben why he lost himself with Amanda. That over the years, life got so very, very difficult, with my mom and his dad and my dad and Leo, and we lost so much, and that when we could have chosen to duck down in a foxhole together, we chose otherwise. It didn't happen with one fell swoop, and it was so gradual that neither of us realized it had happened until we found ourselves here, dividing a lifetime. Maybe it would be easier to pinpoint a moment and say: *If only we could go back there and choose differently.* But it's like a plane crash: a series of critical but small things all went wrong, and suddenly you're in a million pieces on the ground.

I have never been one not to do the work, not to roll up my sleeves, but I suppose now I can see that the one place that it mattered most—with Ben—we simply didn't.

I chose this.

I just didn't realize I was choosing it at the time.

I love Ben in ways that are still unexpected, still surprising. It wasn't what I felt on New Year's Eve, and it wasn't what I felt when we fell asleep under the vast Arizona sky in the back of our Jeep because I'd been stubborn and run out of gas, and he'd forgiven me. It's hard-earned, it's complicated, it's also probably indelible.

Though I am fraught with nerves and also the terror of heartbreak, I have told myself that I would show up today and tell him. Lay myself bare; let it all ride on this.

I still love you. I am showing up for you. Please, I don't want to sign the divorce papers. Please, can we try again?

I head halfway down the stairway, scanning the dull sands of the beach until I see him. He is staring out at the horizon, just as I'm staring at him. Lost. I found him here, and yet we're just as lost as ever. He removes something from his pocket—cigarettes—and taps the pack against the butt of his hand, then pulls one to his mouth.

Ben's smoking? When did Ben start smoking? I knew he dabbled after Leo died, but as a habit, no, I had no idea.

I narrow my eyes into slits. How have we gotten so far apart that I don't know that my husband has taken up smoking?

I know how, of course, but that doesn't mean I want to remember.

"Write something for me," I used to say, like it was all I ever wanted in the world.

He never did.

He checks his phone with his free hand, then shoves the phone back in his pocket. Is he hoping it's me? I reach for my own phone and consider, fleetingly, typing . . . I don't know what.

I put my phone back into my own pocket. I don't want to text him, I don't want to communicate in parsed words like that anymore. I want to go to him, down the rest of the steps, tell him that I'm here, that we should start over. But I find that I can't move. Not yet. *What if he doesn't want me? What if he says no? What if he doesn't see in me what I see in him now?*

A blond surfer washes up next to him, then tucks her board beneath her arm and turns left down the beach toward the empty lifeguard station. It's dangerous out there in the surf with no one watching. Doesn't she know this? I want to run down there and tell her to be careful, to protect herself. I wouldn't, not just because it would seem paranoid, pushy. But because I've stopped enjoying the casual company of strangers, of small talk or chitchat with the Gelson's cashier, because everyone watches me now, and nothing can truly ever be casual. It's all documented and photographed, and even if someone isn't holding his phone aloft with the camera app open, someone is tweeting about it.

All a choice, my therapist reminds me. *Move to Montana,* she'll say. *You could.* I could, but I choose not to. Instead, I've constructed this protective bubble around me and allowed that to convince me that I am safe.

Ben turns, heads back toward me, and I duck, like this stair railing can conceal me. I right myself. *No. I'm here, I'm here because I wanted him to see me, to know that I showed up to honor him and Leo and us.* I inhale, exhale, steady myself and start down the remaining steps, still watching him, still wondering if maybe he'll see me first.

He slides on his flip-flops, then freezes, peering at a runner pointed toward him.

I recognize the swoosh of her red hair—I'd spent enough time googling her—even from here.

She stops right in front of him, the surprise on his face morphing to happiness.

Amanda.

Heat rushes to my cheeks at the embarrassment of witnessing this. He'd told me it was over between them; I'd chosen to believe him.

Fuck. Fuck, fuck, fuck, fuck, fuck.

I spin and race up the steps, race back to the Escalade, fat tears startling me in the reflection in the window before I pull the door open and slink inside. I thought I'd prepared myself for heartbreak. Yet even after everything, I hadn't realized that Ben and I would really split in two.

37

BEN

NOVEMBER

Amanda stretches out in her sleep, rustling the duvet, shaking the mattress. I'd forgotten how she did this, even back in New York all those years ago—a lifetime, really—when we'd mostly stay at her place—a one-bedroom off Astor Place, because I was living with my parents. How she'd hog the bed as if she were the only one who should be in it. I watch her sleeping, then her toes scrape against my shin, and she sighs—eyes still shut, red hair spilling over my pillow—and drifts back to wherever her dreams have taken her.

I ease out of bed and then peel off my shirt, then boxers, and step into the shower, trying to wash off the saltwater and the sand. Also to rinse off a film of something else: that I had been waiting for Tatum, yet I left with Amanda, as if they were interchangeable.

We'd barely made it back to my apartment. She'd jogged to the beach, so we'd taken my car, driven back to my place in some sort of frenzy, like dogs in heat. She'd told me that she didn't really expect to see me there, mourning Leo, but then when she did, she couldn't not stop, she couldn't not say something, because seeing me was the entire point of coming.

"Like, I'd gone that far," she laughed, then moved her hand across the headrest of the seat and rubbed my neck. "I guess I figured what the hell, what did I have to lose? You'd already ended it with me two and a half years before. So, like, why not?"

She knew about my marriage, of course. Most of the planet did. I hadn't called her when Tatum and I split, hadn't even thought of her much other than in the context of her being the last woman I fucked other than my wife, before I learned how to navigate the one-night stands that weren't too frequent anyway.

But she had shown up, and Tatum hadn't, and I figured *Maybe that means something*, maybe I misread what Tatum had wanted recently—to try to sort things out, to quit with the lawyers, and maybe I underestimated Amanda, so we drove home like a tornado was chasing us, abandoned our clothes by the door, and fell into bed like star-crossed lovers in a movie where they'd been kept apart too long, like they were foiled by every obstacle in their past and could finally now, desperately, be together.

The spray of the hot water hits my face. I know it is nothing like this; I know ours is not the stuff that inspires fairy tales. Fairy tales do not start and end with your ex-mistress showing up and rescuing you when you were waiting for a sign from your wife, whom you miss desperately and whose trust you have detonated perhaps beyond repair. I wonder what Leo would say about all of this. Probably that I am being an idiot—I can hear him say this: *Dude, you are being such a fucking moron. Tater-tot is the best, why aren't you just telling her?*

He would have been thirty-six today. His face, beautiful and unlined, plays over and over again in my memory. Who would he be now? Would he be happy?

I lean over, try to touch my toes, stretch out my hamstrings and back. It's harder than it once was, though I am also taking better care of myself, now that I have free time to go running, hit the gym, lay off the scotch that had helped nurse my wounds for the first year or so. I consider that happiness is a moving target: how can I possibly know if Leo would be happy when I don't even know how to define this for myself? With Amanda. With Tate.

I'd held it against her—that she knew about his relapse and kept it from me—for a long time, the better part of that first year when I had this new apartment, and I fell asleep with my empty tumbler in my hand. I wore it plainly on my sleeve, like it was a bruise that shouldn't heal, that couldn't heal, and that she'd pelted me and caused permanent damage. I pulled out old photos of Leo, reread e-mails he'd once sent. It was as if this revelation of his relapse reopened the grieving process for me, as if I could trip down endless what-ifs that I had mostly put to bed after we buried him. I replayed all the what-ifs now: how I'd have sent him back to rehab, how I'd have ensured that he stayed the course.

I flew back to New York for a weekend when Tatum had Joey, stayed with my mom and Ron, found myself sleeping in Leo's bed, milling about his room, which was unchanged from when he lived there, from when he was in high school and filled with possibility.

It was a perfect spring weekend in the city. The trees were blossoming, the air had just rounded the corner from the winter chill, the sun was bright and optimistic. My mom and I walked the loop in Central Park, which we hadn't done since I was probably eleven, when I needed to burn off energy and Leo was too old for a stroller but would fall asleep in it all the same as we walked.

"You have to forgive yourself for this, Ben," my mom said. "You have to let it go."

I didn't realize she knew.

She read the surprise on my face.

"I'm not an idiot. It's not like I stuck my head in the sand and didn't know about what he was doing."

"I . . . he'd wanted to protect you from it; hadn't wanted you to know." I swallowed. "I'm sorry. I didn't mean to keep it a secret."

"Yes, you did," she corrected me. "And that's OK too."

I blinked too quickly, tears mounting, and it occurred to me that what I'd done to my mom wasn't so different from what Tatum had done to me. Different motivations, perhaps, but tacit secret keeping all the same.

"I'm his mother, Ben," she said. She still did that: spoke about him in present tense, like he was still among us, which in some ways he still was. "And I tried to help in the best way I could."

We stopped at a crosswalk as the park traffic whizzed by. Fallen petals from the newly sprung trees littered the pavement and swirled in the air around us.

"I didn't know," I said. I reached out and tried to grab a white petal that was circling in front of me, held aloft by the wind. "I guess I didn't have any idea."

"About me? Or about Leo?" The light clicked, and we moved ahead.

"About both," I said. Though what I really think I meant, when I thought about it later, lying in his old bed, my elbows splayed behind my head, my eyes staring at the trophies he'd accrued at Dalton, the Bruce Springsteen posters he'd pinned up, is that I really didn't have any idea about *me*. About what I was made of, about who I'd become. About how I'd stopped aspiring for greatness because the less risky, less ambitious middle ground was all that I'd been offered lately, about how I'd lost sight of Tatum because it was easier to focus on all that I'd thought she'd taken from me—Leo, time, trust—than what she'd given back, which was actually just about everything. I'd even started to blame her for taking Amanda from me—all those years back on New Year's Eve, when, in a different version of my life, Amanda called, and I wouldn't have been with Tatum, and Amanda and I would have found our way back to each other. Which was dumb because I didn't love Amanda like I loved Tatum; that deep, resonant love that isn't exactly passion anymore but is so much a part of you that you don't know where it ends and begins, where to turn it off, even if you wanted to.

My mom knocked on Leo's door.

"One last thing I should have said earlier." She pressed her lips together and seemed to consider what came next. I heaved myself to my elbows and waited. Finally, she offered: "Your dad pushed you toward success. Relentlessly at times, I know."

I waited.

"But what he didn't tell you—though I think he tried to show you, and I can see now may have failed at, is that there is more than one way to define success." She sighed. "He brought me flowers every Friday, Ben. Do you remember that?"

"I do."

"He was a real pain in the ass," she said. "But he loved me unequivocally. And if he were here, he would say that loving someone wholly is success too. Frankly, it's probably the one that matters most."

I didn't know what to say, so she nodded and retreated from Leo's old room, closing the door so quietly, I never heard the latch click.

I flew back to LA and started writing again. For Tatum. Also for me. It came to me suddenly, like a tsunami of awakening that almost makes it hard to breathe. I'd spent years avoiding it because I couldn't see any of it clearly; I couldn't see *her* clearly, and I couldn't see myself either. That's the funny thing about memory, hindsight, nostalgia, and self-perception: sometimes, many times, it gets in the way of knowing how to tell the truth.

I replayed all our years together. I wrote them down. I started in the present, how far we'd gotten from each other, and tore through the years and tore through our past. I tried to be fair, and I tried to be honest, and I tried to honor the love and the mistakes and the mess and the beauty that we'd created. I wrote about the road trip through Arizona, not the one with Joey when we'd already started to splinter, but the one with just the two of us, which I thought was a catastrophe but turned out to be perfect. I wrote about her Oscar, and I wrote about my jealousy, and I wrote about the first time I viewed her through my directorial lens in *Romanticah* and knew she was a star outside my galaxy. I wrote about her dad, and I wrote about mine too. I wrote about how you build a life together and how you let that life together crumble into dust.

I called it *Between Me and You*, because that was all that used to matter once, what was between us. And because maybe it should be *Between You and Me*, but we hadn't quite added up to perfect, so being a little off made me smile every time I read the title page. And I promised myself—because I thought I could still read her, but I was no longer sure, not since she started concealing parts of herself in ways that she hadn't in years—that if she showed up today at the beach, on Leo's birthday, I would finally tell her what I'd written, tell her that it wasn't too late, tell her that the weight of regret I bore on my shoulders was sinking me, but that I was ready to heave it into that gray ocean where I'd rebaptized myself this morning and many mornings prior.

But Tatum hadn't shown. It turned out that I read her wrong. I *couldn't* see her like I thought I could, like I used to.

Instead, it was Amanda.

I spin the handle of the shower, turning the temperature up until it is nearly scalding. I want to feel it, I need to feel it. It's been so long since I've felt much of anything. Now it's good to feel the burn.

38

TATUM

DECEMBER

Work keeps me busy, of course. Work, work, work, work, work. That's what I tell myself, what I've done since I was barely old enough to be employed. I have been working for almost thirty years, and I will work through this too. Work can't be everything, though. Luann thinks it's important that I start dating again or at least that I give the appearance that I've started dating again, even though the divorce isn't final, even though neither of us has been able to sign the papers.

"*He's* dating again," she said a couple of months ago, even before I saw him on the beach with Amanda. "A friend saw him leave a bar the other night with someone who was way too young for him."

"It's sex," I said. "It's fine." Now, I wonder when he had time for casual sex if he is back with Amanda. If their relationship is something casual, or if theirs is now something that has morphed into more. I can't bring myself to ask; I can't even bring myself to say her name to him.

"Well, you need to be having some sex too," she replied. "Or at least make people *think* that you are. If he gets the upper hand here with the media, poof, there goes your sex appeal."

"He's not trying to get the upper hand, Luann. He's a head writer on *Code Emergency*. I really don't think he gives two shits about what *Us Weekly* is reporting about him."

"Well *I* give two shits," she said, ending the discussion. "That's why you hired me."

So I shot the December cover for *Elle* wearing little more than a turtleneck sweater that had LED lights sewn into the cashmere and thus lit me up like a Christmas tree. The headline screams *Tate Expectations!* and the ebullience on my face nearly completely disguises the evidence of my broken heart.

In my high-ceilinged, open, gargantuan kitchen, I thumb through the magazine now, lingering on the glossy pages, the blown-up images of me in ridiculously expensive evening gowns, in tiny skirts with too high heels, in makeup that morphs me into someone I am not. It's all part of the fantasy of my celebrity, of course, but it has nothing to do with real life.

The security bell buzzes, and I flip the magazine closed.

I've agreed to a setup tonight. Lily Marple, of all people, had a guy in mind, and when she mentioned it at a "Women and Hollywood" luncheon last week, Luann was practically apoplectic with joy. Lily and I have formed a tentative friendship over the past year, mostly out of respect for each other's craft and probably born out of the adage of keeping one's enemies close, but it's not as if I have so many friends these days, and besides, sometimes she makes me laugh with her utter contempt for the world at large. So I agreed to the date.

"He's gorgeous," Lily had promised me. "Certainly at least worth a one-nighter."

"I don't do one-nighters," I'd said.

"You didn't before, but you haven't met Damon." She winked and sipped her chardonnay, her liquid lunch, because she was off solids until awards season was over.

Luann has assured me that it doesn't have to mean anything, but it's important to at least pretend, because the pull quotes from the *Elle* article sing about how ready I am to dive back into life! And how much I'd like to find a partner to share that life with because I am so! dang! full of zeal! That my breakup didn't gut me, that men all over the world should still want to fuck me, that their wives and sisters and moms should still want to be my best friend.

I've halfheartedly tried dating over the summer when I took a break from work to decompress with Joey and just be, you know, a "mom." But it was impossible to grab a casual coffee without being gawked at, impossible to make small talk with someone who already knew the entirety of my life with a simple Google search. Google didn't tell them who I was, only what I'd done, but assumptions were made long before I even shook a hand, kissed a cheek. Not that the line of suitors was all that long. A cinematographer friend of Mariana's; a lawyer whom Susan McMahon thought I'd like. He was fine, decent enough, but I was the one who was on edge, jumpy, wondering what he knew, what he thought of me, how exhausting the notion was of overcoming someone's preconceptions over a martini.

Instead, I retreated to Joey. We spent the summer lingering in the pool until our hands pruned, riding bikes through Italy because I'd never really been to Europe just for fun. He was almost old enough now to start to get sick of me, and I'd spent so many of his recent months and years working—working, working, working—that I didn't want to squander these last precious moments before he realized he could start to live outside our bubble. Like Ben had with Amanda. *Stay in this bubble with me forever,* I wanted to say to Joey. *Stay eight years old forever.*

The doorbell buzzes again, and Constance calls from upstairs, where she is playing an Xbox game with Joey. "Miss Tatum, do you want me to get that?"

"No," I call back. "I have it. I won't be out late. Have fun."

I swing the door open, flap my hands to my sides, and say, "Hi, I'm Tatum," in more of a sigh than a statement.

Damon laughs and kisses my cheeks. "Your enthusiasm is infectious." He laughs again, and his bellow echoes through my giant foyer, loudly enough to penetrate, just slightly, my protective armor.

I smile. "OK. Let me try again. Hi, I'm Tatum Connelly. Let's go have a normal date and pretend this isn't really awkward."

That laugh again. It's deep, baritone, and his smile, of perfectly straight, perfectly white teeth, illuminates his already handsome face, his smooth cocoa skin, his eyes that glint like he is game for anything.

Lily has given me his résumé: grew up in Harlem, put himself through Georgetown and his first year at Fordham Law, only to discover that he didn't want to be a lawyer after all. He worked at the Gap while saving up to start a furniture company; at first, working nights and crafting all the wood by hand, welding the iron in a garage near his apartment—something Lily told me he learned from his grandfather. Then he assembled a team, a few people at first, that is now a small empire. He relocated to LA last year for more space (his warehouse takes up half a block downtown) and for the weather too. Lily had filled her living room with his pieces, which is how he landed in my foyer for a blind date. I like that he was a little lost in his younger years; I like that he had to take some time to figure out who he was, is. This makes him feel safer, like he won't disappoint me like Ben had. I also like that he had to earn his keep, just like I did.

"So where are we going?" I ask, when he has escorted me to the driveway, slipping a hand on the small of my back, then opening the car door.

"Surprise," he says. He grins again, and I feel another piece of my armor chip away.

"You realize that there is very little in my life that can be spontaneous."

He waves a hand. "Everyone can be spontaneous."

"You don't live inside my bubble."

"I don't," he says, then points a finger at the air and jabs it forward. "Pop."

∞

He takes me to a hole-in-the-wall place in Koreatown where I get a few double takes, but no one stops me for an autograph or asks for a photo.

"I think my publicist wanted somewhere a little splashier," I say. "Wanted an accidental sighting."

"Oh fuck your publicist," he says, laughing again. "Lily filled me in: I know exactly what she wanted. But I tried to think about what you might have wanted instead."

We are seated in our own booth with a hot grill on the table. He hesitates before sliding in—sitting next to me or across—and rightly, gives me some space.

"Ever done this?" He rubs his hands together. "It's my favorite thing. Literally, my favorite thing in the world." He articulates all the syllables in *literally*, and it makes me grin.

"I'm a pretty terrible cook," I say. "You'll probably have to do mine for me."

"No," he says. "If you want to eat tonight, you have to do it on your own."

I push out my bottom lip and pretend to pout.

"That doesn't work on me either." He grins. "I have a ten-year-old daughter. Do you think I'm that easily manipulated?"

"You have a daughter?"

He nods. "Her mom lives in San Francisco. I have custody." He shakes his head. "It was very complicated for a while, and then, I guess, it wasn't." He reads me. "You seem surprised."

"I . . . I guess I am. Lily didn't mention it."

"I'm not as easy to google as you are," he says with a smile.

"You are," I say. "I just didn't."

"Figured this was going to be a bust before we even got started?"

My cheeks redden. "No, I mean . . ." I wave a hand, fiddle with the skewers on the table. "I'm just not very good at dating."

"I think if you're very good at dating, you probably do it forever," he says.

"Like tennis? Like, if you're very good at tennis, you play it until you're eighty?" I laugh now too.

"Golf," he says, just as the waitress approaches with a plate stuffed with beef. "Golf is what you play until you're eighty."

"Well, I don't play golf," I say.

"Good," he says. "I don't either."

∽୭

He drives me home at a respectable hour, after we walked from the Korean BBQ place to a bar next door for a drink. A few heads turned in my direction, and he saw me squirm, and we agreed, regrettably, to rush up I-10 back to reality. I find that I don't want to, though, that I'd like to draw out this safe bubble for as long as I can until it's punctured for real. Which it will be inevitably because that's my life. *Pop.* We listen to a classical station he has the radio tuned to and settle into a comfortable silence until he veers off the freeway and onto the back roads toward my enclave.

"It's difficult dating me," I offer eventually, because I like him enough to want him to know the truth.

He says nothing.

"I'm not saying that I don't want to . . ."

"You have a lot of walls," he says, making the sharp turn up the hill to my house. "I get that."

"That's not what I meant. There are just always people watching."

I don't say, *And I'm still married,* though the divide in our lives is likely large enough to remain permanent—and after seeing Ben with Amanda last month, it's clear I need to be done with us. I need to get it: that he has moved on, that I'd misread his hesitation with moving forward with the divorce. I need to absorb this so deeply that it shifts my DNA.

I tell myself that I will call Ben tomorrow and tell him that we need to sign the papers; that this has been going on long enough—I saw them together over a month ago at the beach. How long can I put myself through this, hoping he'll come back to me? I thought that if I found the nerve to find *my* way back to him that he'd want me, be ready with open arms. But she was there that day, and now, that's that.

The car slows to a stop outside my security gate.

"Do you want to come in?" I ask.

He smiles his beautiful smile. "I would love to come in, but I won't."

"I don't have walls," I say. "I mean, I do. But I guess I'd like not to."

He seems to consider this. Leans in closely, kisses my cheek, his smooth skin against mine.

"Sometimes I get a piece of wood in my studio, and I can tell that it's going to make the perfect, just the absolute slam-dunk of a perfect piece. A tabletop, a chair . . ." He eases back in the driver's seat, away from me, away from my cheek and his kiss. "But, man, that piece is going to take so much work. The sanding and more sanding and the staining and the polishing . . ."

"I'm the wood," I say, and I nod because I am and because it has been so long since anyone has seen through me. Not since Ben. Then: "Maybe you can make a piece for me? Out of one of those perfect slabs of wood?"

I think of all the times I asked Ben to write something for me, of all the times he failed me.

"Actually," I say before he can answer, "maybe I could come down to your showroom, see how it's done? Try my hand at it on my own."

"It's not the type of thing you pick up after one visit." He smiles. "But sure."

I think, *You don't know what I'm capable of, what I can do if I dream it.*

I say, "I'd like that. To at least try."

He doesn't reply. Instead, he leans forward and kisses me for real. I step out of his car, and he drives off into the night.

I linger in my driveway, under the shadow of the impenetrable wall that I moved behind because of the stalker and also because it shielded me from the cameras and from lingering eyes and from probably a lot more than that too. I gaze up at the sky and wonder, for the first time in years, if perhaps I didn't mistake isolation for safety, if I didn't get confused and think that walls protected me, when what I learned at Tisch and a million times since then—in rebuilding my relationship with my dad, in sleeping in the open air under that Arizona sky—is that sometimes the only way to free yourself is to learn what you thought you couldn't know. To knock everything down and start over.

39

BEN

DECEMBER

"Jesus Christ!" Tatum screams when she finds me sitting at the kitchen island, nursing a glass of merlot from a bottle I'd found open in the wine fridge and flipping through the December issue of *Elle*, for which she's the cover model. Her hand flies to her heart, and her heels click against the bare wood floor as she skitters in surprise.

"Sorry, shit, sorry," I say. "I didn't mean to scare you."

"What are you doing here? Is everything OK?" She exhales, regaining her breath, drops her purse on the island, and reaches for an empty wineglass of her own in the cabinet.

"I brought over Joey's gifts to put under the tree. Figured I'd stay. Sent Constance home."

Her brow furrows, then relaxes. "Oh, OK. I mean, sure, that's fine."

I was doing this from time to time now: stopping by unannounced, with the honest intention of spending time with Joey—our custody agreement was fluid, and Tatum never minded—but then often loitering for longer, inviting myself to stay for dinner, suggesting we all watch a movie.

Tatum pours the merlot, swirls the wine, sips deeply. I know she's been on a date. I can tell by the cut of her dress, by the hint of her makeup. Not the piled-on stuff she wears for work when a professional comes and fluffs her, not the uncomfortable heels and dress she'd wear for a junket or a dinner where she has to be *on* all the time.

"What?" she asks now, catching my stare.

"You look nice," I say. "That's all."

"I was just . . ." She waves her hand while holding the glass, and the wine tumbles over the lip, onto the white counter. "Shit, shit, shit, shit."

I scramble off my stool and grab the cleaning solution from underneath the kitchen sink, then pass her the paper towels too. It's as if nothing has changed, even though everything has. Or maybe it's as if I wish nothing had changed, but really, it's all gone to complete shit. I'm jealous, of course. I'm fucking jealous that she was on a date, spent an evening sizing up a guy who could occupy the space in her life that I once did. Amanda is working tonight; otherwise surely she'd be at my apartment, on my couch, in my bed. It's happened so quickly, how we picked up like years hadn't passed, like I hadn't burned my old life to the ground and we were just, like, who we were back at NYU. It's nothing like that: Leo is gone, and my dad is gone, and I've lived a whole life between then and now, a life with Tatum, but it's easier to pretend that this isn't true. Amanda hasn't spent time with Joey yet; I haven't mentioned her to my mom (and Ron) yet. It's been only a month since we reconnected that afternoon on the beach, five weeks if we're being specific, and to make those introductions feels too permanent, too real.

I know this is what Amanda wants. Permanence. She tells me she finally feels complete, like she always knew we'd find our way back to each other. I refrain from reminding her that she left me for a residency in Palo Alto, regardless of who officially broke up with whom. I refrain, also, from telling her that when she tumbles into sleep after a long shift in the ER and after we've slept together in ways that were akin to how we used to sleep together when we were twenty-five, I slip out of the bedroom and retreat to my computer, where I hone the manuscript I am writing for Tatum. Finally. I want to give it to her for Christmas, which leaves me ten days to get it right, prove to her that I didn't overlook that promise I made to her for years on end.

It's as if losing Tatum—even though we lost each other so slowly for so many years now—losing her for good has finally made me realize, stupidly, romantically, what I wanted all along. Amanda keeps me company; Tatum has my heart. It's like a ridiculous romantic comedy that years ago, I'd never have even entertained, never deemed good enough to watch, much less embody. But we have detonated what we had, and in the rubble, I've seen the beauty of it too. Maybe the fact that I can finally uncover a silver lining in all that has gone wrong means that I'm growing, growing up. At forty-fucking-two. But finally. If I can't, if all I can do is get mired down in the shitty ways that life has failed me, or I've failed life, I'll never point myself back toward happiness. Not quick-sex happiness with Amanda. That high lasts only until I make it into the shower. Real, resonant happiness with Tatum that can't be washed off in the shower because its grit and its depth has sunk into my pores.

Tatum cleans the mess on the counter, then winds her way into the living room, where the white lights on the Christmas tree bounce off the walls and make the whole room sparkle. The three of us had gone together, driving north toward Santa Barbara, to find it. Joey had run from tree to tree, screaming each time: "This one is perfect!" but Tatum wouldn't settle until she found one that actually was. It was a rare afternoon when no one hassled her, when we could tromp through the tree farm and not encounter another soul for swaths of time that led us all to feel a little normal.

"This really was the perfect tree," she says, staring up at the lights. Then: "Remember that tiny one we had years ago?"

She means the three-footer we plopped in the corner of the bungalow on Ocean Avenue our first year out here. I was working too much on, *what*, I jigger my brain to remember now. *All the Men* or *One Day in Dallas*? Maybe *Reagan*. All those hours and years spent obsessing, as if I were chasing the crown to please my dad. Amanda had been the one to point this out to me recently, but I wonder if Tatum didn't understand that too; maybe she just wanted me to figure it out on my own. Anyway, whatever it was that I was working on, it felt so important then, important enough that I didn't have time to properly shop for a tree with her, despite her nudging me three, four, five times. Instead, I dragged myself home one night and found a pitiful little tree in the corner of the living room. Tatum had bought it at the grocery store and stuffed it in the back of the Prius. She'd spiraled swirls of popcorn around it from the bottom to the top and found an illuminated star to place atop; it flashed on and off every other second so our living room looked like it was constantly on the verge of losing its electricity.

I laugh now. "I'm not even sure that could be defined as a tree. It was more of a plant."

She stretches back her neck, takes in the span of the tree. "God, you know, my mom always said, 'If you can dream it, you can be it.'" She rights herself. "I'm not sure that this tree was part of that plan. I mean, I liked that *plant* that we had back on Ocean Avenue. It's hard, now, to see exactly what was wrong with it."

The air catches in my throat. This is the moment, the one where I can tell her: *I haven't forgotten, I'm still writing something for you.*

Instead of being honest, though, I deflect, because it's second nature now and because I don't think I can *see* her like I used to, even though I feel that I can all the same. How do I bridge what I think and what I feel? How do I figure out which to trust?

I say, though there is so much else to say: "Well, I mean, it was basically half dead. And those popcorn strings . . ."

She laughs, not particularly happily. "I guess it was a long time ago."

"Well, this tree is a work of art."

"Decorators came out, did the whole thing from top to bottom." She flops her shoulders again, then circles the front branches. "I don't even know where they put all the ornaments, the ones from my mom . . ." She trails off, her eyes searching. Now she's the one to deflect: "How's work?" Then: "Sorry, we don't have to talk about work."

She knows as well as I do that it's a sticking point between us: how apparent my insecurities were, how frustrated I was—unfairly—at her success. But also, how she almost always chose her own work over me in recent years, like maybe I did with her back when we first started and she bought a half-dead plant at the grocery store and considered it a Christmas tree.

"It's fine," I say. "I mean, Cassidy is screwing Paxton, and they think no one knows even though their trailers are literally shaking every time we call cut."

Tatum giggles at this, and she has never looked more beautiful. "Well, you know, two hot actors on a set, what are you gonna do?" She quiets. "I mean, not me. That was never my thing but—"

"Listen, you can always ask me about work," I interrupt. "It never should have been otherwise."

Her face stills. "OK." Then more quietly: "OK."

Something shifts between us then, a collective passing of regret, of all the mistakes we've each made, of all the times we scarred each other, of all the ways, too, that we loved each other for so long. Maybe still do.

"Do you miss her?" I ask.

"Who?"

"Your mom," I say. I'm as surprised that I'm asking as she appears to be asked. Tatum and I haven't spoken nakedly in such a long time. I almost feel as if I'm probing a stranger or a new girlfriend, pressing her for personal details that she might not be ready to divulge.

"All the time," she replies, wide open, a map as easy to read as when she was back at Dive Inn, a million years and memories ago.

Of course she would answer me honestly. Tatum never was one for secrets. Until she was. Until I was too.

I tell myself to reach for her, to tell her of all my regrets, of all the ways I would do it differently. But then her cell rings in the kitchen, and she scurries from the room, refocusing on her other life now, and I stand there underneath the glow of the Christmas lights, and I ask myself again: *What do you feel? What do you think? Whom do you see?*

The last question, for so many years, was the one that mattered most.

40

TATUM

DECEMBER

I can't sleep after Ben leaves.

I debate texting Damon, thanking him for the lovely, unexpected evening, but I'm not sure if that's too forward, too needy after just one evening together. I'm new at the dating thing, and besides, I don't even know if I want to be forward or needy or see him again. Luann has texted me three times, desperate to know how it went, but I don't have the energy to tap back: *He kissed me and my knees went a little weak, and then Ben was waiting for me in our kitchen when I got home. And then I discovered that I was glad to see him there, that I didn't really want him to leave. That part of me wanted to say,* Stay forever. *But part of me knew that was just a line someone wrote in a romantic comedy. Not real life.*

I fling off the sheets, slide my feet into the slippers some designer gifted me, and pad across my bedroom toward Joey's room. He doesn't like me to sleep in his bed anymore. *Eight going on fifteen,* I tell anyone who asks. I crouch next to his sweet face instead, running my hands over his forehead, then cheeks. He is warm, Joey is always warm—*He runs hot,* I also say when I have to explain why he refuses to wear long pants or a sweater—and he's stripped off his PJs, flung them to the floor. I try to remember if my own mom would ever slip into my bed because she needed comforting or if I ever woke to find her watching me. Nothing comes, no reassuring memory to call upon.

My mom believed in taking your licks and rising back up. She didn't tell me not to get that first job at twelve; she certainly wished that she hadn't gotten sick, but she didn't shy away from how working made me resourceful, independent, a caretaker too. She still called me "Deflatum Tatum," even though she knew I hated it: she didn't do it to mock me, she did it to arm me, so I could know myself, understand my flaws, and figure out how to best use them to my advantage. When to nurse them, when to let them go. She protected me from my father, locking him in their bedroom or throwing him into a bathtub and turning on the shower until I was old enough to understand his erraticism, his instability. She also taught me how to protect myself.

I kiss Joey's forehead and stand. I want so very much to lie next to him, to use him as a shield from all of my thoughts from the moment— *Why is Ben here, why do I want him here, why is he with Amanda if he is lingering in my kitchen, why am I not asking him about all of this, how have we made such a mess so that I can't even ask him in the first place*— but I conjure up my mom and I try to honor what's now best for Joe. His space, his freedom, giving him an inch or two to discover who he is, while I stand in the shadows, ready with an outstretched hand for when he stumbles.

I wind my way down the spiral staircase into the kitchen, pour myself another glass from the opened bottle of merlot, flip the *Elle* cover so that I stare at the perfume ad on the back.

My mom didn't leave my dad until it was bad. Truly awful. Blackout drunkenness and fired from his job and nights when he never made it home and we weren't sure if he ever would. That was what it took to break her.

I wonder if she'd be surprised to see him now. Eleven years clean. A doting grandfather, a committed husband, a sober coach, an excellent golfer. I wonder if she'd think I gave up too easily with Ben. Then I wonder if perhaps I'm the one who actually believes that. If my dad is proof of anything, it is that anyone can remake himself if he tries hard enough. I remake myself several times a year for whichever part I'm playing. It's easier than you'd think, really. Maybe Ben and I could have remade ourselves too.

Tonight, I could have said: *You're back with Amanda. Let's sign the papers, be done with it.* I could have said: *I wish it were anyone but her.* I could have said: *I feel so alone in my little bubble, and I want you to permeate it.* I could have said: *I just met an amazing man who took me to Koreatown and surprised me in a million ways. Tell me for the last time that it shouldn't be you instead.*

But I didn't. Because every time I think I can read him—showing up at the beach that day, sharing how much I miss my mom tonight—it turns out that maybe I read him wrong. *Show me the map of who you are again,* I want to say. But I haven't. I don't.

I open the recycling bin, drop the copy of *Elle* on top, flip the lights off in the kitchen, and wander to the living room.

I find Ben's presents for Joey under the tree. I sift around for a minute, wondering if he'd left me something unexpected as well. I'd purchased a rare, signed script of *Love Is in the Air*, Reagan's first film, from an antique collector online—it had been nearly impossible to track down, and I had it sitting in a drawer in my office, ready to be wrapped and gifted if I were bold enough or if I thought it could help. *Help what?* I shake my head. *What a stupid notion.* Ben was with Amanda now, and he hadn't gotten me anything, and I was probably turning this into something it wasn't, a fantasy that we could be what we once were. I'd always been good at that, God knows. If I was an expert in anything, it was concocting a world of make-believe. That's why they've anointed me out here, that's why they call my name and give me awards and pay me a ludicrous amount of money for playing a part.

There is a thumping in the hallway, and Monster rounds the corner to find me. His gait is so slow now, but his tail beats in rhythm as he makes his way to rub against my leg.

"Hey buddy, hey, guy." I nuzzle his graying nose.

He folds himself into a ball at my feet, so I flatten myself beside him on the hand-spun Egyptian rug that cost too much; my designer picked it out, and I must have approved it when she did so, but I have no memory of that now. The lights from the tree dance off the ceiling, like a starlit sky, like that wide expanse a lifetime ago in Arizona.

I narrow my eyes to slits, then peer through my fingers to shift my perspective. Maybe if I stare long enough, I can make believe that we're still back there, that we haven't detonated between then and now. Maybe, I can make believe about that too.

41

BEN

DECEMBER

"Come back east with me," Amanda says, forking her eggs. We'd slept late and walked to a late breakfast at a bistro with a garden a few blocks from my apartment. "I have that whole week off between Christmas and New Year's."

I push around my own omelet, pick out the onions. Amanda had ordered for me while I took a call from Eric—our lead actress, Cassidy Rivers, was threatening not to return to the set after the holidays if we didn't fire the lead actor, Paxton Fisher, with whom she'd been sleeping until last week—and Amanda had forgotten (or didn't know) how much I loathed onions.

"I don't know if I can get away." I use my knife to point to my phone. "Cassidy is threatening mutiny."

"Screw her. Call her bluff. Isn't she contracted for the next decade? I think I read that in *People*."

"It doesn't really work that way," I say. "Besides, I'm not really sure that calling people's bluffs is the best way to cultivate a relationship that indeed needs to last the better part of the decade. Honesty might be better." I say this but what I am really thinking is: *Tatum. Why weren't we more honest with each other when we had the chance?* I recalculate. *Why wasn't I more honest with her when I had the chance? How I was threatened by her success, how I resented her blind trust in her dad, how I found a new spark with Amanda because it was easier than struggling to relight whatever had faded between us?* It all seems so stupid now, trivial even, that I let these dishonesties pile up until they were too high to surmount, and now, I don't know what she wants, what she sees, what she feels.

Amanda misses all of this. She takes another bite. "Oh, you know whom you should hire?"

I find a square on my omelet that is onion free. "Who?"

"Lily Marple. I am obsessed with her right now."

"She doesn't do TV. Much less a show that's been around for years."

"But if she did . . ." She sips her coffee too enthusiastically, and it spills on her chin. "I'm just saying. Do you know her? Can I meet her?"

"Years ago," I say. "I worked with her years ago." *One Day in Dallas,* when she shoved her hands down my pants and made it clear she was up for anything. A lifetime ago when I wouldn't have dreamed of being unfaithful.

"I'm completely obsessed with everything she's doing. Like, I literally googled her boots the other day."

"This coming from a highly lauded doctor," I say.

"I know," she laughs. "I'm only telling you. Don't breathe a word to any of my patients."

"I think Tatum is friendly with her now. I can ask her if you really want."

Amanda freezes for a flick of a beat, then catches herself and pretends that she hasn't. I know this is a sore spot with her, that I am newly close with Tatum again, that I sometimes stop by for dinner

unannounced or that I still wear the watch she gave me for my fortieth
or that the lock screen on my phone is a photo of the three of us. I tell
Amanda it's because of Joey: Tatum and I are committed to providing a
united front for him, and even if it's an excuse, it's also true. I am trying
not to skirt the lines of untruths now knowing, with hindsight, how
badly they can unmoor me.

"No," Amanda says, her jaw firming. "It's OK. I didn't really think
I could meet her or anything. It's not like Lily Marple and I were going
to be best friends. God."

I pick out a few more onions with my fingers.

"Do you not like them?" she asks. "Since when?"

"I don't think I ever did. It's fine. I'm just eating around them."

"Shit, sorry. I didn't know. I don't remember that at all."

What she could actually be saying is: *We don't remember a lot of
things about each other.*

Though we've been back together only for about six weeks, Amanda
practically lives at my apartment now. At first, like many firsts with her,
it was exhilarating. We screwed constantly; we stayed up late eating
Chinese food in bed like we had when I was twenty-five; we went to the
gym together, we showered together, we did, well, everything—other
than when she was at work, or when I was with Joey—together. But
then the tug of the manuscript, *Between Me and You*, and the promises
I made with that manuscript, called me back, and with that, the tug of
why I was writing it—*for Tatum*.

Then I remembered that I was firmly *not* twenty-five anymore,
and there were concrete reasons why part of me preferred adulthood.
That Chinese food at midnight leaves you with heartburn, and screwing constantly distracts you from real life. Amanda is needier now
than she used to be, or at least how I remember her to have been.
She'll straddle my lap when I'm writing or she'll pout when I tell her
I'm checking in with Tatum. She's older too—almost forty, and I

know she wants kids of her own, so I get it. I get that she wants me to be all-in, but it's impossible to be all-in when I'm not even sure if I'm all-out with Tatum. Of course there are the divorce papers, and we've finalized all the decisions, neatly sliced our life in half—*This is yours, this is mine, thank you very much.* But it doesn't feel as final as it seems, though maybe this is just another lie I've convinced myself of rather than facing the stark truth: Tatum doesn't love me anymore. This is at least half the reason I haven't finished the script yet: I rewound our collective history and wove it into the fabric of the pages, but I have no idea where we'll go from here, no idea how to finish it. If the characters will end up happy; if in turn, Tatum and I can end up happy.

"Listen," I say today at breakfast. "Even without this crisis with Cassidy, I can't come back east with you. It's Christmas, and I have to be with Joey."

"And Tatum," Amanda replies flatly. "I thought they were going away? To Hawaii?" She says *Hawaii* like it is Siberia, an absolute punishment of a vacation.

"Not until after Christmas. Her dad comes, and her sister . . ." *Be honest, be more honest,* I tell myself. "It's not just that. I want to be here. Not that I *have* to, but I want to."

"Fine."

"He's my son, Amanda."

"And she's still your wife, after all." She wipes her lips with her napkin, pours some of her coffee over her food so she won't eat the rest, then covers the mess with her napkin. She does this whenever she thinks she's had enough but doesn't trust herself to stop; I remember it from back then too. Old habits can be tough to change. "God knows I can't compete with that."

I wish I could pour coffee over us, throw a napkin atop the two of us to stop whatever is about to come next. I don't want to hurt her; I don't want Tatum to hurt me. There is so much damage in this world already. Wouldn't it be nice if we stopped bruising each other and could untangle our messes without leaving more marks?

"Amanda," I say, but have nothing else to soothe her.

"I'm sorry about the onions," she says. "I guess I should have known."

42

TATUM

DECEMBER

Monster collapses on the kitchen floor while I'm pouring myself coffee. I hear a loud thud, and it takes a moment to register because Joey is at school, and the house is otherwise quiet, just as I need it to be to go over the towering stack of scripts this afternoon. I've promised my team I'll make a pick on my next three projects—line up my entire next year— by Christmas. Piper and Scooter and the kids are arriving in two days; I've left myself no time to consider the next twelve months of my life.

I race around the kitchen island and see him, helpless, shaken, in a pool of his urine.

"Monster! Oh baby boy, oh sweet boy, no, no, no, I'm here." I sink to my knees and cradle his head.

His lost eyes find mine, his nose nuzzling my lap.

He is too big for me to carry myself. And I promised myself I wouldn't call Ben. It's a stupid thing: my pride, the welt that sits with me because he's with Amanda, and I'm still alone. There's Damon, but that isn't much of anything yet, just a second date where he kissed me again, and I felt woozy with desire, but then I said good night and returned to my cocoon, behind my wall, figurative and literal. I can't call Damon because my dog is dying.

I find my cell in my back pocket and dial the vet.

"My dog, Monster Connelly Livingston, he . . . he collapsed, and he's breathing and I guess he's alert, but he's a hundred pounds, and I can't get him to you, and I don't know what to do now . . ."

I don't even realize I'm crying until Monster licks my fallen tears off his snout.

"Ms. Connelly," she says, because she always knows when Hollywood royalty calls—it happens this way all over town. "We'll send someone with a van out to you immediately."

"You can do that?" I hiccup.

"We provide the service," the receptionist says. What she means is *We provide the service to people who are special.* "Our driver will be to you within fifteen minutes."

"OK," I breathe. "OK."

It turns out I don't have to call Ben, or Damon, or anyone who can penetrate my bubble. The vet will send a van. I kiss Monster's snout and tell myself that I won't fall apart when I say good-bye to him alone.

❦

The vet assures me that I have time. If I'd like, he says, I can take Monster home, make him comfortable with pain meds, but he has a tumor that is untreatable, and it will one day, literally, explode his heart. It's cancer. Fast-moving and vicious. But he can live for a few months until it ultimately eats him from the inside out. They've sedated him for now so they could do all the proper scans, take a closer view of the tumor on his heart.

"I'm sorry, Ms. Connelly, this is difficult news," Dr. Britton says, resting his hand on my shoulder. I jump, and he pulls back. "I apologize, I didn't mean anything by that . . ."

"No, I just . . ." What can I say? That other than my son or when faking love with costars, no one touches me anymore, Damon's two kisses notwithstanding? I miss those lazy days in bed with Ben from so many moons ago; the way he held me even in his sleep, the way he'd massage my ankles after the long shifts at P. F. Chang's. "I'm sorry," I say. "I'm just falling apart a bit."

"Everyone does," the kind man says. "This is the impossible part of loving a dog."

"How do I bring him home, knowing that his heart will explode?" My voice breaks, and the tears come quickly.

"Can you call someone? That will help. This decision doesn't have to be on you."

I shake my head no.

"Are you sure? Going through this alone can be very tough."

I wonder if he's read about me: surely, he knows I have a (semi-ex-) husband, a son, an entourage. There is no anonymity for me any longer, even in my dying dog's vet's office. He doesn't mean to pry, and he doesn't even mean to allude to all the details he knows about me without actually knowing anything. That's just how it is now. When Damon takes me to a jazz club for our second date and heads turn, when I show up for Joey's birthday celebration at school and eyes widen, when I bring my cancer-laden dog to the hospital.

"He was the best dog I ever could have asked for," I say.

"If we could find a way to make them live forever, we would," he concurs. "Let me give you a minute. I'll check back and you let me know what you decide."

He closes the door behind him, and I'm alone again.

My shaking hands find my phone in my purse. *I don't want to call Ben, I don't want to call Ben, I don't want to call Ben.* He's moved on, and I need to *get* that, that calling him is needy, emotional, is something you do with your partner, which he's not now. But who else is there? Daisy is in New York, and Luann is on my payroll, not a friend for the sake of pure friendship. I haven't spoken to Mariana in weeks. Lily Marple? Has it come to me calling Lily Marple when my dog is dying?

I remember how I brought Monster home, back to our Ocean Avenue bungalow, how I thought a dog would be a great idea to prepare for kids, how Ben was skeptical and not on board, so I promised to do all the work. I didn't, of course. He rose early to walk him and feed him because of my late shifts at P. F. Chang's, and he'd take him to the beach to burn off his endless energy, and he caved and let him sleep in our bed after the first month, when I'd already ignored that rule anyway.

I'd promised that Monster would be mine alone, but I'd broken that promise to Ben—probably knew that I would from the start—and he graciously, openheartedly accepted it.

And now our beloved dog has a tumor on his own heart.

I consider this, and how maybe I feel like I have a tumor on my heart too.

But I don't. I'm lucky enough that I don't.

My poor, poor boy. I love him so very much, love him as if I've birthed him.

I realize that so does Ben. And if I ever have a moment to excise this tumor that Ben and I have grown for each other from my own heart, it's now.

I press his number into my phone, and pray that Amanda doesn't answer, and pray that Ben can hear that the pain in my heart is nearly suffocating me. And that he might be the only one who can heal me.

43

BEN

DECEMBER

I'd answered on the first ring. I was rereading the script and second-guessing everything: if writing it for her had been a mistake, if she'd read it and say: *Ben, we're done with us, I thought that was obvious,* if that would finally be our death knell.

But then my phone rang, and caller ID said *TATUM*, and I answered it, and she was wailing.

"Ben," she said. "Please. Please come, it's Monster. I didn't have anyone else to call."

And I said: "You should have called me. I'm glad you did. I'm still your person."

And I raced to the vet, and we agreed that Monster deserved better than waiting around for his heart to explode, so we sat with him, each of us cradling his face, each of us spilling an unending waterfall of tears, until he went to sleep.

Back home, in our old (new) home, she curls herself into a ball on the white sectional her designer picked out, despite its impracticality for a home with an enormous dog who jumps on all the furniture, and a nearly nine-year-old boy with a fondness for spilling anything that can be spilled.

"Thank you for coming," she says for the hundredth time. Like I wouldn't have. Does she think that I wouldn't have? That we're so far removed from who we used to be that I wouldn't have shown up to help with Monster? She wipes her nose with her sweater, tries to slow her tears.

"Tate, I would never not have come." I shift closer, rest my hand on her leg. She startles but then places her own hand atop of mine.

"I know, I know." She inhales sharply. "It's just . . . I know you're with *her* now, I know you're over all this drama with me."

I slide my hand back to my own lap. I haven't said a word about Amanda to her, partially because I have no idea what I'm doing, partially because it's *Amanda*, and she is not a badge of honor I wear proudly. Also, partially, because I know if Tatum had her pick, she'd be OK with just about any other woman besides the one I'm sleeping with.

"I . . . I didn't realize . . . how'd you know?"

"I saw you guys." She floats her snot-covered sweatered arm aloft, then flops it down. "On the beach. On Leo's birthday."

"What?"

"On the beach last month, OK? I saw you guys, and I mean, I get why you didn't say anything, but—"

"You were there?" My heart accelerates. It hadn't even occurred to me that she was there. Why would it? I waited, and Amanda showed, and that was the end of that and the start of something else.

"I wish it weren't her, Ben. I know I have no control over whom you date, but I wish it weren't her."

My brain freezes, and my tongue does too. I was waiting for Tatum on the beach. I was waiting for her and promised myself that if she showed up, I'd tell her how much I missed her, how wrong I'd gotten so many things. And she *had*. She had shown up, but like a million other moments that I'd missed in these past few years, I'd overlooked this too.

Jesus, I'd been so chickenshit. Waiting for her. *Why didn't you just do it, go to her and say,* Please, I love you, can we try again? I wanted everything to be different, yet I hadn't changed as much as I'd told myself.

The script, though. That is putting it all out there. That will be the point of no return, when I prove how far I've come, or perhaps how much I'm like the old self I used to be. When I made promises I still kept; when I didn't have to wait for her to say *I love you.* I said it first so long ago when her mom died, as I watched her pack to go bury her.

But words have run their course. We've avowed ourselves, and we've told each other everything, and still, we landed on this dead-end route.

Now, the only way to really say it is through what I do.

I say, "Tate, I'll always take your call, pick up the phone if you need me."

This makes her cry harder.

"Monster is the one consistent thing I've had for a decade."

I start to reply, *You've had me,* but this isn't true in so many ways. Not just when we separated, but years before then too.

"How about if I stay here with you until Joey gets home? We'll order in a pizza, watch a bad movie."

She sniffles and nods.

"I hear Lily's new one is terrible, a real shitbomb," I say.

She laughs at this, so hard that mucus projects from her nose.

"Sorry," she says. "God, I'm gross."

"I don't mind."

"I should probably stop crapping on Lily. We're friends now," she manages.

"With friends like those . . . ," I start.

"I don't have all that many," she says. "Daisy is in New York half the time. Mariana is filming in Asia." She picks at her thumbnail. "I take them where I can find them."

I lean in closer to her, wrap an arm around one shoulder, ease her next to me.

"He was such a good dog," Tate says, her head resting on my chest.

"He really was kind of a pain in the ass," I laugh. "Remember how for the first few years he tore up every garbage can we had?"

I feel her grin against me. "Fuck, he was irritating."

"And how his gas was so bad we had to constantly leave the room?" Her shoulders shake, and I let out my own chuckle. "But we loved him anyway."

"In spite of everything," she sighs. "We loved him anyway."

I let her sleep and go to straighten up around the house. She has a housekeeper come in three times a week, so I mostly just try to busy myself, because this is no longer really my house, and I don't want to sit and watch her sleep. I clean up Monster's urine in the kitchen, put his bowl away in the cabinet, tuck his toys into a bin by the back door. I hope she doesn't mind, hope she doesn't think that I'm already trying to erase the imprint of our imperfect dog. I'm only trying to make it easier. I find that I'm enjoying this, not the grief of losing our dog, but the comfort in taking care of her, and I further find that I don't want to leave. Not just for the evening, but forever. That, after everything, I want to take care of her forever. Let her take care of me forever too.

In her office, I find an old photo of the three of us—Leo, her, me—from when he came out to visit us shortly after we'd landed here. She's framed it and displayed it alongside so many other happy family memories: Piper's wedding, Joey's birth, her dad's five-year sobriety ceremony, us on the Oscar red carpet when she won—before we got the call about Leo, of course. In that one, I'm smiling beside her, but I can tell that my heart isn't in it; that I'm panicking on the inside, as if I somehow believed that she'd outgrown me just by being anointed. I stare at the picture of the three of us on the beach, with the blue waves behind us and the golden sky wide open above us and Leo's smile that made him seem invincible. I wish, as I do more often now, and certainly as I have most viscerally tonight, that we had done it all differently.

I don't hear her come up behind me.

"He was so beautiful, Ben."

I rest the photo back on her bookshelf.

"Why didn't you tell me back then?" I ask. "I know it's because I was absolutely horrible about your dad, and that it seemed like I couldn't understand—no, I couldn't forgive what I thought was a weakness." I drop my head. "I mean, I know that. But . . . he was my brother, Tate. Did you not think I'd look past that to try to help him?"

She considers this, and I nearly reach for her hand until I catch my impulse and thwart myself. "I should have told you. It's on my list of regrets, if that means anything. I just . . . Well, there was my dad, how unwilling you were to give him a chance. But also . . ." She trails off.

"It's OK," I say. "I can't imagine that you could say anything now that could hurt me in any way that we haven't already done to each other."

She nods, understanding. "I guess I wanted something you didn't have."

I frown. "You had a ton of things I didn't have. I feel like your whole life was made up of things I didn't have."

"I didn't . . ." She waves a hand. "I was wrong, you were wrong. About a lot of it. But I guess I wanted to do it my way, God knows I've gotten stuck in that habit, and I take responsibility for it." She meets my eyes. "I do. But I guess I thought that your way with him, I mean, with some things, was so rigid, so unforgiving. You were mad at a lot of things back then—and I don't mean that blamefully. But you and I had started keeping score by then, right? I mean, hadn't we?" I nod, and she inhales, then exhales. "I guess this was me keeping score, like I wanted to keep something from you to put in my arsenal, on my scorecard. Like, I knew something that you didn't, and I knew, or I thought I knew, that I'd be proven right. And you'd never know the difference.

But *I'd* know. That he could be rehabilitated, just like my dad, and knowing that I was right, and you weren't . . ." She glances to the floor. "I guess that made me feel smug, in a good way. Self-satisfied."

"Funny, I always thought you were plenty smug." I grin, and she grins too.

"Well, only *after* the Oscar, right? Before that, you took the cake there," she says.

"If we're getting specific, I think it started when you became a big-shot director."

"Well, I learned from the best. You were downright *insufferable* on *Romanticah.*" We both laugh easily, then harder.

"Guilty as charged," I say between hiccups. "Guilty. As. Charged."

I exhale, find my breath. Then lean back against her desk.

"We've really fucked things up haven't we?"

She looks at me now, her eyes already misty again.

"We really were happy once."

"I remember," I say, thinking of my script, considering saying more, but knowing that words aren't enough now, promises aren't enough when we'd broken so many before. "I remember all of that too."

44

TATUM

DECEMBER

We order a pizza and watch *Ferris Bueller's Day Off*, Joey's favorite, even if it's not totally appropriate for an almost nine-year-old. He sobs when we tell him about Monster, and I realize this is the first real death he'll remember. He was too little to recall the day we buried Leo, even though he was there, holding my hand. And my mom and Ben's dad will always just be faces in photographs for him, stories we'll tell.

I promise him we'll get another puppy soon. Go to the shelter after Hawaii and bring home whichever dog he chooses. I can already hear Luann in my ear, excited about the notion of a photo op, all the ways my unselfish act for Joey can be marketed.

Joey falls asleep right when Ferris is serenading the city of Chicago. His head lolls into Ben's lap, his arm splayed off the couch. Ben rests his palm over Joey's chest, as if he can intuit the beats of his heart, and then laughs out loud at the screen. This was always his favorite part: the parade. The pure ridiculousness of it, the total joy and inanity of Ferris's antics.

"Let me wake him, take him up to bed," I whisper. "He has school tomorrow."

"I'll carry him," he says. "In a few."

I nod. Neither of us is in a rush to disrupt the bubble, false as it may be, that surrounds us.

I think of Damon, how on our first date he told me that was what I needed—to live *outside* of my bubble, that getting out of my comfort zone could be the best thing that ever happened to me. He's right, of course. But challenging yourself to be uncomfortable, especially when so many people think they know you, think they *see* you, is complicated. It means that you disrupt their perception of who you are to them, and that means you disrupt your perception of who you are to yourself too.

"Hey," I whisper again. "When we were happy, happier, do you think I had walls up? Like, do you think that as things got bigger for me, that I shut you out?"

He considers this. I watch his hand rise and fall on Joey's chest.

"When we first met—remember in the bar?"

"Dive Inn," I interrupt.

"At Dive Inn, I guess I thought you were the most fearless person I'd ever met. And then with *Romanticah*, I thought you were the best actress I'd ever seen . . ."

"So the answer to my question is yes."

"Tate, you know you do, have walls. I mean, you had to. You're *you*, the great Tatum Connelly. Of course you had to put up barriers."

"I never cared about being famous."

"I know." He reaches out, touches my knee.

Joey stirs, and Ben's hand returns to him. He gently hoists him up, wrapping our son's limbs around him to carry him upstairs.

Ben guides Joey's head onto his pillow, and I pull the duvet up to his chest. We watch him wordlessly for a minute, maybe two. I'm surprised to find my cheeks wet again, missing Monster, missing all of this: how easy it could be, how deeply I once loved Ben, how difficult it was to destroy it, and yet we did.

Ben sees my tears. "Do you want me to stay?"

His question catches us both off guard. I can see it in the quiet alarm behind his eyes; I can feel it in my quickened pulse as I reach for an answer. Then I remember: *Amanda*.

"You have a girlfriend now. You should go home to her." I hate that I've said it so coldly; I hate that I mentioned her at all.

"You guys come before her," he says.

I want to say, *Of course you should stay,* but his nonanswer, that we come before Amanda, is not exactly a proclamation of unrequited devotion. I don't want to be the first one to say it, to say, *Stay.* Also, I have no clue whether Ben's implying anything more than sleeping on the couch, eating a cold piece of pizza.

I say, "I have to be up early anyway. I skipped all those scripts today." I sigh. "Shit, I have so much work to get done before Piper gets here."

"OK," Ben says. "I have work too."

"*Code Emergency?*"

He shakes his head, plunges his hands into his pockets. "Something else."

"Mysterious."

"I'm stuck on the ending," he says as we tiptoe out of the room, down the hallway and then the stairs.

"Want me to read it?"

"Eventually," he says. "I promise."

45

BEN

DECEMBER

Amanda leaves for Boston early. Changes her shifts at the hospital so she can fly on the twenty-second, a few days sooner than planned. She doesn't have to tell me that this is a giant fuck-you mostly to me, not that she wants more family time with her extended clan; she just wants less time with me. She'd asked me to come one last time a few nights ago, implored me to be spontaneous, grab a ticket and join her, but I was resolute.

"There's Joey," I said. "We're going to get a new puppy too once they're back from Hawaii."

She crossed her arms and left the room. We'd both understood that this wasn't just about spending Christmas back east; it was about starting new traditions and a new chapter. And we also both knew that because I was unwilling to do either, even if simply disguised as a last-minute plane ticket, that we were all but done.

She e-mails me from the plane to say that I shouldn't call over the holiday, shouldn't be in touch.

I e-mail her back to say: *I understand.*

She wrote back: *I thought it would be different this time.*

And I reply: *I'm sorry.* Because I am. Though I find that I am enormously relieved once I hit Send. It was a passive way to break up, I suppose, but I didn't need fireworks, and she didn't need the bullshit. We'd been through enough of that.

Then I return to my laptop to finish the manuscript.

I'd decided last week, after I left her on the night Monster died, that I was going to go for it: lay it out for Tatum, project what I hoped the ending would be, could be. I hadn't been this bold in my writing in years, hadn't had to pour any vulnerability or raw honesty into *Code Emergency* (obviously), hadn't really had to on any of the other scripts either. When was the last time I wrote something just for myself? I hunched over my laptop and considered this. *All the Men* and *One Day in Dallas*, even though they earned me early accolades, the countless, uncredited rewrites on other people's work, the *Alcatraz* series—none of them laid me bare like *Romanticah*, which I'd written to get over my breakup with Amanda, which I'd written because I allowed myself to be vulnerable. Since then, I've been so much less so in my work. Less human. Less open. Less brave.

Not unlike Tatum, I'd erected my own walls, placed myself in my own bubble. For different reasons, sure, but when you've burned everything around you and no longer have the protection of those safeguards, do those reasons even matter anymore? Tatum and I had both insulated ourselves from each other, and the only way, *the only way*, to find each other again is to stand there, bare, with the ashes of our wreckage at our feet, and acknowledge that we see each other's nakedness.

And so I write the ending I hope for. Maybe she'll see it as a cop-out, that I had to put it in writing rather than standing in front of her proclaiming my regret. And maybe she'll reject me all the same because I have been a shitty partner, and I have cheated and been unsupportive and been petty and unkind. But I love her. I still love her, and now I can only hope that this is enough.

She and I are past words. Now we are on to promises.

So I'm finally writing something for her, the promise that I made too many years ago that has gone unkept.

I'm keeping it now.

I type faster than my brain realizes is possible.

A happy ending. That's what I'm going to give us. I'm going to rewrite that day in November, Leo's birthday, when I waited for her, hoped she'd come. I change it now: that I didn't see her there, at the fence by the beach on the chilly morning, so instead she called to me—*Ben! Ben!*—and I glanced up toward her, squinted and then saw her clearly, and suddenly, she was there all along.

Not Amanda. Tatum.

She showed up that day, and I saw her.

I rewrite the truth of our history until we find ourselves happy again.

I hit Save.

I press Print.

Between Me and You.

I compile all the pages, find gift wrap in a kitchen drawer, tie it in a bow.

Maybe it will be something. Maybe not enough. But maybe it will be too.

46

TATUM

CHRISTMAS

I make Joey wait until Ben gets here to open his presents. He's been up since five a.m., jumping on my bed, demanding that we start, but I insist. Instead, I make him pancakes (from a mix, but it's the best I can do on my own), let him dump out his stocking, and log him in to Petfinder, where he keeps squealing that he wants to adopt all the dogs. *All of them, Mom! All of them!*

Finally, at eight, Ben, holding a tray of gourmet coffees, lets himself in with his key, and Joey races through the house into the foyer to throw himself at Ben.

"You're finally here! Thank you, thank you, thank you, thank you, thank you. Mom was making me wait," Joey shouts, then untangles his limbs and races into the living room.

"Latte?" Ben asks, holding out a cup.

"Necessary," I reply. "He's been up since five."

"Ouch."

Piper, Scooter, and Emily come down the steps, Piper with the new baby, Harry, on her hip.

"I'll call Dad," I say. "Tell him we're starting."

To Joey, I shout, "Hey, Joe, before you dive in full frenzied, are you packed like I asked?"

Joey doesn't answer. Instead, he's neck deep in gift wrap, in all sorts of toys that he certainly doesn't need and that might go unused before Constance earmarks them for charity.

"I can check," Ben says. "If you want to call your dad."

"I gave him a list, told him to take everything out that he wanted to bring, and pack. Told him no allowance if he didn't do it by this morning." I've been trying to instill more responsibility in Joey. Remove him from his own bubble that we've inflated around him with the divorce, with the perks that are given to him because of my fame, the deference of being my kid, the special treatment.

"It's Christmas, Tate, let's give him a break." He kisses my cheek. "Oh, before I forget." He rests his coffee on the foyer table, reaches into his bag, removes a gift in silver wrapping, a white bow. "For you."

"Ben . . ."

"I know I didn't have to. I didn't do it because of that. I wanted to."

I meet his eyes and nod. "I have something for you too. It's under the tree."

I decided only last night to give it to him, the signed *Love Is in the Air* script. I'd tracked it down through three auction houses, had to place a special hold on it, spent a small fortune. I wasn't even sure why I was doing it at the time: Hope? Forgiveness? An apology for all the ways we wronged each other? Last night, though, I knew. Absolution. Maybe even a new start.

It had been sitting in my desk drawer emitting a muted radar signal that became louder, then louder still after the night Monster died. *Do it. You love him. Show him.* He was with Amanda now, yes, and so maybe it would be a gesture that meant only that we could be good for each other, kind to each other, in new ways. Not as spouses, but still as partners. I loved him. I wanted him. I had shown up on the beach in November to say that, to demonstrate. That he has moved on hasn't changed how I feel. This was the surprising discovery I made last night while I was fingering the worn pages of the script, remembering how I used to read Ben's drafts of his *Reagan* screenplay, how he'd pull a blanket over my legs, how he'd pace behind me waiting for my feedback. Because my opinion mattered, because we valued each other in so many ways. I shut the leather-bound script quietly, then retrieved the wrapping paper from the hall closet, and folded the corners, taped them just so, wrote a card that I signed *with love*. I found a grosgrain ribbon in the closet and tied it in a perfect bow, which I'd learned years ago during a holiday season spent gift-wrapping at the mall for extra pay.

He'd been there for me when Monster died; he'd been there for me for so much more. Nearly two decades now. Just because he is with Amanda doesn't detract from any of that. And so I padded downstairs and placed the script, wrapped in silver and gold paper, under the tree. I stared at it for a moment. It was luminous. The present, yes. But the choice I was making in giving it too.

"You got something for me?" Ben cranes his neck toward the tree and grins with such surprise that he reminds me of what he looked like when we first met, back at Dive Inn.

"It's nothing," I say. "I mean, not nothing. But I just saw something, and I thought of you."

"Well, thank you. I can't wait to see it."

I start to undo the bow on his gift, slip my fingers under the seam of the paper.

"Wait, no, please don't open it here." He almost seizes it from my hands.

"What? Why?"

His cheeks turn crimson.

"I just . . . can you do it once I'm gone?"

"But you're staying through dinner, right?" It occurs to me that I don't want him to leave, not after we're done unwrapping the gifts, not for a long while.

"I'm staying for dinner," he says. "This is the only place I want to be."

"I'll open it on the plane." A week in Hawaii with Joey, Piper, Scooter, Emily, Harry, my dad, and Cheryl. *It should be enough,* I think. *All of their company, without Ben.*

"That's what I envisioned." He smiles. "You opening it on the plane."

"I don't even know what that means."

"You don't have to," he says. "Because I do."

47

BEN

CHRISTMAS

I kiss all of them good night and wish them a safe flight. Tatum promises to call when they land.

"And after I open this mysterious gift of yours," she says.

"Take your time with it," I reply. "It's OK. There's no rush."

She wrinkles her brow. "OK."

"OK," I say, and then kiss the top of her head.

Dinner had been perfect, like we were a family again. Daisy had started it, broken the tension. Told the story of how Tatum and I first met, over a bet, and Joey's eyes got wide and then he laughed until apple cider came out of his nose.

"Mom, you bet Aunt Daisy that you could get three numbers?" He looked at her cockeyed. "No offense, Mom, but really?"

"I know you think I am over-the-hill," Tate said, laughing. "And embarrassing and horrifying, but let me tell you, I could put on an act and pour a beer with the best of them."

"She could," I concurred. Tatum and I locked eyes, and we both remembered that this was the truth.

"And then I got the chicken pox," Daisy said. "And maybe if I hadn't, I'd be the Oscar winner and not on my gajillionth season of *New York Cops*."

"But then you'd have had to marry my dad," Joey said, rolling his eyes.

And I said: "Yeah, no offense, Daisy, but that wasn't happening."

And Tatum said: "Yeah, now that I think about it, why *weren't* you into Ben back then, Dais?"

And Daisy laughed and said: "Uh, no offense, Ben, but nice guys were never my thing." But she raised her eyebrows at the irony.

And Tatum snorted but in a funny way, and I laughed because we'd all gotten it wrong, and we raised our glasses to Daisy's chicken pox.

I'd waited to open Tatum's present to me until I was home. She'd asked me to. I sink into my couch and place it on my lap, then slide my fingers under the immaculately folded corners. I tug it from the paper and stare at it for a moment, then a moment longer, aware of the rise and fall of my chest, of how my hand has moved to cover my mouth in my astonishment: a signed script of *Love Is in the Air*, Reagan's first film. It must have been nearly impossible to track down.

After so long, after all the scars we have inflicted, Tatum still knows me best. That even if I hadn't penned the script about Reagan I'd hoped for, part of me would always be connected to that dream—of who I wanted to be when I first stepped foot out here, of who I hoped to be to make my father proud and, concretely, to make myself proud too. And Tatum. She'd never asked for me to win an Oscar; she'd never cared. She simply wanted me to keep dreaming. I'd stopped for a bit. I'd stopped a lot of things along with it.

My phone buzzes in my back pocket. The screen tells me that it's Amanda, maybe regretting how perfunctorily we'd ended; maybe regretting we'd ended at all. I decline the call. I'll try her back later, tell her the truth, even though the simple e-mail was easier. I'll tell her that I wrote something for someone else, that I am dreaming now of something different, that I am dreaming now of Tatum.

Now, in my empty apartment, I ease my head against the back of the couch and squeeze my eyes closed. I've done everything else I can. There is nothing to do but wait.

48

TATUM

NEW YEAR'S EVE DAY

The beach is deserted now. It's nearly sunset, and the families with little kids have taken them inside to tend to sunburns or to stave off full meltdowns; the retirees have returned to their condos for early dinners or, in my dad's case, a nap. There are a few stragglers, a young couple who keep chasing each other into the water, a father and his teenage son still tossing a football. But mostly I'm alone. Something I'd grown used to, even if I resented the isolation I'd brought on myself.

I tug my Tisch baseball hat lower, hug my tunic closer as the wind kicks up. I reach for my straw bag and rest the script inside.

I'd opened it on the flight over. Everyone had fallen asleep, so it was just me, in a darkened cabin, with the overhead light aglow. He'd written a note on top:

For you, just for you, Tate. I should have done it years ago but maybe now was the only time I was ready. Take your time. Don't rush. Be sure. But now you know how I feel, now you know, I hope, that I can still keep my promises.

I'm not sure if I breathed from the first page to the last. I must have, of course, but my heart was so tight, my pulse so quick, that I wouldn't be surprised if I hadn't. I closed the last page and stared out the window for I don't know how long. The darkness of the night passing by, the ocean so far below us that it was impossible to see.

"Mom?" Joey poked me.

"Sweetheart, I didn't realize you were awake," I said.

"Are you OK? You're crying."

I pressed my fingers against my cheek. I was. Unlike so many times in scripts, in rehearsals, on screen, when I wedge myself into an emotion and play it out, this time I hadn't even realized how deeply it had cut.

"I'm fine, love. Just thinking about something."

"Monster?" he asked.

"Him. Lots of other stuff too." I squeezed his hand, and he nodded, then closed his eyes and tumbled back to sleep. I turned back to the window and the vastness of the world we were cutting through.

Now, on the white beach in Hawaii, I've sat with it for five, nearly six, days now. It's a masterpiece, of course, and it's his masterpiece that he wrote for me. Or for himself. That's not for me to say. But I know what he's trying to say in these pages, and I understand that it is now up to me. He made his plea, he wrote down his version of us—all the ways we hurt each other, all the ways we loved each other too—and he got a lot of it right. The beginning when we couldn't get enough of each other, the middle when we began to splinter, when we faced loss and triumph and should have used each other as both shelter and foundation but instead lost our way, and then the end, of course. The end was messy with his infidelities and regrettable with my own untruths.

He wrote it all down, and he showed me his nakedness.

He told me to be sure. So I've waited to call, waited, just as Tatum does in his script, to know that I'm certain, ready to be what we once were.

342

I watch that young couple fall on themselves as a wave crashes over them.

No, not what we once were. Because we were foolish and selfish and shortsighted. Can I believe that we can put all of this aside and evolve into something better? How can you ever be certain of that?

The couple emerges from the waves, and he says something that delights her. She throws her head back and laughs, and he reaches for her hand before they set off down the beach.

Maybe you can never be certain. Maybe all you can do is reach for the other's hand and go.

I inch up from the chaise, let my feet sink into the warm sand, then stride to the water's edge. I haven't gone in this whole trip. The ocean has always scared me for reasons that I never really probed or even wanted to understand. Leo was always jumping in, diving under. Ben too. But I usually just sat and watched, called out to them if I thought they were swimming out too far. It was the unknown, of course. How the blue turned black, how it was shallow and then suddenly you couldn't find your footing. How it is something bigger than you, and it always will be, no matter how big you get on your own.

I stare out to the horizon, the sky now a blistering shade of pink and fuchsia and orange and blue. I think of my mom, of how she told me I could be anything I dreamed of. I always thought she meant with my life; it only now occurs to me that she also meant with my heart, that there has to be room for forgiveness and second chances, along with everything else. If I dream of loving Ben that much, we can become whatever we imagine our dreams to be.

I have room in my heart for Ben. If I am brave enough to open up that sliver that remained there through everything, I can peel it back and find him.

I wade deeper into the water, up to my knees now, then to my chest. I push myself into discomfort; I push myself into my fear.

It's a shame, I realize, that everyone has gone inside for the sunset.

They've given up, turned their backs right before they got to the best part.

⟲

I dry off in the open air.

I reach for my cell at the bottom of my bag. I've missed seven calls from my team but it's my holiday, and I'm giving myself this.

Instead, I punch in Ben's number, just as he wanted me to.

He answers on the first ring.

"We're an ocean apart, but I can see you clearly, all the way from here," I say, staring out to the horizon, then up at the darkening sky, the stars beginning their nightly dance.

"I see you too," he says. "All the way from here."

"It feels like it took us forever to get this right," I reply. "Get here as fast as you can."

"Not forever, just a few more hours," he says. "I'm already on my way."

49

BETWEEN ME AND YOU

BY BEN LIVINGSTON

(FINAL DRAFT)

INT. BEN'S BEDROOM—DUSK

Ben, our hero, sits on his bed in his small apartment, stunned. Fading light ekes through his window. From his expression, it's obvious that he just received news that he can't get over. Then a joyful—the happiest—grin spreads across his face. In one quick instant, he grabs the phone off his bed, lets out a hoot, and runs to the front door, where his suitcase is already packed and ready. He races down the steps to the waiting taxi.

BEN:

How quickly can you get me to the airport?

DRIVER:

Traffic's not bad. It's New Year's Eve. Everyone's at home getting fancy, ready to party. So twenty minutes, no problem.

Ben checks his watch.

BEN:

Twenty minutes is perfect.

DRIVER:

Gotta be somewhere by midnight?

BEN:

Gotta kiss a girl by midnight.

The driver laughs, guns the gas. We pan out to see the taxi racing down the 405.

50

TATUM

NEW YEAR'S EVE

The sky is bigger than I ever dreamed it could be. That's what I keep thinking from my chaise, tucked under a blanket on the empty Hawaiian beach as midnight nears. That the world is so immense, and we are so small, and isn't it a miracle that we find someone to love amidst its expanse? That Ben and I found each other? That we found our way back to each other again?

I check the time on my phone. He'll be here in time. I know it.

"Hey, Tate, you coming in?" Piper shouts from the open patio door. From behind her, I can hear the pulse of music, the sound of heightened laughter from my family, as they dance and celebrate and wait to ring in the new year, the new chapter.

"Mo-o-o-o-ommmm," Joey yells beside Piper. "I'm addicted to sparkling apple cider! It's. The. Best!" He toots a noisemaker in triumph.

"I'll be in soon, don't worry," I call back to them.

"You OK?" Piper says.

"I called him," I say. "He's coming."

"HOLY SHIT!!" Piper screams, running down to me, kissing my face all over until I can't stop giggling.

"OK, now let me have a moment of peace," I say.

She clutches my cheeks and says, "God, I'm proud of you, Tate. I know none of this has been easy."

I nod and sink back into the chaise, and she retreats. She must have shut the patio door because the noise from inside is swallowed up.

I check my phone again. This is how he wanted it, how he wrote it, with him waiting for me, with me calling and telling him to come—and without even realizing it, this is how I wanted it too, how I would have asked him to write it if I were still asking.

For him to fly across an ocean for me on New Year's Eve, for us to stand under the stars as the clock ticks down to a new start, a rebirth, just as it had so many years ago.

The patio echoes with revelry again, the door reopening. I hold my breath and wonder if it's him, if he's made it in time, just as he'd written, just as I'd hoped.

He drops his bag next to the chair, and I tilt my gaze upward, and there he is.

Ben.

"You made it," I say. My smile spreads nearly to my heart, if that were the type of thing a smile could do.

"I promised." He reaches down, pulls me to my feet, presses my hands to his own heart.

"You wrote it backward," I say. "So you could see where we got it right."

"I wrote it backward," he says. "So I could see everything clearly again."

"Hey you two lovebirds," Piper shouts from inside the patio door. "We're counting down!"

"I think she might be tipsy," I laugh.

"Well, it's New Year's. Maybe we should all be tipsy."

"Remember Leo at Times Square?" I laugh harder, and he does too. "And that girl, that poor girl he brought, and how he, like, practically ate her face off at midnight?"

Ben's shoulders shake, and he howls.

"Jesus," he says through his laughter. "I'm so glad we did that."

From inside, they are cheering *Ten! Nine! Eight!*

"So are you going to kiss me?" I say, looking toward him, batting my eyelashes.

"You already know how this ends," he says. "You know how I wrote it."

And then we are at *Two!* And then we are at *One!*

And then Ben is kissing me or maybe I'm kissing him, and just like so many years ago, before we loved each other and before we broke each other, we lose ourselves in the moment when the past becomes the present and the calendar is nothing but a clean slate.

Ben pulls back and stares at me, like he's seeing me for the first time. Then he says: "Come on, let's go inside. We have a lot to celebrate."

I nod. "OK."

But neither of us moves, neither of us breaks from our embrace. My hands stay knotted around his neck; his stay knotted around my waist. I rest my head against his chest and listen to his heartbeat, the fireworks above, and the waves lapping in and out, in and out, in and out.

Finally, I push back and say, "You ready?"

And he says, "I am."

Then, under the unending sky in our tiny corner of the galaxy, where we have found our way back to each other, I braid my fingers into his, and we go.

ACKNOWLEDGMENTS

This book could not have been written without the counsel of my agent and friend, Elisabeth Weed. After countless drafts filled with structural problems and obstacles that seemed insurmountable, and when it would have been easier to throw in the towel and write a more traditional novel, Elisabeth said, *Keep going, you can do this,* and so I did. I am enormously grateful for her words and support.

Tiffany Yates Martin provided editorial insights that elevated the plot and characters beyond my initial musings and in ways that I could not have done on my own. Thank you, thank you. It was a joyous collaboration.

Danielle Marshall, Kelli Martin, Dennelle Catlett, Devan Hanna, Gabriella Dumpit, Nicole Pomeroy, and the entire team at Lake Union have offered the best possible cushion for a writer: a bubble of support and enthusiasm and kindness, and I am appreciative of their hard work and expertise every step of the way.

Kathleen Carter Zrelak is a dream publicist. Truly. Just wow.

Michelle Weiner at CAA, thanks for your advocacy; Laura Dave, thanks for your wise notes. My mom, thanks for your incredible copyediting eye and your hours spent with the manuscript and a red pen. It's true that I use way too many commas.

Brandon Flowers, who doesn't know me and will never likely see this, provided the inspiration for the book's title through his music that

I often listened to on long walks, mulling over Ben and Tatum and their messes. Thanks! Everyone should go listen to his excellent song, "Between Me and You."

My dogs, Pele and Paco (and the late Pedro), get a thanks for helping to bring Monster to life. (Also, I've always wanted to thank my dogs.)

And to my husband, Adam, and my children, Cam and Amelia. Between me and you, I couldn't ask for more.

ABOUT THE AUTHOR

Photo © 2015 Kat Tuohy Photography

A *New York Times* bestselling author, Allison Winn Scotch has published *The Department of Lost & Found*, *Time of My Life*, *The One That I Want*, *The Song Remains the Same*, *The Theory of Opposites*, and *In Twenty Years*, a *Library Journal* Best Books of 2016 selection. Her novels have been translated into twelve different languages. A freelance writer for many years, Allison has contributed to *Brides*, *Family Circle*, *Fitness*, *Glamour*, *InStyle*, *Men's Health*, *Parents*, *Redbook*, *Self*, *Shape*, and *Women's Health*. A cum laude graduate of the University of Pennsylvania, where she studied history and marketing, Winn Scotch now lives in Los Angeles, where she enjoys hiking, reading, running, yoga, and the company of her two dogs, when she's not "serving as an Uber service" for her kids.

Follow her at www.allisonwinn.com, on Facebook at www.facebook.com/allisonwinnscotch, or on Twitter at www.twitter.com/aswinn.